The Summer Wind

"Distinct, complex, and endearing characters ... Mary Alice Monroe continues to make Charleston proud with her authentic and purposeful writings."

—*Charleston Magazine*

"Monroe's vivid imagery of the Lowcountry's smells, tastes, and sights brings you up to the door of the Sea Breeze, so even if you're at home far from the ocean, you can imagine yourself there."

—*The Herald-Sun*

"Monroe deftly explores the unique problems each woman faces. . . . These are modern women addressing the prickly questions of identity and purpose in today's world, a world very different from the one their grandmother knew as a young bride. . . . Written with convincing Southern charm and thoughtfulness, *The Summer Wind* explores the bonds of sisterhood and the challenges of modern womanhood with warmth and genuine affection."

—*BookPage*

"A series I urge everyone to get into, it makes the perfect beach read and I know you will be fully invested in this family as much as I am."

—*A Southern Girls Bookshelf*

"The second book in the Lowcountry Summer Trilogy, *The Summer Wind* . . . pulls at your heartstrings even more than the first."

—*Posting for Now*

The Summer Girls

Mary Alice Monroe

A Lowcountry Wedding

A
LOWCOUNTRY
SUMMER
NOVEL

G

GALLERY BOOKS

New York London Toronto Sydney New Delhi

G

Gallery Books
An Imprint of Simon & Schuster, Inc.
1230 Avenue of the Americas
New York, NY 10020

First Gallery Books hardcover edition May 2016

GALLERY BOOKS and colophon are registered
trademarks of Simon & Schuster, Inc.

For information about special discounts for bulk purchases,
please contact Simon & Schuster Special Sales at
1-866-506-1949 or business@simonandschuster.com.

The Simon & Schuster Speakers Bureau can bring authors to your live event. For
more information or to book an event contact the Simon & Schuster Speakers
Bureau at 1-866-248-3049 or visit our website at www.simonspeakers.com.

Manufactured in the United States of America

10 9 8 7 6 5 4 3 2 1

Library of Congress Cataloging-in-Publication Data is available.

ISBN 978-1-5011-3682-5
ISBN 978-1-5011-2544-7 (ebook)

For Angela May
My lowcountry girl, with thanks
for her never-failing faith and her smile
that lights up even the darkest day

A
Lowcountry
Wedding

MRS. EDWARD MUIR
REQUESTS THE HONOR OF YOUR PRESENCE
AT THE MARRIAGE OF HER GRANDDAUGHTER

Carson Colson Muir

TO

Blake Waring Legare

SATURDAY THE TWENTY-FIFTH OF MAY
TWO THOUSAND AND THIRTEEN

THE LEGARE WARING PLANTATION
CHARLES TOWNE, SOUTH CAROLINA

SIR JEFFREY AND IMOGENE JAMES
REQUEST THE HONOUR OF YOUR PRESENCE
AT THE MARRIAGE OF THEIR GRANDDAUGHTER

Harper Muir-James

TO

Mr. Taylor Archibald McClellan

SUNDAY THE TWENTY-SIXTH OF MAY
TWO THOUSAND AND THIRTEEN

WILD DUNES GRAND PAVILION
ISLE OF PALMS, SOUTH CAROLINA

Prologue

Be kind, my darling girl. And be happy!

Spring was in the air—ripe, verdant, full of promise. And with the spring came the rush and clamor of weddings.

Marietta Muir stood on the porch of her cottage in her nightgown and robe. Across the gravel drive was the main house—her Sea Breeze. The old white wooden house with its black shutters and gabled windows was dark and quiet in these early hours. It was a handsome house, she thought, taking in the gracious staircase that curved out like a smile of welcome. To the left was the unsightly, leaning wood garage. In the center of the courtyard an immense, ancient live oak tree spread low-drooping boughs that to her appeared as a great hand protecting them all from harm. The tree and the house had survived generations of Muir ancestors and countless storms and hurricanes. That it could weather them all, scarred and bent perhaps, yet endure, was testament to the strength of the family.

Marietta lived in the small white cottage that had once been the home of her longtime maid and companion, Lucille. To her mind, it would always be "Lucille's cottage." Marietta had moved to the cottage when her granddaughter Harper had purchased the house from her, thus keeping Sea Breeze in the family. It was a good decision. Living in the quaint guest cottage, Marietta was free of the hassles and distractions of caring for that big house and all those possessions. She'd spent a lifetime tending the house, closing shutters for rooms filled with antiques, cooking meals, presiding over parties or going to parties, decorating for holidays, and celebrating the milestones of her family's lives. She no longer had the energy, or in truth the desire, to do all that. Running a household and raising children were tasks for the young!

She held a cup of coffee in her hands and sipped slowly, enjoying the warmth. Now she could enjoy the peace of a lowcountry morning such as this when the air was heady with scents. She lowered her cup from her nose and breathed deep. Coffee still lingered in the air, but there was the pervasive scent of pluff mud this morning and the cloying sweetness of jasmine and other spring flowers that tickled her nose. Salt tinged the moist breezes from the ocean. Smacking her lips, she could almost taste it. And, too, there was that delightful freshness of mist and dewy grass that lingered like spirits at dawn.

Marietta awoke with the sun most mornings now. Nights were restless and she was eager to rise from her bed and greet the new day. At eighty-one years of age, each day granted was a blessing. And today was especially exciting. Carson was arriving home. Harper and Dora were positively spinning with anticipation. Now they could begin the wedding festivities in earnest, for in only two months' time, both Carson and Harper would be celebrating their weddings.

Just the thought gave Marietta palpitations. So much had to be done. So much she wanted to say to the girls before they took this important step in their lives.

But *what*? What wise words could she share with them that would inspire? What words could she say that they could pull from their memories when times were tough and they needed reassurance and guidance to persevere?

When Marietta was soon to be married, her mother, Barbara, had taken her to tea for a private mother-daughter tête-à-tête. Marietta's wedding day was only a week away, and a flurry of parties were being given by friends and family. Barbara had set aside this time alone with her daughter, to share with her the advice that only a mother could. That afternoon over Darjeeling tea, her mother had presented Marietta with a book of etiquette by Emily Post. Now that Marietta was setting up a home of her own, her mother said, she wanted her to have guidance at her fingertips for any question she might have regarding the correct deportment of a lady with a well-appointed house. Marietta had already been thoroughly instructed on the rules of conduct, the customs, and the expectations of Charleston society. "Yet," her mother had told her, "refinement and charm are more elusive."

She had placed the book in Marietta's hands and said, "My dear girl, remember that this book only outlines for you the thousands of detailed instructions and protocol of polite society. But at the root of all etiquette and manners is kindness. These rules were not contrived to make one feel important or better than another. As Emily Post said, rules can be learned by anyone. Every human being—unless dwelling alone in a cave—is a member of society of one sort or another.

"Rather, think of etiquette as a philosophy of living and enjoying life with grace, compassion, and respect for others. If, say, someone at your dinner table uses your bread plate, do you make a fuss? Of course not. You must be gracious and make no mention of it. Why? Because you would not want to embarrass the other guest. To do otherwise is the gravest breach of etiquette. You see, while etiquette provides the rules for socially accepted behavior, good manners are how we apply those rules. Being a gentleman or a lady is a code of behavior that draws on decency, integrity, and loyalty—not only to friends and family but to principles. So be kind, my darling girl. And be happy!"

Marietta had held her mother's words close to her heart throughout her long marriage. *Emily Post's Etiquette* had guided her through thank-you notes, birth announcements, the introductions of dignitaries, baptisms, weddings, and funerals. But her mother's words were the spirit behind them.

Mamaw smiled and snapped to action. With two weddings approaching, she knew exactly what she had to do.

She closed her robe tight and hurried back into the cottage. Inside, the walls and sparse furniture were all white. Splashes of color brightened the room in the lowcountry art and the blue linen drapes at the windows. She went directly to the one wall lined with bookshelves. This was the only change she'd made to the cottage after her granddaughters had redecorated it following Lucille's death. Marietta loved her books and had had a difficult time choosing which to keep from her vast library. The furniture she had no difficulty parting with. But the books were like old friends.

Marietta knew the book was here somewhere. She'd never throw it out. Her fingertips slid over the spines of dozens of books packed side by side on a shelf. At last she found it. *Emily Post's Etiquette*. She pulled it out and caressed the well-worn blue binding with satisfaction. Opening it, she found the folded book cover and the inscription on the opening page, *With best wishes! Emily Post*.

She went to the sofa, flicked on the lamp, crossed her legs, and, after slipping on her reading glasses, began to read, going through the chapters: "Introductions," "The Art of Conversation," "Entertaining at a Restaurant," "Balls and Dances," "Preparations for a Wedding," "Table Manners," "Protocol in Washington," and so on. The tone was encouraging and concise, the instructions thorough and direct. She felt again the same awe and wonder—and trepidation—at reading the countless rules for specific situations that she had experienced as that young bride sixtysome years earlier. Marietta had to admit she'd forgotten some—such as calling cards—but for the most part, the rules of etiquette were as ingrained in her as her DNA. She read until the sun brightened the sky, her coffee cup was empty, and her eyes grew weary. She paused, slipped off her glasses, and let her hand rest on the book.

Were these rules relevant to a young bride today? she wondered. Would Harper and Carson find them daunting? Would Dora have utilized these in her marriage to Cal?

They were not her daughters, but her granddaughters. They affectionately called her Mamaw and their bond was strong, indeed. She had done her best to instruct the girls in proper manners when they'd spent summers with her at Sea Breeze, but she didn't oversee their upbringing or guide them day to day. She had no worries that Harper knew her etiquette. In England, her family was in *Debrett's*. Dora's mother, Winifred, bless her heart, did her best. Even if Winnie knew the letter of the law and not the spirit. Carson, however, was a wild card. Raised by Marietta's son, Carson might as well have been raised by wolves. Looking back, Marietta saw that she'd failed Carson by not insisting that the young girl live with her in Charleston rather than with her father in Los Angeles. Yet the girl had a natural grace and a passion for living that no amount of education could teach. Carson knew enough manners to get by. Marietta sighed. How to set a table, at the least. The rest, Marietta knew, Carson could learn.

Mamaw tapped her lips, considering. Certainly for the parties and the wedding ceremonies, protocol played an important role. Especially in the church. Goodness, without protocol they'd all be walking around utterly clueless what to do next. Protocol was reassuring in such times, and Mamaw was confident that she could guide the fledglings in the proper procedures for the ceremonies. With a slight lift of her chin she thought that sometimes being old had advantages.

As for the rest . . . it might be true that some of the rules of etiquette from the past were outdated. Yet didn't etiquette, like language and customs, evolve and adapt to current times? Treating others with kindness, consideration, and respect was timeless. All should be aware of how their actions affect others in their daily lives.

Marriage was hard work. As in the vows the young brides and grooms were going to say, there was indeed *sickness and health, poverty and wealth, till death do us part.* Only in the wisdom of experience could one hear those words and understand the depth of their meaning.

Marietta had lived a charmed life in many ways. Yet she'd also endured the sadness of miscarriages and the crushing blow of the death of her only child. Edward had been her support during those trials, but when he died, it was her dear friend Lucille who had seen her through the darkness to the light. Then Lucille, too, had passed, and Marietta was alone again. Her granddaughters were a solace, true, but she'd also discovered a different sort of comfort and companionship in an old friend, Girard.

So, perhaps, marriage wasn't the only answer for a compatible relationship? she wondered. Partnership and friendship were important ingredients. Still, she believed marriage was an institution set up by society to protect the concept of family. Marriage offered security and stability in a world quickly losing values, customs, and traditions. This she wanted for her granddaughters.

Yet, in the end, her mother had only wanted Marietta to be happy. Happy with her husband, happy in her society, happy in her home. Isn't that what every mother wished for her daughter? Shouldn't she wish only that for her Summer Girls?

She sighed and cupped her chin in her palm. So what to say? *Lord*, she prayed, *help me find the words*. Then she smiled again and the answer came readily. She would tell each young bride the same words her mother had told her so many years ago. Simple words that had withstood the test of time. *Be kind, my darling girl. And be happy!*

Chapter One

It's never too late. Not to begin again. Not for happy ever after.

*I*f the lowcountry was her heart, then the salt water that pumped through all the mysterious and sultry creeks and rivers was her life's blood.

Carson sat in a window seat of the small jet staring out at her first glimpse of the lowcountry in six months. From the sky she stared out the portal window at the estuarine waters snaking through the wetlands looking every bit like veins and major arteries. Carson was heading back home. Back to Sullivan's Island, South Carolina, like so many of the migrating birds and butterflies journeying along the coast. She was so close she could almost smell the pluff mud.

Carson had been traveling for over fifty hours from New Zealand to Los Angeles, then from there to Atlanta, and now, at long last, on the final puddle jumper to Charleston. The past days had been one long blur of plane changes, long lines, endless waiting, and hours cramped in crowded airplanes. She thought she might sleep on the red-eye from Los Angeles, but she'd reached that odd point of being too exhausted to sleep. She couldn't turn off her brain.

She was drained after four months of film photography in the wild forests of New Zealand followed by extended post-production work. Her life had been a series of breakfast, lunch, and dinner meetings where the powers-that-be debated over the best shots for the film's press and publicity. The film's star was a major A-list actor with a high "kill shot" allowance, which meant he could select those photographs he liked and reject those he did not. This prima donna had killed 75 percent of Carson's best work because he had an issue with his nose. In all that time Carson didn't have a free moment to surf, kite, or even stick a toe in the Pacific Ocean. Not even during her two-day stopover in Los Angeles. She'd packed up her few belongings from storage, had them shipped to Sullivan's Island, knocked on a few doors to bid farewell to friends, then called a cab and headed to LAX. Too long a time away from the water put her in a dismal state of mind. She felt fried. She couldn't wait to get home to the good ol' Atlantic.

Home.

Carson tried to stretch her impossibly long legs in the cramped space of economy seating, wondering again if she'd really been so clever to exchange her first-class seats and pocket the money. Resting her chin in her palm, she stared out the small oval window, marveling how, after years on the road, she'd actually been homesick. Carson was lucky to have had a successful run of gigs with shooting on location and long flights back to LA. She'd been good at her job, cooperative, indefatigable on the set. Her personal life consisted of long-term friends and countless short-term suitors. By the time she hit thirty-four, however, the long hours and endless partying, the ever-present alcohol and drugs, began to take their toll. Her work got sloppy, she was drinking too much, and her work ethic grew lazy. When she'd overslept and missed a major scene, it was the last straw for the director and he fired her on the spot. Word got out and her reputation was ruined. No one would hire her.

It had been a long dry spell until that same director, Kowalski, himself a recovering alcoholic, learned Carson had joined AA and offered her a second chance. Carson had given this film her best work, and despite the frustration of the many setbacks and the prima donna actor, she'd stayed clean. Kowalski noticed. At the film's closing he shook her hand, then offered her another film job. That offer had meant the world to Carson. Not only had her reputation been restored, but she'd proved to herself she could stop drinking under pressure. She'd felt validated and proud—and hopeful.

Carson blew out a stream of air. Now she was in a quandary. She'd promised Blake that this would be her last film gig. That she would end her wandering, return in four short months to settle down with him in Charleston to marry and start a new and different life. A life that meant she'd have to begin the dreaded task of searching for any work she could get in a tight job market. That was the plan. Yet when Kowalski offered her another film job, she couldn't flat-out refuse. Instead, she'd asked him for time to consider the offer.

She shuddered at the thought of once again joining the ranks of the unemployed. She'd been out of work so long she'd lost her self-esteem. This time, rather than spend recklessly,

Carson had saved money from this gig to tide her over until she got another job. Whatever and whenever that was. But it wasn't enough. Not nearly enough. She had to land a job soon. Carson was too proud to enter a marriage penniless, jobless, and completely dependent on Blake.

Carson looked down at the small diamond bordered on either side with a sapphire resting on her ring finger. Her engagement ring had been Blake's mother's ring and her mother's before her, thus all the more meaningful to Carson. This symbol of his love, of continuance and commitment, had been her touchstone during the six months they'd been apart. She'd held tight to the ring and all the promises it held whenever she'd been tempted to drink—and she'd remained sober. It had been hard, there was no denying it. At times she'd almost slipped. But she'd held on to the promise of the ring.

She covered her hand with her other palm, squeezing tight as she took a deep breath. Was love enough to calm her fears? Could she maintain her independence, her sense of self, if she relinquished her career? She couldn't bear falling back into the wallowing self-pity of the previous summer.

Her racing thoughts were jarred by the grinding noise of the wheels lowering beneath her. Her heart quickened as touchdown approached. Almost there. Across the aisle a young couple sat, shoulders touching, holding hands. She recognized them as a couple that had boarded the plane with her in Atlanta. The young man's hair had been shorn by an energetic barber. He wore a crisp blue gingham shirt under his navy blazer and a sweet smile as he looked into the woman's eyes. Her blond hair was long and curled, and she wore the classic pink Lilly

Pulitzer dress and matching sweater, and the ubiquitous pearls at the ears and neck. Looking up at him, she beamed. They had to be newlyweds, Carson thought. Or another in a long line of couples who came to Charleston to get married.

Like me, she thought, and the notion surprised her. This was more than a return home to Sea Breeze. She, too, was a young bride flying in to get married. Carson studied the young woman. She was in her early twenties, and fresh as a dewdrop. Utterly enamored with her beau. Is that what I should look like? Carson wondered. Brimming over with dew and sunshine?

She glanced down at her California-chic style of clothing. Faded jeans torn at the knees, a long boyfriend shirt, rows of bracelets on an arm, and strands of beads at the neck. Turquoise and silver hoops at the ears and cowboy boots on her feet. Her long dark hair was twined into a thick braid that fell over her shoulder. She hardly thought anyone would use "dew and sunshine" to describe her. To begin with, she was at least a decade older than that sweet Georgia peach. Studying her dewy-eyed expression, Carson couldn't help but wonder if the young woman shouldn't wait a few years before getting married. Experience more of life before settling.

After all, girls were getting married later now. She'd read that twenty-seven was the average age of today's bride, closer to Harper's age. In bigger cities such as New York, Washington, and Los Angeles, women were disinclined to tie the knot before they were well into their thirties. At thirty-four, Carson wasn't completely sure she was ready even yet.

With a great thump and screeching of brakes the plane landed at Charleston International Airport, jolting Carson's thoughts. Soon the plane was filled with the sounds of seat belts clicking and rustling as restless passengers stood and anticipated an escape from confinement and the continuation of their journeys. She felt herself awakening at the prospect of seeing Blake again. She needed to freshen up before she faced him after so long a time.

In the ladies' room Carson stood in front of the industrial mirror under the harsh light. She saw the ravages of long hours of travel and exhaustion in the chalkiness of her skin. Her blue eyes, usually brilliant, appeared dull and bruised by the dark circles. After rinsing her face with cold water and patting it dry with paper towels, she dug into her large leather bag and pulled out her makeup. She added just enough blush to look healthy, a smattering of shadow and lip gloss. Then she untwined her braid and brushed it until it fell like glossy dark silk down her back. Blake loved her hair, liked to wrap his fist in it when he kissed her.

She stuffed everything back into her bag and straightened her shoulders.

"Dew and sunshine," she said, feeling the bride-to-be at last. She grabbed her suitcase and strode into the corridor. When she reached the exit guard to the terminal, she heard Blake's voice.

"Carson!"

She swung her head toward the sound, surprised. She'd expected him to pick her up at baggage claim. But there he stood at the exit, looking very much the same tall, slender, and tanned man she'd left last fall. Over the winter his dark hair had grown longer. Thick curls amassed on his head, not yet shorn for the summer. His eyes were the color of chocolate and they were warm now, bubbling over with anticipation. When their gazes met, he lifted his hand in a boisterous wave, revealing an enormous bouquet of white roses.

All her nervousness, worries, and fatigue fled the moment she saw him. Like a light at the end of a tunnel, his gaze called to her.

"Blake!"

Suddenly she was grinning wide, face flushed, trotting in her boots to close the distance between them. In a rush his arms were around her, holding her tight, her lips smashed against his in a devouring kiss that was filled with discovery, reconnection, and promise.

"Baby, you're home," he said against her cheek.

Hearing the words, she felt the truth in them. She was home.

He grabbed her bags, eyes only on her, oblivious of the glances they were gathering, mostly from young girls and older women with smiles on their faces.

The drive from the airport in Blake's pickup was filled with catch-up conversation, questions fired and answered, mixed with laughter. Outside, the day was dreary. Rain whipped the windshield while the wipers clicked like metronomes. They crept along Coleman Boulevard, past shops lit up like night, though it was barely one o'clock in the afternoon. Blake kept a firm grip on her hand, releasing it briefly only to shift gears, then clasping it again, as though afraid the bird would fly off again. As they left the mainland and headed over the wetlands, she looked out to see that the tide was so high only the tips of grass were visible, like some great green lawn seemingly ready to overflow with the rain. She knew that in twelve hours the powerful tides would turn and the water would recede again, exposing mounds of mudflats with glistening black, sharp-tipped oyster shells, an army of fiddler crabs, and, if the storm was over, regal snowy egrets. These, she thought, were the seaside sentinels welcoming her home to the lowcountry.

They went directly to Blake's apartment on Sullivan's Island. Once a military barracks, the long, white wood building had been converted to apartments. The history of a military presence on the island went back to the Revolutionary War. Passing Fort Moultrie, Stella Maris Church, her hand went to the window, as though to caress these touchstones. If she turned here toward the back of the island, she'd head toward Sea Breeze, she thought. But Blake drove straight down Middle Street.

They held hands as they climbed the stairs to Blake's apartment, then paused at the door and smiled. They both knew what awaited them on the other side. Once the key entered the lock, Hobbs began his deep-throated huff of warning. They heard the dog's nails clicking on the hardwood, then the exploratory deep sniffs at the door.

"Are you ready for your welcome?" Blake asked, turning the key.

Carson smiled and nodded, bracing herself. When the door opened, the giant golden Labrador licked Blake's hand, then immediately went to sniff the new person—Carson's boots, her jeans, her extended hand. Then, with a high yelp of recognition, Hobbs began barking and whining with excitement, his tail waving back and forth. Carson couldn't have asked for a warmer homecoming. She bent low to scratch behind his ears and pet his fur.

After Blake settled his dog and they entered the small two-bedroom apartment, a moment of tension came between them, the first since she'd seen him. The air around them felt charged with energy and want.

"I'll put the flowers in water," Blake said, taking the roses from her.

She brought them to her nose, inhaling their heady scent once more before relinquishing them to Blake. He was watching her, his pupils pulsing. He stood motionless for a second, then in a sweep tossed the roses to the nearby sofa and stepped forward to place his long hands on her cheeks and draw her lips to his.

He drank from her lips like a man parched. His tongue probed, separating her lips and plunging into the moisture he'd not tasted for months. She welcomed him, clasping herself tighter to him with a soft moan in her throat. It was always like this with them. A kiss was like spontaneous combustion. Neither of them could stop now, nor would they want to. Outside, lightning flashed, and seconds later, thunder rumbled close, loud. The lights flickered. Hobbs whined and curled up in his bed.

Blake pulled back from Carson's lips, let his hands slide down her arms to her hands, and said, "I've missed you."

"I've missed you, too."

He took her hand and, without another word spoken, led her to his room and to his bed. The cold front gusted at the windows, rattling the frames as rain sluiced through the air. But inside, the small apartment welcomed the lovers and protected them from the storm.

"It's still raining," Carson said.

She lay on her back, her long dark hair spilling over the pillows, one arm flung over her forehead. Her breathing had calmed, and spent, she felt suddenly tired, as if she could sleep for hours listening to the rain pattering outdoors. Lovemaking often had this effect on her. Unwinding like a tight coil, the passion gave her a great release.

"It's supposed to rain all day, then move on tonight. Tomorrow should be sunny." Blake rolled to his side and propped his head on his palm. He reached out to shift the sheet up over her naked breasts. "You must have jet lag. Rest."

"I *am* tired."

"It was a good idea to stop here first, before going to Sea Breeze. Give you time to decompress. Besides, I want my time first, before I have to share you with everyone else."

Carson lifted her arm to gently slide her hand along the side of his head. "True, though I miss them. Especially Mamaw. But, yes, we need this time alone. To talk."

"And sleep. It's a good day for sleep."

"Yes." Her lids blinked slowly, listening to the patter of rain on the roof. She felt safe here, with Blake, protected from whatever ill winds blew outside this apartment.

"Oh, Blake," she said in a choked whisper. "I'd forgotten what it was like here with you."

He smiled. "Then don't go away again."

He gathered her closer to him so she could rest her head on his shoulder. They lay entwined in each other's arms, listening to the softer roll of thunder compete with Hobbs's snores.

Carson's fingers played with the hairs on his chest. Furrowing her brows in consternation, she sighed heavily.

"What?" he asked, alert to her shift in mood.

"Oh, I've been wondering. . . ." She looked at Blake and saw his alert expression. Like a man waiting for the other shoe to drop. She paused. Carson had hurt him before. She couldn't hurt him again. She tried to couch her words.

"While I was away, the work was hard, yes. Demanding. Frustrating. That cyclone that hit really slowed down production. I've lived through Category One hurricanes here on the island before, but this cyclone was worse. There were moments I wasn't sure we'd make it. We were all pretty scared." She snorted. "I don't know if Kowalski was more afraid of the storm or the cost of the delay."

Blake waited without speaking, his hand stroking her bare arm.

"All those delays. I know I swore I'd be back earlier. I'm months late. I couldn't help them. I'm sorry."

"I know. We talked about it. It's done. You're here now."

Carson hesitated. "I also said that I wouldn't take another film job."

Blake's gaze sharpened. "Did you?"

"No." She took a breath. "Not yet. But Kowalski offered me another job. A good one, with good pay. He told me I did an excellent job." Her lips turned up. "That applied to my not drinking, too."

Blake nodded slowly, his brow furrowing as though he wasn't quite sure what she was getting at, but he knew he didn't much like where it was going. "That's what you wanted. Validation. Your self-esteem back. You succeeded."

"Yes. And it feels wonderful. It's like I got myself back." Her hand touched her heart. "The strong, confident me. Feeling that again, I . . ." She took a breath. "I can't go back to the way I was last summer. Lost, penniless, unable to get a job."

"The way you felt last summer had a lot more to do with all

that you learned about yourself than the job issue. You joined AA. That took a lot of personal strength. And your bond with your sisters. I like to think I was part of that, too."

"You were. Of course you were. But learning that about myself and going out into the world, testing myself and succeeding, are two different things. I'm a recovering alcoholic. I'll never be cured. The temptation to drink is present every day, and every day I have to have the personal strength to say no. To do that, I have to be centered and strong. Blake, I'm terrified of going back to that woman I was last summer—broke, wallowing, unemployed. So I'm wondering . . . why do I need to go through that when I was offered another job? One perfectly in line with my career, too. I know people who would kill for that job offer."

Blake gently disentangled himself from her arms and rose to sit on the bed. He crossed his legs and looked out the window a moment, but she knew he wasn't looking at the rain.

"How long would this job take you away for?"

"I'm not sure of the details, but probably two months."

"Does that mean four?"

"Hey, a cyclone doesn't usually hit while filming."

"But there are delays."

"Sometimes. Of course."

Blake shook his head. "You said this was your last film job."

"I know. At the time I thought it was. But I'm not sure now. I have nothing else here."

Blake snorted derisively.

"I don't mean you. You know that."

"You haven't looked."

Carson scrambled to rise and sit across from him, unaware

of, unconcerned about, her nakedness. "Yes, I have! Last summer. All summer. I had to take pity donations from Harper." Carson shook her head violently. "I can't do that again. And why should I? Why should I take a job I don't love when I have a job that I do love?"

"Aren't you forgetting something?"

She looked at him questioningly.

"We'll be married. You'll be my wife. You won't be penniless. What's mine is yours. That's what a marriage is."

Carson took a deep breath and turned away from the sincerity on his face. The room was half-dark with the lights off and the dark sky outdoors. "Please understand," she began, trying hard to keep her voice calm and reasonable, "that I appreciate that. But I can't sit back and let you take care of me. I need to feel I can take care of myself. You know how I grew up—my father took me away from Mamaw when I was a little girl and moved me to Los Angeles, where he was going to make his name and fortune. He was always trying to write or sell something. By then he'd given up on his dream to write the great American novel and got into screenplays, magazine pieces, ghostwriting, anything he could so that he could pay the rent. And when he couldn't, he took what little money we had and got drunk. I learned pretty early to depend on myself. I had to hide his money to buy groceries. I cooked, cleaned, got myself to school. I was more the parent than he was. When I turned eighteen, I'd had enough and left. When he died a few years later, I was sad. But I also felt a little relief." She shrugged, a physical effort to remove the guilt she carried. "It's always been me, taking care of me. That's all I've ever known."

"First, I'm not your father. I come from a long line of steady,

hardworking stock. Secondly," Blake said with a hint of humor, "independence isn't the key to a good marriage."

Carson shivered, feeling chilled. She reached out to pull the sheet up over her shoulders. Carson knew that commitment of any kind, much less marriage, was difficult for her. She didn't like long-term leases, jobs that kept her tied to one city, one place. In the past, whenever a boyfriend had started getting serious or mentioned the word *ring*, she'd run. Only with Blake had she found herself able to consider a pledge of commitment. For better or worse, through sickness and health, till death do us part. Blake never had any doubts, was steadfast in his belief in her. In them. But she was beginning to feel shackled by the promises she'd made last fall, bound not only to marry but to give up her independence.

Carson answered seriously, "I know you're not my father. You're as far from him as a man could be. But . . ." She looked down and tugged at the sheet, pulling it closer.

"But what?"

"But as for my independence, I'm worried." She twisted the sheet in her hands, taking a breath, looked up, and met his eyes. "I'm not prepared to give it up."

Blake's dark gaze sharpened. "What are you saying?" Then, visibly paling, he said with caution, "Are you breaking our engagement?"

Chapter Two

*It is always a stressful situation when the wedding of a daughter—
or a granddaughter—brings together parents who are divorced.
It is especially difficult when both families are bitterly estranged.*

To Harper's mind, planning a wedding was not much different from studying for an end-of-term exam. Considerable research had to be done—traditions, venues, music, cake designs, flowers, recipes, decor, goodie bags. Though she admitted to being surprised by how many books and magazine articles had been written on the topics. She'd always been an excellent student and felt up to the challenge. People had to be consulted, lists made, files kept.

What she had been unprepared for, however, was the emotional challenge of wedding planning.

Harper sighed and closed her laptop screen, then leaned back in her chair. It was no use pretending she was working. She'd spent the past hour searching the Internet for still more ideas for her wedding bouquet. Her wedding was only two months away and she hadn't yet selected her flowers.

Harper's venue was decided on, thank heaven. Charleston was the number one destination-wedding location in the country, an accolade that had venues booked two years in advance. This made it frustrating for local girls such as herself hoping to plan their wedding within a year's time. Harper's wedding was scheduled for late May—peak wedding season. She'd gotten lucky and scored a prime venue even though she was late booking. Some bride had canceled a May date at Wild Dunes Resort for a Grand Pavilion wedding the very day Harper's grandmother had called. So Granny James immediately booked it and laid down her deposit—without consulting Harper. Harper's fingers drummed the desk. Most of the wedding was being planned by Granny James, all the way from England. Harper sighed again. It was rather like studying for the exam and having someone else take the test.

Harper let her gaze wander across the room to the bookshelves. Dozens of wedding books lined them. Burgeoning manila folders were stored in the pale Tiffany Blue boxes, each neatly labeled and filled with clippings and photos. Her sisters teased her about her passion for organization and the pretty boxes she was always buying. Harper owned this was true. But what good were all those carefully filed ideas when no one was paying attention to them?

Granny James had been over the moon at the prospect of planning the wedding for her only grandchild. Harper's mother, Georgiana, was Imogene James's only child. Georgiana's wedding to Parker Muir had been a hasty, impromptu affair in New York that had marked the marriage a disaster from the start. They divorced five months later, before Harper was born. Granny James had tucked away her visions of a formal wedding at the family estate, Greenfields Park in England, to save for her granddaughter.

Harper, however, became engaged to a lowcountry boy, moved into Sea Breeze as her home, and intended to live out her life on Sullivan's Island rather than in England. She wanted to be married here, too. On that point she would not budge.

Granny James took Harper's decision with disciplined good nature. Georgiana had prepared Granny James well for disappointment. With her dreams of staging a formal wedding unrealized, she had rallied and launched herself into the task of a beach wedding.

"We love the beach, don't we, darling? Just think. It will be a destination wedding for all the family in England," she'd exclaimed. "So different. We have to have it in the spring so they can escape all the rain. They'll all come. You'll see. What fun!"

A beach wedding was not what Harper had envisioned for herself. Still, knowing how important planning a wedding was to Granny James, she'd bitten her tongue and tried to remember all that Granny James had done for her. Her mother had distanced herself from Harper ever since the engagement. She strongly disapproved not only of the match but of Harper's moving to the lowcountry. Georgiana had always been angry whenever Harper didn't meekly obey her wishes, but when she'd revealed to her editor mother that she was releasing a book with another publisher, the line had been drawn in the sand, and it seemed neither woman was yet willing to cross it.

In contrast to Georgiana, Granny James had been there to wipe Harper's tears all throughout her youth and, after a testy period of interrogation, finally welcomed Taylor into the family. And most significant, Granny James had adroitly engineered Harper's inheritance so that she could purchase Sea Breeze when Mamaw had put the house on the market.

After all that, Harper didn't have the heart to tell Granny James that what she really wanted was a small lowcountry-style wedding at one of the southern plantations in the Charleston area. She'd envisioned ancient oaks dripping moss, winding creeks, a long flowing dress and veil, flower-draped verandas.

The wedding that Carson was having, basically.

Her older sister had also gotten engaged at summer's end. After a tumultuous love affair, the capricious Carson had finally said yes to Blake Legare. Just before she took off for a job as a stills photographer on a film being shot all the way over in New Zealand. Carson was supposed to have returned at the end of January. Yet here it was March, and her feet hadn't touched the lowcountry. Not everyone was surprised. Money had changed hands with friends betting whether Carson would return at all. Not that Harper had placed a bet, but she had to admit that at almost two months late in returning, Carson had everyone's teeth on edge. All except Blake, who'd maintained a stoic faith in his fiancée.

Oh, Carson, Harper thought with a shake of her head. Her heart pumped with affection. She adored her freewheeling sister. Envied her enthusiasm, her lust for life and fearlessness. Carson had taught Harper how to swim, to row a boat, to run wild along the coast of Sullivan's Island playing pirates. But that very independence carried a streak of recklessness that could be annoying, too. Their weddings were to be a means to play new games together—choosing wedding gowns and bridesmaid dresses, bouquets and goodie-bag items, *together*.

In typical Carson fashion, however, she found herself too busy and had blithely left her wedding plans to Mamaw and her future mother-in-law. In an e-mail from New Zealand, Carson wrote, "Do whatever you think best. I know it will be beautiful!"

What normal young woman would hand over her wedding plans to someone else? Harper thought. Then, with chagrin, Harper realized she had done virtually the same thing.

But all that was the past. Carson was coming home now at last, and the wedding plans would kick into high gear.

Harper felt a fluttering in her stomach. Placing her palm there, she wasn't sure if it was nerves, anticipation, or anxiety over what all was left to be done. Truth was, Carson's return home after nearly six months signaled more than just the beginning of a blitz of wedding plans. Tomorrow night Harper was hosting the first family gathering at Sea Breeze since that mass departure last September.

She glanced at her watch and with some alarm saw that it was nearing five. Her mind stopped dallying and sharpened on the immediate. Taylor would be home soon, and so much was still to be done for the party. She rose quickly and strode across the thick carpet to the door. Harper took a final sweep of her office. The hearty pine-paneled floors, the walls of bookshelves, the Oriental rug, a painting of the sea. This had once been the house's library, the male bastion of her grandfather Edward and her father, Parker, complete with hunting paintings, mounted rifles, and the air redolent with pipe smoke. When she and her half sisters began spending summers at Sea Breeze, the feminine accoutrements of dollhouses and pink toys chased the men from their cave. Soon after it became Harper's makeshift bedroom. As years passed, the west wing of the house became known as "the girls'" wing. Mamaw kept the paneling and books and the room was still referred to as the library, but everyone knew it was de facto Harper's room.

Harper made her way down the west hall, her gaze sweeping the rooms she passed to make certain all was ready. At the end of the hall was Carson's bedroom, the largest of the girls' rooms, with a spectacular view of the Cove. This had been Carson's bedroom since she was four years old. Carson's mother had died in a tragic fire, and Mamaw had stepped in to take care of the motherless girl. Mamaw had been more than a grandmother to Carson. She'd been the only mother Carson had ever known. Their relationship was uniquely special, and neither Harper nor Dora resented their bond . . . much. During the summers when the three young girls gathered at Sea Breeze, Carson naturally claimed her childhood room as her own. Harper had every intention of reassuring her sister that this hadn't changed now that Harper owned Sea Breeze. Her sister would always have a place here.

Harper and everyone else were excited to welcome Carson home. But the elephant in the room that no one was mentioning was how Carson resented that her wealthy half sister could afford to purchase Sea Breeze—the only house that Carson had ever considered home.

Harper didn't want any arguments or resentments to mar what she hoped would be a happy time for the family as the weddings approached. Satisfied that everything in the room was just as Carson had left it the previous September, Harper closed the door, reminding herself to add fresh flowers to the room before Carson arrived.

The second bedroom was smaller and faced the front of the house and the ancient live oak tree that shaded the house under its protective foliage. This was Dora's room, one Harper had shared with her sister for a time. Pink and French in design, it suited their oldest sister. Now living in her own cottage on Sullivan's Island, Dora didn't need a bedroom at Sea Breeze. So Harper had decided she'd put Granny James here when she arrived in a few short weeks.

She entered the living room and paused. Carson would notice the changes here. The large, airy space with lots of large windows faced the front courtyard. Harper had freshened up the room a bit, making it younger in appeal with an icy-blue, and white-trim, palette. Mamaw's Early American antiques had been placed into storage for Dora and Carson. Having assumed ownership of the house, Harper felt it only fair that her sisters receive the furniture. Besides, she was inheriting a boatload of antiques from her grandmother's estate in England. More than Harper could ever use. She had selected a few favorites for Sea Breeze—the gorgeous secretary, several side tables, a dining-room table and chairs, and paintings. She'd purchased two new down-filled sofas. She'd spent a lifetime growing up with hard, creaky antiques and was determined to have a comfortable place to sit in her own home.

Home.

The thought never failed to take her breath away. Growing up, she'd been carted from one home to another depending on the season, complete with an assortment of faceless nannies. She'd never felt that any one of them was home.

Except for Sea Breeze. The historic house was so named because it sat perfectly situated, high and proud on the southern tip of the island, facing onshore Atlantic breezes from the front and the racing currents of the Cove in back. This house felt like home because of Mamaw's consistent love and Harper's sisters. And her ancestors. Memories were embedded in each nook and cranny of the house that went back more than a hundred years. Harper often felt the whisperings of the past when she wandered the halls, her fingertips delicately stroking the walls, the furniture, the glass.

This house—this *place*—had planted the seeds of her love for the lowcountry. A stirring passion that had bloomed with her love of Taylor. And, herself. Harper felt she belonged here. Here at Sea Breeze she'd discovered the strength of family. Continuity. Security. Harper was a wordsmith. And, as of last month, a soon-to-be-published novelist. She wanted to write books that shared her love of these words, their profound influences, and, of course, the lowcountry.

She caught her reflection in the large Venetian mirror. She saw the same slender, fair-skinned woman who had returned to the lowcountry the previous May. A clever but timid girl without direction. An obedient daughter seeking love. Her red hair was longer now, pulled loosely up in a clasp. Her eyes the same brilliant blue she shared with her sisters. But staring at herself Harper knew that she was not the same girl at all. She had grown up. She'd found her voice. And regardless of what Carson or Dora or anyone else might want or say or think, she was the mistress of Sea Breeze now. Soon to be a wife.

A short while later Harper was standing in the kitchen before the great Viking stove. A storm had blown in, coloring the sky a gunmetal gray. Looking out at the Cove, the choppy gray water mirrored the sky. A gusty wind whistled, rattling the windows. A cold front was moving fast over the island bringing with it icy rain. She shivered, feeling the damp to her bones. She looked in the nearby corner at Thor, Taylor's behemoth of a black dog, part Labrador, mostly Great Dane. The dog would curl up on his cushion by the warmth of the oven in inclement weather.

"Don't you worry, boy. The weather promises to be all blue skies tomorrow," she told him. Thor raised his head to look at her with deep brown eyes, and his tail thumped the floor in a heavy staccato. "At least I hope so," she muttered to herself. Carson couldn't abide cold weather, either, and Harper wanted her sister to be in the best spirits possible.

Harper's small hands moved quickly, efficiently, to add the sautéed okra, celery, bell pepper, garlic, onion, and chicken to the roux. She lowered her head and inhaled the scents, tracing a finger over the gumbo recipe on the counter. The old recipe was one of dozens created by the family's former housekeeper, Lucille. They were handwritten on index cards and assorted sheets of paper. Yellowed and stained, some of the pencil lettering was so faint Harper could barely read them. She had spent months attempting to re-create the recipes as a gift to her sisters.

Thor's head shot up, ears alert. In a leap he was on his feet, trotting to the door, his nails clicking on the hardwood floors. A moment later the door swung open and a gust of cold, wet air swept through the room.

"It's colder than a witch's tit out there."

Harper turned at the sound of Taylor's voice, a wide smile on her face. His tall, large frame filled the entryway. He carried a large green cooler in his arms. Thor whined with joy at his side, torn between greeting his master and sniffing the shellfish inside the cooler.

"You're home late."

"Crazy day. My meeting finished early, so I headed up to McClellanville and got that shrimp you asked for." He set down the large cooler on the floor, stretched, then slipped off his rain jacket. He stood a moment, shaking off water that splattered the floor. "Mama and Dad send their love."

Again she felt fortunate that Taylor's father was once a shrimper. Like many others, Captain McClellan had tied his boat up at the dock and looked for work on land. He couldn't afford to stay in the business. Imported shrimp was priced too low and diesel fuel was priced too high. Shrimping was a vanishing southern industry. But he still knew the few shrimpers left and could always get his hands on fresh shrimp right off the boat.

Taylor hung his jacket on a peg and immediately crossed the room, slipping his arms around Harper's waist. "How's my girl?"

Harper leaned back against him, relishing the feel of his strong arms around her. Over six feet, his broad frame dwarfed her slender five feet two inches. From the moment she'd met him, Taylor had made her feel safe. It was a new sensation for a girl who'd never known security. She ducked away when he nestled his lips at her neck.

"Stop," she protested. "I'm cooking!"

"I'm starved." He leaned over her shoulder and sniffed loudly. "Smells good."

"This isn't for tonight." She turned in his arms to slip her own around his neck. "It's for tomorrow night. For Carson's welcome-home party. I thought . . ." She laughed when he dove in for another nibble at her neck.

"I told you I was starved."

She laughed again and pushed him, this time more firmly, away. "Bide your time, man. You're going to make me burn my gumbo." She turned again, this time successful in being released. "I thought tonight we'd have chicken salad."

"Nope." Taylor walked to the fridge. He tugged it open, pulled out a beer, and flipped off the top. "Salad isn't going to do it. I need something that'll stick to my ribs."

"How about you order a pizza?"

"Done."

While she stirred at the stove, she watched as he moved with easy familiarity to the kitchen drawer and drew out a wine cork, then walked to the pantry, where bottles of wine were stacked. Such a domestic scene, she thought contentedly. They could already be husband and wife. Taylor had moved into Sea Breeze last September after the papers were signed and Granny James returned to England, Carson flew off to LA, and Dora moved to her own cottage on Sullivan's Island. Mamaw had promptly declared that she didn't want to be a third wheel in the main house and had taken up residence in the guest cottage. Taylor had felt awkward at first, tiptoeing around as though he were a guest. She enjoyed seeing him comfortable at Sea Breeze now, accepting that this was his home.

Taylor's large hands grabbed a bottle of wine from the rack. "Red okay?"

"Don't pour me any wine." Harper reached out to lift her mug. "I'm drinking hot tea. It's so chilly."

Taylor set the bottle down, then returned to the stove. He reached for a spoon and dipped it into the gumbo. He blew on the sauce, then tasted it, eyes closed. After a second he said, "Tastes good, baby, but it needs something. Not spicy enough."

Harper trusted his palate when it came to lowcountry dishes. She picked up a pen and bent over the recipe.

"I'm still making adjustments on Lucille's recipe. It's trial-and-error. She was, shall we say, creative in her measurements." Harper lifted the recipe and read aloud, "Toss in some oregano, basil, onions, garlic."

Taylor laughed as he walked to the wooden kitchen table where a pile of mail sat. "Lucille probably learned these recipes at her mother's or grandmother's knee. Watching them *toss* things in. She wrote those directions for herself. There was no need for her to be specific."

"I, however, have to make an educated guess. Thus lots of tasting." Harper brought the spoon to her lips, tasted, then reached out to add a generous pinch of oregano. "I want everything to be perfect for tomorrow's party."

"It will be. You've been planning for weeks."

"It's the first time there's been a gathering here at Sea Breeze since we've bought it."

"Dora's been here plenty of times."

"Well, Dora, yes. Of course. She lives so close. But not Carson. She's the one who's most attached. And the one who had an issue with me buying it." Harper stirred more rapidly as she felt the nervousness tighten her stomach. "She'll want every-thing to have stayed the same." Including Mamaw's still owning it, Harper thought.

"Hey, it's done. All water under the bridge now."

"She can't help but resent the fact that I own the house she loves. Me, the least likely candidate."

"Why the least likely?"

"I was the least connected to the house. To the South for that matter. I only came here as a child for a few summers. I was the sister from 'off.' The Yankee from New York. Then I come barreling in last summer and buy the place right from under their noses."

Taylor scoffed, "Hardly the scenario. You were the only one who could afford to rescue it. I figure they're all thinking you came riding in on your white charger to save the day. Other-wise strangers would be living in this house right now. Carson has to accept that fact and be grateful."

Harper didn't reply. In her experience, emotions ran high in family matters and clouded judgment. "She'll resent any changes I made. Think that it's not my place, especially while Mamaw is still alive."

"Maybe at first. It'd be only natural. But she'll get over it." Taylor reached in for a second taste. "Better. But it still needs a little more heat." He put the spoon on the counter and reached for the mail. "She's getting married, too, don't forget. She'll be moving into her own place with Blake. He was talking about buying a house. She'll have enough on her mind."

"Blake's not moving. He's keeping his apartment on Sul-livan's."

Taylor stopped sifting through the mail and set the pile

back on the table. He and Blake had become close friends since the engagement. Their shared interest in dolphins cemented a natural affinity.

"Not moving? I thought he was heading out to James Island. Closer to NOAA."

"Carson doesn't want to leave Sullivan's Island. At least she's firm about something."

Taylor kept silent but his brows gathered.

Harper turned off the stove and lay the wooden spoon on the counter. She knew Taylor's silences held back a lot of words. As quick as Harper had been to imply one of Carson's faults, her defense of her sister came naturally. "It's not like Blake doesn't want to live on the island, too. It's *his* apartment."

Taylor took a long swallow from his beer. "When's Carson arriving, anyway?"

"Tomorrow afternoon. Blake is picking her up from the airport, then bringing her here." Harper chewed her lip. "Her room is all freshened up. I'll put fresh flowers in tomorrow and some lowcountry snacks . . . benne wafers, pralines."

"You're doing a lot, honey. Is it really all necessary?"

Her face lit up as she caught his gaze. "I want to. Taylor, it's beginning. The weddings."

Taylor's eyes kindled. "I only care about the one wedding. Ours."

He leaned against the table and rubbed the back of his neck. Harper knew this as a signal that something was on his mind. She leaned against the counter, crossed her arms, and waited for him to speak.

"I was talking to my parents," he began.

Harper said nothing.

"We were getting our ducks in a row. Do you know how long Granny James will be staying here?"

Something in his voice made Harper glance up sharply. No love was lost between those two when she and Taylor were dating, but peace had been made.

"She'll stay until the wedding for sure. After that, as long as she cares to." Her voice sounded more unyielding than she'd intended.

"Of course," Taylor hastened to reply. He looked down, his fingers drumming the table behind him. "The reason why I was talking about dates with my parents is that my mother thought it might be nice for me to return home for a while. Before the wedding. Sort of a last chance to be with her boy again before I become your husband."

Harper relaxed again and moved closer to Taylor to slip her arms around his waist. "I've always assumed you would go back home for a while before the wedding. It'll be a flurry of estrogen and lace here. But I'll miss you. How long would you guess? About a week?"

He looked down and his eyes caught hers. "Actually, I was thinking of leaving soon. Before Granny James arrives."

"What? But that's next week!"

Taylor nodded.

Harper was stymied. "But . . . but why? There's no need for you to leave that early. It's insane. Getting to work every morning all the way from McClellanville will add hours to your commute."

"It'll only be for a short while."

Harper released him and strode across the room for her tea, feeling a sudden need for its warmth. She closed her hands around the heated ceramic and stared at the dark brew. "I don't understand," she said softly.

"You remember how things were between your grandmother and me."

"That was last year. She loves you now."

"Love?" he said dubiously. "Tolerates, maybe. Accept, possibly. She raked me over the coals."

"Granny James was just being protective. She didn't know you and wanted to be sure . . . well . . ."

"That I deserved you."

"Yes." Harper's lips twitched.

"And that I wasn't after you just for your money."

Harper shrugged. "That, too. And you passed with flying colors. So what's the problem?"

"I don't think it's a good idea for me to stay here, living in this house, sleeping in your bed, before we're married."

"It's no secret. She knows you're living here."

His eyebrows shot up. "She does?"

"Oh, for heaven's sake. She's no prude."

"She is when it comes to you. I don't want to be on the receiving end of her cool glances. That woman could kill a charging rhino with one look. I'd rather deal with hours of traffic. Or rent a room for a few months."

Harper put her cup on the counter and crossed her arms against an irrational panic growing inside her chest. She felt her heart beating faster, and it felt as if all the worries she'd squelched deep inside were pounding to get out. "I can't be left alone here! They'll all be here—Carson, Blake, Granny James, Mamaw, Girard, Devlin, Dora, Nate. . . . They'll be constantly in and out, asking for things, meals to prepare, laundry. Not to mention the wedding plans. How will I ever cope?"

"You don't have to take care of everyone. They can take care of themselves. It'll be the same as last summer."

"But it won't! This is my home now. It'll be expected that I make the decisions. Plan the meals. Be the one in charge. I can't, Taylor," Harper blurted, tears springing to her eyes. Taylor came forward to put his arms around her. As always, she felt safe in his arms. She needed him now more than ever.

Taylor smoothed the hair from her face, damp with tears.

"I'm sorry. I don't know why I got so emotional. I'm actually very happy they're all going to be here. I just feel a bit over-whelmed. It's just, I can't do it without you here. I need you. Especially now."

Taylor's hand stilled. He slid back, holding her arms in his hands and studying her face. After a brief silence he said faintly, "Why especially now?"

Harper drew a breath and wiped her face with her finger-tips. Her face broke into a smile. "Because"— a gleam was in her eyes—"we're going to have a baby."

Chapter Three

Like any young southern bride, she had visions of being the perfect wife, the best mother, and a creative hostess worthy of the pages of Southern Living magazine.

The streets were collecting water on Sullivan's Island by the time Dora made her way home. It had been raining like the Lord's flood all afternoon without sign of stopping. It didn't make her life any easier on a day Dora had to rush all morning arranging after-school care for Nate and squeezing in a few extra, much-needed final minutes of study. Now the day was done, the test taken, and she was on her way home. It felt as though all the energy she'd bottled up had spilled out on the test, leaving her feeling empty. All she wanted to do on this chilly, wet night was to change out of this constricting dress into comfortable clothes and slippers, drink a glass or two of wine, curl up on the sofa, and watch mindless television.

The cold rain splattered the windshield of her car so hard

she could barely see the little house nestled among clusters of palms, oleanders, and old oaks. She turned off the engine and sighed in the sudden silence, eyes closed. The rain beat the roof of her aging Lexus like a drum. This was the first moment of peace she'd had since she'd opened her eyes this morning. She felt weary, as if she'd run a marathon—only, she thought with chagrin, without having lost an ounce.

Her brief moment of peace concluded, Dora began to revisit in her mind the questions on the exam, second-guessing her answers. Dora had never been a great student. Not like Harper with her razor-sharp intellect and Ivy League education. Dora had to study, hard, for a test. Yet no matter how much she studied, when the test was put before her, she felt a panic build in her chest and a pounding in her ears that made it difficult to think clearly. Her teachers had called her a "poor test taker." Because of this her grades had suffered in school, but that was a lifetime ago, and she'd never been all that worried about her ranking in academics. She hadn't finished college so she could marry Calhoun Tupper after her junior year. As her friends had joked, who needed a BA when she got a MRS?

This test was different, however. Passing the real estate exam meant the difference between starting a new career that she loved and trying to support herself and her son on minimum wage. She placed her fingertips to her temple, feeling the old fear of failure rear up in her heart—a cold shiver, a tightening in the chest. Paralyzing.

Her marriage to Calhoun had been a dismal failure. For the ten years of their union, Dora had struggled to be the wife she'd always believed she should be. She had exalted expectations set by her mother and her mother before her for generations. She and Cal had pulled together their savings and borrowed to the hilt to purchase an old Victorian house in the historic section of Summerville, South Carolina. They'd thought it was the first step toward the life they'd planned for themselves. Like any young southern bride, Dora had visions of being the perfect wife, the best mother, and a creative hostess worthy of the pages of *Southern Living* magazine. With the naïve excitement of youth they'd made great plans to lovingly restore what they saw as a grande dame of an old house. Oh, the plans Dora had! All she'd needed was a little money and a little time for her dreams to come true.

Time, however, had not been kind. The old treasure of a house was in fact a money pit of mold, rotting foundations, and rats in the attic. Cal's meager salary and lack of promotions at the bank meant there was never the money to begin restoration. And Cal, it turned out, didn't know a hammer from a paintbrush. They lived in a run-down house in an aura of disappointment. If that wasn't depressing enough, she'd had one miscarriage after another. When at last her prayers were answered and she gave birth to her son, Nate, she'd thought things would at last improve. But she knew something about her son was off, and at three years of age Nate was diagnosed with Asperger's, a high-functioning autism.

Naturally, Dora lost interest in the house and focused on what was important—helping her son. She withdrew from local volunteering and began homeschooling. She didn't realize that she was becoming isolated and lost interest in herself, as well. Meanwhile Cal, too, lost interest, not only in the house but in his wife and son. Then, last summer, he had asked for a divorce.

When Cal left, Dora felt she'd failed at everything that had mattered to her and fell into a deep depression, which led to broken heart syndrome, also known as cardiomyopathy, which landed her in the hospital. Mamaw's invitation to Sea Breeze had saved her. She'd moved to the safety of her grandmother's and sisters' arms. With their support, she'd begun her long journey to healing.

Now, her divorce was final. She was, for the first time in her life, truly on her own. The sensation was both heady and daunting. Dora knew she had a lot to prove—to herself, and, too, to her son. Yet she'd never felt so stressed. Money was tight. The tuition for Nate's private school was costly, and Cal was often lagging behind in contributing his share of the payments. He kept telling her he had to spend money to get the house in shape for sale. That albatross had been on the market for nearly a year without a serious offer. If only it would sell, she'd be free of it and maybe have a little money left over. *Don't count your chickens before they hatch*, her mother would tell her. It was true, Dora knew that. She had to concentrate on what she could do right now. Such as getting her real estate license.

Dora squeezed her eyes tight and said a quick prayer. She just had to pass this exam. For once in her life she didn't want to depend on anyone else or any turn of fate. She wanted to make it on her own.

But it was hard being a single parent. Between caring for Nate, cleaning the house, shopping and cooking, working full-time, and finding time to study, the one she'd stopped taking care of was herself. Again. She was falling into a dangerous trap. She'd stopped exercising on the excuse she didn't have time. She ate take-out food. And the wine . . . The pounds she'd lost were slowly piling back on. She felt like such a failure for slipping into old, bad patterns.

Relax. Don't beat yourself up, Dora told herself. She took a deep cleansing breath, then exhaled out the noxious feelings of self-hatred and failure. She looked out the car window and saw the little cottage peeping out from the wet, drooping foliage. *You're home now,* she told herself.

This feeling of homecoming was hard-won. She loved this little cottage. Devlin, her boyfriend, had purchased it a year earlier when the real estate market crashed. When they'd started dating, she'd helped him remodel it, even rolling up her sleeves and working alongside him. Dora had poured into the cottage all she'd dreamed of doing all those lonely years in Summerville. Devlin not only appreciated her suggestions but had incorporated them. And more, Devlin knew how to wield a hammer. Together, they'd rehabbed the house by the creek into something special. This cottage was one of her successes. Devlin had then let Dora rent the house at an amount she could afford while he waited for the market to improve. They both knew it was his way of helping her through this rough time.

Devlin was waiting for her inside now. Feeling buoyed by the thought, she pushed open the car door and ran along the winding walkway, clutching her raincoat close to her neck, to the front door. It was thankfully unlocked so she pushed it open and scampered into the dry shelter.

"Surprise!"

Dora stopped in the entryway, mouth agape. Yellow light from the lamps filled the small living room with golden light. Hanging from the ceiling, from corner to corner, were ribbons of crepe paper in blue and white, and under them, her boyfriend and son stood wearing party hats and blowing paper horns that sounded like duck calls.

Dora brought her hands to her cheeks. "What's all this?" she exclaimed, dripping in the front hall.

"Congratulations, baby," Devlin shouted as he came to her side and planted a firm kiss on her cheek.

"You don't even know if I passed the exam," she protested.

"I know you will," he replied confidently as he helped her out of her raincoat. "You studied harder than anyone I've ever seen, plus you had me as your tutor. You're a shoo-in."

Nate hurried toward her, and looking down, she saw his face flushed with a wide grin of excitement. That in itself was unusual, and she felt a rush of love. She wanted to bend to hug him in her arms, to squeeze his small, slender frame with all the love she had to offer, but she held back. Dora knew that part of his autism meant that her son didn't like to be hugged or touched and accepted kisses only rarely, when he was in the right mood. She played fair and instead lowered herself to meet his gaze, matching his smile.

"Are you surprised?" Nate asked.

"I am. Very."

"Was it a good surprise?"

Her heart melted at seeing his blue eyes, the same Muir color as her own, shining. "The best."

"I have another surprise. I'll show you!"

"Hold on, fella," Devlin told the boy. "Give your mama a chance to take off her coat and get dry. We've plenty of time for more surprises."

Nate's face clouded. He didn't like to wait. But to his credit he didn't begin a litany of stubborn whines. He merely frowned and nodded his head, then stomped off to the table to wait for dinner. "I'm hungry."

"I am, too, pal," Devlin said.

Dora was still surprised at Devlin's effect on her recalcitrant son. Cal had never spent time with Nate. He saw his son's autism as some kind of failure, hers naturally. Cal never attempted the normal father-son activities or explored other possible ways to connect. In contrast, Devlin accepted Nate for who he was, appreciated Nate's unique talents, and, more, enjoyed his company. He took Nate fishing and taught him how to clean a fish and steer a boat. How to ride a bike and not cry when he fell off. How to identify snakes and spiders, set up a tent, bodysurf the waves. Thanks to Devlin, her pale, thin child was becoming a golden-skinned, wiry lowcountry boy. Although Nate rarely displayed affection, she knew her son liked Dev, even respected him. Devlin was the male influence—she didn't dare say the father—that Nate so desperately needed.

"Come sit down, pretty lady," Devlin said to Dora, walking to the table and pulling out a chair. "I fixed us something special. Your favorite. Shrimp and grits . . . the good grits, too. Not that watery stuff you make. Stone-ground, cooked with cream and bubbling with cheese. Now don't give me that worried look." He waved his hand dismissively. He was in the kitchen, visible from the dining room. She watched him hover over the stove, giving his grits a final stir before preparing the plates. Devlin loved to cook, and most of the time he was mindful of her healthy-heart diet. They'd all been frightened last summer after the scare that had put her in the hospital. But he knew she yearned for butter, bacon fat, and any meat that came from a pig.

"Your diet can skip a day," he said. He went to the gleaming stainless-steel fridge to pull out a bottle of champagne. With the speed of experience he twisted the cork, and they cheered at the sound of the reassuring pop. "Tonight's special." Devlin walked over to hand her a flute of the bubbly. "You're a bona fide real estate agent!" Devlin bent to kiss her lips with a proprietary air.

"Almost," she reminded him, accepting his kiss. She was touched at his thoughtfulness. It was typical of Dev to prepare an impromptu party. He loved a good time. Thought life was too short not to enjoy the special moments. She got swept up in his enthusiasm and felt her anxiety ease.

"Hey, Mr. Cassell, I guess this means you're my new boss."

"Welcome to Cassell Real Estate. Where *your home is your castle*," he added, raising his glass with mock seriousness as he recited his company's slogan.

Dora always thought the phrase a bit corny, but it seemed to work. People remembered his name, and his was the most successful real estate company on Sullivan's Island. To her, though, Devlin would always be the adorable surfer that she'd fallen in love with at sixteen years of age.

She enjoyed the delectable shrimp and grits, forcing herself to ignore the calories. She saw tonight as a well-earned treat, promising herself she'd get back to her diet the following day. Across from her, Nate was wolfing down the grits, which were on his select list of approved foods. Though he wouldn't allow the shrimp to touch the grits or a drop of the gravy. She drank another glass of champagne, then another, enjoying the buzz after the months of studying and the completion of her course. Once she got her license, her plan was to quit her job at the clothing store and begin her new career as a real estate agent. She lived in a house she loved, had a man she loved and a son she loved more than anything else in the world. She felt her world shift and suddenly life looked promising.

Nate squirmed in his chair and kept eyeing the hallway to his bedroom.

"What's putting ants in your pants?" she asked.

"All right, big guy," Devlin told him. "I reckon it's time to give your mama your big surprise."

Nate's face lit up as he bolted from his chair and ran down the hall.

"What in the world?" Dora turned to Devlin. "Please don't tell me he's giving me a video game. That is the only thing that fires up the boy like that."

"You'll see," Devlin replied mischievously, a grin playing around the corners of his mouth.

A moment later Nate returned, walking slowly, cautiously, down the hall carrying something in his arms. When he was closer, she heard a faint, high-pitched mewling. Dora glanced sharply up at Devlin and saw him looking at the boy, grinning. Whatever it was, Dora knew that Devlin was part of it.

Nate stopped before her, his blond head bent, cradling a small ball of fur—white, black, and brown. He held it so tight she didn't know if the poor thing could breathe. Her heart sank and she didn't know what to think. They'd never had pets, afraid of how Nate would react to anything climbing on him or, worse, licking him. Not to mention the hair, the litter box. A kitten was the last thing she'd expected to see Nate walk in with tonight—and her face showed it.

"Look!" Nate exclaimed.

"A . . . a kitten!" she stuttered.

"Yes," Nate replied matter-of-factly. He was looking at the kitten. "It is a calico kitten. It's a girl. Did you know that all calico cats are girls? I learned that."

"Where did you get her?" Dora tried to keep her voice cheery.

"We got her at the animal shelter. The ASPCA." Nate looked at Devlin for confirmation.

"That's right," Dev said.

"It's your present," Nate told her.

"Mine?"

"Yes. But I will have to take care of her. She needs a lot of care. I will give her food in the morning and at night, too. It's dry food. They call it kibble. We also got some cans because she is so little. And a litter box. Dev got you the litter box. That's his present for you, and the kitten is from me. But I will take care of it for you."

Dora shot a level glance at Devlin. He was still smiling and winked at her. "Wait for it . . . ," he said sotto voce.

"She got her shots already. And she's really good. She already peed in the litter box." Only then did Nate look up, slowly, his eyes shining in appeal. "Do you like her? Do you want to keep her?" His brows knit and he reminded her, "She is *your* present."

Her present? Dora almost laughed aloud. She peered at Nate clutching the kitten as if his life depended on it. The mother in her knew that in fact *she* would be the one caring for the kitten. She would be the one to change the litter box, to pick up the hair balls, to despair at the tears in her curtains and newly upholstered sofa. The kitten was one more responsibility for a single mother. Dora didn't think she could handle one more.

Dora shot a glance at Devlin laced with accusation that he'd put her into this position of being the one who had to say no. Devlin stared back at her with wide-eyed innocence while a small smile of encouragement lingered on his face.

When she turned back to Nate, she watched as the kitten began crawling up his chest. Its tiny claws dug into his sweatshirt as she made her way up to his neck. Dora tensed, poised to leap, waiting for Nate's scream of "Get her off!" There would be tears, maybe even a meltdown.

But none of that happened.

The kitten reached Nate's shoulder and, after mewling a bit, settled there, curled beside his neck. Nate reached up as though it were the most normal thing in the world to have a cat curled by his neck and stroked her gently. In the stunned silence, Dora could hear the kitten's soft purring. She sat staring, not believing what she was seeing. Her son, a boy that didn't like to be touched, was allowing this kitten's claws to dig into his clothes and its fur to rub along his neck. And he was petting her! He seemed to be enjoying the physical contact. Dora's heart expanded with wonder, and in that moment Dora knew she would keep that sweet calico kitten no matter if it tore up the whole cottage. She turned again to Devlin, tears of disbelief in her eyes.

"There's your gift," he said softly.

Dora loved Devlin in that moment more than she ever had before. He really got her son. Knew what he needed and how to handle him. Devlin knew, too, what made her world light up.

Thank you, she mouthed.

He smiled and nodded in mute acknowledgment.

"Yes, of course you may keep her," Dora told Nate. "She's very sweet. I've never received a better gift. And I know you'll take very good care of her. Thank you."

"Good!" Relieved, Nate slowly extricated the kitten from his neck as it mewled piteously. Nate was not the least off put by the kitten's complaints. He put the kitten firmly back into his arms, holding tight. "I am going to put her to bed now. Oh, she needs to sleep in my room. So I can take care of her."

"Does she have a name?" Dora wanted to know.

"Miss Calico."

"Will you call her Callie for short?"

"What do you mean? Like a nickname?"

"Yes. Something short and easy, for when you call her."

Nate considered this. "Okay. Callie for short."

They watched him walk with care from the room and close his bedroom door behind him.

Dora turned to Devlin. "How did you ever manage that? I want the whole story. All the details."

The candle was burning low and the rain continued to patter on the tin roof, a mild drumming that was a soothing white noise. Devlin poured more of the champagne into their glasses, then put his elbows on the table and leaned forward. "Are you really okay with the kitten?"

"It means a bit more work. But I couldn't refuse. My lonely, remote, difficult-to-touch son was just cuddling that kitten. He was hugging it!" Dora sipped her wine. "That's a first. To see him love like that meant the world to me. Of course I'm okay with it."

"I thought it might. But, hey, if it doesn't work out, I'll take the kitten. Seems only fair."

Dora set her elbows on the table and leaned toward Devlin. "So tell me."

Devlin swirled the wine in his glass. "Well, you know I've been looking for a rescue dog. So I go to the pound from time to time, to see if one speaks to me. Last week I took young Nate with me. He was curious and wanted to go. There we were walking around and looking. Truth be told, I was hoping he'd find some dog he liked and I could get that one. But what happens? I turn around and find him squattin' down in front of a kennel filled with a litter of kittens staring like a coon dog on the scent. He was smitten, I could tell. I tried to persuade him to come see the dogs, but you know Nate when he's got his mind made up. He wanted a kitten. Period. And not just any kitten. There was a black one, a gray one, and a gray-and-white-striped one. All furry and bright eyed, one cuter than the other. But he had his eyes set on that there calico."

"So you asked the attendant to let him hold it."

"Sure I did. I couldn't refuse. I was a mite worried, him being so skittish and all about touching. The minute he held the kitten in his arms, he started petting it. And that kitten just sat there and licked his fingers. I knew he had to have it. I saw what you just saw, and I'm not ashamed to tell you I had tears in my eyes."

Dora reached out across the table and took his hand in hers. She squeezed it tight. "Thank you."

"Yeah." Leaning back, he crossed his boot over his knee and gave a sorry shake of his head. "But I'm still lookin' for a dog."

Dora picked up her wineglass and leaned back in her chair. "Maybe I should return the favor and find you a dog."

"No, ma'am. A man's got to choose his own dog."

"Is that some unwritten code in the world of men?"

"It is for a lowcountry man."

"I see." She rolled her tongue in her cheek. "Well, just remember that you're responsible for my gift," she said, exaggerating the word *gift*. "And you're also my landlord. So I don't want to hear one peep from you about litter-box smells or accidents on the carpet."

He laughed his low, rumbling laugh. "I know, I know." He paused to swallow a long drink from his wineglass. "That brings up another subject. Hear me out before you jump to conclusions, okay?" He looked at her, demanding an answer.

His tone had changed. She could tell that he was a bit nervous and it wasn't about the kitten. "Okay, you've got my attention."

"Good. Real good." He set his glass on the table and left his hand there, his fingers drumming. "You remember how we arranged things for this cottage. I told you I'd have to put the house on the market when things picked up."

Dora froze.

"Well, this spring things have really picked up. The market's good. Especially for a house on the creek."

Dora's heart beat harder, fearing where this was headed. "You're selling the house?"

"I might have to."

"Oh." She felt all the joy of the evening fizzle.

"Honey, I have no choice. I'm carrying a lot right now after a slow season, including two houses. This one and the one I'm living in. Oceanfront usually sells good, but the price on my place is a lot higher than this one and the damn beach is eroding. Dora, the simple fact is I can only afford to keep one. One has to go."

Dora wrapped her arms across her chest. She'd known the day would come that this cottage would have to be sold. Her rent didn't nearly cover the mortgage. It had all been arranged from the start. But the thought of losing it . . .

"I'll buy it."

Devlin's face softened. "You can't afford it, baby."

As much as it hurt to hear, Dora knew that was true but had to ask. She found her voice. "Can I pay a higher rent? At least until I sell my house in Summerville? I could give you a down payment then."

"I don't want to do that to you. You're stretched so thin as it is."

She looked out the window. The night was dark and rainy, but in her mind's eye she could see the grassy slope to the salt marsh, the long wooden dock that stretched far out into the creek. All her dreams for this place were like driftwood, caught in the racing tide. She chewed her lip, lest she burst into tears.

Devlin reached out and took her hand. "Hear me out, now," he said, gently reminding her of her promise. "See, then I thought . . . if we moved in together, it wouldn't be an issue. We'd sell one, but still keep one. Together."

"Dev," she said near tears. "You know we can't live together. Not with Nate. The scandal . . ." She didn't need to elaborate. This was still a small, old-fashioned town at heart, and gossips would reach his school eventually. Kids could be cruel.

Devlin sat for a moment looking at her hand, playing with her fingers. Longer than normal.

Dora was attuned to a subtle shift of mood. She waited, breath held. He lifted her left hand and held it in his, letting his fingers stroke her ring finger. Then Devlin reached into his pants pocket and pulled out a small black velveteen box and set it on the table in front of her.

"I understand that you don't want to live together. And I don't want to be your landlord any more. I want to be your husband." He paused. "You know how I feel about you, Dora. I've loved you and only you since we were sixteen years old. When you came back into my life, I swore I'd never let you leave me again. I got to thinking. . . . Your two sisters are getting married. I know how close y'all are. Why don't we join them? Make it a threesome? It'd solve everything. Aw, baby, say you'll marry me and make me the happiest man in the world."

He flipped open the jeweler's box and slid it closer to her.

Dora gasped. The ring was stunning by any standards, but more, she recognized it as one she'd admired in a magazine ad months earlier. He'd casually shown her the ad in the Sunday *New York Times* and asked her which of the four rings pictured she liked best. She'd told him not to get any ideas, but when he prodded, she'd pointed to the three-carat, cushion-cut stone wreathed with small pavé diamonds. What woman wouldn't want that?

And there it was, sitting before her. All she had to do was pick it up and let Devlin slide it on her finger. Dora looked at Devlin's face, flushed with anticipation. So sure of his answer. When she'd first fallen head over heels for the wiry, tanned surfer boy on Sullivan's Island, he'd been poorer than a church mouse. Devlin Cassell was a self-made man. She saw in his face the pride that he could buy her such a ring now, when years before, back when they'd dated, he didn't have one dime to rub against another. She hoped that he knew she'd accept a ring from a Cracker Jack box when the time was right.

But the time wasn't right.

"Oh, Devlin. It's a beautiful ring. The most beautiful ring I've ever seen."

"You did see this one." He pulled the ring from the box. "In that ad, remember? You told me how pretty it was. I kept that ad and ordered the ring in your size."

She smiled tremulously.

He reached for her hand. "Let's put it on and see if it fits."

"Wait." She slid her hand back. Her heart was pounding in her ears in a way that felt very much like panic.

Devlin froze and studied her face. There was an awkward moment. Then his face fell and he put the ring back into its place in the box. "Right."

"I love you, Devlin. You know that."

"But you're saying no."

Dora shook her head. "I'm not saying no. I'm saying not right now."

"Aw hell, woman. We've been through this before. You told me last September that you needed to wait till the divorce was final and I waited. Did I pester you to get married? No. I bided my time. Dora, you're a free woman now." Frustration bubbled under his words. "Your divorce is signed, sealed, and delivered."

"I'm only just divorced. The ink's barely dry. I still am figuring out who I am, what I want out of life, what I can do on my own. I need to love *me* before I can give myself to you. Fully and without doubt. It's not about you. It's about me."

"That's not what I'm hearing. I hear you saying that you don't love me enough. Not yet."

"That's not at all what I'm saying."

"Well, that's what I'm feeling."

"Dev . . ."

"What's next, Dora? Tell me. What are you going to need before you say yes?"

"I don't know. I . . ." She thought. "My starting work as a real estate agent is a big step closer. That's good, right? I suppose the last thing I need is to be financially settled. Once that damn house sells in Summerville, I can pay off my debts and feel like I'm well and truly done with the past."

Devlin furrowed his brows, listening hard.

"Dev, honey, I love you. I want to marry you. I just need to stand on my own two feet. I want you to be proud of me. Then I'll wear that ring. I'll hoot and holler and show it off to anyone and everyone. I promise."

Devlin closed the top of the box with a snap. It sounded ominous to her ears. He tucked the box back in his khaki pants pocket, then rose from the table. "Well, darlin', you put me between a rock and a hard place. Something's got to give. I'll put my house on the market. And I'll put the cottage on the market. As planned. See what happens."

She knew impatience, with herself and with him. "Fine."

He pursed his lips and looked at her, as though holding back words. In the end he only looked toward the door and sighed. "It's getting late. I have an early showing."

Dora watched him walk to the door and grab his jacket from the hall tree. "Don't leave mad."

Devlin slipped into his jacket, stuck his hands in his pockets, and pulled out his keys. He looked at them in his palm, then lifted his head to her. "I'm not mad. I'm disappointed," he said in a flat voice. "I just asked you to marry me and you turned me down."

Dora lowered her head but didn't respond., wincing as she heard the front door shut firmly behind Devlin's retreating figure. There was nothing more she could say.

Chapter Four

Love . . . acceptance . . . forgiveness . . . commitment.
These are the cornerstones of marriage.

*T*he Reverend Atticus Green paused to smile warmly at the young couple before him at the altar of the Ebenezer Baptist Church. The young bride was swathed in white tulle. The groom was smartly dressed in a black tuxedo and gray waistcoat. Atticus winked at his best friend, Kwame, the groom.

Kwame was one of his basketball-team friends from their days at Howard University. Kwame was a big man with as big a heart, appropriately the team's power forward. Beside Kwame stood a line of tall athletic men, handsome in their groomsmen suits. Marcus, whose long arms could sink a basket from any distance, was the shooting guard. Standing beside him was Beau, a bull both in frame and attitude. He was the small forward. Atticus, though neither the tallest nor broadest, was fast and clever. And like his idol, Michael Jordan, Atticus had a winning smile that endeared him to the fans and ladies alike. He played the team's leader as point guard.

Atticus loved these men as brothers. He felt a rush of emotion at being able to marry Kwame today. It was a privilege and an honor. Clearing his throat, he lifted his prayer book and began the service.

"Love . . . acceptance . . . forgiveness . . . commitment. These are the cornerstones of marriage. We stand together, before God, to witness this couple pledge themselves to one another. Please, take each other's hands."

The over-the-top wedding reception was at the St. Regis, a five-star hotel in Atlanta. No expense was spared. There was mood lighting, tall silver candelabras blown out with flowers, and a seated dinner with prime rib and seasonal foods. Atticus didn't want to think of the cost nor how much his church could have done with that money. He wasn't being critical. Everyone had the right to the wedding of his or her choice. He'd held services at most every venue imaginable in the Atlanta area. Formal, like this one. In the country with horses, on beaches in bare feet, and even on boats cruising the river. Yet there was no evidence that a wedding that cost $100,000 could guarantee a successful marriage any more than a $10,000 wedding or, for that matter, an elopement.

As the hour grew late the guests thinned out and the music had changed to the soul funk he loved. Beyoncé, Estelle, Jill Scott—ladies who could really blow. The lights dimmed and people shouted over the loud music to be heard. Someone called out his old college nickname. Atticus cringed hearing it, hating it now as much as he did back then.

"Hey, Attaboy!" Beau called, waving him over.

Following the voice, he spied Beau standing beside Kwame with his arms around his groomsmen. Their ties and jackets were off and each had a drink in his hand.

"Big Beau!" Atticus called back.

"Get your ass over here and link arms. Forget the four cornerstones of marriage. We got to get a picture of the four cornerstones of the Bison basketball team."

Kwame laughed, waved over the photographer, and said, "You got that right. We're the four cornerstones of the Bisons." Kwame opened an arm for Atticus. "Our team was the stuff of legends."

Atticus laughed softly as he slipped off his tie and unbuttoned his shirt collar. They were ribbing him, borrowing his phrase "the cornerstones" from his service. It was true. The four of them were the power players for the four years they were at Howard. Atticus joined his basketball brothers, slipping arms over Kwame's and Marcus's shoulders, feeling the old camaraderie that he knew would always be between them. They'd all taken different paths in life. Kwame was a sports reporter for CNN. He was just married, wanted a family, he was on his way. Marcus had gone into medicine. Beau was a manager for a construction firm. His wife was at home, too far along in her pregnancy to come to the wedding. Atticus had taken a different turn after college and gone to Yale Divinity graduate school. In his black wool jacket and open-collared black shirt, he looked cool and available. No one would guess he was a minister.

He and his friends met on the basketball team their freshman year and were inseparable for four years. Though Marcus and Atticus had gone off to graduate school, after graduation they'd returned to Atlanta to work. It was quietly understood that they'd all stay in Atlanta . . . stay in touch. On weekends they played pickup games of basketball. They stood up for each other's weddings and funerals. Atticus couldn't have gotten through his mother's funeral were it not for them. If all that wasn't enough to bind them for life, the car accident the fateful night of their college graduation was. They were blood brothers.

The photographer did his duty and got the picture. Two of the bridesmaids, seeing the action, came running over, their high heels clicking on the wood floor.

"Wait," one called out, arm waving. "We want a picture with us in it."

They trotted up to the men, giggling and smoothing out their dresses, while the men gave them the once-over. The two women were young and sexy in their off-the-shoulder, silver-sequined gowns that reflected the light and accentuated their ample curves. Keisha, a sloe-eyed beauty, wiggled in beside Atticus, leaned her ample breasts against him, and pressed her cheek against his.

"That's the way," Marcus teased him, chuckling low. "Real close now."

When the photo was done, Keisha turned in Atticus's arms, her body close to his. "You're Atticus Green, aren't you?" she asked coyly.

"That's me."

"I heard about you."

"Oh yeah?"

"Yeah. I heard you've got the most beautiful eyes. And know what? It's true." She pressed closer. "I could look in your eyes till kingdom come." Her intonation clearly indicated that she'd look at them at least until morning.

"You like them blue eyes?" Beau teased her. "Them's white-boy eyes. Look at mine, deep, dark chocolate. Not too sweet. African grade." He laughed.

Atticus smirked and said nothing. All his life his blue eyes had been the butt of jokes among the boys. And a magnet for the girls.

"Hey, Atticus," Marcus said. His arm remained around the other bridesmaid. "Mattie and I are going out after the wedding. Come with us."

"Oh, yes," Keisha urged, wiggling closer.

"Can't," Atticus replied. "Sorry."

"Why not?" Kwame asked, slapping his back. "Keisha wants to go out with you, don't you, baby?"

She nodded. "Sure do."

Beau complained, "Why aren't you asking me to go out with you?"

"'Cause you're married, fool," Marcus shot back. "Your wife's home about to have your baby."

"So what? Don't mean I can't have a good time." Beau laughed as Marcus slapped his back.

"Not with me you can't," Keisha said in his face. "Come on, Atticus. We'll have a good time."

"Wish I could, but I have a service first thing in the morning."

"All work and no play makes Atticus a dull boy," Keisha said, twiddling with his collar.

"I'm sure it does." He gently removed her hands and kissed them before returning them to her. "Maybe another time." He ignored the loud groans of disappointment from his friends.

"But don't you be forgetting me now." Keisha slipped a piece of paper in his pocket, then patted it. "Call me," she whispered in his ear before slowly disentangling herself and strolling off with her friend.

"Are you crazy?" Beau asked him when they were out of earshot. "That was a sure thing. Back in college you never let an opportunity pass."

Atticus shrugged. "I'm not in college anymore."

"No. You're a priest now," Beau fired back. "Celibate."

The men laughed at his expense.

"Not a priest." Atticus gave them their laugh. "And not celibate. Just more choosy."

Marcus gave him a gentle punch. "Yeah, right."

"Hey, I get that," Kwame said, wrapping both arms around Marcus and Atticus. "I knew when I found my Letitia, she was the one." Kwame got teary eyed and looked across the room at his new wife. "Look at my bride. She's so fine. Gentlemen, my days of trolling are over."

Beau hooted and Marcus patted his shoulder. "That's real nice," Marcus said patronizingly. "Give it a few years. As for you . . ." He pointed at Atticus.

A roar from the crowd interrupted them as music for the Electric Slide broke out. Marcus let out a whoop and turned to dance his way to join the lines forming on the dance floor.

Kwame took off after him, looking for his bride.

Beau grabbed Atticus's arm. "Come on, brother. Let's show 'em how it's done."

The weather was cloudy and cool when Atticus got out of the pizza joint. The pizza was only okay, but the run-down restaurant was close to home and the only place still open. The warmth of the pizza felt good on his hands, and the scent of tomato sauce and crust floated up to him, making his mouth water. With his free hand he turned up his collar, hunched his shoulders, and began walking.

Seeing his friends again, feeling the pull of the bonds of his youth, left him feeling unsettled. Kwame, Marcus, Beau—they all seemed content with their lives; even Big Beau, who talked a good game but was devoted to his wife. They sensed Atticus's loneliness, as best friends could. And knew that he'd changed after the accident. Sometimes, he felt they tiptoed around him. He caught the hooded glances they shot to each other when they were worried, such as tonight when he didn't go out with Keisha. They were always trying to set him up, somehow thinking finding the right woman would end his searching. Atticus appreciated their concern, but didn't they get that he wasn't looking to get laid? He'd sowed more than his share of wild oats in college. He wasn't the same popular and conceited kid he was back then. The car accident *had* changed him. A life-and-death experience did that to a person. And what bothered him most was that the conceited, skirt-chasing Atticus was the man his friends missed.

From far off he heard the high-pitched scream of car brakes. Atticus stopped abruptly, his head reared up, and his heart rate accelerated. In a flash he was back to that night eight years earlier.

It was another damp spring night, like tonight. The night of college graduation. It had been raining hard and they'd been drinking hard. Marcus and Beau were in the backseat of Atticus's new BMW, a graduation gift from his parents. Kwame was in the passenger seat. Atticus remembered the new-car smell mingled with the scents of cologne and whiskey. It was almost midnight when they'd left the graduation party, and bored, they were headed to a nearby club. They were just a bunch of young bucks, feeling no pain, out to celebrate. The night was black and starless. He shouldn't have been driving, but he was cocky and young enough to believe he was invincible. Back then, Atticus felt he knew better than his mother, his teachers, and, hell yes, his father. He'd found all the advice he needed in the lyrics of hip-hop, the heated whispers of girlfriends, the late-night drunken wisdom of his friends, and the amber magic he'd discovered in a bottle.

The last thing he remembered was losing control of the car as it hydroplaned across two lanes. The tree came out of nowhere. Suddenly there it was, looming large in the headlights. Atticus awoke days later. Blinking heavily, he felt as if he were swimming up from underwater. Sounds were muffled and he saw the world through a watery veil. Someone called his name, "Atticus, Atticus," over and over, pulling him out from the depths.

"Mama."

They said it was the first word he'd spoken in nearly a week. The police came to take his statement. His friends had been spared with minor injuries. The car was totaled. Atticus was the only one not wearing his seat belt.

By all accounts, Atticus should have died from his injuries. When the doctors found him to be in good health without resulting damage, it was generally accepted by all to be one of those rare occurrences in the medical world that could only be attributed to a miracle. The doctors said this tongue in cheek. They explained how no one knew the hidden strengths that lived in any individual.

Atticus knew in his heart that the doctors were right the first time. It had been a miracle. Something had happened to him in those days teetering between life and death. Images, voices that he could not yet discern because his earthly experiences could not relate to what had happened to him in that other realm. It was otherworldly, outside his nomenclature to explain. Yet as he healed, he felt the nagging sensation that he'd been granted some sort of reprieve. A second chance to make his life meaningful. Atticus tried to brush off the feeling, second-guessing the experience. He was only twenty-one. He didn't want to change his ways, to take the hand held out to him. He didn't want to go down that path.

Atticus sighed now as he walked the empty street, remembering the futility of his denial. He'd been pursued by the Hound of Heaven. A lost soul, racked with guilt and indecision. Peace only came to him once he'd accepted that he'd been called. The first thing he did was to accept that he had a drinking problem and begin his recovery. After he was sober, he applied and was accepted to Yale Divinity School. And he never again touched another drop of alcohol.

Yet despite all the positive changes made in his life, Atticus still felt an emptiness inside, a deep loneliness that going out with a girl tonight wouldn't have filled. His mother had died a few months earlier, his father three years before her. It could be he was still mourning. But though he kept busy and loved his work, Atticus couldn't shake the feeling that something was missing in his life.

He strode at a clipped pace west on Auburn past the Martin Luther King Jr. memorial park with its brick-and-concrete plaza, arch-covered walkway, and reflecting pool. Usually he walked through the garden, but it was late and the pizza was getting cold, so he pushed on past the Ebenezer Baptist Church, where he served the congregation. At an older redbrick building near the church he rented an apartment made available at an affordable cost to him as one of the church's young ministers. Pushing open the building door, he spied on the tiled floor a FedEx box waiting for him. He picked it up and, squinting in the dim light, made out that the package came from the law firm that had handled his mother's estate when she'd died. He put it on top of the pizza box and climbed the stairs to the third floor, then balanced the boxes precariously while he unlocked the multiple locks on his door.

Once inside, he set the boxes on the dining-room table, then turned to relock the door. He couldn't be too safe in this neighborhood. He rubbed his hands together, one warm from the pizza, the other cold, and looked around the small apartment, one typical for a bachelor of limited income. The apartment had come with furniture he was sure was donated to the church. Mismatched sofa and chairs were clustered around a wobbly wood coffee table in front of the television. The electronics he'd bought for himself. He was particular when it came to audiovisual. The decor wasn't creative, but the place was clean and comfortable and would do until he finished his training and was assigned to a congregation permanently. He was barely in the apartment, anyway. His work kept him out all hours.

He'd tried to make it his own, however. His mother had collected art, especially African-American art. If only by osmosis he'd learned to appreciate fine art. He'd hung a few favorite paintings from his mother's collection. Looking at them made the place feel a bit more like home. His bike leaned against the wall by the door, his books filled several shelves, and a silver-framed photograph of his parents sat in a place of honor on the mantel. His parents were all the family he'd had. And now they were both dead.

He shook out his damp, sleek raincoat and neatly hung it in the closet. Atticus was careful with his appearance. Growing up, his father, a successful lawyer, had taught him that "a man's worth was noted not by the value of his suit or shoes, but by whether the shoes were polished and the suit pressed." Baptist ministers didn't wear the collar, but they were expected to wear somber attire appropriate for his profession. Atticus took pride in his appearance, and though he didn't buy many, he bought quality suits and took care of them. He hung his black wool suit jacket beside his coat, then pulled out his phone and checked for messages.

An hour later he had showered, put on his pajamas, and eaten the pizza. He rarely ate much at the weddings he officiated. He had to spend the evening talking to guests or, more likely, listening. If it was a Baptist wedding on the church premises, no alcohol would be served. For him, however, at any wedding, the drinking of alcohol was never an option.

Sated, he went to the kitchen to make himself a cup of coffee. The heady scent filled the kitchen. Having poured a cup, he returned to the dining-room table. The caffeine woke him a bit and at last he felt ready to tackle whatever was in the mystery package.

What could be from the lawyers now? he wondered as he began to tear at the tape binding. His mother's will had been read. Her estate had been left entirely to him, her only child. His father, a high-profile Atlanta attorney, had died years earlier. He had left his widow with an estate that gave her the option to stop working and live a comfortable lifestyle. Zora Green had a successful career as a magazine editor and continued working at what she loved until the cancer that would take her life forced her to retire.

When Atticus inherited his estate, he'd donated a significant portion to charities that helped the poor in Atlanta. He also made a generous pledge to the Ebenezer Baptist Church stewardship fund. What he'd do with the rest, however, Atticus didn't know. He was a newly ordained minister and committed to his calling. He lived a modest lifestyle. Not married. He liked to take women to dinner at nice restaurants, take a trip once in a while. Other than that, he had no need for it. So until he received some message from God about what he should do with the money, he had arranged with the law firm to put the funds into safe investments. Atticus knew how fast that money would have flowed through his fingers if he'd inherited it when he was twenty-one.

Atticus felt a little apprehensive when he opened the box. He pulled out a glossy black folder bearing the insignia of the

Pearlman & Pearlman law firm. There was also a plastic bag—filled with two bundles of envelopes of different sizes and colors, each bundle tied with red ribbon. Glancing at them, ever more curious, he set them aside and turned back to the folder. Opening it, he found a formal typed letter in the left pocket, a sealed envelope in the right. He reached out to take a sip of his coffee. It was hot, black, and sweet. Then he pulled out the typed letter to read.

Dear Atticus,

Following Mrs. Zora Green's (your mother's) instructions, we waited until all the business of the will and estate were settled before embarking on her final wishes. To date, all outstanding debts, taxes, and funeral expenses have been paid.

Which brings us to her second request. Mrs. Green gave to our safekeeping certain letters that were to be delivered to you after her death. The said letters are enclosed. A sealed, personal letter from your mother, located in this folder, is addressed to you and should be read first. The bundles of letters in the plastic bag can be read at your leisure.

The aforementioned letter is written in Mrs. Green's own handwriting and signed by her in the presence of my secretary and a clerk. Mrs. Green also provided us with all the necessary legal documentation to substantiate the claims she makes in her letter. Please contact me at your convenience and we will send you the complete set of documents under separate cover.

Again, I am here to assist you in any way possible. My sympathy again on the passing of your mother.

Sincerely,
Robert Pearlman
Pearlman & Pearlman LLC

Atticus set the lawyer's letter on the table, then pulled the sealed envelope out from the right side of the folder. He held it in front of him with two hands, immediately recognizing his mother's beautiful script. On the envelope she'd written only his first name, as was her habit for all birthday and holiday cards she'd sent during her lifetime. Just *Atticus*. Underlined with great flourish.

His mother had told him with pride and a certain conceit that she had chosen his unusual name. He hadn't liked the name as a child. There wasn't an easy nickname for it, not a good thing for a boy. He'd wished he'd been named for his father, Tyrone, a good, strong, popular name. His father had once told Atticus he'd never wanted his son named after a famous white literary character, but he'd finally approved once Zora reminded him Atticus Finch was a lawyer. Zora had pushed hard for the name as hers was a literary background. Her favorite novel was *To Kill a Mockingbird* and her favorite male character Atticus Finch. When she was young, Zora, then an editor at a major New York publishing house, was in a commuter marriage with Atlanta-based Tyrone, but left the city when she learned she was pregnant and returned to Atlanta to settle there. She continued working in publishing, rising up to become publisher of a local magazine. Both Atticus's parents were highly educated, but he got his love of books from his mother.

Atticus looked at the envelope as though he could see right through to its contents. What kind of news could it carry that required legal documents and a lawyer on call for questions? His mother had lived to see him change his life, become a minister, and fulfill her dream for him. God knew how hard he had struggled to find this peace. Did he want to risk shaking the emotional terra firma of his world with whatever his mother felt he needed to know in some cryptic letter from the grave?

He resigned himself to the inevitable. Picking up a knife, he slit open the envelope with one smooth sweep. On the letter, written on pale blue parchment, her name was engraved in navy script: *Zora Middleton Green*. Atticus took a deep breath and began to read.

> *My darling Atticus,*
>
> *I'm writing this letter with the intention that it be delivered to you after my death. It contains information that I should have told you years ago. It's important you understand that I had promised your father that I would never tell you. I kept that promise in my lifetime. I feel, however, that you have the right to know your history. In these modern times, genetic histories are critical for one's health and welfare and I do not want to deprive you of these important facts.*

Atticus lowered the letter, swallowing hard at what the words indicated. He reached to pick up his coffee and took a bolstering sip. His cup clattered when he returned it to the saucer. Then, picking up the letter, he continued reading.

*Tyrone Green is not your biological father. He has
been your father in every way since your birth, and he
could not have loved you more if you were his flesh and
blood. Your biological father was a decent man. He never
met you, never held you in his arms, never participated
in your life. His name was Parker Muir.*

*Allow me to tell you the circumstances of your birth.
As you know, I was an assistant editor for the executive
editor of a major publishing house in New York City.
What you did not know was that we were already
married and that Tyrone and I were separated at the
time—he was living in Atlanta working on his law
career. While working I met the husband of my boss,
Georgiana James. He was a writer by the name of Parker
Muir. He and Georgiana James were recently married,
but it was obvious they were having a hard time of it.
There was little love lost between them. Parker had hoped
Georgiana would edit his manuscript. But instead she
tossed it on my desk and asked me to do the job. I found
the situation awkward, to say the least. But Georgiana
James was not a woman whose orders were not obeyed.
Thus it was I began editing Parker's novel.*

*Parker was a wonderful storyteller. When he spoke,
his eyes lit up and with his delicate southern accent he
made his story come alive. I could listen to him for
hours. And did. Unfortunately, he couldn't bring that
same enthusiasm and life to his printed words. To be
fair, the novel had undergone too many revisions. Like
a body that had one too many surgeries, its life's blood
had been drained. Yet he was so in earnest I tried to*

encourage him. We would go out in the afternoon to a nearby coffee shop and discuss the book, and eventually, our lives. Over the course of months of working together, we grew close. We were both lonely. He learned of my separation. I learned that his marriage was doomed. He wanted to leave but Georgiana was pregnant. She had little interest in Parker, his manuscript, or their marriage. She was constantly working, and when she wasn't at the office, she was out at luncheon and dinner meetings, never inviting her husband to join her. Neither of us knew many people in the city and thus we spent evenings together as well. In short, we fell in love.

Georgiana found out about our affair. When she confronted Parker, he asked her for a divorce. I believed Parker when he said he would marry me. I know he loved me. But I did not want to marry him. Though I loved him, I knew his weaknesses. You see, at this same time I discovered I was pregnant. Atticus my darling, you were the child I desperately wanted. Tyrone could not give me a child. This was one of the reasons we separated. To his great credit, when I called him and explained my situation, without hesitation Tyrone told me to come home to Atlanta.

I'll spare you the drama. Suffice to say it all ended quickly in New York. I was promptly fired. Georgiana and Parker were divorced. After the debacle I traveled to Atlanta and Parker to Charleston. He did not know that I carried his child.

Tyrone agreed to raise the child I was carrying as his own provided I promised him that I would never tell you or anyone that the child wasn't his. A point of pride, perhaps. I agreed. When you were born, no one questioned that he was your father, and in every way that mattered, he was. Your skin is fair, like mine. Though your blue eyes are the same color of Parker's. So many times when you were young you asked me where you got your blue eyes from. Now you know. I wondered if every time Tyrone saw those eyes he was reminded of my infidelity. We both know that Tyrone was an exacting man. Even cold, at times. That was his nature, not you. He wasn't the kind of man that showed affection readily. I know this was hard for you, especially when you were young. When you grew older, it made my heart happy to see the two of you playing golf, watching basketball games, bonding. Believe me, Atticus, he did love you in his own way. Very much.

I never told Tyrone this—not long after I'd returned to Atlanta, Parker Muir wrote to me asking to see me again. Naturally I couldn't allow that. Parker would take one look at you and know you weren't Tyrone's child. So I told him the truth, that I'd given birth to his son, and just like that he offered to marry me. He was a good man. I explained to him that I'd reconciled with my husband and how he'd agreed to raise my child as his own. I asked Parker for only one thing—his silence. I made him swear never to see you or contact you.

He kept that promise. Though he never met you or contacted you, every year on your birthday he sent you a card in my care, and every year I tucked it away, unopened. I think he hoped that someday I would tell *you and when that day came you would know that he'd remembered you. I saved these cards for you and instructed Bobby Pearlman to give them to you with my letter. They are yours to do with as you wish.*

Now it is done. I hope I've not made a mistake in telling you the truth of your birth. I've given the subject twenty-eight years of thought and always I have come to the same conclusion—you had a right to know. You had a self-centered youth which you turned around. I am very proud of you. In retrospect, I wonder if you didn't suspect something was amiss between you and your father. I hope this information answers any questions stirring in your brain, resolves any shadowy doubts, and quiets any unrest in your heart. You are a strong man and I have every confidence that you will figure out what to do with this knowledge.

My dear Atticus, I have loved you from the moment you were conceived, completely and unconditionally. No mother could love a child more than I have loved you. I hope you'll understand and forgive me for not telling you earlier. I've learned in this life that one cannot foresee the future. We must place our trust in God. After all, I was given you, the greatest gift of my life, without expecting that miracle. So trust that He has His plan and that you will come to understand it, in God's good time.

I am tired. At last I am free to die with a clear conscience and peaceful heart. In the end, my child, regardless of who your parents are, your life is your own. We all enter and exit alone.

Farewell, child of my heart. You carry my love in yours.

Always,
Mama

Atticus's hands were shaking as he let the last page of the letter drop. He brought his hands to cover his face and wept. He missed his mother, longed to talk to her about all she'd revealed. He wanted to hear her melodious voice comfort him, hear the gentle inflections of her southern accent, which he'd committed to memory. Needed to feel her hand on his shoulder, her kiss on his cheek. She'd written how she hoped learning this *resolves any shadowy doubts, and quiets any unrest*. Just the opposite! He'd never felt so alone.

After a long while he dropped his hands, emotionally spent. Atticus mopped his face with his palms, then brought his fingers to the bridge of his nose and took a long, shuddering breath as his composure returned to him. Quickly, efficiently, he gathered the pages of his mother's letter and neatly tucked them back into the envelope. This he placed into the right side of the folder and closed it, resting his palms upon the table.

He desperately wanted a drink. More than he could remember wanting a drink in years. He reached for the coffee and gulped down the final dregs. It had turned cold and bitter. Atticus rose from the table and paced the room. His mind was spinning with unanswered questions. Chief among them was who this Parker Muir was. His biological father.

He went to his desk and opened his laptop to begin an

Internet search on Parker Muir. There was scant information. Just an obituary.

So his father was dead. This gave him pause. He rested his hands and closed his eyes. While he didn't feel an emotional loss, never having known Muir, he nonetheless felt a profound regret that he'd not met him. Another vacancy in his life that couldn't be filled. He returned to the obituary, devouring the scant information there. Searching further, he discovered a notice about some adult film Muir was involved in. Some articles written by him had been published in newspapers and magazines. Apparently Parker Muir was published; he just never got that novel published. In the end Atticus had not learned much. Parker Muir was from Charleston, part of a historic family. Parker's surviving relatives were listed as father Edward Muir, mother Marietta Muir, and three ~~sisters~~ *daughters* Eudora Muir Tupper, Carson Muir, and Harper Muir-James.

Atticus paused at that revelation. The name of Parker's then wife in New York was Georgiana James. So the last one was the child she was pregnant with when Parker and Zora had begun their affair. Atticus was shaken, too, by her first name. Harper. It couldn't be a coincidence that she bore the name of the author of *To Kill a Mockingbird*, the very same novel featuring his namesake, Atticus Finch. Atticus swallowed the distaste that Parker Muir obviously had something to do with his mother's choice of his name.

He shut the computer, frustrated that he'd learned so little about this man who was his biological father. Atticus grew up the only child of two compulsively hardworking parents. They were a solid family, celebrated the usual holidays, milestones.

There was love between them. Yet now that his parents were dead, and just when he felt most alone, he was informed he had this other family living in Charleston.

Another family. Maybe this is what Atticus had felt was missing his entire life. What he'd been searching for.

Before he fell asleep that night, Atticus knew that the following morning he would call the Pearlman law office to find out more about the Muir family. He needed details. He needed his birth certificate.

He needed an address.

Chapter Five

All couples have issues to get through. That's what marriage is all about. Taking the good and bad, the hard and easy. And making it work.

March is a mercurial month in the lowcountry, but as promised, the rain and wind blew off island during the night. The sun rose on clear skies and warmer weather than the residents had experienced so far this spring. Carson opened her eyes and stretched languidly. The sheets were warm and scented of love. Sighing, she patted her hand on the mattress beside her. Blake's side was empty. Fear fluttered through her. She kicked off her sheet and in a mild panic half rose to let her gaze dart around the room. Soft breezes from the open window caressed her naked skin.

"You're awake."

Her gaze shifted to follow Blake's voice. He stood at the

door carrying a tray. She let her eyes feast on his long, lean frame as her body slumped softly with relief. "You're here."

"Where else would I be?" He walked toward her.

Carson didn't reply. When she'd found the bed empty, she felt a sudden terror that he'd left her.

Blake was already dressed in his usual khakis and dark green polo shirt bearing the logo of NOAA. She thought to herself that if he lived in Los Angeles, he'd likely wear black jeans and a tight T-shirt to show off his swimmer's body. She chuckled to herself, knowing Blake would never be so fashion-forward. Blake put on his clothes in the morning without thought. From the moment he woke up, his mind focused on getting outdoors as quickly as possible. Blake had a long waist with taut and sinewy muscles across his chest, shoulders, and arms from hours spent on the ocean, not the gym. The scent of the sea, mud, salt, these were home to him. Like her, he needed to be near the water and spent as much time as he could out on the waterways researching the animals that lived in the depths. Blake was a marine mammal specialist at NOAA, and their shared love of dolphins had initially cemented their relationship.

She smiled up at him as he set a tray on the bed beside her.

"*Merci,*" she said, letting her fingers stroke his hand.

She gathered her long dark hair in her hands and pulled the locks from her face, remembering with a flush the long afternoon and longer night of talking, arguing, and making love. She gave him a slanted look. "I feel rode hard and put up wet."

She got the hoped-for smug smile as he straightened and caught her gaze.

Carson hid her own smile of satisfaction by looking down at the tray. He'd remembered her favorites. Wheat toast, yogurt, fresh berries, coffee.

But, oh, she needed water.

"I'm parched," she said in a raspy voice. "I'm so dry I can barely speak. Could I have some water? You've run me dry, boy."

She detected another faint smile of self-satisfaction as he ducked out of the room. She sipped the coffee, and in a moment he returned. Hobbs pushed past him into the room, trotting to the bed, and immediately began sniffing the sheets with keen interest. Carson giggled as Blake shoved him away with a gruff "No." Hobbs backed off with a snort of displeasure and sat a few feet away, staring at Carson with baleful eyes.

Blake handed Carson a tall glass of icy water. "I'm pretty sure when a dog snorts like that it's dog language for 'Fuck you.'"

Carson laughed, then drank thirstily. Again, she felt a breeze flutter the curtains and slide across her body like water.

Blake sat on the bed beside her. She felt the dip in the mattress with his weight, then his cool hand as it slid across her body. "I've missed seeing you in my bed."

"Oh, I've missed this, too. You by my side. The soft island breezes. I slept like I haven't slept since I left."

He snorted. "I should hope not."

"When you let me sleep, I should say."

He leaned forward to kiss her. The moment lips met the spark ignited, as it always did for them. She felt the telltale trembling of his lips as his tongue pushed hers open.

"No, no, no," she whimpered, pushing him back. "I don't have the energy. Or the time. They're expecting us for lunch."

He released her, but still leaning close, his dark eyes searched hers. "Carson . . ." He hesitated, and his tone implied he wanted to talk.

"Yes?" She picked up a slice of toast. She bit into the buttery bread, using the action to disguise her sudden wariness.

Blake pushed back and placed his palms on his thighs. "We need to talk."

She knew that look on his face. She felt her guard go up. "I thought we'd done enough talking."

"You took off your ring."

Carson glanced at her ring finger, barren of the diamond. "We're still engaged. Sort of. We're going to be promised to each other. While we work things out. No pressure."

"Last night when we were exhausted, it seemed a decent compromise. But in the light of day . . . What the hell does *promised* even mean? We're sort of engaged? We're promised to do what? That puts us in limbo." Blake shook his head, moving his dark curls, longer now after a winter's growth. "I can't do that."

"But we said—"

"I can't face them."

"Who?"

"Your family. I can't go to Sea Breeze and be with your family and talk weddings as if it's all going to happen when you're not wearing my ring."

"But we went through this." Carson sat up. "I'm still wearing your ring. Around my neck."

"Not on your finger. Not in a way that matters." Blake shook his head. "The way I see it, we're either engaged. Or we're not."

"I don't see why you're making a federal case of this." She

felt her fuse light up. "It's up to you. I have a job offer. It will take me away for a few months and it'll pay well. Then I'm home again. I'm okay with that. Lots of married couples are separated for a while."

"Not me. Not for months at a time. We both know the temptations you'll face. And when you come back, how long will you be home? How long before you accept the next job? And the next?"

"We'll have to work out the ground rules. I'll only take one or two jobs a year depending on the length. No more than a few months at one time."

"That's what you told me about this last job. Four months. You swore by it. But it took six."

Carson flushed. There was no denying it, but she was tired of apologizing for it. "So I'll only take one job a year."

"I don't want to have a marriage where my wife is gone for six months of the year. I don't want to take those odds."

Carson raked her hair with her fingers, then clutched it in fists while she counted to ten. He was being unreasonable. They sat across from each other, stiff shouldered, eyes blazing. "And I don't want to sit around jobless. I told you that. I can't. I won't," she said emphatically. She dropped her hands. "Why should I be the one to give up my career? You could move to California, you know."

He reached out to take her hand. "I know," he said in a low voice.

When he lowered his tone, it immediately diffused the tension between them. Blake could cool quickly, and in doing so, he could always bring her down from the edge as well. It was a gift, she knew. One she appreciated. He managed wildlife

as readily as he did the humans who worked under him with that same calm and easy manner. But she'd seen his temper flare, too. When he got truly angry, he was formidable. He could be terribly stubborn. As, she knew, could she. Harper referred to them as Scarlett and Rhett.

"Here's the thing," he said in that soothing tone of voice. "I've thought about this all morning."

She looked into his face. His brown eyes appeared so black she couldn't tell where the pupils ended and the irises began.

"We have things to work out," he acknowledged. "Our schedules may be tough to manage. But all couples have issues to get through. That's what marriage is all about. Taking the good and bad, the hard and easy. And making it work. The way I see it, if we can't get through this now, then what's the point of being engaged or promised or whatever you want to call it? On the other hand, if we love each other, and we want to be together, to get married, you should wear the ring and together we'll figure something out. We have time. Then, if we can't find a solution we can live with"—he shrugged in the Gallic manner—"then you can give the ring back to me before the wedding and we'll call it all off for good."

Carson could only stare back, mute. The thought of breaking her engagement had crossed her mind. But the reality of it was too cold. She shivered.

Blake saw her reaction and took both her hands. "But I don't believe that will happen. Because I love you, Carson Muir. And I believe you love me."

"I do," she said softly though urgently.

"We've been through worse."

Carson's mind whirled back through a series of traumas

that she'd fought her way through the past year. And each time Blake was there, enduring it all with her.

"Yes, we have."

"Have faith, Carson. Wear my ring."

Carson smiled tremulously. She stretched far across the bed to the small marble-topped bedside table to grasp the diamond-and-sapphire ring that Blake had given her the previous September. The ring she'd removed during the night with the intention of slipping it on a chain and wearing it around her neck. She was unaware of the beautiful, long line her slender, athletic body presented to Blake, but she felt his hand once again slide across her curves. Sitting back up, she held the ring between two fingers. Then, in one movement, she slid the ring back onto her left ring finger and smiled up at him.

"Carson!" Harper exclaimed, grinning wide. "You're here!"

Carson looked much the same as she had the previous fall. Tall and exotic with her long dark hair, brilliant sapphire-blue eyes, and her finely tuned body that turned heads wherever she went. Yet she appeared different, too. The restlessness had settled and her manner had a new softness. She wore no makeup yet had the glow of a woman well loved.

"You look beautiful. Rested. It must've been an easy trip."

"I caught some z's on the plane." Carson moved through the open door into the house, her eyes scanning Harper. "You look different, too. Less sleek New York and more French country. I like it. Careful, though. Don't go too Suzy Homemaker on me."

"I think there's a compliment in there somewhere," Blake said to Harper, stepping into the house.

"Harper knows I swing from the hip, don't you, Sis?"

"I do." Harper laughed, closing the door behind them. Carson was always honest, sometimes brutally so.

Carson leaned forward to give her sister a hug, then pulled back and asked, "Where's Mamaw?"

"Oh, she's here somewhere. Probably in her cottage. She'll be up in a minute."

"The cottage?" Carson asked with surprise.

"Yes." Harper paused to kiss Blake and offer him a hug, then turned to Carson. "Mamaw moved into the cottage. I thought you knew that."

"No," Carson said coldly. "Why would she move into the cottage? This is her house."

Harper's smile fell, replaced by stunned surprise.

Carson immediately realized her mistake and quickly amended, "I mean, it's *your* house, of course. But it's still her house, too. In a way. I mean . . ." She let her words slide away feeling sure her meaning was understood.

Harper's stare was defensive, as was the stiffness of her smile. "I would never ask Mamaw to move to the cottage," she said with some heat. "In fact, I begged her not to. But she insisted. And you know Mamaw when she's made up her mind."

Carson grinned wryly. "That Muir stubbornness."

Harper paused, assuaged a bit by the humor. "She said she wanted to have a smaller space of her own. Mamaw has free rein of the house, of course. She comes and goes as she pleases. She still likes to sit on the back porch, the same queen as always." Harper's tone grew thoughtful. "But more and more, I find her sitting on the porch of the cottage, rocking, reading a book. I think she finds comfort there, where Lucille lived."

"But isn't it, I don't know . . . weird? Sleeping in her room?"

"At first, maybe. But not anymore." Harper met Carson's gaze squarely. "This is *my* home, after all."

There it was. The line in the sand. The house now belonged to Harper. She'd bought it free and clear. In doing so, she'd not only provided Mamaw the opportunity to remain at Sea Breeze rather than move into a retirement community alone, but the generous purchase offer had provided Mamaw a comfortable income to live on for as long as she lived. It was extraordinarily fortunate for all of them that the house could remain in the family.

The tension was broken when Taylor entered the foyer, a huge black dog at his heels. Blake and Taylor greeted each other warmly, leaning forward to slap backs and mutter words of welcome. They were both tall, but the resemblance ended there. Taylor was broad shouldered and muscled and bore the upright stance of a man who'd spent years in the Marines. When Harper had first met Taylor, his hair had been shorn close to the scalp. Now the light brown hair was longer at the top and she'd been amused to see it had a slight wave.

"Carson!" Taylor stepped forward to wrap her in his strong arms for a firm hug. "Good to see you again. Welcome home. Here to stay now, are you?"

Carson flushed with pleasure at his hearty welcome. "I'm good. Glad to be home."

"You look good."

"I stopped at Blake's place to freshen up." She glanced at Blake, who met her gaze with a conspiratorial smile.

"Well, be prepared," Taylor said ominously. "Harper's been revving up, just waiting for you to get here. And her grandmother arrives next week. Whoooeee, Blake"—Taylor patted Blake's shoulder—"there's going to be a sea of estrogen bubbling over wedding details here. You and I have to make ourselves scarce and get out of their way. Let's start with getting ourselves a beer."

As the men chuckled and walked off to the kitchen, Harper glanced at Carson and could see the anxiety in her face, the awkward looking around the room, unsure of where she should go.

"Well, I guess I'd better get settled. Where do I sleep?" she asked Harper, in a nod to her authority over Sea Breeze.

Harper visibly relaxed. Her smile bloomed with enthusiasm. "In *your* room, of course. It will always be your room, Carson. That will never change."

Carson heard the sincerity in Harper's words and moved to wrap her arms around her.

Harper smelled the oriental scent of Bal à Versailles, Mamaw's scent and now Carson's as well. Harper always associated the scent with love and security, and it brought her instantly back to the days of their girlhood summers. In that moment all the tension vanished and there was only her and her sister, back at Sea Breeze, together again.

Chapter Six

*When a woman lives long enough to see her
grandchildren married and settled, she feels blessed.*

*L*ater that evening, when the moon rose over the earth and
the stars sparkled in a crisp, cool sky, Mamaw stood at the
kitchen window peering out at the Cove. The moon shed
dreamy light across the water, creating a ribbon of light on the
rippling tide. Her granddaughters were sitting together on the
dock—Eudora, Carson, and Harper. This early in the season
that water would be nippy, so instead of dangling legs in the
sea they sat huddled in blankets against the chill. Occasional
yelps of high-pitched laughter sang out in the quiet night. In
the moonlight, they could be young girls again—her Summer
Girls. Her heart expanded as she said a prayer of thanks that
the summer before her plan to bring the girls back together
at Sea Breeze, after their being scattered to the four corners
of the United States, had worked so well. Far better than her

expectations. Here they were once more, happy, connected. Sisters.

True they were half sisters. The daughters of her only child, Parker, and his three wives. Not that she blamed him for wandering. Though she loved her granddaughters to distraction, her daughters-in-law were a disappointment to say the least. Dora's mother, Winnie, was a small-minded, prejudiced woman Mamaw found annoying at best.

Then there was poor Sophie, Carson's mother. Mamaw couldn't help but feel sympathy for the eighteen-year-old French nanny, even though she broke up Winnie and Parker's marriage. But then again, if it wasn't Sophie, it would have been someone else. Her son had a wandering eye, and Sophie was too young and too weak to withstand his charms. Her tragic death had scarred young Carson, but in consequence, the four-year-old was delivered to Mamaw's care. And for that special bond she shared with Carson, Mamaw would always be grateful.

Mamaw only had disdain for Harper's mother, Georgiana James. A more arrogant, self-righteous harridan she'd never met. And a negligent daughter and a narcissistic mother to boot. For the scant few months she was married to Parker, Georgiana was also cruel. The best Mamaw could say about that union was that Harper was born—and a sweeter child never walked the earth.

But Parker, bless his heart, though a dear boy, had displayed little restraint or sense of responsibility to himself or his daughters. Mamaw had done her best to support him, but in the end she'd only made excuses and cleaned up his messes. Edward was furious with his son, then disgusted, then finally apathetic. He'd wanted to cut Parker off since college, but Mamaw wouldn't hear of it. In her day, a mother did what she could to help her child. Yes, she'd spoiled him. But Parker was her only child. She'd made mistakes, she knew that now. Her therapist had taught her the word they'd coined for what she was—an *enabler*.

Mamaw had her regrets, true. But one thing she had no regrets about was inviting her three granddaughters to Sea Breeze each summer. She gathered her Summer Girls together like precious seashells and helped them to connect as sisters should. Mamaw sniffed. She couldn't count on their mothers for that! Besides, with Carson in California and Harper in New York, how else could she be certain they'd know where they were from? To remind the girls of their southern roots.

And they did come. Every year, from the time they were young girls until they reached their teens. Then, typically, each of the girls made other summer plans, and before too long they stopped coming to Sea Breeze. The slim thread that bound them together was broken.

They visited rarely. In fact, only for the funerals of their father and a year later, their grandfather, her dear husband, Edward. She received letters and phone calls, but Mamaw had felt lonely, even neglected, by the girls. She reasoned it was all part of the selfishness of youth. Yet when she reached the ripe old age of eighty and realized that she could no longer care for an estate on the sea with all the nips and tucks necessary for maintenance, she brought the girls home once more to celebrate her eightieth birthday and bid farewell to Sea Breeze before it was sold.

She had hoped they would all come for the weekend. But

the girls had ended up staying the summer. . . . Mamaw sighed in memory, hardly able to believe how perfectly everything had come together. She owned that it was due to her admittedly manipulative ways. Lucille had pointed her finger at her and accused her of "foolin' around where you ought not."

Mamaw shifted her weight and sniffed. She saw her actions as simply the determination of a devoted grandmother to protect her beloved granddaughters. Sometimes one had to be creative, eh? And what did it matter now, anyway? Mamaw smiled again as she looked out at the girls sitting shoulder to shoulder on the dock, a unified block of family. She'd succeeded. Far more than she'd thought she would, even in her wildest dreams.

"Penny for your thoughts."

She turned and smiled when she spied Girard approaching. In his presence she was not Mamaw, the name her granddaughters affectionately called her, but Marietta. Ageless, still attractive, full of life. A woman in love. Girard was a courtly figure. At eighty, with his tanned skin and white hair streaked with dark gray strands, his blue eyes that always held a hint of mirth, he still turned her head. She recalled her friend Sissy's comment the night they'd first met Girard and his wife, Evelyn, fifty years earlier. Sissy had nudged Marietta and whispered how Girard reminded her of Cary Grant. Mamaw laughed to herself. God help her, he still did. She and Girard had been friends back then. Good neighbors. But all these years later, he a widower and she a widow, they'd reconnected, thanks to the charms of one beguiling dolphin.

Girard stepped closer and placed his arm around her shoulders. She leaned into him with a long sigh.

"I was thinking how I look out there and see my Summer

Girls talking like sisters should and know how lucky I am. We're all back together again at Sea Breeze. They seem happy. And in a short while Carson and Harper will be married to good and decent men. Dora, too, in her time. When a woman lives long enough to see her grandchildren married and settled, she feels blessed. I feel quite content. My life has come full circle. I am complete. I want nothing more in life."

"I hope I'm part of that circle."

She rested her head on his shoulder. "A very important cog in the wheel, my dear. And a wheel that is still turning. We'll have weddings soon, then births, baptisms. We'll begin the circle again."

"Together."

"Yes, together." She smiled once more when she felt his hand squeeze her shoulder.

Carson closed the door to her bedroom and, leaning against it, sighed deeply in the peaceful darkness. Dinner was over. Blake had left for his apartment. It had been a wonderful evening with the family. A long one, too. Carson yawned and began unzipping the sleek silk dress. She let the dress slide from her body to the floor as she walked toward the window. Her bra and panties followed, also left on the floor. Carson opened the window to the spring-night air, chilled and moist with the remnants of winter. She breathed deep the scented air and spread out her arms. She was home. At Sea Breeze.

Her Sea Breeze. The attachment to the place was visceral. Impossible to let go. Yes, this was Harper's house now. Intellectually Carson knew that. Accepted it. Harper couldn't have been a more welcoming sister and hostess . . . thus far. Yet by virtue of being Harper's house, Sea Breeze was no longer Carson's. She crossed her arms and jutted out her chin. In her heart, Sea Breeze would always be hers. Her touchstone. The only place that had ever made her feel secure. The only house she had ever called home.

She'd thought going away again would lessen the ties, but the moment she'd seen Harper open the door as mistress of the house, when Carson was served dinner at the table, ever so graciously, by Harper and Taylor, she had felt more a guest. The thought occurred to her—how long could she stay? Could she help herself to something from the fridge? Did being a sister allow her to drop in or were reservations required? She supposed they were. This was the new reality at Sea Breeze.

With a groan she fell back onto the bed, spread-eagled. The soft mattress of her youth wrapped itself around her like a cocoon. Lying on her back, Carson glanced idly around her room—the four-poster rice bed, the long mahogany bureau, the two brass-and-crystal lamps, and directly across from her bed, the elaborately framed portrait of her great ancestor Claire Muir. Her lustrous dark tresses curled to her shoulders in an elaborate coiffure complete with a charming hat spilling over with lace and feathers. And speaking of spilling over . . . the great lady's endowments were barely concealed by the lace and velvet of her eighteenth-century blue velvet gown and the rows of lustrous pearls that revealed her wealth.

Still, it was her eyes that drew Carson in. A blue so unique and brilliant, a color so dominant, that it defied being recessive through generations and was inherited by each of the three Muir granddaughters. Legend claimed that Claire's blue eyes had first captured the attention of the rogue Gentleman Pirate when he reached port in Charleston. But her wit and fiery spirit were what had won his heart and caused him to give up a life on the seas and settle in Charleston. Their love was fabled. How much was true and how much conjecture was uncertain. But Mamaw loved the stories and told them to the girls with relish, especially how their illustrious ancestor had left treasure buried somewhere on Sullivan's Island. Carson and Harper had spent much of their youth searching for it.

Carson would never forget the evening that Mamaw had entered Carson's room to say her usual good-night and found Carson crying bitterly. She was in the turbulent, angst-ridden preteen years. She'd been an ugly duckling with her long, skinny body, her big feet, and untamed, thick dark hair that other children had teased was a "rat's nest." Carson had wept that she would never be the southern belle that Dora—or Mamaw—was.

Without a word, the following morning Mamaw had driven to her house on East Bay Street in Charleston and returned with the painting of Claire in tow. With Lucille's help, Mamaw had hung it so that Carson could look at the famed beauty every day when she awoke and every evening before she fell asleep, so that Carson would appreciate the beauty of her own dark hair and blue eyes. Mamaw understood that the mother-less girl needed a role model to emulate, someone with spirit and courage.

Carson had stared into her ancestor Claire's eyes when she'd needed to find her own courage, or to confess her heartbreaks, the changes in her body, her thoughts, her dreams. The times a girl needed her mother. This painting had been the one thing she'd most wanted from Sea Breeze, and the previous summer Mamaw had given it to her. Someday, Carson knew, the portrait would hang in her own home. But that was a ways off. For now, the portrait of Claire would remain at Sea Breeze, in Harper's good care.

Yes, Carson thought begrudgingly, Harper was taking good care of Sea Breeze. Thanks to her, the house and property had stayed in the family. And from the looks of the extensive gardens and the scents of wax, soap, and polish, Sea Breeze was being lovingly tended. Carson would like to say it was easy for someone with as much money as Harper to keep up a property, but that would not be true. Harper's personal touch was everywhere. She loved Sea Breeze, as much or, perhaps in her own way, even more than Carson.

Resentment aside, Carson was grateful. Looking around her room, she saw that Harper had kept everything just as Carson had left it. Even her messy drawers and closets. Carson chuckled to herself, thinking how knowing that mess lay there behind a closed door must have driven her fastidious sister crazy these past months. It was a symbol of her respect for Carson's place in the house. And it meant a great deal.

With her head on the pillow and staring at the ceiling, Carson brought to mind all the surprises she'd learned throughout the evening. Dora had passed her real estate exam! Carson had never seen her so chuffed. And Nate was blooming. Carson thought he'd shot up at least two inches. Mamaw seemed quite content staying in the cottage. She was, Carson thought, even glowing. Dora had confidentially whispered that the reason had nothing to do with the cottage but with the continued presence of a certain gentleman caller whom the girls had all been introduced to last summer. Carson liked Girard and found that tidbit most interesting.

The one who'd changed the most, however, was Harper. She had softened, not only metaphorically, but literally. Her face, her contours, were rounder, softer. If she were painted in a portrait, she'd have to be a Rubens. No, Carson amended. Perhaps not a Rubens—those curves were more Dora. Perhaps a Monet or a Renoir. Harper was an impressionistic vision of a country maid, her red hair tumbling down her shoulders, her large blue eyes wide.

Was the change wrought by love? Carson wondered. Or merely the prospect of being a bride? Harper was positively giddy with wedding plans. Carson had never seen her so animated. Surpassing even Dora with exuberance. In fact, Dora seemed surprisingly subdued tonight on the whole topic of the weddings. Harper, however, was a force of nature. She'd already scheduled them for cake tasting. When Carson had complained of jet lag, feisty Harper told her to "get over it" and reminded Carson that she was already ridiculously late in getting her wedding gown. Or choosing the bridesmaid dresses, selecting items for the goodie bags, and countless other decisions that had Carson's brain swelling. And apparently, Harper believed all these decisions had to be made "together."

Harper was determined not to make another wedding decision unless Carson was involved. She'd even gotten a bit teary eyed about it all. Carson's objections were silenced by that. Who knew the cool, collected Harper could be so emotional? Or that the seemingly remote Taylor would be so protective? To see him place his arm around her shoulder and plant a gentle kiss on her head was touching. Sweet, Carson thought. She'd glanced at Blake and could tell that he'd noticed, too. He was as emotional about the upcoming vows as Harper. Blake's eyes had smoldered and he winked at Carson from across the table. Perhaps, she thought with a yawn, some of Harper's romantic wedding spirit would rub off on her. Thinking again of the message pulsing in Blake's smile, she felt a slight shiver of pleasure and thought it might already be.

Carson moved to slip under the thick down blanket, bringing the softness over her chilled shoulders. The sheets were crisp and scented with lavender. She smiled again, realizing Harper must have freshly laundered them before Carson's arrival.

She closed her eyes, suddenly awash with nostalgia and feeling a little emotional herself. How many nights had she fallen asleep in this bed to the sound of palm fronds rustling in the breeze? Or heard the roar of a restless ocean pounding the beach? These were the lullabies of her childhood that could woo her to sleep. Soon, she fell into a deep slumber listening to the gentle music of Sea Breeze.

Dora folded the kitchen towel and laid it on the counter. At last, the dishes were done. She glanced around the kitchen before turning off the lights. Everything was neat and tidy, like Harper herself. Lemons and avocados filled the wire basket, spices were organized in the rack, a to-do list was on the chalkboard. The leftover red velvet cake, another of Lucille's recipes, sat under a glass globe. Dora resisted the urge for one last piece.

She flicked off the lights and walked through the living room to collect Nate from the library where he slept. It was late and past time to go home. Sea Breeze was blanketed with a hush. Taylor had taken Thor for a walk. Mamaw and Carson had already retired. Dora was the last to leave. She was dragging her feet, not ready to go back to the empty cottage.

Tonight she'd felt happy. After dinner she and her sisters had gone out to the dock, bundled in blankets, and talked and laughed as they did last summer. She'd missed that . . . missed them. Missed this house and the feeling of security and support that surrounded her in these walls. So real she could almost smell it.

Dora laughed to herself. Tonight, security smelled like gumbo. Darn, but that Harper made a mean gumbo. Along with warm corn bread and red velvet cake for dessert. All accompanied by stories every bit as rich, filled with the myriad details of what had transpired in their lives over the six months since they'd last been together. All in all a note-perfect family gathering.

Dora had to ask herself, was there anything that Harper wasn't good at? She was an Ivy League scholar, a former New York editor, fluent in three languages, and if she didn't know something, she always had her trusty computer nearby to look it up. Tonight, Dora felt a little as she had last summer when Harper had arrived from New York. She appeared sleek and polished in her Armani suit and Louboutin shoes, dragging her Louis Vuitton luggage. Dora had felt like a sea cow beside her. Over the past months, Harper's style had relaxed, and so had Dora's diet. She'd put on weight again and it only made her want to eat more. Tonight her eating was out of control—she'd had seconds of gumbo and rice, several glasses of wine, and she'd sneaked a second piece of cake in the kitchen while doing dishes.

She wrapped her arms around herself, feeling the love handles she despised. When she reached the library, she opened the door. Her eyes grew accustomed to the dim light and her gaze swept the room. The library was where Nate had slept when Mamaw owned Sea Breeze. It was Harper's office now, filled with furniture Harper had brought over the pond from Greenfields Park. Papa Edward's heavy desk had been replaced by an antique desk with feminine curves. Valuable side tables held a printer, scanner, and other office equipment. The bookshelves were filled with Harper's books.

Dora's gaze rested on her son, sleeping on the twin bed. It spoke of Harper's infinite thoughtfulness that she'd kept the twin bed in the room so that Nate would have a place to sleep at Sea Breeze. Harper knew that any change in routine was difficult for Nate. Dora drew near her boy and reached out to sweep a lock of hair from his forehead. She could do this now, while he was asleep, without his shooing her away.

A voice came from the door: "Everything okay?"

Dora startled and stifled a yelp with her hand.

Harper laughed softly as she entered the library. "Oh, I'm sorry, Dora. I didn't mean to frighten you. I saw the door open."

Dora laughed, too, embarrassed. "I'll bet you're waiting for us to leave so you can go to bed."

"Not at all," Harper replied, but she couldn't stop a yawn. "Forgive me, I might be a little more tired than I thought. But I won't sleep for a while. I'll be up remembering bits of conversations."

"You're a wonderful hostess. You make us feel so at home."

"That's because this is your home. I'm just sorry Devlin had to miss it."

Dora stammered, "Ah, yes. Me, too. His work is keeping him busy nights now."

"Should I pack up some gumbo for you to take to him?"

"No, I don't think I'll see him for a few days. Crazy busy . . ." Dora was glad for the darkness. It cloaked her lies. She'd told everyone that Devlin couldn't come to dinner tonight as planned because he was working. In truth, he didn't want to come. He'd said he needed some time to think, and that had terrified her.

Dora pushed on, plastering her face with a practiced smile. "I have to tell you, the gumbo you made was delicious." She put her hand to her face in the manner of telling a secret. "I'll deny I said this, but it was better than Lucille's."

Harper was pleased. "That's high praise, indeed. I just added a little more of this or that. The recipes were, shall we say, loosely written."

"Will you share the recipe?"

"Of course."

Dora pursed her lips and shook her head. "Listen to us. I'm asking *you* for a recipe. Girl, you've really come a long way from the city girl who'd arrived last summer. Back then you needed my help with the garden, and you even asked me to teach you how to cook. Remember?" Dora shook her head. "Now look at you. Your garden is simply amazing and now I'm asking *you* for recipes. You never fail at anything, do you?"

Harper shifted her weight and looked at Dora with concern. The compliment had somehow morphed into something akin to an insult. "Dora, where's this coming from?"

Dora looked away, embarrassed for her outburst. "Oh, Lord, I'm sorry. I didn't mean for it to come out like that. I admire you. I do. I guess I'm just feeling a bit insecure."

"Why?" Harper's voice filled with empathy. "Everything is

dovetailing for you. You passed your real estate exam. You're a bona fide real estate agent!"

"Probationary," Dora amended. "Oh, it's nothing," she said, sidestepping a discussion of Devlin. "I'm just a little nervous. New job and all." She looked down at her sleeping son. Her heart bloomed with love for him. "Nate is my biggest success," she said softly.

"Dora, is it so wonderful to be a mother?"

"Oh, yes. There are no words."

Harper's eyes grew wider and shining in the soft light. "If I tell you something, you have to promise not to tell anyone."

Dora, always loving a good secret, perked right up. "I promise."

"I'm pregnant!" Harper blurted out.

"What!" Dora squealed. She slapped her hand across her mouth and cast a wary glance at Nate. He stirred but remained asleep. She reached out to hug Harper. They rocked back and forth with sisterly joy in the shared moment.

The mood shot skyward as they walked to the two upholstered chairs and settled in, feet tucked under their thighs, leaning toward each other.

"Does anyone know?"

"Only Taylor. And now you. I'm so glad I told you. I have so many questions and you're the only one I could ask."

Dora felt smugly happy that she was the one Harper confided in. She felt the bond between them strengthen, and this helped her feel better about herself. She cupped her chin in her hand, eager to hear every word, her mind whirling with advice she could share.

Neither of them would go to bed for quite a while.

Chapter Seven

Weddings bring out the best and the worst in people.
You can't believe what people say and do—to their own
family members—under normal circumstances. It's not
wise to expose a long-held family secret into the mix.

Atticus was on his way to the lowcountry. He had struggled with this decision ever since he'd read his mother's cryptic letter from the grave. The terra firma of his life had been shaken, and a huge hole had been punched in his identity. He'd prayed on the subject, talked to his pastor, then, with his blessing, packed his truck and whizzed east to find answers to the questions. Pros and cons whirled in his head as he passed by the green fields and long stretches of white fences of the Augusta horse country, then crossed the Savannah River. Traffic was light and he was making good time. By the time he reached Columbia, South Carolina, and the signs heralded Charleston, his rationalizations had blown away with the light breeze. He began looking forward to his first visit to Charleston in years.

Though this was far from a pleasure trip. He had a lot of facts to dig up, people to meet, and soul-searching to do. He needed to learn more about this Parker Muir—a stranger to him. When his mother died, he'd thought he was alone in this world. Now he'd learned he had a living grandmother, Marietta Muir, and if the Internet was to be believed, three half sisters.

Atticus was an only child. His parents had told him that they couldn't have more children. But now he knew that it was his father who could never have a child. Atticus supposed that was one of the hurdles his parents had faced when they'd separated. He scratched his head and wondered what kind of a man would take his wife back, pregnant with another man's child, then raise that child as his own.

A pretty damn good man, Atticus thought as he pushed forward along Interstate 26. Tyrone Green had been a formidable personality. With a big voice and staunch principles he could be intimidating in the courtroom. And in the home, as well. He was generous with charities, a deacon in the church, and took on a lot of pro bono cases. Atticus had always admired him and knew his father loved him. But they were never close. Part of the reason was because Tyrone worked so hard and rarely had time. But even if he did, he wasn't the type to play catch in the yard or take his son to a game. Not because he didn't care. The thought had probably never even crossed his mind. But he was a good father in his own way. He did his best, and Atticus, now knowing the circumstances of his birth, thought Tyrone did better than most men would have done.

Atticus looked out the passenger window as he approached

the Ravenel Bridge. It spanned the Cooper River like two giant, glistening steel sailboats. Beneath, the blue waters sparkled in the sunlight. His thoughts stilled as he became another tourist gawking at the sight of the shimmering water below speckled with pleasure boats and, beyond, great hulking cargo ships in dock. As he soared over the bridge, the fabled city spread out beneath him. He spied the multiple church spires that gave Charleston the name the Holy City.

As he crossed the bridge into Mt. Pleasant, his thoughts shifted from the Green family he'd grown up with to the Muir family he would soon meet. He stretched his fingers against the steering wheel as he felt a surge of apprehension. The Muir family of Charleston was historic. His search had come up with a long family tree, and annotations of papers held by the Charleston Library Society. He'd felt a quiver of disquiet when he'd read the old slave purchase records. He knew it was likely that a wealthy Charleston family in the eighteenth and nineteenth centuries would have had slaves, but to read it—to read in unforgiving print that his own ancestors had owned slaves—was hard for a black man to accept.

At long last he crossed the wetlands from Mt. Pleasant to Sullivan's Island. The shadow of his Silverado pickup truck traveled on a parallel path to it. The truck was a far cry from the flashy two-seater sports coupe of his youth, but it had a powerful engine, was cushy inside, and was the southern man's dream car. Plus it suited his new lifestyle. He used the truck for church business, carting food, clothing, and supplies from one place to another.

The low tide exposed the rich black mudflats and mounds of black, sharp-pointed oysters. White egrets perched elegantly on long sticklike legs, feasting on fiddler crabs and a cornucopia of insects. Some good fishing was back in those creeks, he'd wager. He smiled ruefully, trying to remember the last time he'd picked up his rod. He couldn't. Sullivan's Island was similar to the barrier islands he frequented off the coast of Georgia, the beautiful Sea Islands—St. Simons Island, Sea Island, Jekyll Island, and of course Tybee Island and the magical Cumberland Island.

Yet each island had its own history and unique flavor. Crossing onto Sullivan's Island, he spotted first a small green space on his left separated from the road by a small chain. A handsome sign declared it to be an African-American cemetery. He knew that Sullivan's Island had played an important role in African-American history. But had never heard of this cemetery. A number of slave cemeteries with unmarked graves were on the barrier islands, some of them only recently discovered as a result of development of coastal property. He made a note to research this cemetery later. For now, his attention was focused on one house on the island, Sea Breeze, home of the Muir family. His map showed it to be on the back side of the island, facing a small body of water called the Cove.

Turning onto Middle Street, he crawled at a snail's pace past a few blocks of small restaurants and shops in lowcountry-style buildings. Once beyond the strip, the streets were thickly lined with palmetto and oak trees covered with the spring-green softness of new leaves. Even a stranger such as him could detect a sense of neighborhood. As well as an air of privilege. Charming historic cottages and imposing new mansions nestled in the foliage, side by side.

His navigation system led him off Middle Street to the narrow side streets along the back of the island. When he hit a gravel road, he checked his map. Yes, this was the correct way. He drove slowly forward, slowing when he noted the mailbox number before a property hidden behind a tall green hedge. This was it.

He paused at the entrance, modest yet subtly imposing. Atticus recalled his mother telling him, "Those with real money don't need to advertise." His mouth went dry and he could feel his heart pumping in his chest at the prospect of meeting the Muir family.

Atticus had decided to arrive without calling them first. He didn't want to give them the chance to refuse him. And, perversely, he wanted to see what kind of a reaction a black man at their front door would receive before he told them of his family connection. He'd rehearsed in his mind what he planned to do. He would knock on the door, and when it opened, he'd politely introduce himself, then tell them that his mother was a great friend of Parker Muir's. How she had spoken of him so often that he was curious to see where he'd lived. This would give him the opportunity to gauge for himself how he was received, to get a feel for them before he boldly told them that he was Parker Muir's illegitimate son. News like that had to be presented carefully. Anyway, he thought, blowing air through his lips, that was the plan.

Atticus wiped his palms on his thighs. A pretty flimsy plan, he knew.

He shifted into drive and passed through the hedge. The house was what was called by Charlestonians a beach cottage, a place a wealthy city family had come to in the sweltering summers to escape the heat. Over the years the small house had to have been raised on pilings and renovated, yet it had kept all the grace of the original. Solid, elegant, but not ostentatious. He caught in the air the unmistakable whiff of old money.

On either side of the main house stood a small white wooden building. The one on the right was the picture of a lowcountry cottage, with a red tin roof and front porch complete with rocking chairs. To the left sat a sorry-looking garage that appeared to be tilting. He grinned, thinking that building at least appeared to have weathered one storm too many.

Standing proud in the middle was an enormous live oak tree, its boughs drooping low and laced with moss. The magnificent tree was ancient, budding countless green leaves that would provide welcome shade in the summer. Atticus drove around the gravel circle to park near the line of bright pinks of azaleas that bordered the front of the house. Stepping from the car, he paused to breathe in the cool, moist air that tasted of salt, and stretched his neck after the five-hour drive.

So this was Sea Breeze. Home of the Muir family. He wondered if his illegitimate tie to the bloodline would earn him a welcome here. As he climbed the front stairs to the veranda, he noted that the tidy house was well maintained with a fresh coat of paint on the trim, green ferns already hanging in large baskets over the railing, and black iron urns spilling colorful, cool-weather pansies on either side of the door. Staring at the closed glossy black door with the striking brass knocker in the shape of a shell, Atticus wondered which of the Muirs he'd meet when the door opened. Perhaps Marietta, his grandmother. She was widowed and had lived alone in this house for over a decade. Though recent real estate reports revealed that the house had recently been sold to a Miss Harper Muir-James. This would be his youngest half sister. Quite a purchase for a single woman about the same age as himself, he thought.

He stood at the door. *No more stalling,* he told himself. There was only one way to meet the family, and that was to knock on this door. He took a moment to compose himself, breathing deep as he did before a sermon. Then he rang the doorbell.

In the tense silence he heard the sound of footfalls in the house. His stomach tightened. Too late to change his mind. The front door swung open.

An elderly woman stood before him, tall and slender and with the straight carriage of confidence. His first impression was of an elegant woman dressed in a quality tan sweater with a crisply ironed white blouse. A coral scarf softened her appearance, as did her white hair, which seemed to float around her head like a halo. She had a pretty face, even kind. One that was open and welcoming. She had a mug in her hand, and Atticus was relieved to see warmth in her clear blue eyes as she offered him a smile of welcome.

"Hello?" she said inquiringly.

His shoulders began to relax.

Then suddenly her expression froze. Her eyes rounded as though startled. "Parker!"

The mug dropped from her fingers, tumbled, crashed on the floor, shattering.

The mention of Parker's name shook Atticus to the core. He stood momentarily frozen as Marietta gasped and rushed to pick up the broken pieces of the cup.

"Please, wait one moment," Mrs. Muir said, flustered. Her

cheeks were pink and she cast several curious looks at his face, trying unsuccessfully to be discreet. "I'll just dispose of these. I'll be right back." She hurried off, leaving the front door open.

Atticus rammed his fists into his pockets and stared unseeingly over his shoulder at the scenery. He was stymied, unable to think of what to say or do next. All he could hear in his mind was the woman's startled cry of her son's name. *Parker!* The poor woman was clearly upset. She'd left the door open to a complete stranger.

"Forgive me," Mrs. Muir said on returning. She appeared once again composed, though her eyes betrayed her, shining unusually bright. "You reminded me of someone I knew." She added airily, "I don't know what came over me." Mrs. Muir extended her hand and approached him. He saw her long fingers with clean, short, polished nails and only a simple platinum wedding band. "I didn't catch your name."

Atticus cleared his throat and lifted his hands from his pockets. "I'm Reverend Atticus Green, ma'am. My mother was a friend of your son."

"Really? Of Parker's?"

In his mind he heard her startled cry of that same name and knew what they were both thinking of that moment. "Yes. She often talked about him. And how he described this place. Sea Breeze, correct?"

"Yes." A soft smile relaxed her features. "Did he?" The comment pleased her and he felt another stab of guilt.

"I was in Charleston on business and thought I'd drive by and see it. I shouldn't have come by uninvited." He broke a quick smile. "My mother would be very angry with me. Truly, I'm sorry I disturbed you."

"Any friend of Parker's is welcome at Sea Breeze. Please, Reverend, won't you come in? Mind the tea," she warned him, indicating the spilled liquid on the floor. "I'll get to that later."

He followed her into a large living room that was all creams and blues, the colors of the sea. Atticus appreciated the refinement and wealth reflected in the well-appointed room.

"Won't you sit down, Reverend Green?" Marietta led him to a Chippendale cream sofa. "Would you like something to drink? Water? Coffee or tea?"

Atticus felt his first relief that she'd welcomed him into her home as any genteel lady would a guest, even an uninvited guest as he was. He felt the first flush of shame that he'd put her into this awkward position by not calling first. His mother had taught him better.

"No, thank you." He sat straight backed on the linen sofa, uncomfortable in the strange surroundings that were, he knew, his family's home.

"It's a lovely home."

"Why, thank you." Mrs. Muir joined him, sitting on the matching sofa across from him, her hands folded tightly on her lap. Blue-patterned pillows bolstered her back, lending her a regal air. Yet despite her outward composure, two bright blotches of pink stained her pale cheeks, a sign of heightened alertness. "So, Reverend, what can I help you with?"

Atticus hadn't planned what to say once he'd gained entry to the house. And now that he'd met Mrs. Muir—his grandmother—the inclination to tell her the truth sat at the tip of his tongue. Especially since she'd seen in him a resemblance to her son. He ventured the topic by saying, "I'm sorry I startled you."

Mrs. Muir looked at her hands. "You're probably wondering why I called out the name Parker?"

"Well, yes."

She paused again, studying his face as an expert would a portrait. She put her hand to her heart, as though she still couldn't get over it. "Parker was my son. He's passed now. When I saw you, I thought you were him. The resemblance is uncanny."

Atticus remained silent, enduring the scrutiny.

"What was your mother's name?"

"Zora Green."

"Another literary name," she noted, seemingly pleased by the fact. "You know, my son, Parker, named his daughters after his favorite southern authors—Eudora Welty, Carson McCullers, and Harper Lee."

"He must've loved books. My mother did."

"Oh, he did." Her face softened in memory. "He was a writer, you know."

"Yes, that's how he got to know my mother. She was an editor. They met while she was helping him with his novel."

"Zora . . ." Marietta paused to think back, then regretfully shook her head. "I'm sorry, but I don't recall Parker ever mentioning your mother's name."

That rankled. "Oh."

"We rarely discussed his friends or personal life. So that's not to be taken as a slight in any way. You see, my son and I had a serious falling out after his first divorce. Later we reconciled, but from that point on it was tacitly understood that his personal life was not up for discussion. And, to be honest, I was more comfortable being kept in the dark. Let's just say Parker was a very handsome and charming man. He had three wives, you see."

"And you have three granddaughters."

"Tell me about your mother," she said.

This was a subject he could speak about readily. A small smile crossed his face as he pictured his mother in his mind. "She was lovely in every way. And bright. She was the publisher of *Atlanta* magazine until she died."

"It's a very good magazine. Small world."

He nodded in agreement, then looked idly around the room in the heavy silence.

"Reverend . . . Atticus, do you have something in particular you'd like to ask me?"

Atticus felt the heat of her searching stare. "Not particularly. As I said, my mother was a friend of Parker's and I was curious to see where he grew up."

Mrs. Muir looked at her hands. "I think, perhaps, an intimate friend." She lifted her eyes.

He met her gaze sharply. "I didn't say that."

"You didn't have to."

As they stared at each other, his blue eyes searching into hers, Atticus knew without a doubt the game was up. This was a wise old bird, biding her time.

To her credit, she released a knowing smile that revealed more compassion and wisdom than he felt he deserved, under the circumstances.

"Atticus, you are the very image of my dear son, Parker. Tell me, child. Did you come here, to Parker's home, searching for answers? If so, I have a burning question of my own." She closed her eyes as though to gather her strength, then, opening them, she held his gaze and said with heart, "Are you my grandson?"

Atticus's defenses were shattered. The vague responses he'd meant to give melted away under the heat of her gaze. Open and vulnerable, she looked at him. She'd laid her cards on the table and now waited for his response.

He blinked slowly. "Yes."

Her hand flew to her lips as her composure fled. Tears filled her eyes, appearing as two deep lakes about to overflow. With the truth out, Atticus felt her stare intensify as she examined him with open curiosity, even hunger, clearly searching for signs of her son in his son.

Atticus felt uncomfortable under the scrutiny. "Are we really that much alike?"

She smiled with self-effacing charm. "Enough that I thought you were him when I first saw you. Scared the living daylights out of me, I must say."

"Alike, except with a different skin color," Atticus said wryly.

"Well, yes." Marietta leaned forward and peered into his face. "Now that I look at you more calmly, there are differences, of course. The nose isn't his. Your forehead might be a bit broader. And though he was tall, he wasn't as tall as you. But overall the resemblance is absolutely profound. Your facial structure, slender frame, and of course your eyes. It's the Muir blue color," she said with a hint of pride.

Atticus listened, soaking in the information like a dry sponge. He'd not looked like Tyrone and only somewhat like his mother. "I had always wondered where I got my blue eyes from."

Marietta shook her head, seemingly dazed. "But this is

extraordinary! I wonder why he never told me. You're his only son. My only grandson."

"My mother asked him not to tell anyone. I have to respect him for keeping his promise. He never met me. I didn't know about him, either."

"Then how . . . ?"

"My mother died a few months ago. After her estate was settled, her lawyer sent me, per her instructions, a letter she'd written to me before she died." He steepled his hands. "It was a shock."

"My dear boy, I can't imagine."

"I didn't see it coming." He paused at the understatement. "My parents were separated when she met Parker. My father was working as a lawyer in Atlanta. My mother went to New York to work as an editor for a major publishing house. According to the letter, it was there she met your son. I gather she was helping him with his book, they spent a lot of time together, and one thing led to another." Atticus shrugged. "She says they fell in love."

Marietta's eyes widened with a sudden realization. "Did your mother work for Georgiana James?"

"Yes, I believe that was her name. She was, according to my mother, a cruel woman."

Marietta's eyes narrowed. "It was Georgiana," she said with certainty.

"In any case, once her boss found out about their affair, she fired my mother and divorced your son. Only, by this time my mother was pregnant. She returned to her husband in Atlanta, where they reconciled. He raised me as his own son."

"When did Parker find out he had a son?"

"My mother wrote to tell him before I was born. You should know, he offered to marry her."

Marietta's face was somber. "It was the honorable thing to do."

"For a white man to marry a black woman in your society here in Charleston almost thirty years ago, it would have meant a scandal. In New York? It might have brought a few raised brows, but they could have done it. My mother loved your son, and he loved her. But she didn't want to marry him. She chose to go back to her husband. My *real* father."

Mrs. Muir didn't respond.

"Let me be clear. I'm not here in search of a father. Tyrone Green is my father. He's the only father I've ever known or need to know. And he was a good man. A good husband to my mother."

"I've no doubt. Meeting you is proof enough."

"Thank you." He was relieved that his loyalties were clear. "But they're both gone now. As are their parents, my grandparents."

"Do you have any brothers or sisters?"

Atticus shook his head. "I'm an only child. I'm alone."

Mrs. Muir smiled gently. "Well, you have three sisters now."

He took a deep breath, exhaling with wonder at that reality. "Right. Half sisters, anyway."

"Blood is blood." Mrs. Muir brought her hands up and clasped them near her heart. "I have a grandson," she said with disbelief, feasting her eyes on him.

Atticus felt emotions long held in check come surging up now. "I didn't know if you'd be glad to learn about me. If you'd want me."

"Oh, dear boy, I'm overwhelmed with joy. I didn't know you existed. My son's son." She put her fingers to her lips. "You are the sole male heir of the Muir family."

Atticus put up his hands, suddenly feeling a little trapped. "Whoa . . . I didn't come to interfere. The Muir granddaughters might not appreciate that. Laws of primogeniture notwithstanding, I didn't come here to be one of the Muir clan."

"But you *are* here, Atticus. And you are a Muir."

When she put it like that, it made his arguments sound trivial. He looked at his hands. He didn't want to expose the fragility of his emotions. Having a family meant more to him than he'd realized. He had been feeling lonely since his mother's death, a man adrift without a family to anchor him. Now this woman, his grandmother, was including him in his new family, and it was a gift, as welcome as it was daunting. How did he feel about embracing this family as his own? That was not clear yet.

"You're curious about us," Mrs. Muir continued.

"That's why I came. It's only natural that I'd want to know my genetic history. My health records."

"And you'll have them. Do you have children?"

"No. I'm not married."

She leaned back, surprised. "A handsome man like you? Goodness, in that respect you're not at all like Parker."

Atticus looked at her with surprise, then saw that she was laughing. Parker had married three times and had three children, one with each wife. He sounded like a womanizer. That she could make a joke of it showed character, and he liked her all the more.

"You'll want to meet your sisters, no doubt."

Atticus blew out a stream of air and leaned back against the sofa. "Honestly? I don't know. They might not be thrilled to meet me."

"Why ever not?"

"This is all happening so fast. I hadn't meant to tell anyone about my family connection today. Not even you."

She lifted a brow speculatively. "So this was a scouting mission?"

He half smiled as one caught in his game. "Exactly."

"But then I recognized you and ruined your plan."

His grin widened. "I didn't expect that." He was aware she was watching him with a thoughtful, appraising expression.

"I think you should meet your sisters. Why waste any more time on doubts? You'll like them."

"Are they anything like you?"

Marietta laughed shortly and said, surprised, "Why, I should think they are. I hope I'm like them."

"Then I know I'll like them."

She lowered her chin coquettishly. Atticus thought she must have been quite something in her heyday.

"How will they react to a surprise brother? Even a half brother?"

"It's not a new experience for them."

"Not even a black half brother?"

"That might be a surprise, perhaps. But it won't matter."

Atticus crossed his legs. "It might."

"Let's risk it. What choice do we have?"

"Mrs. Muir . . ."

Marietta put her hand up. "Please, that's much too formal

under the circumstances. Call me Mamaw. That's what the girls call me."

He swallowed, touched by the offer, but shook his head. "I'm sorry. It's a kind offer, but I'm not ready to go that far yet."

"Marietta, then?"

"Marietta," he conceded.

"I hope that someday you'll feel comfortable calling me Mamaw."

Atticus accepted the statement with a tilted nod of the head. Mamaw's breath momentarily caught in her throat as she recognized the gesture as a mannerism of Parker's. "I hope I will, too."

Marietta made a move to rise. "This is going to be such a great surprise for your sisters. You'll be here to celebrate Harper's and Carson's weddings!"

Atticus put up his hand in an arresting motion. "Hold on a minute, please."

Mamaw settled herself back on the sofa and waited, eyes alert.

"When are the weddings?"

"They're coming up right quick. May. Not a double wedding. One on Saturday and one on Sunday with a joint rehearsal dinner on Friday night here at Sea Breeze."

He could see the excitement taking hold of her. "With the weddings so close, I don't think the timing is right to spring this on them. Weddings are a roller coaster of emotions. The last thing they need to deal with now is a brother they knew nothing about. Mrs. Muir . . . Marietta . . . I'm a minister. I deal with the ups and downs of weddings all the time." He made a face. "Weddings bring out the best and the worst in people. You can't believe what people say and do—to their own family members—under *normal* circumstances. I don't think it's wise to expose a long-held family secret into the mix. Not now."

He could see the older woman was having trouble accepting this possibility. She wanted to pop the champagne and celebrate the return of the lost grandson. Still, his argument wasn't lost on her.

Marietta brought her hand slowly to her neck. "I didn't think of it that way. Perhaps you're right. This is a delicate time for them." She rolled her eyes for effect. "And we have a few issues to deal with already." She sighed, not quite ready to give up the argument. "But you're here now. It's a shame to wait."

"We must. My mother died only recently, and I only just learned that Parker was my father. That's a lot to take in. I need time to digest all this."

Marietta appeared resigned. "I suppose it would be a lot for all of you to face. At least immediately."

"Exactly. I'm still grieving my mother and have to reason why she never told me or sought you out. And . . . I hope you'll respect that I may, in the end, choose to keep my distance."

"I can't promise that I'll never let your sisters know."

"I understand. I'm only asking you to wait." He checked his watch. They seemed to have reached an impasse.

He was about to stand and leave when she turned sharply toward him, her face brightening. "I have an idea!"

He looked at her dubiously. "What's that?"

"You said you're a minister? What kind of minister are you?"

"Southern Baptist."

She pursed her lips in thought. "I'm an Episcopalian. Dora

is, too. But Carson and Harper, the brides, aren't members of any church as far as I can tell. I'm not sure about Harper. Being from England, she might be Anglican, but in any case I can tell you that neither girl has stepped foot in a church since she's arrived." Marietta sniffed, which gave away her opinion of that. "I think we can make this work," she said with confidence.

"Make what work?" Atticus asked dubiously.

"What if I introduce you to the girls as an old family friend? We'll have to come up with some history, but that shouldn't be too hard. And"—her eyes brightened further—"as a friend, I asked you to officiate at the weddings."

Atticus couldn't speak for a moment. She looked at him with an expression of innocent delight when what she was asking him to do was to get involved in a lie.

"But it's not true."

"It's not a lie if you actually are the minister at the weddings. You'll be able to meet the girls and act as their counselor. It will involve talking to the girls, meeting their fiancés, spending time with them." Marietta straightened her shoulders and said in utmost seriousness, "Reverend Green, I'm asking you to marry my granddaughters. Will you?"

"They're not members of my church." Atticus was grasping for an excuse.

"We both know you can get around that for special occasions."

"I don't know. . . . It would mean being involved in a lie."

"Say yes to marrying them. Then it's not a lie. It's an omission."

"Which is also a sin."

"We are not deceiving them. We are simply withholding certain information. Temporarily."

Atticus looked at her askance. "That's the definition of a sin of omission."

Marietta tossed her hands up in frustration. "Let's not split hairs, Atticus," she entreated. "Please don't be obstinate. You forget how important it is to me to have you be a part of the weddings. You're my grandson. And I've only just met you."

He felt the emotion in her words and had to admit, he felt them, too.

Her voice quivering, she continued softly, "You see, I will need time to fully comprehend all this, too." He thought she might cry, but she rallied, forcing a gallant smile. "Oh, but you're here now."

Marietta rose, came to his side, and sat beside him. "Dear boy, we must choose a course of action. You started the ball rolling by coming to Sea Breeze and knocking on my door. We cannot turn back from the truth now." She took his hands. "We must be strong. Together. Either we tell the girls right now who you are and let the chips fall where they may—"

He shook his head. "No."

"—or I introduce you as the minister who will preside over their weddings and we give all of you time to get to know each other first. Which will it be?"

Atticus released his hands and crossed his arms. This was one strong and determined woman, he thought. She reminded him of his mother. He knew that he could—maybe even should—get up and walk out and never see any of them again. She held no authority over him. And yet . . . remembering the warmth of her welcome, the longing in her eyes, his gut instinct was to go along with her plan, at least for the time being. She was his grandmother. That was the unarguable fact. Plus, he felt an odd alliance with this woman, this stranger who was his father's mother. Did the ties of blood overcome his objections?

Atticus closed his eyes and prayed for guidance. He didn't believe in doing the wrong thing for all the right reasons. Yet this didn't feel like the wrong thing. Or at least, not a bad thing. In truth, he did want to meet his half sisters. Talk to them, get to know them. But he wasn't ready to declare himself their brother. By agreeing to be their minister, he could get to know them slowly, give them—and himself—time to form opinions without the shock of their father's infidelity and a surprise brother popping up. Not right before their weddings. When looking at the situation from this light, the plan felt more like a kindness.

"If I agree," he said warily, "will you agree to wait until I say I am ready to tell them the truth about being their brother?"

Marietta's eyes shone with the light of expectant victory. "I agree."

Atticus stared at Marietta as a wry smile crossed his face. "I'm guessing you win a lot."

"Me?" she asked innocently. "Why, Atticus, I'm just a li'l old lady."

Chapter Eight

Soon everyone will be in wedding mode. Aka hysteria.

*M*amaw? Are you here?"

Marietta's and Atticus's heads both swung toward the sound of the voice, then toward each other in silent agreement. Atticus felt his insides do a slight flip—he wasn't sure if he was quite ready to play the role they'd only just created.

A moment later a woman strolled into the room, an enormous black dog at her heels. Atticus was alert and immediately sized up the dog—was it friendly or a guard dog? But he needn't have worried. On catching sight of him in the living room, the woman immediately turned and gave the dog the order to stay. To his relief, the gargantuan animal dropped to the floor at the entrance—though not without a sorry whine—and put his head in his paws.

"Harper!" Marietta exclaimed, and opened her arms.

So this was his half sister, Atticus thought as he watched her come to her grandmother's side and place a kiss on Marietta's upturned cheek.

"I want you to meet someone," Marietta said, indicating Atticus.

As he rose to his feet, Atticus's stomach tightened under the appraising gaze of this stranger, his half sister. He braced himself for another round of startled recognition of their father, but it didn't come.

"This is the Reverend Atticus Green," Marietta said, delivering a megawatt smile toward him that spoke clearly of her expectations. "Atticus, this is my granddaughter Harper Muir-James. One of the brides-to-be."

She stepped closer and suddenly he was looking into eyes the exact color of his own. Hands were extended and he caught a glimpse of an enormous diamond on her slender finger. They murmured greetings in the usual polite manner.

"Atticus is an old family friend," Marietta continued. "Very dear." She turned to Harper. "I have a surprise for you."

"I love surprises." Harper's eyes sparkled.

You have no idea, Atticus thought to himself as he rocked on his heels. He looked at Marietta, his eyes pulsing with the message *Do not tell her who I am.*

Marietta said, "I wrote to Atticus and asked a favor of him, if he would please come to Charleston to marry you and Carson. And he has agreed! Isn't that just too wonderful?"

Harper was momentarily stunned by the unexpected announcement. Then her face lit up with astonishment. "Really?"

Atticus managed a stiff smile and a nod of his head.

Marietta, in contrast, was at ease. "You know how we worried about who would officiate. And now we have our answer.

Atticus drove all the way here from Atlanta to meet you and Carson."

Harper put her hand to her heart. "I'm speechless. I'm so happy! So you'll really marry us?"

Atticus swallowed. "Yes."

It was done. One word and he'd tied himself to the story that would bind him for the next few months.

Harper clasped her hands together. "That's super! Amazing, actually. Mamaw!" Harper turned on her heel to face Marietta. "Why didn't you tell us you had this card up your sleeve? You clever old girl."

"I didn't want to make the announcement until Atticus agreed." Marietta cast a searching glance his way.

A furrow creased Harper's smooth brow. "I'm not a member of any church. Is that a problem?"

Atticus shook his head. "No. I'm a Baptist minister, but it shouldn't be."

Harper sighed. "What a relief. I didn't want to get married by a justice of the peace. And if you're a family friend, it makes it all the more special, doesn't it? I don't know many people here, you see. I moved here from New York only a year ago. Most of my family is in England."

"You're a Muir, dear," Mamaw reminded her. "You have family connections here."

"But I don't really know them. Nor they me. Did you talk to Granny James about this?" Harper turned to Atticus. "My grandmother is giving the wedding. Her name is Imogene, but we call her Granny James. She'll be flying in from England soon, and I can't imagine she'll have any objections."

Mamaw scoffed, "I should think not. And, no, I didn't talk to her about it yet. This is my contribution to your wedding. She's been rather miserly about sharing duties, after all."

"Now, Mamaw." Harper cast an embarrassed glance toward Atticus. Apparently this was a tender subject. "You're throwing the wedding for Carson. It's all decided."

"Yes, well. There are things I can help with, being here and all. And don't you have a say? Are you happy with the arrangement?"

"Very."

"Then it's decided. Atticus will say the service." Marietta sniffed. "Unless Imogene's bringing a member of the clergy in tow from England."

"She's not." Harper laughed lightly. She turned to Atticus. After a brief pause she tilted her head. "How are you a family friend, by the way? Are you a relative of Lucille's?"

Atticus was caught unawares. Lucille? Who was Lucille? The first stumble already. Atticus turned to Marietta with a challenging stare.

"He's met Lucille, of course," Marietta jumped in smoothly. "Long before she died." Marietta stressed that important point to Atticus. "But that's not the connection. Atticus's mother, Zora, was a great friend of Parker's."

"My father's?"

Atticus prudently kept silent.

"Yes," Mamaw replied evenly. "Zora Green is a writer, too." She lowered her head in respect. "Or was, may she rest in peace. While she was alive, we kept up over the years, Christmas cards and such. Not nearly as much as we should have. But I thought of Atticus when you were searching for a minister and"—Mamaw paused and held out her arms—"here we are!"

The answer seemed enough to satisfy Harper. She turned to Atticus, her smile radiating warmth. "I'm so delighted. And Carson will be thrilled."

Atticus thought to himself how the young woman had not an ounce of guile. The genuineness of her joy was endearing. Yet beneath the smile she had a sophistication and innate grace that revealed class. This was the young woman who had purchased Sea Breeze from her grandmother, after all. No small change could have done that.

"Does Carson know?" Harper asked.

"Not yet," Marietta replied breezily. "He's only just arrived. Where is she, by the way?"

"Out on the dock. Again. Probably yearning for Delphine."

"Go fetch her, will you?" asked Marietta. "I'd like her to meet Atticus."

"You'll love Carson," Harper said to him. "Everyone does. Be right back."

Harper turned and hurried from the room, clapping her hands for the dog to follow her. He leaped to his feet and trotted happily behind.

Marietta smiled broadly, clearly pleased with the turn of events.

"She's lovely," Atticus said.

"I told you. Each of them are. Are you sure you don't want to tell them?"

"Yes," he said firmly.

"Oh, very well." Disappointment flooded Marietta's features. She went to the sofa and sat, fingers tapping her lap.

Atticus walked around the room, filling the empty silence

with random questions about the art on the walls. With relief, a short while later they heard footfalls in the hall. Both of them turned toward the noise expectantly.

Harper entered, followed by a taller, striking woman of uncommon beauty. This must be Carson, he realized. She was a study in contrasts with Harper with raven hair and a southwestern-chic style of dress. But as she drew near, he saw the same blue eyes that he now knew were dominant in the Muir line. Those eyes studied him with cool appraisal.

To usher Carson closer, Harper held out her arm, acting as if she and Atticus were already old friends. "Carson"—she waved her sister closer—"come meet Reverend Green, an old friend of Mamaw's. But we call him Atticus."

Carson walked closer with long strides and held out her hand. "So you're the man who's going to marry us?"

A bold move, he thought, appreciating it. He took her hand. "If that's okay with you?"

Her handshake was firm and he liked that she looked him straight in the eye. He could tell that she was recognizing the eye color, working it out in her mind, but her smile remained in place as she politely withdrew her hand.

"It's okay with me," she said nonchalantly. "You should know I'm not much of a churchgoer."

"So I've been told."

She ventured a curious smile at that. "And I've been told you're a Baptist minister."

"Southern Baptist," he confirmed.

"One's the same as another. Blake's family is Baptist," Carson said. "They'll be pleased as punch."

Atticus held his tongue. He didn't want to get into an argument about her comment "one's the same as another," at least not yet.

"Shall we all sit down? I'll make coffee," Marietta offered.

"Mamaw"—Harper reached out to stall her with a soft touch on her arm—"I'm sorry but Carson and I have an appointment at the bakery. To taste the cakes. We have to leave." Harper looked at Atticus. "I'm so sorry to cut out on you."

Atticus wasn't sorry. He was relieved. "No, that's all right. I have to leave anyway. I need to go and check into a hotel."

"Where are you staying?" Harper asked with alacrity.

"I don't know yet."

"Stay here! With us," Harper exclaimed.

Carson swung her head to deliver her sister a hard stare of warning.

Atticus immediately backtracked, "No, I couldn't impose."

"It's no imposition at all, really. We have loads of room," Harper said, ignoring Carson. "Well, at least until the weekend when my grandmother arrives."

Atticus glanced at Carson in her pale blue shirt regarding him from under furrowed brows. She was clearly wrestling with the invitation. He looked at Marietta, and her eyes were shining with reassurance, even hope, that he would accept, reminding him of her warm and sincere welcome.

"No. Thank you," Atticus said more firmly. This was all moving far too quickly for him. He needed time alone to reflect on all that had transpired—possibly life changing. "I have other business to attend to while I'm in town and will be in and out. I'll need my own place. But again, thank you for the invitation."

"Of course. We understand," Mamaw said firmly, putting the invitation to rest.

Harper reluctantly accepted this, but wasn't through yet. She took a step closer. "How long are you in town?"

Atticus had taken a leave of absence from his ministry. After a long discussion, his pastor had advised him to take all the time he needed to get answers, to ponder them and come to conclusions before he returned to work. But of course Atticus kept this to himself. Even with Marietta's warm welcome, he didn't know how long he could bear to stay in Charleston, caught in this web of lies.

"Undecided. For several weeks. Possibly longer. My, uh, research is just beginning."

"Then you absolutely must come for dinner Saturday night. I'm having a pre-wedding gathering at Sea Breeze. All the usual suspects will be there. Taylor, my fiancé, Carson and her fiancé, Blake. Our other sister, Dora, and her boyfriend, Devlin, and her son, Nate. And all the parents and grandparents. You can meet us all in one fell swoop. This Saturday. Six o'clock cocktails. Seven o'clock dinner. Casual attire. Please say you will come. You're the minister, after all."

He felt the force of Harper's invitation and thought how much like her grandmother Marietta the young girl was. Gracious and warm, with an underlying will of iron. He felt the lie closing in on him and began to make his exit, subtly backing toward the door.

"Six o'clock. I'll be there." He checked his watch. "But now, I really must go. It was nice to meet you, Harper." He offered his hand.

Harper stepped forward to take his hand, then leaned in to kiss his cheek. The kiss surprised him. He nodded, mumbling some agreeable parting comment.

"Good-bye. See you Saturday," Carson told him.

Atticus looked to Marietta. Her blue eyes were still shining. With joy or triumph—or both—he wasn't sure.

"Good-bye," he said to her. His smile was sincere. "It truly was nice seeing you."

Marietta couldn't be restrained. She rushed across the space between them to put her hands on his arms and squeezed tight with a gentle shake. The kind a grandmother might give to her grandchild. Once again she seemed at risk of crying.

"Atticus. You have no idea how happy you've made me."

Atticus couldn't get to his truck fast enough. The emotions were too strong, too confusing. As soon as he stepped from the house, he took deep breaths of the fresh air and stretched out his arms, not realizing how stiffly he'd been holding himself. He looked behind himself at the closed door, not quite believing all that had transpired in the past hour.

Atticus turned the collar of his suit coat up around his neck and quickly descended the stairs. His heels dug deep half-moons into the gravel as he marched to his truck. He needed some time alone to think. With a yank he swung open the door and had one foot in the truck when he heard a voice calling his name.

"Atticus! Wait!"

He lowered his head, his hand on the truck, and sighed. Not fast enough, he thought. With resignation he dropped his foot back to the gravel and turned to see Carson hurrying down the stairs after him.

"I'm glad I caught you!" she called out, arms tucked, trotting to his side.

"Did I forget something?"

"We don't have your contact information while you're here. Mamaw asked me to come fetch it."

There was no way he couldn't give the information to her. "Right. Let me give you my card. It has my cell phone number." He patted his pockets but remembered he hadn't brought his card case. "I keep a box in the glove compartment. Hold on."

He climbed up into the truck and stretched across the driver's seat to open the glove compartment. He pulled out a small cardboard box. From this he pulled out several cards, then returned to face Carson. "These ought to do it." He handed the cards to her. "You can reach me on my cell."

"Okay. Great. Thanks." She looked at the card. A brisk breeze blew a strand of hair across her face. She brushed it away, then looked up at him warily. "Will we have to do those pre-wedding discussions?"

"I recommend them. If you were a member of my parish, it would be mandatory."

"To be honest, I'm not so keen on the idea."

"I'll leave that decision up to you."

The March wind gusted, icy and damp. Carson wrapped her arms around herself and shivered. "I hate the cold," she said through chattering teeth.

He searched her face and sensed anxiety lurking behind her question. Intuition was an important aspect of his work, and he'd learned to trust it. "Do you have anything in particular you'd like to discuss? Something bothering you?"

She looked off a moment, and when she turned back to him, she nodded curtly.

"Step into my office." Atticus grinned. He leaned over the seat again and pushed open the passenger door. He then closed his own door and started the engine, boosting the heat. Carson climbed into the passenger seat and spent a moment rubbing her hands together in front of the surge of warmth.

"It's sure cold today," she said, blowing on her fingers. "Feels like winter. Just when you think it's spring."

"To be fair, official spring hasn't arrived yet. But the promise of spring is in the greening trees and flowers."

She tilted her head and smiled at him, liking his answer. "True."

He waited for her to begin. It was close quarters in the front cab of the truck, and the heater was barely doing its job. "So, what's on your mind?"

"It's all this wedding business. Now that I'm home, it seems all anyone thinks or talks about are the wedding preparations. When Harper's grandmother arrives in a few days, everyone will be in full wedding mode. Aka hysteria."

He had to chuckle at this.

Carson sighed. "You met Harper. Sweet, elegant, thoughtful—right?"

He nodded.

"Be forewarned. She's turning into a bridezilla. She's got us all on a short leash. Her favorite new expression is *chop-chop*. I hardly recognize her."

"And you?"

Carson shrugged noncommittally and tucked her hands between her knees. "I care, of course. But honestly"—she looked up at him—"I'm not all that interested in wedding plans. Frankly, I've got so much on my plate right now, I can't be bothered."

This was often a warning flag for him that something else was amiss. "Are you feeling pressured into getting married?"

"No, it's not that. Well . . ." She pursed her lips. "Maybe a little."

"How are you feeling pressured?"

Carson looked out the windshield and said miserably, "Blake and I just went around the block on this. There are outside issues that are causing problems. Schedules." She paused, then turned to look at him. "Do you have time to listen to all this? I thought you had to go."

"I have time."

She heard this, glanced at the front door of the house as though she expected Harper to come running out for her. "We can't agree on my working situation. I have a job as a stills photographer with a film company that takes me away for months at a time. Usually eight to nine weeks. But it can go longer with delays. Blake doesn't want me to continue working that job after we're married. Thinks it's not a real marriage if I'm gone a lot." She puffed out air. "And to be fair, when we got engaged, I promised him I'd quit after this last gig."

"I hear a *but* coming."

"But . . . I got offered another job. It's great money and I love what I do."

"Sounds very cool."

"It is. At first. The travel gets old after a while. But more than that, I don't have another job waiting in the wings. Frankly, I've been unemployed, and it freaks me out to face that possibility again. I mean, why should I give up my career just because he doesn't want me to travel? So I can wait tables again? I don't think that's fair of him to ask me to do that."

"Is he asking you that? I thought you just said you'd promised him you would."

She lowered her head, seemingly contrite. "I did. That's why I suggested we change our engagement to a promise that we want to get engaged. Just until we work this out. But Blake won't do that. He says we're beyond that point. We're either engaged or we're not."

"Sounds like he's a pretty strong guy. Do you feel comfortable with that? Safe?"

"Oh, sure. I don't want you to get the wrong idea. Blake is not opinionated as much as he has strong convictions. I like that. He's old-fashioned about some things, like marriage. But he can be pretty flexible, too. And fair." She smiled at some memory. "Always fair."

"Are you in love with your fiancé?"

"Yes! Intensely. Loving Blake is the only thing I am sure about."

"Intense feelings are pleasurable and desired," Atticus said evenly, "but they're not a measure of compatibility for marriage. Whether or not the relationship is solid requires time and personal conversations. That's part of what I hope we can do when we all sit down together. To help you navigate whether or not you feel whole in your relationship, secure enough to voice your private thoughts and truths and know you're heard. To evaluate your relationship with your heart *and* your head."

"But if we find out we have problems? What then? We simply break up?"

"No, not break up. Perhaps postpone the marriage? Give yourselves more time."

"That's what I'd suggested."

"Carson, you say you're worried about quitting your film job. Are you more worried about losing that particular job, or about not finding another? There's a difference."

Carson took a deep breath, and he could see she was seriously considering what he'd asked.

"That's hitting the nail on the head," Carson answered with finality. "I'm worried that I won't find a job that's as rewarding. That gives me validation." She looked down at her hands, and her long dark hair fell over her face like a veil shielding her expression. Her voice emerged from behind, shaky and soft. "I know I come across as strong, but I'm not. I have a soft underbelly. The thought of floundering without a job, without a sense of purpose or of who I am and what I want out of life leaves me feeling lost and frightened. That leads to feeling angry and frustrated. And that leads to . . ."

She paused and blew out a plume of air, one that indicated a long story that she wasn't sure she wanted to tell. She tucked her hair behind her ears and turned to look at him. "This is between us, right? Is this like a confessional? With a priest?"

Atticus chuckled and shrugged. "I suppose. But I don't want to hear your sins."

She laughed. "Thank God. We'd be here all night."

Atticus liked her all the more for her openness. He'd always found that someone with a good sense of humor had a sharp brain as well.

"I'm afraid I'll start drinking."

Atticus snapped to attention. "What do you mean?"

"There's a family curse. And I don't mean the one that was placed on the head of our ancestor the pirate. Though, who knows, the disease may have its roots there. I'm an alcoholic. And so was my father."

Atticus went very still. The news that Parker—Carson's father . . . *his* father—carried the genes for alcoholism was not so much a shock as a brain-searing epiphany. There it was. The answer to the question that had dogged him since he tasted his first liquor.

Atticus closed his eyes tight and took a deep breath. He was an alcoholic. For so long he didn't know why he'd had the disease. Neither his father nor his mother were alcoholics. Nor their parents. Genetics accounted for only about 50 percent of alcoholism; the other 50 percent was due to environmental factors or poor coping mechanisms. But he'd grown up in a strong home with lots of support. So he'd wondered, *Why me?* Now he knew. The taste of the revelation was bitter in his mouth. This was his gift from his biological father. *Thanks, Dad.*

"Atticus?"

He blinked and brought his attention back to Carson, who sat across from him studying his face, concerned.

"Sorry." He brought himself back to the moment.

"I lost you for a minute."

"Yeah." He rubbed his eyes and then, dropping his guard, said, "I feel it's only fair to be honest with you, too. I'm a recovering alcoholic."

Carson stared back at him, then asked quietly, "How long have you been sober?"

"I haven't had a drink in eight years."

"Impressive."

"Being a Baptist helps. We don't drink." Atticus cracked a grin. "Maybe you should consider converting? I can help you out with that."

She smiled. "Maybe, but AA is working for me now. I'm going on eight months."

He nodded, acknowledging it. "Does Blake support you?"

"One hundred percent."

Atticus rested his hands on the steering wheel and looked out the windshield as he spoke. "So, let me see if I've got this right. You're a recovering alcoholic with a fiancé who is supportive. But you're afraid that if you quit working, you'll lose your identity and fall apart, which, for you, would mean falling off the wagon and starting drinking." He turned to face her. "Does that sound about right?"

She pulled her long dark hair up with both hands onto the top of her head in a loose pile, then, with a groan, she let her hair drop and faced him. "Yep. That sums it up," she said flippantly. "You're good at your job, you know that?"

He recognized that she was covering up her soft underbelly with humor. He respected her confidence too much to play along. He said seriously, "And you're afraid because . . ."

Her face shifted and after a moment she said, "Because Blake deserves better than that. Come on, we both know this is a lifelong struggle. I see the life that we could have together if I stay sober, and it's glorious. I get all rosy eyed about our future. But I know there's a chance I'll slip. A good chance. If I'm on the road, then I'm only hurting me. If I stay here and fall apart, I hurt Blake, too. And God help me, children down the line." Her eyes were red around the edges and she looked away, as though trying to hide them.

He reached out to gently touch her shoulder. "And yet—as an alcoholic—you have to accept that a certain loss of control over drinking is inevitable. Carson, it's simply not reasonable to believe that you can completely control your drinking. No matter where you are. And when a failure does occur, you can't make that a measure of your self-worth."

Carson asked with pain in her eyes, "Why make him go through that?"

"That's for Blake to decide. *You* have to focus on yourself now. What will keep you strong and healthy, in mind and soul? What will help you stay sober? You can start by establishing a bottom line. That's not a threat, mind you, but a position that supports and protects your self-esteem. A bottom-line position defines what you can accept and still feel good about the relationship, the other person . . . and most of all, yourself."

"I don't have a lot of time to figure that out."

"You have all the time you need."

Carson looked at Atticus's business card in her hand. "I can call you?"

"Anytime."

She looked at him. "And Blake?"

"Of course. We should talk about this again. Later, when we're all together."

She looked so anxious that he made himself smile. "You'll be fine." Looking up, he saw Harper standing on the front porch, looking out at them. "And you'd better go. Harper's looking for you and she doesn't look pleased."

Carson swung her head to see Harper waving at her from the porch. She returned a quick wave, then turned back to Atticus. "Do you know what's worse than a bridezilla?"

Atticus shook his head.

"A southern bridezilla." She pushed open the door and climbed from the truck. On the ground, she stopped to look at him, her head tilted in thought. "I'm glad you're marrying us. I feel so comfortable with you, like I could tell you anything. That's rare, trust me." She smiled again. "We must have been great friends in a former life. Bye, Atticus."

He watched her leave the truck and mount the stairs easily. Once on the porch, she turned to offer a final quick wave, then disappeared behind the closing door of Sea Breeze.

"Jesus take the wheel."

Atticus said the words of the country song like a prayer. He said it in times like this when he didn't know what his next step should be. Where he should go. Atticus believed that when he prayed, he was heard. It was a child's faith, one he held close when he was a boy in Atlanta, out in the Georgia woods, lost in the streets of the city, or tucked safe in his bed before falling asleep. He'd believed in a God that watched over him. Guardian angels. Good and evil.

When he was a teenager, however, he was too cool to believe in the fables of childhood. When he was a young buck, he relegated God to the backseat while he took the wheel of his destiny. Or so he'd thought.

Atticus crossed the northern tip of Sullivan's Island and

pulled off in a small parking area beside a bridge that led to another island. Isle of Palms, he thought. He didn't know . . . didn't care. He just had to stop the truck.

He parked the car in the lot slick with rain and staggered from the truck, taking deep gulps of the crisp air gusting from the sea. He walked to the edge of the lot to a small green space. Below, the dark, murky, turbulent water seemed to have no direction, swirling and whipping up whitecaps that crashed against the shoreline. Across the inlet, colorful houses sat back on the beach, one more large and beautiful than the next. The inlet opened up to the Atlantic Ocean. The breadth of it, gray and infinite, stretched out ahead of him.

"Lord, what do you want me to do?" he asked in abject humility. "Give me a sign. Something."

Atticus lowered his head. He'd come here thinking he was in control of the situation. Such conceit. He should abide by his own advice that he'd given Carson. By the time he'd arrived at Sea Breeze he had his plans in place. Then, in the space of a moment, an old woman—his grandmother—had wrested control away. When would he learn humility? The final words of his pastor before he left were to "accept what comes and remain open."

He paused and looked out at the restless water as a new thought took hold. Perhaps a power bigger than both Marietta or him had led them to this path? Marietta's immediate recognition of him . . . the bond he felt with his sisters . . . the welcome that was more akin to a homecoming. Atticus tucked his cold hands under his arms. That possibility was as disquieting as it was reassuring. So much of his life sometimes felt mapped out since the accident. There was another word for it: *preordained*.

The wind gusted, rattling the icy palm fronds, clicking like bones. He shivered. It felt as if someone had walked over his grave.

He was living on borrowed time. That he was standing here, alive and well, was nothing short of a miracle. A second chance from God. He knew that. But with that knowledge came the daunting realization that he had a job to do in the remaining days he was granted. God wanted something from him, and his life's effort was to figure out what that was. Intuitively he understood his task was to make life better—not for himself, but for others. He'd confessed this to his mother when he'd awakened from the coma in the hospital room.

"You have to earn your wings," his mother had told him.

"I'm no angel," he'd replied dismissively.

"What is an angel? We don't know the form they take. We only know they are doing God's bidding. You were my miracle." She kissed his cheek. "And now, you have to find out what God is asking from you."

"What, Lord?" he cried out now, feeling as helpless and alone as he'd ever felt. "Why did you lead me here?"

Seagulls huddled along the beach took flight at the sound, calling back their mocking laugh.

Atticus stared out at the gray sea churning before him and caught sight of a lone dolphin slicing through the waves with ease. He watched the dolphin's dorsal fin rise then disappear, to rise again a short time later. The dolphin was swimming in from the sea toward the bridge and the calmer waters of the Intracoastal Waterway. He continued watching as the dolphin drew closer. Atticus walked down the grassy slope to the small patch of beach below. The dolphin reemerged nearer the shoreline, and rather than continue on, the dolphin lingered near the shoreline where he stood, swimming back and forth. *What luck,* he thought, *to be here to witness this. It must be fishing in the turbulent waters.*

But this dolphin wasn't fishing. It wasn't diving. It coasted along the shoreline, and he had the sense the dolphin was watching him with the same curiosity as he was it. Atticus could see the dolphin's sleek gray skin glistening in the water. Stepping closer to the water and squinting, he saw long gray lines of scars crisscrossing its body. As the dolphin drew closer to the shoreline, it tilted its head. Atticus held his breath as he looked directly into its knowing eyes. Without question he knew he was looking into the eyes of a thinking, aware creature. And this dolphin was undoubtedly communicating with him.

The moment fled as quickly as the dolphin when it suddenly dipped beneath the water again. Atticus peered out at the sea, searching for the dorsal fin to reemerge. It did so, farther away by the bridge. Then it arched, dove, and he lost sight of it.

A short laugh escaped his lips. Was that his sign? The connection was powerful, to be sure. But what possible meaning could a dolphin have? Nothing for him. Yet, as Atticus turned and walked back to his truck, the feeling of tightness in his chest eased. Did it matter if it was a sign or not? He felt instinctively that Sullivan's Island was where he was supposed to be. He had a mission here, not only to benefit himself, but someone else.

Was it Harper? Or Carson? Or even Marietta? He was supposed to find out. He felt sure of it. And what better way than by being the minister at the Muir weddings? Good ol' Mamaw, he thought with a chuckle as he climbed into the truck. She'd come up with a pretty clever scheme. He'd have to be careful of that one. He could tell she was good at manipulating others to do her bidding. He fired the engine. Immediately the truck roared to life. Heat blasted from the vents, taking away his chill. Atticus rested his hands on the wheel and looked out a final time at the narrow inlet that separated the two islands.

He thought again of the sleek dolphin gliding through the worst of the turbulent waters, navigating the currents with skill and an enviable ease.

Sometimes, he thought, you just had to have a little faith.

Chapter Nine

It's a family wedding. That's what weddings really are. And as such, they are events filled with compromise.

Dora sent the tines of her fork slicing through the layers of the yellow cake. The lemon curd filling oozed out. She raised the cake to her mouth and slipped it inside, groaning, "Oh, Lord, I've died and gone to heaven."

Carson looked at her and shook her head ruefully. "You're going to die, all right, if you don't stop eating seconds of all the cakes."

"I'm not eating seconds," Dora protested, between chewing. "I'm taking a second bite, that's not the same thing."

Harper shared a glance with Carson.

Dora caught the glance and flushed. "I have to be sure which cake I like best." Dora set down her fork on the linen-covered table.

"And which of the cakes do you like best?" Harper asked, trying to soften the tease.

Dora rolled her eyes with a short laugh. "I can't decide. They're all so good!" She picked up her fork. "Maybe I'd better taste a few more."

The three Muir sisters were seated at a table in the charming tasting room of the Charleston bakery Harper had selected. They'd made an appointment and had preordered the five different cakes that sat in front of them. Neatly, and without fuss, each of the five cakes were sliced and served. Then they were left to discuss their choices.

"I'm getting them confused. Tell me all the flavors again?" asked Carson. She was turning one of the cakes around to get a better look at the filling.

Harper reached for the printed list. "Lemon buttercake with lemon filling, buttercake with chocolate Kahlúa filling, and almond buttercake with fresh-raspberry filling. The one you're looking at, Carson, is a hummingbird cake."

"My personal favorite." Dora slipped a forkful into her mouth.

"It says here that this bakery only uses European Plugrá butter."

"What's that?" Carson asked.

"It's a slow-churned process that creates less moisture content and a creamier texture, thus a flakier pastry," Harper answered. "It's so much better. The word Plugrá comes from the French *plus gras*. 'More fat.'"

"Of course it does," Dora said woefully, wiping a bit of the chocolate-cream filling from her lips with her pinkie.

"And last but not least," Harper said, "is the fresh-grated-coconut cake. Which, by the way, is the one I'm going with." Saying that, Harper pushed back a bit from the table. "It's a Charleston classic and I'm mad for it. I fell in love with it on one of my first dates with Taylor at the Peninsula Grill."

"Hummingbird cake is very traditional, too," Dora said, digging into another bite of it. She pushed the slice of cake toward Harper. "Try it again."

"No, I'm decided. Plus I couldn't eat another bite."

"But you hardly ate any."

"You had enough for both of us," Carson said.

Harper gave Carson a stern glance of warning. "Think of cake tastings like wine tastings."

Dora set her fork on the table, feeling suddenly embarrassed that she had attacked the cakes like a woman starved. If this were a wine tasting, she'd be drunk now. "I know that. I was just hungry. I skipped breakfast," she said, trying to salvage her dignity. "What about you, Carson? Did you taste the hummingbird cake?"

"I did, thanks. They're all mouthwatering. But honestly, I'm thinking of going with cupcakes."

"Cupcakes?" Harper exclaimed, clearly shocked. "But you're getting married at the Legare Waring plantation. You could do the cupcakes at a beach wedding, like mine. But for a traditional wedding location, you should go with a classic cake to go along with the theme of your wedding. You have to follow tradition!"

"What if I don't want to? I don't care if the dessert is non-traditional." Carson was getting her back up. "Unconventional is more my style."

"That doesn't matter," Harper said archly. "You chose the Legare Waring House. You're having a formal wedding. You set the theme, tone, and vision for the day, and everything must follow. Including cakes." She smoothed the pleats in her skirt. "You should have chosen a beach wedding. Then you could have been more relaxed about things."

"Oh, please . . ." Carson slapped her hand over her eyes with a groan. "I don't think I have to follow all those rules. What does it matter? I should get to choose something for my wedding, don't I? And I choose cupcakes."

Dora shot her hand in the air as if she'd just seen Jesus. "Oh. My. God. I had a vision, ladies. First, Carson, that's positively inspired. I have a friend who owns a wedding-cupcake shop on wheels—Sweet Lulu's Bakery. They have a nontraditional vintage trailer that's decorated real pretty. They'll put those sweet little cupcakes in those cute mason jars. How's that for southern?"

"I like it." Carson smiled smugly. "Done. Cross that off the list for me."

"Wait." Harper made a faux pout. "Now I want that. Mason jars would be adorable."

Carson looked back at her, incredulous. "But will it work for a beach-wedding theme?"

Harper and Dora both burst out laughing, and eventually Carson joined them.

Dora relaxed, glad to see the three of them finally seeing some humor in all this wedding charade. "I'll give you Sweet Lulu's contact information."

Harper beamed. "I've been waiting for months for you to get home so we could make these decisions together. Isn't it fun?"

Dora nodded.

"Like a barrel of monkeys," Carson replied, tongue in cheek.

Harper's smile faded. "The wedding is only two months away. Really, Carson, it means a lot to do this with you."

Carson reached out to place her hand on Harper's arm. "I'm sorry. I didn't mean to get you upset."

"Sometimes I don't think you care."

"Of course I care. I care about getting married to Blake. I just maybe don't care about all this cake business. At least not as much as you do." Carson rallied and said cheerfully, "So, what do you recommend?"

"Well," Harper said, taking the question to heart, "if I were you and having my wedding at the Legare Waring House, I'd go with the hummingbird-cake cupcakes in mason jars. Just as you said. It's brilliant and as lowcountry as you can get."

"That *is* the theme of my wedding," Carson said.

"I'm a little jealous, to tell you the truth. I love those mason jars." Harper twiddled her fork between two fingers. "But I love my coconut cake, too."

"The coconut cake. Must taste the victor." Dora reached across the table to take a forkful of the coconut cake. "By the way, do I have to remind you that you're going to be eating both cakes anyway? You're the bridesmaids for each other's wedding."

"Along with you, matron of honor," Carson said to Dora. "And if you keep eating like that, you're not going to fit into your dress."

Dora stuck out her tongue, then slipped the cake into her mouth.

Harper put her napkin on the table and moved aside the plates. "Now that we have the cakes decided on, let's talk about what we should put in the goodie bags. They should reflect the different themes, too." Harper reached down into her enormous bag and pulled out two manila folders. "These are the goodie-bag choices. I've narrowed them down to these few. So look them over and let's make our choices."

"This is a few?" Carson's eyes went wide with horror at the bulging files.

Harper ignored Carson's outburst and put the files on the table, flipping them open to reveal countless photos of items ripped from magazines and more downloaded from the Internet. Dora thought Harper seemed quite pleased with her organization.

"Dora, will you write our choices down?"

"Absolutely." Dora pulled a pen and paper from her purse. She, too, moved the cake plates back, but not before a long, lingering look at the lemon curd. "It's like a shower," she said with a giggle.

Carson stared at the thick piles, then pretended to roll up her sleeves. Her fingers flipped through the photos as fast as a croupier did cards. Dora went through the photos more slowly, wondering which ones she might have chosen for her wedding a decade earlier. Hers was a traditional Charleston wedding, and all the stops were pulled out. Her wedding was held at the venerable St. Philip's Church, her rehearsal dinner at Mamaw's impressive house on East Bay, and the reception at the exclusive yacht club. Dora's mother spared no expense for the grand wedding. Dora had felt like a princess that day in a gown of satin and tulle. She'd never been thinner, either. Despite the marriage's failure, she'd always hold that one, beautiful day as a highlight in her life.

She was daydreaming about her wedding when Carson handed her a small pile of photographs and announced, "Done! I choose fans, flip-flops, suntan lotion, saltwater taffy, bottles of water, sun hats, and, if there's enough money, beach towels."

"Wait, you're going too fast," Dora said, writing on the paper. When she finished, she looked up. "Okay. Got it."

"That wasn't too hard, was it?" Harper asked with innuendo.

Dora, not wanting to get off topic again, said, "Harper, your turn."

"I've been through these for weeks now. I already know what I want. Ready? Jars of tupelo honey, bug spray, pralines, and a canvas bag. And since Carson gets the cake in mason jars, I'm going to give away scented candles in mason jars."

Dora finished writing Harper's choices, then reviewed the selections. She tapped her pen against her lips and double-checked the lists. Her face became thoughtful. She set her pen in her lap, looked at her sisters, and made a face.

"Did you see what y'all did? You selected items for the other bride's wedding. Not your own. Harper, all your things are for a plantation wedding, and Carson, you chose things for a beach wedding."

Carson and Harper each looked at their own selections, then at the other's, and started laughing.

"I just chose the things I wanted to give away," Carson said. "It came naturally. My mind always goes straight to the beach."

"Me, too." Harper grew introspective. "I always wanted a tra-ditional wedding. I'm drawn to the formal weddings in bridal magazines. And when Prince William and Kate got married, I was glued to the television." Harper looked at her sisters, her expression perplexed. "I don't know what to do for a beach wedding."

"Then why are you having a beach wedding?" asked Carson.

"It's what Granny James wants."

Dora said, "But, Harper, it's *your* wedding."

"I know, but it makes her happy to plan it. She's been so generous with me. I owe her this much. Besides, I'm getting married to Taylor, which is all I really want."

Dora wasn't buying it and gave Harper a look that told her so. "That's hooey. No one who does this much research and collects this much stuff doesn't care."

Harper blushed. "Okay! I admit it. I want a plantation wedding complete with an elegant wedding gown, live oaks dripping with moss, winding creeks, scented candles in mason jars." She put her hands to her face. "Carson, I want the wedding you're having. The Legare Waring plantation has so much lowcountry history and tradition. That's more who I am. I guess I always thought I'd get married some place like that."

"I know what you mean. I always saw myself getting married on some beach. Just him and me and a few people I really cared about." Carson wiggled her brows. "Preferably in Hawaii."

Dora scratched her head. "Hold your horses. Let me get this straight. Carson, you want a beach wedding, but Harper is having that. And, Harper, you want a plantation wedding, but Carson is having that." Dora crossed her arms, pointing her fingers at each of them. "You two are having each other's wedding?"

Both brides looked at each other, then giggling, nodded.

"How in heaven did that happen?"

Harper leaned back against the chair. "That's what comes of letting someone else plan your wedding."

"Or not caring enough to get involved," Carson said.

"But that's just crazy," Dora argued. "These are *your* weddings."

"Not really," Harper said with finality. "It's a family wedding. That's what weddings really are. And as such, they are events filled with compromise."

"Well, look on the bright side," Dora said. "You both wanted a lowcountry wedding and that's what you're both getting. Carson's having the lowcountry plantation wedding. And, Harper, you're having the lowcountry beach wedding. You've got the lowcountry wedding theme covered. It's too late to change venues now, anyway. Money's been put down and the invitations have gone out. So we might as well have fun helping plan each other's wedding."

The baker, Mr. James, returned to their table with a flourish of smiles. A slender man, he had well-trimmed, longish hair and was stylishly dressed in slim black pants and a crisp white shirt. Dora couldn't imagine how a man could bake cakes for a living and still be so slender.

"So, ladies," Mr. James said, a polite smile on his face, "do you have any questions before you make your selections?"

Carson told him she was undecided, but Mr. James wasn't the least flustered. He focused his attention on Harper. He sat at the table with sketch paper and discussed with her the wedding themes and colors and tossed around ideas for design. The women clustered around him as he sketched his ideas for Harper's wedding cake right in front of them.

Harper clasped her hands together at the sight of a three-tiered cake with Tiffany Blue icing and long, arching sea grass, shells, and coral. "It's perfect. That's the cake I want."

"Done! Now it's time to celebrate." At Mr. James's signal, a waitress carried out a tray with three glasses of champagne. "For you!" he said gaily. "Congratulations!"

"None for me, thank you." Carson held up her hand.

"Me neither," Harper said. "Thank you."

"I'll have some!" Dora exclaimed, taking a glass.

The waitress carried away two flutes of wine.

"Coffee then?" Mr. James asked. When Carson and Harper nodded, he said, "Very good. I'll be right back."

Carson watched him leave the room, then gave Harper a long, searching look. "I know why I'm not drinking wine. Care to tell us why you're not?"

Harper shared a glance with Dora.

"Okay," Carson said, catching the look. She sat straighter. "Tell me."

Dora pinched her lips tight under eyes shining with knowledge.

Harper spread out her arms in announcement. "We're going to have a baby."

Dora could not be contained. Even though she'd already been told, fresh tears filled her eyes and she fluttered her hands in the air like butterfly wings. "We're having a baby!"

Harper looked searchingly at Carson, who sat wide-eyed and speechless. Dora felt a flash of worry Carson might take the news poorly in light of her own miscarriage. Dora needn't have worried.

Carson yelped with joy and wrapped her arms around Harper. "Congratulations! Wow, I didn't see that one coming. When are you due?"

"Not till the fall. Late September."

Dora counted back on her fingers. "Someone had a merry Christmas . . . ," she joked.

"Does Mamaw know?" Carson asked.

Harper shook her head. "Only Taylor. Dora. And now you. I've been waiting till Granny James gets here. Two birds with one stone and all that. But I'll need your support. I'm not sure how they'll respond to my being pregnant before I'm married. Them being from another generation and all. Do you think they'll be upset?"

"I can't speak for Granny James," Carson said, "but I don't think it will be an issue with Mamaw. After all, it wasn't when I was pregnant. All she cared about was my health and happiness. She stood right by me."

"I agree with Carson. Times have changed. Besides, honey, what do you think they can say? Cancel the wedding? Ship you off somewhere? You own your own house! Your only worry, frankly, is fitting into your wedding gown. Though I have to say, I'm relieved I'm not the only one with that on my mind." Dora peered past the table to Harper's midsection. "You had me fooled with those loose tops. I never would have guessed."

"Everyone will guess by the time the wedding arrives." Harper frowned and cried in a forlorn voice, "I'll be that pregnant bride."

"You'll be beautiful," Carson said. "Don't worry."

"I'm happy . . . but I'm kind of pissed, too. All my life I dreamed of my wedding day. Now I can't eat the tuna tartare or sushi I like or drink champagne. I can't even drink much caffeine. And if all that's not bad enough, I don't think my dress will fit."

"Aw, poor baby," Carson teased while pretending she was playing a violin.

Dora took Harper's worries seriously. "Can they let the dress out?"

"They can try. But the way it's constructed . . . I have my doubts. I actually thought about canceling my wedding and just having a quick ceremony."

"No!" Dora blurted out. "Don't do it. Who cares if you have a baby bump? Besides, it's too late. We're tasting cake, for heaven's sake. The invitations went out!"

"No, it's not too late," Carson fired back. "She can cancel anytime she wants. Even the day of, if she wants to."

Dora was at a loss at Carson's emotion on the topic. Dora had struck a nerve and it made her wonder about her runaway-bride sister. So Dora tempered her comments to restore peace: "Of course she can cancel." Then Dora turned to Harper. "But only cancel if you don't want to get married at all. Not because you're pregnant. Lots of women get married with a baby bump."

"I know," Harper said dejectedly. "I must've read every blog on the topic. Most days, I'm confident that I made the right decision to keep the wedding in place. But there are other days I'm not sure. Like when I see models in wedding dresses looking so gorgeous with their tiny waists."

"Don't worry. You can always get another dress," said Carson.

"But the wedding is in two months!" Harper cried with exasperation. "What choices will I have?"

"Hey, take it easy. I haven't found a dress yet, either."

Harper scowled at Carson. "Who's fault is that? At least I had a gown. You waited till the last minute, then tried on every gown in the last two shops we visited and still rejected them all."

Carson picked at her nail. "I didn't feel like any of them were right."

"You looked beautiful in every one of them." Dora sucked in her rounded stomach. "Damn you both."

The girls all shared a laugh, and the tension was broken.

"You know what I read in one of Harper's magazines?" said Dora to Carson in a know-it-all tone. "A bride who cannot choose a wedding dress often has some underlying issues and she may not want to get married."

"You read that, did you?" Carson asked mockingly. "You just keep on reading your magazines. You'll find an article saying that everyone should just get off the bride's back and let her find a gown she likes."

Dora barked out a laugh.

Harper clapped her hands. "Let's stay positive. We've got the cakes done. Granny James arrives in two days, and we're going to dress-shop with the grandmothers. I'm meant to show them the final fitting for my gown." Harper looked at Carson sternly and pointed her finger. "You have to stop stalling and choose a gown. Do you understand?"

Carson's lips twitched. "I do."

Chapter Ten

In enduring the unendurable pain and coming out of it together, they'd formed their unbreakable bond.

Carson stood on the upper dock of Sea Breeze, her arms folded across her chest against the stiff breeze, staring out at the water of the Cove. There was a break in the rain, but a chilly, wet breeze stirred the waters, creating ripples and making her huddle deeper into her Windbreaker like a turtle. She never could abide the cold. She felt it straight through to her bones. Yet, she took heart at the signs of spring taking hold in the lowcountry. This morning she'd seen the brilliant yellow, trumpet-shaped blossoms of Carolina jessamine, her favorite flower, along Mamaw's fence.

Looking out at the water, Carson imagined Delphine must be out there somewhere. She ached to see the dolphin's familiar face, to look once again into her dark, soulful eyes and to hear her nasal *eh eh eh* calling her to the dock. At times in the past months when she was alone on the photo shoot, far from anyone she knew or loved, she wondered if she'd only imagined the bond she and the dolphin had shared. Standing here now, though, the memories came back fresh and erased any doubt. Delphine had saved her life, that was true. Yet not only physically when the rogue shark had been circling Carson's surfboard and Delphine had distracted it, but emotionally as well. There was much to learn from the wisdom of the wild. Delphine had taught her through example how to endure pain without blame, how to forgive, to let go of the past and to live fully in the moment. To remember to laugh. Carson smiled remembering Delphine's riding the wake of Blake's boat.

She sighed, missing her dear friend.

"You miss Delphine, don't you?"

Carson swung around to see Nate standing near. He wore his navy parka with the hood over his head and bright red flannel pants. Soft pants, of course, with an elastic waist. A must for him. His Asperger's caused him to be particular, but also perspicacious, beyond his young years. No one knew better than Nate the longing she felt for Delphine.

She came closer to the boy and patted the soft padded top of his hood. She didn't think that was the same as touching him, something he wouldn't tolerate. Nate didn't back away. She looked into his eyes, blue not brown, but every bit as soulful as Delphine's.

"I do," she confessed.

"So do I."

Her heart lurched for the boy. Last summer he'd been lonely, without any friend save for that beguiling dolphin. Delphine had brought the boy out of his shell. But Dora told her that Nate had been excelling at his new school and making friends. He'd moved on.

As had she. So she was oddly comforted that he, too, still felt the hole left by the dolphin's absence.

"It's a good thing we have each other, isn't it?"

"You have Blake. You're getting married."

A short laugh escaped her lips. "From the mouth of babes."

Nate scowled. "I'm not a baby."

"No," she said apologetically. "You most certainly are not."

Nate appeared mollified by this. She had to remember that he didn't understand metaphors or sarcasm but took what people said quite literally.

"I see her sometimes, you know."

Carson startled. "Who? Delphine?"

"Yes."

"Where?"

"Sometimes when I go out on the dock to fish, I see her. Sometimes I just go out there. I like to be near the water. I see lots of things. I have a pelican friend now, too. I call him Pete. He looks like a Pete."

She watched Nate's fingertips tap his jacket as he paused. He's thinking about Pete, she thought, and smiled at the whimsical workings of the mind of a boy.

"And Delphine?"

"Yes. Sometimes I see her, too. Swimming by. I don't call her," he said with urgency, wanting Carson to know that he'd not broken their strictest rule: not to try to communicate with a wild dolphin. "But I know it's her. I can see her scars."

"Oh." A pang of guilt struck deep.

"She's good. I think she's happy."

"Really?" Carson couldn't believe that she, a grown woman, was seeking affirmation of Delphine's welfare from a ten-year-old boy, but because it was this child, she knew that he would sense it more than anyone else. Nate, for all his struggles, held a wisdom beyond any measurement ascertained by schools.

He looked at her with a hint of longing. "Do you think she'd come if you called her?"

Interesting question, Carson thought. One she'd been thinking herself. "I don't know. It's been a year."

"I think she would. She's very smart."

"She sure is." Carson looked at the boy. "Do you want me to call her?"

He nodded. "Yes. I miss her."

Sweet boy, she thought. She wondered if he tried to call her himself from his own dock, despite insisting otherwise. Yes, of course he did. Maybe once. Naughty boy, she realized with a hidden smile.

"I can't do it. I promised I wouldn't and it was a very big promise. If I love Delphine—if you love her—we will let her be wild. We both remember what happened to her when we did call and she came."

Guilt clouded the boy's expression as he nodded solemnly.

She heard the heavy footfalls reverberate on the wooden dock and looked up to see Blake walking toward them. Over his jeans Blake wore his navy peacoat. His hands were deep in his pockets, and a day-old scruff of beard lined his jaw. He took her breath away.

"We didn't call Delphine," Nate shouted out almost defensively. "We kept our promise!"

"Good decision," Blake called out as he approached. He came up to her side and delivered a kiss that spoke clearly of his gratitude for her decision. "I'm marrying a good woman, do you know that?"

Nate said, "Of course she knows that. She's the woman."

"Right again." Blake slipped his arm around Carson as naturally as breathing and turned to Nate. "Do you ever see Delphine?"

"Yes, sir."

"She look good?"

"Yes."

"I'm glad you think so. Because I have some news. She's pregnant."

"What!" Carson felt the news like a bolt of lightning. "Pregnant? How?"

Blake chuckled. "Oh, the usual way."

Carson slapped his coat. "Silly, I mean how far along is she? How do you know?"

"One look at her and you can tell. She's wide and full. I'd say she's due in a month or so. Dolphins give birth every month of the year, but around here a larger number of them give birth in the spring."

Carson did the calculations in her head. "So she got pregnant last spring?"

"Yes."

Carson held Blake's gaze. "Through all that pain and trauma, she kept the baby."

A shadow of pain flashed in Blake's eyes. He squeezed her shoulders, and in that moment they shared the grief of their lost baby. Carson had found out she was pregnant the previous summer, and just as she and Blake were becoming used to the idea, she'd had a miscarriage that had ultimately broken the couple up until they realized they couldn't live without each other. In enduring the unendurable pain and coming out of it together, they'd formed their unbreakable bond.

Carson's smile trembled. "I'm glad. She's so strong."

"Like you."

His concern touched her, and she smiled weakly to tell him that she was all right. "Blake, I need something to do to connect me with her. Something helpful. What can I do?"

Blake's eyes sparked as he released her and turned to face her. "That's what I came out to tell you. I just got a text from Ethan at the South Carolina Aquarium. You remember him?"

"Of course. Your cousin. Married to Toy."

"Right. He told me that they're looking for another person for the aquarium's PR team. They were really impressed by you and he thought you should apply."

"If they were so impressed, why didn't they hire me last year?"

"They had specific needs at that time. Now they're expanding."

Carson looked at Blake with suspicion. "Did you set this up?"

"No," he said sincerely. "I wish I had that kind of clout. I put the word out that you were looking for a job and I just got the text. Here, look." Blake pulled his phone from his pocket and showed her the message.

Carson had spent the previous summer waitressing at a local pub and, after getting fired, searching for a job. Waitress, secretary, temp . . . It was ignominious to be impoverished and living with her grandmother. She would have returned to LA except she couldn't afford to leave. On the flip side, she was able to mend wounds that had festered for too many years and build bonds with her family. When she was offered the stills photography job, she swore she'd never be stuck in that limbo again. This job could be perfect for her. Her work as a stills photographer was to take the vitally important photographs of film sets or studio shoots that were used to create the press and publicity for feature films. If the shots were good and used well, they could significantly contribute to a film's box office and international sales success.

"I'll reach out and set up an appointment today." She could feel her blood racing with hope.

Nate reached over to tap Blake's sleeve. "What about me? What can I do to help?"

Blake slid his hands into his pockets and looked at the boy staring up at him, his eyes wide with hope. Carson held her breath. The history of the boy and the dolphin went deep. Carson and Nate both needed to feel the connection in an appropriate way.

Blake studied the boy awhile, deep in thought. Then his long face relaxed and his eyes brightened. "Of course. I should've thought of it sooner."

"What?" Nate said eagerly.

"You're young so you'll need a sponsor. Someone to work with you." He looked meaningfully at Carson.

She immediately understood that this was an adult job, and that if Nate was going to do it, she would have to do it right along with him. Carson nodded in acquiescence.

Blake looked again at Nate. "You and Carson can work together. I'll hook you up with the Marine Mammal Stranding

Network. You'll be the point team along these beaches for any strandings of cetaceans. That means those that wash up ashore. The network will call Carson when they get notification that an animal has washed up on the beach. She has to be the one to go check it out, okay? Nate, you can go with her if you're not in school. But you can't touch anything, got it? Your job is just to check it out and report back to us. Then you basically hang around to keep curiosity seekers away until someone from NOAA gets there. It could be a short while or an hour, depending on where the team is. Interested?"

"Yes," Nate replied with alacrity.

Carson put the brakes on. "When you're not going to school," she reminded him. She looked at Blake. "Sure, we'll do it." She gestured with her finger. "It's you and me, Nate." She crossed her fingers. "Together."

A loud bark sounded from the house. Turning, they spotted Thor galloping like a horse down the slope toward them. He thundered down the wooden dock to their side, tail wagging, tongue lolling from his mouth, delighted to be out of doors. Nate took a step back from the probing, icy nose, but Blake leaned over to pat the dog's black barrel chest and murmur, "Good boy."

"I'm freezing," Nate announced, slipping his hands under his arms.

"Me, too," agreed Carson. "Come on, Thor. Back home," she ordered with a hand gesture.

The dog shot off and ran, nose to the ground, blazing the trail. They followed him down the dock toward the house, their footsteps echoing on the wood.

"Now let's get inside and warm up. Your aunt Harper's going

to boil over if I don't go shopping with her this afternoon." Carson rolled her eyes at Blake. "More wedding stuff."

"That reminds me. My mother wants to schedule a time for you to see the Legare Waring House."

This was the historic plantation home of his ancestors. Held in family hands for generations, in recent years it had been sold, and now, with the stately house, the impressive line of live oaks and lush gardens and its long Charleston history, the plantation was used for events, such as weddings. Blake's family members had been married there for generations. This beautiful location was where Carson and Blake would be married.

"I'll call her today," Carson promised.

Blake wrapped her in his arms and looked down into her eyes. His own were shining. "We're getting married," he said, and stooped to kiss her, quick and sweet and proper.

Granny James arrived with the spring weather. The long stretch of gray skies and rain ended at last. The day opened with a glorious sunrise of surreal pinks and blues that chased away the doldrums. Frowns turned upward as people raised their faces to the warm sunlight, removed windbreakers, and headed out of doors.

The birds came out as well. In the trees winter-resident mockingbirds, thrashers, and cardinals tweeted out territorial tunes while woodpeckers drummed, heralding breeding season. Higher in the sky the ospreys were already busy repairing their large nests. Small ruby-throated hummingbirds were brilliant flashes in the garden, and on the beach assorted gulls were returning from Florida. Love songs were in the air.

Harper was a whirling dervish in preparations for Granny James's arrival. She wanted the house to look its best. She'd raked every inch of the property, planted her spring garden, and refilled the hanging baskets of ferns along the front porch. Inside the house the aromas of oil soap on the floors and lemon-scented furniture polish competed with the sweetness of the fresh flowers arranged in vases in every room. Even Thor had a good scrubbing and was not allowed to roll around in the pluff mud.

Taylor's horn honked lightly as he pulled into the circular driveway of Sea Breeze. Harper stood at the front window and knew a moment of panic. This was her grandmother's first visit since last September when she had helped Harper purchase the house. Harper felt her responsibilities keenly. She was considered by her family to be efficient, organized, and tasteful. She wanted everything to be perfect for her first family gathering as mistress of Sea Breeze. Yes, Mamaw and her sisters had helped, but she was the hostess. Her emotions were running high; she was pregnant, after all. Taylor kept telling her to relax but wasn't that just like a man? What did he understand? When someone saw a well-organized home they complimented the wife. When the house was a mess, well, they pitied the husband. And who would be more critical than Granny James? Her grandmother excelled at running a large estate. Even if she did have a staff that carried most of the weight. Harper wrung her hands and stared out the window at the car. She saw Taylor coming around the car to open Granny's door. Oh God, she wasn't ready.

Mamaw floated through the living room in a cloud of perfume. She was wearing a pale blue dress with a brilliantly colored Ferragamo scarf around her neck that lent a vibrancy to her appearance. She had dressed carefully for Imogene's arrival, like any queen would a foreign dignitary. For all their friendliness post Harper and Taylor's engagement, there was still the whiff of competition between the two ladies.

"Come, darlin', they're here!" Mamaw exclaimed, waving her fingers to hurry Harper along.

Harper placed a practiced smile on her face and followed Mamaw to the front door. When they opened it they saw Taylor helping Granny James down the high truck step.

Granny James was dressed for travel. Her tan Burberry trench coat, dark slacks, and sensible shoes were simple but smart. Harper noted that her hair was shorter, a blunt cut tucked around the ears. Younger in style, she thought, though Granny looked pale with fatigue. Granny James appeared a bit disconcerted from the effort of getting out of the truck. She adjusted the belt of her coat with crisp movements as she looked around to get her bearings. Harper knew a pang of guilt since she didn't go with Taylor to pick her up, but she had fallen behind in dinner preparations. She could only imagine Granny James's reaction when she saw Taylor pull up with his pickup truck.

Harper rushed down the stairs. "Granny James!"

The moment Granny James spotted Harper her face blossomed with a wide smile of adoration. "There she is! Come here, my darling bride!" Granny James exclaimed. "I've traveled a long way for this moment."

Harper ran the distance into her grandmother's arms. Catching her scent, joy blanketed Harper and her earlier worries dissipated. She felt enveloped in her grandmother's love. "Oh, Granny, I'm so glad you're here."

When they separated there were the usual polite questions and complaints about the trip, enough for each of them to catch their breaths and regain composure. Granny James looked around the compound, her eyes bright. She sighed with pleasure when her gaze rested on the cottage.

"Welcome, Imogene!" Mamaw called from the front porch, where she'd waited to give the two a moment alone.

"Marietta!"

Mamaw began her trek down the stairs to greet her. "Come in and put your feet up! I have a pot of tea waiting especially for you. You must be exhausted after that long flight." She came walking across the gravel, arms extended in welcome. Granny James stepped forward to receive a warm hug of welcome and a kiss on the cheek.

"It's so good to be back," Granny James said. "You don't know how many times I've thought of Sea Breeze in the past months." A flutter of sadness shadowed her eyes. "But I'm here now."

"As we thought of you," Mamaw replied. "Lord, we have so much to catch up on. And plan. And celebrate. I hear wedding bells!"

"Isn't it all too exciting?" Granny James replied, though her tone was weary. "I simply must get out of these travel clothes first." She turned to Taylor. "Thank you for hoisting all my luggage. It's at moments like these I'm delighted my granddaughter is marrying such a strapping young man."

Peering into the rear, Harper saw a steamer trunk and two large suitcases.

"Good Lord, Granny, what did you bring?"

"Only the necessities, dear. We're having a wedding, after

all. Parties and dinners. One can't be too prepared." She lifted a white leather bag with a heavy, locked clasp. "I carry my jewels in my hands, of course. One can't be too careful." She sniffed and said as an aside, "My other things will come along at a later date."

"Other things?"

"Why yes, dear. We'll talk about that later," she said in a hushed voice before turning to Marietta with a beaming smile.

Taylor headed toward the front stairs with the two suitcases.

"Oh no, dear," Imogene called after him. "I'm staying in the cottage." She turned to Harper. "Isn't that right, dear?"

Harper froze like a deer in the headlights. "Uh, no. I've put you in the main house. Closer to me."

"Oh." Granny James's smile fell. "But I do love my little cottage."

Harper exchanged a quick glance with Mamaw.

Mamaw spoke up. "Actually, Imogene, I've moved into the cottage. To give the young ones space of their own."

"You've moved into *my* cottage?" Imogene asked with no doubt of her displeasure.

"I wasn't aware that it was your cottage," Marietta replied, taken aback.

"But of course. It was understood. I said I'd be back."

"And so you are," Marietta replied evenly. "And you have a lovely room for your visit."

Harper watched the exchange, felt the sudden chill, and worse, saw the old competition between the Grande Dames spark again.

"My darling grandmothers," Harper intervened. "We are all here, together. That is what matters. Not where one sleeps."

Pink blotches appeared on Granny James's cheeks as she pinched her lips tight.

"Let's not spoil your homecoming with arguments of where you're going to sleep. It's only for a short while. And besides," Harper added, slipping her hand under Granny James's arm with a gentle squeeze. "I want you close to me, Granny. So we can have lots and lots of chats about the wedding."

Granny James smiled weakly and patted her granddaughter's hand. She really had no choice but to appease the bride after such a tender declaration.

Harper guided Granny James to the front stairs. "You'll love the room I've prepared for you. And it's closer to the pool. I heated it already. Extravagant, perhaps, but if I know you, you'll be swimming every day."

Imogene cast a lingering glimpse at the cottage, but her final gaze rested on Marietta—and her eyes narrowed.

Chapter Eleven

Men get caught up in the wedding whoopla, too. We women tend to forget that. They don't talk much about it, pretend they don't notice, but they do. They're like little children—big ears that don't miss a word.

"Well, here we are," Dora said, pushing open the door.

Atticus followed Dora into the three-bedroom condominium on Isle of Palms she was showing to him for rent. He'd decided to extend his stay and asked Dora to help him find a convenient place for short-term rental. He'd had enough of hotel living. Dora was thrilled to help, calling him one of her very first clients.

He stepped onto the tile of the condo into the great, wide-open room with the veranda beyond it. Two halls went from left to right but he was struck immediately by the wall of windows overlooking the ocean. The brilliant blue became its own glittering world and called to him. Ignoring the rest of the condo, he went directly to the sliding doors and pushed them open.

Atticus stretched his arms out to rest on the iron railing of the veranda. Before him the Atlantic Ocean filled the horizon as tender a blue as the sky. He breathed deep the cool, crisp air. "Now this is more like it."

"Nothing like oceanfront." Dora joined him on the veranda. "It's pricey, but we're moving into spring season. By summer, whew." She lifted her hand for emphasis. "The rents go sky-high. You're also getting a good deal," she told him sotto voce. "This happens to be my first listing. The owner wants to sell so he only wants short-term rentals."

Atticus watched the waves roll in, soft and gentle, to the delight of the two lone male swimmers standing knee-deep in the chilly water. Atticus had to laugh. "Look at them. It is so damn cold out there, but those two young bucks are hell-bent to get their money's worth and go surfing." Behind them, two girls, shivering in bikinis, egged them on. "They're probably trying to impress the ladies."

"Coming from the North, it feels warm to them."

Atticus noted a volleyball net farther up the beach with more young guys battling in a game and more girls shivering in bikinis watching. He wondered if the volleyball net was open to the public.

"We call this area Front Beach. Everything you need is here. Shops, restaurants. And you're close to Sea Breeze."

Clusters of people were on the beach, some in swimsuits, some in jackets. He pointed to a young family walking along the shoreline gathering shells. They looked like a family of ducks, Mama carrying the bucket and leading the three little ones, Dad bringing up the rear. "Families come, too?"

"Oh, Lord, yes. We're a family beach." Dora turned to look at Atticus. "Are you close to your family?"

The truth that she was his family lay at the tip of his tongue. It would be so easy to tell her the truth now, he thought. So natural. But he'd promised Marietta he would wait. "Both my parents are dead."

"Oh, no! I'm so sorry."

"I was close to my mother. But to be fair, both my parents provided me with a safe home, a great education, and supported my ambitions." He smiled and, crossing his arms akimbo, leaned against the railing. "Even if neither understood my love of sports. They were more academic," he explained, remembering their efforts to show up and cheer at his games. "My mother didn't speak sports. I'm pretty sure she didn't know the difference between a basketball net and a hockey net." He shrugged. "And then they were gone."

"You must feel robbed to lose both parents so young."

"I do. I never had the chance to share major milestones with them—my wedding, my children." He looked at Dora and thought to himself how God had provided him with this second opportunity of a family. Surely this had to be part of his destiny. "Family is destiny," he said. "You don't get to choose your family. It's a crapshoot of genetics. But you deal with what you get."

"It's an interesting way to look at it. My son, Nate, has Asperger's syndrome. That's genetics for you. I thought it was a curse when I first found out. I mean, no mother thinks she wants an autistic child. But now, I don't think of Nate as autistic. He's just Nate. I love him exactly for who he is. He's not so big on sports, either." Dora laughed. "His coordination isn't so great. But he's good at so many other things unique to him. So if Nate is my destiny, I'll take it as a blessing."

"Well said." Atticus looked again out over the beach. The boys had abandoned their attempt to swim in the ocean. Mother Duck was shuffling her family back toward the beach path and home. Another day was done. Tonight was Harper's party at Sea Breeze. He would meet the Muir family and extended members as well. He'd be welcomed into the fold. By going tonight he would be committing to be the Reverend Atticus Green, friend of Mamaw's who had agreed to officiate the weddings. There would be no turning back.

Atticus breathed deep, stretched, then put his hands on his hips, feeling his decision settle. Inside he felt as calm as the horizon line that married the infinite sky to the sea.

"Well, Miss Dora"—he turned to the condominium and clapped his hands—"I'll take it."

A week had passed in the blink of an eye, thought Mamaw with no small amazement. Imogene had arrived and was settling in, though she made no secret of being displeased at not being in the cottage. Yet Mamaw couldn't be upset about this. It seemed trivial compared to all that was going on in their lives. Their wedding planner, Ashley Rhodes, was calling frequently now, lining up appointments with florists, caterers, and more to confirm the myriad details for the wedding. During the busy days, however, always in the back of Mamaw's mind was her grandson. She held his existence close to her heart. His was the face she thought of when she awoke, and the face that appeared in her dreams. Sometimes Atticus and Parker would become the same person, as happens in dreams.

She'd counted off the days, and at long last Harper's party was tonight. The family would gather at Sea Breeze and he would appear, as promised. She always felt her blood race before a party. But this party! The thought of Atticus's being welcomed into the bosom of his family made her feel quite giddy. Her hands were shaking.

A gentle rap on the front door of the cottage told Marietta that Girard had arrived for the dinner party. She still felt a flutter of butterflies whenever he was near. In the past year their friendship had grown to something far deeper, sweeter, than she could have imagined. Who knew that this late in her life she could discover love again? The kind of gushing girlish excitement she thought she was way past experiencing. She had lived her life with Plan A set in her mind. Now suddenly there was a Plan B and it took her breath away.

On her way to answer the door she paused to check her reflection in the mirror. She wore blue, this time a simple silk sheath with a cashmere sweater in the same color. Girard had once told her he liked her in blue because the color flattered her eyes. So she wore it often, for him.

Opening the door her heart skipped at seeing Girard, tanned and debonair in his dark suit and crisp white shirt, waiting at the door. The porch light highlighted the silver in his hair and the whiteness of his teeth as he smiled at seeing her.

"You look beautiful."

"Thank you." She brought her hand up to smooth her French twist.

His eyes gleaming, Girard leaned forward to kiss her.

Marietta caught the scent of his aftershave and closed her eyes.

The crunching of gravel alerted her to the arrival of a car. They both drew back and turned to see Dora's car pull into the circular driveway. The silver Lexus was once Dora's pride and joy when she'd purchased it after Nate was born. But that was a decade ago and now the car was dented, rusted, and running on a lick and a promise. The sound of car doors slamming sounded in the night followed by the crunch of gravel. Marietta peered in the dim light to see Dora and Nate approach. Dora looked harried. Her hair was disheveled, she was wearing old flats, and her arms were laden down with a large purse and a tray.

Girard rushed forward to relieve her of the tray. "Here, let me take this. Excuse me, ladies." He nodded to Marietta. "I'll bring this right to the kitchen."

"You're my knight in shining armor." Dora sighed heavily. "Nate, you go on with Mr. Bellows, hear?"

"Yes'm." Nate obediently followed the older man to the house.

Dora turned to Mamaw and said in her ear, "Mmm-mmm, that's one fine man."

"Yes"—Mamaw followed Girard with her eyes—"he is."

Dora hoisted her bag. "Well, I'm a hot mess. Harper wanted me to make my mushroom canapés for the dinner. I made some spinach, too." Dora rolled her eyes. "Said I had to get them here early. Mamaw, she actually said *chop-chop*! Carson calls her Bridezilla." Dora made a face. "She kinda scares me."

"I remember her saying the same about you once upon a time," Mamaw replied with humor and a hint of reproach.

"Harper's just nervous because Granny James is here. She feels like she has to pass some sort of test. It's all in her mind, of course, but you know what a perfectionist she is."

"But we're family."

"You know that. I know that. But she has to go through this passage. It's all quite normal for a young bride. Don't you remember?"

Dora conceded with a sorry nod. "I suppose. But, Mamaw, I'm not talking about just dinner tonight. I'm busier than a moth in a mitten. Harper's running me dry with the wedding, fetching this and that. And Carson is MIA most of the time. Being the only bridesmaid for two weddings sucks. Pardon my French."

"Dora!" Mamaw laughed lightly in sympathy. "You're a good girl."

"Well, bad girls have more fun, I reckon. Anyway, I'm just complaining. Glad to do it, but look at me. I'm half-dressed. Can I use your bathroom? I just need to poof up my hair and put on my lips." Dora grimaced. "Granny James is staying in my room."

Mamaw was pleased that despite Dora's having her own house on Sullivan's she still thought of the bedroom she'd slept in at Sea Breeze as *hers*. "Of course." After a quick glance at the main house's porch revealed Girard was already in the house, Mamaw led Dora to the bathroom in the cottage.

Dora dumped her bag onto the small marble bathroom counter and immediately began pulling out a brush, her makeup bag, hair spray. She grabbed the brush and began working on her shoulder-length hair with a vengeance.

"Let me." Mamaw took the brush from her hand.

Dora sighed. "Thank you. I just washed it and it's out of control."

Mamaw began stroking the blond hair.

"Mamaw, why did I get such thin, unruly hair? Carson's hair is so thick she can barely get a comb through it, and Harper's hair falls like silk."

It was true, Mamaw thought. Poor Dora's hair was thin and flyaway. But she had other assets. "We all want what the other person has. When Carson was young, she cried because she wanted to have your blond hair. And Harper buys the best hair products. You might ask her about them. But you, Dora, have the most beautiful skin. Peaches and cream. I doubt you'll have a wrinkle even at my age. Remember, hair can always be managed. But once your skin goes . . . Would you like me to put it up? In a twist like mine?"

A relieved smile eased across Dora's face. "I would."

As Mamaw brushed and styled Dora's hair, she noticed the pensive expression on Dora's face.

"Is everything all right?"

Dora skipped a beat. "Not really."

Mamaw could tell that was a difficult admission for Dora. She was so proud and she'd worked so hard in the past year to get over the divorce. "Do you want to talk about it?"

"I'm starting my new job but no one seems interested in that."

Mamaw lowered her hand. "Of course we're interested," she said, surprised. She placed her hands on Dora's shoulders and lowered to look at Dora through the mirror. "Congratulations! Honey, this is a big step for you."

"I didn't want to take the spotlight off the brides."

"You couldn't and wouldn't. There will be plenty of spotlight on the brides. You have your moments to celebrate, too. I'm so proud of you."

"Thanks," Dora said with a short laugh, mollified. Then she shrugged lightly. "Mamaw?"

Mamaw heard a tone in Dora's voice that she hadn't since the night before Dora's own wedding. The voice was childlike, tinged with fear. Mamaw gave Dora her full attention. "Yes, Eudora?"

"I'm a little nervous about starting the new job. I passed the exam with high marks. But everyone knows I got the job at Cassell Real Estate because of Devlin. They're going to be watching me like hawks, just waiting for me to slip up. And what if I do? I don't want to embarrass Devlin. Or have him see me in a lesser light. Do you think it was a mistake to work for him?"

"No, Dora, I don't. Everyone is nervous before they start any new job. You're facing a new world with its own set of rules, peopled with new characters, some of them nice, others not so nice. You just have to walk in the door with your head held high and do your very best. That's all anyone can ask of you. And let me tell you a thing about Devlin Cassell. He built that business himself. That's his name on the stationery. Don't think for one minute he's only hiring you because he loves you. If he didn't think you would make a great real estate agent, he would come up with a million different jobs for you. He's too savvy a businessman to risk his company."

Dora sighed with relief. "You're right. That's his baby."

"It sure is." Mamaw began to brush Dora's hair again.

"But even if I do okay, I'm still worried I won't bring in enough commission, especially the first few months. It's hard to get started and make contacts."

"I know what to do! I don't know why I didn't think of it before. I'll throw you a nice little party and invite all my friends. Get the word out that you're an agent. People like to know who they're dealing with when they sell something as important and emotional as one's house. You're a Muir, dear. Our name means something in these parts."

"Would you, Mamaw? That would be amazing."

"The hens and chicks will start clucking, don't you worry." Mamaw paused. "You have money problems, child?"

Dora looked at her hands. "Things are kind of tight now and the bills are stacking up. Mamaw, sometimes I wake up in the middle of the night and start thinking of all the bills I've got to pay and I can't go back to sleep. I swear, I'm a breath away from long nights with a bottle of whiskey."

"What about Cal's alimony and child support? I thought that would help carry you through."

"It's supposed to, but he's been late. Says he can't manage it with the house payments and improvements."

Mamaw felt like a bull seeing red. She jabbed the hairbrush into the air. "You tell that no-count skinflint that you're going to call your lawyer if he doesn't assume his responsibilities. ASAP. And you call, hear?"

"You should call him. He's afraid of you."

"As well he should be. He's no gentleman, letting you take on all the worry for Nate. That man's tighter than a gnat's behind."

Dora laughed at the truth in it. "Amen." Then she looked at Mamaw with a wry grin. "I don't believe I've ever heard you so riled before."

"When it comes to my babies, my claws come out. Still"—Mamaw regained her composure—"we can say what we will here when we're alone. But for Nate's sake, when you see Cal, you can offer him a sweet tea and a smile, but do not put up with that man's bull honkey."

"No, ma'am."

Mamaw paused as her mind went to a different man. "Have you told Devlin about your money problems?"

"I did not," Dora answered firmly. "I'm not talking to Devlin about money matters. Or anything else much these days."

"Oh?"

"We had words. He's not coming tonight."

Mamaw stilled her hand as a flood of disappointment washed over her. She liked Devlin a great deal and, more, counted on his humor to keep this particular party afloat. "But why? He didn't come to our last dinner, either. Surely he's not still annoyed with Granny James? I thought they'd buried the hatchet."

"It's not that. He likes Granny James and relishes the chance at another go-round with her. I think they both enjoy it. No"—Dora sighed—"it's the engagements."

"The engagements? I don't understand."

"My two sisters are getting married," Dora said, stating the obvious. "Devlin wants to get married, too." She looked at her hand, bare of any ring. "He proposed again."

"Ah." Mamaw was aware of the tension between the couple over marriage. "And you said . . . ?"

"That I wanted to wait."

Mamaw held her tongue. She could sense that Dora needed to vent.

"I love him. We'll get married someday. I'm . . . I'm just not ready. I only just got divorced. And I have all these bills. . . ."

"I understand, dear. But he's the one that you have to help understand."

"I'm trying."

"Well, try a little harder. Now let's finish this." Mamaw gathered the blond hair in her hands and gently twisted it with the experience of a woman who'd worn her hair in this style for many years. She reached for a handful of pins and carefully set the twist in place. "There." Mamaw eyed her work with satisfaction. "You look very pretty."

Dora turned her head from left to right, admiring her reflection. "Much better. Thank you, Mamaw. For always being there."

"That's a grandmother's job." Mamaw studied Dora's face. "But you need a bit of makeup before you're done. Try some of my pink lipstick, dear. It will flatter your skin tone."

"Yes, ma'am."

The headlights of a car shone briefly through the window.

Mamaw peered through the shutters. "Another guest. I'd better go in and help Harper and Carson. Come up when you're ready. And don't forget to use a bit of hair spray."

Before she left, Mamaw paused at the door and caught Dora's eye. "Weddings are a time of great joy. Families gather to celebrate. There's lots of hugging and kissing. Laughter. Issues that lay dormant emerge again."

Dora looked at Mamaw in the mirror with a worried expression.

"It's all normal." Mamaw smiled. "Men get caught up in the wedding whoopla, too. We women tend to forget that. They don't talk much about it, pretend they don't notice, but they do. They're like little children—big ears that don't miss a word. Bless his heart, Devlin is just getting caught up in the wedding bliss and wants to be part of it. You just need to reassure him that you love him and that your time will come. Tell him that this time round, you can have a great time without all the fuss and worry. Call it your dress rehearsal."

"I'll try."

"Do more than try. Devlin's a good man. Give him a call right this minute, hear?"

"Clair de Lune" sounded from the speakers as Mamaw entered the front door. She clasped her hands together and let her gaze take in the front room dressed up for a party. Canapés were artfully arranged on the coffee table beside bowls of Marcona almonds and shelled pistachios and a plate of cheeses, all displayed with sprigs of rosemary and parsley. She walked through the room, gazing at the paintings and furniture—Harper's things. Her party. It was bittersweet.

Mamaw remembered the many parties she'd thrown over the past decades. Not so many in this house. Sea Breeze had always been a place of retreat for her and Edward. They'd hosted a few small dinners and cocktail parties, nothing grand. But in Charleston! Oh, her house on East Bay had such architectural charm. And the views . . . She used to decorate the house with seasonal flowers and holiday decor with the same doting care that a mother would a beloved child. She left no detail untouched and prided herself on knowing that an invitation to a Muir party was always accepted.

But goodness, she thought, that was all so many years ago. She was only too happy to pass on the torch to the younger generation. Planning parties took great effort and energy. She surveyed the room with an experienced eye. If this were her party, she would have lit a fire, perhaps lowered the lights, added a few candles, set out a few more napkins. She laughed at herself. But no matter. Everything looked lovely just the way things were. These days she was happy simply to be a guest and observe the goings-on through the rosy-colored glasses of experience.

The sound of voices and laughter rang out from the kitchen. Smiling, she followed the happy sounds, thinking to herself that no matter how one tried to lure guests into the living room, they always seemed to gravitate to the kitchen.

The kitchen was warm and festive, redolent with the scents of garlic and rosemary. Harper stood in a butcher's apron at the wood table, her hair pulled back with a clasp, putting aluminum foil over the leg of lamb. Carson was bent at the waist peering at potatoes roasting in the oven. Mamaw had enjoyed watching Harper embrace cooking over the past year, especially southern recipes. All her latent domestic instincts were in full bloom.

Blake and Taylor were standing by the back door talking with beers in hand. Girard and Nate were inspecting a hand-held electronic game. Mamaw paused at the door, soaking in the sight, thinking how these young couples were the family's future. The house, the meal, the arrangements for the evening—all the tasks that had once been in her dominion—were now in the hands of her granddaughters. She could sit back and watch. Rather than its making her feel displaced or unhappy, she felt a surge of gratitude that she'd lived to see this natural evolution of a family unfold.

The doorbell rang. A moment later, Devlin appeared in the kitchen. Mamaw's eyes widened in surprise. Dora stepped in behind him, a canapé in her hand and a smile glowing on her face. "Devlin!" Mamaw exclaimed. "You're here!"

Devlin wrapped his arm around Dora's shoulders. "I wouldn't miss it for the world, Miss Marietta." Then he looked over her head and shouted, "It's party time, y'all! Carson, your in-laws-to-be have arrived."

Chapter Twelve

Acting like adults is something brides and grooms should be able to expect from everyone—including themselves.

Mamaw saw the party scene as a stage set. Each of the characters had a role to play. The brides and grooms with their respective families, the homey setting with candles lit, smiles in place. Tonight the families gathered for the first time before the two weddings. For some, introductions would be made, first impressions struck. It was a time to limit drinks, to not brag on family or pull out the embarrassing story. Acting like adults was something brides and grooms should be able to expect from everyone—including themselves.

Imogene entered the room at last. She held her chin high with hauteur. Mamaw had to admit Imogene looked regal in a long skirt of emerald-green silk and a creamy blouse that set off her pearls. Mamaw sniffed. Even if they were showy. The pearls were the size of quail eggs.

Devlin hurried to greet Imogene. He took her hand, kissed it, and said with a gallant bow, "Your Majesty."

Mamaw stifled a laugh with her hand. Devlin had an Irish sense of humor, the kind that made people laugh by poking at the truth. Usually someone was pricked by the point of the joke.

To Imogene's credit, she played along, eyeing Devlin with a glint of humor. "I see you're still playing the role of jester."

"Yes, ma'am," he drawled. "Still rollicking in the sand and sea."

Imogene's rigid face cracked with a smile of amusement. "Incorrigible."

Devlin's eyes glinted with pleasure.

"Granny James." Dora came up to kiss her cheek. "I'm so happy to see you again. We've missed you."

"How lovely you look, my dear," Imogene said, receiving her kiss. "Tell me, dear girl, why aren't you joining this wedding parade? We could have a triple wedding. What's one more?" Imogene turned to Devlin. "Scoundrel! Aren't you going to make an honest woman of our Eudora?"

Devlin flushed and cast a telling glance at Dora.

"He's tried," Dora explained quickly. "It's my fault, I'm afraid. I'm enjoying being footloose and fancy-free."

"I see." Imogene studied her.

"But don't worry. Wedding bells are coming. We're just biding our time."

Imogene leaned close to Dora and said in a stage whisper, "Just don't wait too long, my dear."

Taylor walked over with a drink and handed it to Granny James, without asking her what she wanted.

Granny took it while eyeing him speculatively. She tilted

her head questioningly then took a sip. "Delicious. Well done. You may do, after all."

Dora gave a little laugh while Mamaw brought Girard to greet Imogene. Girard had the talent to make small talk appear effortless, and Mamaw was relieved to see that Imogene made no attempts to further her outrageous flirtation with Girard from her last visit, which she'd done purely to get a rise out of Mamaw. Harper interrupted to introduce her grandmother to Taylor's parents. Girard stepped away and returned to Mamaw's side with an amused wink.

"Granny, allow me to introduce you to Taylor's parents." Harper, a graceful and experienced hostess, guided them forward. Her emerald-green dress, the same shade as Granny James's skirt, was bateau-necked with a slender, dazzling belt. Pavé diamonds encircled her emerald earrings, which took center stage as her red hair was slicked back in a chignon. With her sleek eyeliner, Mamaw thought Harper's retro look could be on the cover of a 1950s *Vogue*.

"This is Jenny and Alistair McClellan," Harper continued the introduction. "They've been looking forward to meeting you. I've told them so much about you."

"Oh, dear, should I be worried?" Imogene asked with a warm smile.

"Not at all," Mr. McClellan assured her. "Harper sings your praises." He towered over Imogene as he stepped close to take Imogene's hand and shake it hard.

Mamaw hid her smile as she watched Imogene teeter a bit with the force of it. "Well, I see where Taylor gets his strength from!" Imogene said good-naturedly.

And his size, thought Mamaw, seeing father and son stand

side by side. Alistair wore the classic dress attire of a lowcountry man—pressed khakis, a pressed, open-collared shirt, and a navy blazer with shiny brass buttons. Beside him, Harper's influence was seen in Taylor's well-cut camel-hair jacket and Hermès tie.

"We all call him Captain," Harper said with an affectionate glance at her future father-in-law.

"Then I shall, too." Imogene turned to Jenny McClellan and smiled graciously. "Congratulations are in order, are they not?"

Mrs. McClellan was a small, sturdy woman, no bigger than Harper but more substantial. Her green eyes shone with warmth and her brown hair was naturally streaked with gray. Mamaw thought there was no question whom Taylor got his eyes from. Jenny wore a simple navy knit dress that showed off her fit body and plain navy pumps. Though a bit stodgy in dress, her manner shone forthright and open, a woman comfortable in her skin. The two women shook hands warmly.

"And you must be Miller, Taylor's brother," Imogene said warmly to the fifteen-year-old boy patiently waiting his turn.

"Yes, ma'am." The boy made his parents proud the way he stepped up to greet her and take her hand.

Taylor beamed with pride and slapped his brother's shoulder. Miller was tall like his brother but slim and gangly, like a puppy that had not yet filled out to fit his paws. Miller wore a carbon copy of his father's clothes. Even the shoes looked brand-new. Mamaw thought Jenny did her men proud.

The scene was replayed with Carson's future in-laws, Linda and David Legare. Blake looked very much like his father. David was also tall and slender, except his dark hair was more salt than pepper. Behind his heavy-framed glasses, David's eyes were a warm brown. He was a professor of biology at College of Charleston and looked the part in his baggy brown suit and open-collared, plaid shirt.

Blake's mother, however, was rather plump and plain in a mauve, flounced dress that only made her skin look all the more pale. A simple strand of pearls graced her neck, lovely and lustrous, but they appeared minimal compared to Imogene's ostentatious pearls, as any others would. Mamaw thought the show of wealth out of place at a family gathering and was secretly glad she'd decided on topaz tonight. Still, she thought to herself, Imogene was on her best behavior. She was making an effort, it was clear. Imogene was a woman of substantial wealth, stature, and title. She was accustomed to grand fetes with a class of people who had high expectations. Like so many women of her station, she could be utterly charming to those people she found interesting or important. And cold and aloof to those she did not. Thus Mamaw warmed to Imogene's humanity tonight. She had dropped the façade and was behaving as any grand-mother of the bride should, graciously, even warmly, paving the way for healthy, prosperous relationships for her granddaughter.

Linda, however, withdrew her hand quickly from Imogene's and appeared ill at ease. Carson noticed and came to stand by Blake's mother's side with a commendable loyalty. Carson had a natural beauty that needed no adornment. She was a vision in a long ivory silk gown that flowed from one shoulder over her body like water over rocks. She wore no jewelry save for her engagement ring and appeared all the more lovely for her sim-plicity. Few women could carry off a gown like that, Mamaw thought with pride.

"Linda is a primary-school teacher on John's Island, where they live," Carson informed Imogene, prodding a conversation.

"How interesting your job must be, guiding all those young minds," Imogene said.

Linda took heart at the comment and launched into a monologue on the importance of children maintaining handwriting skills.

While Imogene listened with a practiced smile, Mamaw stepped away and got a glass of water. Her throat was parched, more from nerves than speaking. She was anxious for act 2 of the play. Glancing at her watch, she saw that it was nearly seven o'clock. The cocktail hour was coming to an end, and as yet, Atticus had not arrived. From across the room she caught Harper's sharp, desperate gaze. She stood by the fireplace and discreetly lifted her hands as if to say, *What should we do?*

Mamaw froze in indecision.

Harper came to her side, eyes wide with concern, and leaned close to her ear. "Mamaw, I really have to start serving dinner. The meat will go dry."

Mamaw wrung her hands. *Where are you, Atticus?* She'd thought of little else but his visit in the past few days. She'd dug out Parker's old photo album and studied photograph after photograph, her fingertips lovingly caressing his face as she searched for any resemblance to Atticus. It was silly of her, she knew, but by having Atticus in her life she felt she was being given a second chance. To be a better mother—or grandmother. Her heart knew a surge of worry that Atticus had decided not to come to the party after all. And more, that he'd decided not to make further contact with the Muir family. *Please, God, let him come.* Mamaw glanced at the door, willing the bell to ring.

And at just that moment, it did.

From the moment Atticus entered the room, it seemed as though a spotlight shone on him. Everyone in the room paused in his or her conversation to look toward the door. Mamaw's hand rose to her throat as she took in the young man in his well-cut navy suit, a crisp white shirt, and navy tie, worn with every bit as much style and panache as Taylor and the other young men in the room showed. Mamaw felt a rush of pride at his poise and polish. This was her grandson.

"You're here!" Harper exclaimed after opening the door, then reached up on tiptoe to kiss his cheek.

Atticus greeted Harper with a warm smile and said something Mamaw couldn't hear. He handed Harper a bouquet of yellow roses. Taking them in her hands, she ushered him into the room.

While Harper put the flowers on the side table, Atticus adjusted his cuffs, turning his head at a slight angle to let his eyes glance discreetly at the people in the room. Mamaw caught her breath. This was a typical movement of Parker's. Atticus caught her eye, and his smile at seeing her lit up his blue eyes and transformed his face from merely handsome to astonishing.

"Atticus!" she exclaimed, rushing forward to greet him. Her gaze devoured him hungrily. "I've been waiting for you. How handsome you look." She took his hand and held it tightly for a moment. Then, looking into his blue eyes, she said with meaning, "We're all so happy you're here."

He stood beaming at her, their secret sizzling between them. "I'm sorry I was delayed."

"You're here now, that's all that matters." They hugged and

Mamaw inhaled the subtle scent of sandalwood and felt the creamy cashmere wool of his jacket. "Come, let me introduce you around."

"Mamaw," Harper cut in, almost breathless with happiness. She placed her hand on Atticus's sleeve. "Please, allow me."

"Of course," Mamaw replied. She caught the warmth in Harper's expression and was delighted at her and Atticus's rapport. Mamaw released his hand and clasped hers together, enjoying the view from the sidelines.

Carson came rushing forward with long strides, her silk gown sweeping the floor. Atticus smiled broadly, glad to see her again.

"Rev! There you are! At last. I was worried I'd have to chase after you again." Carson leaned forward and kissed Atticus on the cheek. "Come on over here. I want to introduce you to Blake." Grasping Atticus's hand, she turned and looked over the room, chewing her lip. "Where did that man go?" she said with a hint of frustration. "Hold on one minute. I'll go get him."

Carson released Atticus's hand and went in search of her missing fiancé. Atticus chuckled at her nickname for him. It touched a soft spot for the friendliness implied. Beside him, Harper raised her hand, signaling someone. He didn't stand alone long. Taylor came forward to vigorously shake Atticus's hand. Taylor was a big man, as big as Kwame and with as stern a face and as powerful a grip. Atticus wondered what sport he'd played in college.

"This is my Taylor," Harper said, introducing them.

Taylor smiled and his eyes warmed, revealing that the big guy also had a big heart. "So you're Atticus," he said, seemingly eager to be friendly. "I was right glad to hear the news."

"News?" Atticus was taken aback. He darted a look to Mamaw laced with suspicion that she had told them their secret.

Mamaw discreetly shook her head, indicating she had not told anyone of his identity.

"That you're marrying us," Taylor explained.

"Oh. Yes," Atticus said, catching himself. "Hey, man, it's my pleasure."

Carson came hurrying back, Blake in tow. Blake stepped forward with his hand extended. Both men were about the same height, though Blake was more slender in frame. They shook hands firmly.

"Carson's told me that she's found a great new friend," Blake said. "A confidant."

"Did she? Well, then, I guess I am," Atticus replied good-naturedly. "I hope I'll be your friend, too."

"Let's see how you feel about me after those pre-wedding chats," Blake joked.

"Don't worry, I'll be easy on you. You're the one who works with dolphins, aren't you?"

"That's me." Blake took a sip from his drink.

"The weirdest thing happened to me the other day. I was standing by the inlet, Breach Inlet I think it's called, just looking out, when this dolphin came closer to the shore. It stopped right in front of me. Is that normal?"

"It depends," Blake said. "The water's turbulent there and it makes for great fishing for the dolphins. It could've been after one."

"I don't know if this one was. I swear it seemed to look me right in the eye. And I gotta be honest with you, it was a pretty powerful moment."

Carson stepped closer. "How big was the dolphin?"

Atticus shrugged. "I don't know anything about dolphins, but average I'd guess. There *was* something unusual, though. This one had all these scars along its body."

Carson gasped. "Delphine." She looked to Blake and they shared a long meaningful glance.

"You know that dolphin?" Atticus asked.

"Yes," Carson said.

"Did the dolphin stay close or move on?" Blake asked, more interested now.

"It moved on. Really, the whole thing probably lasted only a minute, but I'll never forget it."

"That's good," Blake replied. "It's only a problem if they stay and beg for food."

"Nope, no begging."

Blake was called by his mother from across the room. He excused himself. Soon after, Taylor and Harper went off to do some host duty. Atticus was left standing alone with Carson.

She looked over her shoulder as though scoping out the whereabouts of Blake, then leaned closer and said almost in a conspiratorial whisper, "Do you know how to paddleboard?"

The question surprised Atticus. "Uh, yeah, I can manage a board."

"Good. Come by tomorrow morning. At dawn. We'll go paddleboarding. There's something I want you to see."

The invitation seemed entirely innocent, but looking into her eyes, he saw them dancing as though she were up to mischief.

Carson spotted Blake waving her over. "You can let me know later," she said, and hurried across the room to join Blake with his parents.

Atticus felt uncomfortable with the seemingly clandestine invitation. Sometimes women formed attachments to their minister, especially after a personal conversation. It was always wrong, but in this case with his sister, it was egregiously wrong.

Mamaw stepped up beside him. "I couldn't help but overhear. Do go with Carson. You'll have a wonderful time. No one knows these waters better than Carson. I'm so pleased to see you getting along."

"I like her enormously. But"—he hesitated—"the way she was looking over her shoulder, it seemed she was making sure that Blake didn't know about the invitation."

Understanding flashed in Mamaw's eyes. "She doesn't want Blake to know because she wants to check on Delphine. Your story about the scars prompted this, I'm sure."

"You mean the dolphin?"

"Yes." Mamaw noticed Carson returning. "Ask her to tell you the story," Mamaw hastily added, then walked away.

Carson returned, anxiously awaiting his answer. "So? Can you make it?"

Atticus smiled. "Absolutely. I'm in."

"Good." Carson leaned closer to give him the specifics of what he'd need to bring.

While they were speaking, Harper clapped her small hands together for attention. She licked her lips, then spread out her hands. "If you look on the cocktail table, you'll see Taylor brought out a tray of champagne flutes. Would you all please take one? We have a toast . . . or rather a few toasts we'd like to make."

Amid murmurs of pleasure the guests collected their glasses. In an amusing, and expected, conundrum, Miller reached for a glass only to be thwarted by his mother. He scowled and went off to retrieve another glass of sweet tea.

Taylor approached and handed a glass of champagne to Atticus.

Atticus took the wineglass without comment.

Carson came back to his side carrying two tall glasses. "Here, Atticus, I've brought you a sweet tea."

Atticus took the drink and sent a quiet *Thank you* her way. He discreetly set the wineglass on the table beside him.

"Everyone!" Harper called out. She clanged the side of her glass with a spoon, corralling the attention. Again, the room quieted and everyone looked at her expectantly. She appeared radiant.

"Taylor and I want to thank you all for coming tonight and joining us in celebrating our engagement, and the engagement of Carson and Blake. Our weddings are around the corner now, and this is the first of many celebrations to come."

There was a chorus of "Hear hear."

"I look around the room and I see our growing family, and it fills my heart with great joy. First, a toast to family!"

"To family!" the group echoed, and glasses were raised.

Mamaw quickly glanced at Atticus, delighted with the toast that included him. He kept his gaze straightforward, and she wondered if the toast made him feel uncomfortable, or if he was privately pleased.

"I'd like to introduce to you a very special guest. The Reverend Atticus Green." Harper turned to indicate his presence at her right. "Atticus is a dear family friend of Mamaw's. And now ours as well. So it's all the more special that he has agreed to officiate at our weddings."

A host of muffled expressions of surprise followed. Mamaw scrutinized the reactions carefully. Imogene had a stiff smile on her lips and one brow raised, but she appeared more annoyed that she had not been consulted on the decision. Beside her, the McClellans appeared pleased with the announcement. One more item checked off the to-do list. David Legare rocked on his heels impassively. In contrast, his wife Linda's face was flushed and her lips tightened. Mamaw's eyes narrowed. She preempted any disagreeable comments by stepping forward.

"I'm so very delighted," she said loudly, adding to the toast, "to have someone so dear to my heart marry my darling girls." She raised her glass as her gaze swept the room, resting longer on Linda Legare. Mamaw turned to her grandson. "Thank you, Atticus."

Atticus returned a gracious bow of acknowledgment.

A buzz of renewed talking commenced.

Harper clinked her glass once more. "I'm not quite finished!" When the room quieted again, she smiled. "I told you we had a few toasts tonight." She took a breath, composing herself. "This has been and will continue to be such an amazing year. Epic. Of course, as we all know, in only a few months Taylor and I"—she looked at her fiancé—"and Carson and Blake"—she lifted her glass in their direction—"will celebrate our marriages. Then, come October, we'll pop more champagne to celebrate the release of my first book."

Heartfelt applause and comments of congratulations were renewed, though most of them already knew this news.

"Finally . . ." Harper glanced again at Taylor, who stood beside her, chest out and beaming. He slipped his arm around her shoulders. "Taylor and I will be celebrating another release this fall." She paused, then blurted out in a high-pitched voice, "We're having a baby!"

Mamaw's hand flew to her mouth to squelch her gasp of surprise. Immediately she turned to Imogene to catch her reaction and found her gaping back at her in utter shock. Clearly neither of them had been told. Both of them were relieved by that knowledge. Immediately both women's expressions shifted to reveal their unabashed joy. They hurried to each other and clinked their glasses.

"Well, we are double blessed!" Mamaw exclaimed.

"You have no idea. The family line continues! There were days I wasn't sure. Oh, Marietta, this certainly is a celebration!"

The two women embraced, then Imogene scurried to Harper's side. Mamaw stepped back into the corner to enjoy a moment of peace and watch as the spirit of the evening shot skyward at the happy news. The evening would progress as it should, she was old enough to know. The women would cluck like hens endlessly about weddings and babies. The men about sports, mutual funds, and fishing as though no mention of a baby had been made. And the children . . . She watched as Nate and Miller withdrew to the sofa, both with electronic games in hand. She shook her head, amused. *Typical*, she thought.

Amid the clinking of glasses, the sound of Michael Bublé crooning in the background, the rise and fall of laughter, Mamaw slowly brought her champagne glass to her lips and thought to herself how comforting it was to see life carry on. Tasting the golden sweetness, she could not have imagined a happier ending to this evening's play.

Chapter Thirteen

She felt oddly smug to be free from any entanglements of house and hearth. Even babies. She wasn't married or a mother yet. She was still free to skip out of the house at will.

Carson rose at dawn the following morning and rushed outdoors before Harper could snag her sleeve and involve her in more wedding plans. And before anyone discovered that she was meeting Atticus to go paddleboarding.

The lowcountry was blessed with an upcoming string of exceptionally warm days—a gift to the residents after the cold spell. She slipped into her wet suit; the neoprene was cold against her skin. The air might be warmer, but the water in the Cove would be frigid.

She tiptoed through the house, shushing Thor's inquiry of a low, gruff bark. She silently closed the door and checked out the cottage. Mamaw was an early riser, too. But thankfully there was no sign of her this morning. The sun had risen but only just. Overhead the sky was a robin's-egg blue streaked with pink-tinted cirrus clouds. Her heart quickened as she scampered down the front stairs. This was her favorite time of the day, when everything was fresh, new, full of possibilities. She scurried across the gravel to the garage. The old sliding door was rotting in spots, and chipped paint flaked like dandruff when she moved it. The door rattled noisily along the rusting metal frame. Mamaw would have to replace the door soon, Carson thought, pushing with all her might. Then, pausing to catch her breath, she realized that such things as broken garage doors were no longer Mamaw's concern. They were Harper's.

She felt oddly smug to be free from any entanglements of house and hearth. Even babies. She wasn't married or a mother yet. She was still free to skip out of the house at will. Grabbing hold of her board and hoisting it in her arms, she thought again how she loved being young and relatively carefree.

The sound of a car on gravel sent her running out from the garage. She saw a large gray Silverado Z71 pulling into the driveway. With its fender flares, nerf bars, and chrome trim, she thought of how Blake would love a pickup like that. Who knew the dishy Rev was a country boy at heart?

The truck door swung open and Carson hurried to the pickup. She didn't want him to go to the front door and wake up the house. "Morning, Rev!" she called in a stage whisper.

"Morning," he whispered back. Atticus climbed from the truck and pulled out a bag of gear from the back. He was wearing a full wet suit with a wet-suit jacket and sandals. Wet suits clung to the body, and she had to admit the Rev looked in damn good shape. She, too, wore a sleeveless wet suit with a jacket, her long hair pulled back in a thick braid. She was accustomed to men giving her body a double take.

"Why are we whispering?"

"We don't want to wake everyone up. Did you bring a board?" She looked into the back of the truck.

"No, should I have? I don't have a board here. My stuff's in Atlanta."

"No problem. I have two." She turned and led the way. "Follow me to the garage. The board's probably dusty, but who cares, right? We're going in the water."

Atticus did as he was told. The garage was a hazard, chock-full of stuff. It took a bit of time to get both boards out from behind the clutter. They were wedged behind a golf cart and gardening equipment.

"This place needs a good cleaning out. God knows where my kiteboard stuff is," she said, looking around the dimly lit space. Lines of sunlight flowed in through cracks in the wood. "It's my first trip on the water since I've been home. Careful there!" She pointed to the floor where a stone planter blocked his path.

In the driveway they dusted off the dirt and spiderwebs from the long boards, one blue, the other green, then Atticus hoisted the green one up to his shoulder and followed Carson along a stone path that wound its way past azaleas and jasmine blooming, fragrant in the morning mist to the back of the house. As they rounded the house and emerged from behind an imposing bottlebrush shrub, Atticus came to an abrupt stop. He was unprepared for the power and beauty of the Cove. The sun was higher in the sky now, casting fingers of pearly-pink color farther across the whole sky.

The back of the house was even more impressive than the front. Clearly, he thought, the builder of this house loved the water, then remembered some talk of the Muir family's coming from a long line of sea captains. The back porch stretched across the width of the house, wider at the left where a black-and-white awning shielded a circle of large black wicker chairs. The property sloped to a second tier, where a second deck surrounded a swimming pool. Below this tier, wooden steps led the way through a well-maintained flower garden to the dock.

"Quite a place," Atticus told Carson with awe.

"Sea Breeze has that effect on people," she replied in the breezy manner of someone who had heard that comment many times before. "Come on, Rev, we're wasting daylight."

Her movements were smooth with the skill of experience. Soon she had both boards in the water by the dock, SUP leash attached, and paddle in hand. The water was calm this morning, and sticking her foot in, she shivered. "Damn. The ocean is icy."

"I'm used to cold water."

"Then you'll love this."

She stepped onto the board, finding her balance readily. Using her paddle she easily pushed off from the dock. She turned her head, making sure Atticus was behind her. "You coming, slowpoke?"

"Nag, nag." He stepped onto the board and bent his knees, finding his balance. He was doing well, though not quite as adroitly as Carson. He hadn't been paddleboarding in a few years, and it took him a few minutes to feel comfortable. Carson, however, was a natural. She was already out in the current, getting farther ahead by the second. He inserted his paddle into the water, grateful for his long arms, and dug deep. He took a few strokes on one side, then switched to the other, making a beeline for Carson.

Carson made it all look effortless, as though the board were an extension of her body. She was long, lean, and strong. Her paddle sliced through the water like a hot knife through butter. He had the advantage of strong back muscles, however, and before long he caught up with her.

Once in the current it was easier. Coasting, he took the time to look around and appreciate the tranquillity of the early hours of the morning when the earth was awakening. The paddle made pleasing, soft splashing noises in the quiet morning. White egrets stood in the tall grasses that bordered the water, while overhead, pelicans flew in formation over the creek toward the open sea. The air had a dreamy quality, a purity. Each stroke in the water felt like a prayer.

As they made their way slowly toward the harbor, Atticus knew full well what Carson was praying for. Her strokes were too determined. She had a goal in mind. Delphine. He couldn't blame her. With each pant he, too, uttered a silent prayer that the dolphin would appear.

Carson suddenly raised her paddle and paused, scanning the water. Atticus followed suit, standing motionless, his eyes searching. They were the only ones on the water, and for as far as he could see, it appeared quiet and shimmered in its reflection of the pink sky.

"There!" Carson called out, pointing. "Three o'clock."

Atticus abruptly shifted his gaze to three o'clock but saw nothing.

"There's another one. One o'clock."

He looked but again saw nothing. Too slow. The water was still but he kept his gaze as steady as one of Beau's coon dogs out on a hunt. Suddenly, off in the distance, he spied a pair of dorsal fins of similar size. His excitement shot skyward. "I see them!"

Carson turned to grin over her shoulder, delight lighting up her face. "Come on, city boy, put your back to it." She lowered her paddle and dug deeply, moving forward at a rapid clip.

Atticus laughed, loving the thrill of the moment. The water, the strokes, the hunt—he felt so alive. He kept his eyes peeled. The two fins rose and fell in different spots but remained in the same general area. Carson seemed to know exactly where to go.

"They must be fishing in the inlet," she called back. "If they were traveling, there'd be no possible way we could keep up with a dolphin's speed."

He thought she was doing a pretty good imitation. He kept digging his paddle in the water, breathing hard, trying to keep abreast.

As they drew nearer the inlet, both dorsal fins disappeared. Once again Carson lifted her paddle, watching, listening, coasting with the current. They waited for several minutes. Atticus figured the dolphins had moved on, then a noise caught his attention. From behind them, soft and muffled. Carson heard it, too. She raised her hand over her eyes and peered toward the sound.

There it was again—the unmistakable sound of air through a blowhole!

Carson anxiously scanned the water.

Atticus could feel his excitement bubbling. Then he saw the dolphin break through the water twenty feet behind them. His heart was beating hard. "There!" he called out.

Carson held up her hand to indicate they should remain still. Suddenly a dolphin emerged again, closer. Atticus swung around and teetered on his board. Arms out, he just managed to keep his balance and not fall into the water. Taking a breath, he lowered to his knees.

One dolphin had swum off. Only one was here now. It swam toward his paddleboard, close enough for him to get a good look at its glossy and sleek gray skin in the sunlight. It dove again, but not before he saw the crisscrossing of pale scars across the glistening body.

His heart raced. He paddled closer to Carson. "It's her! "Delphine. I saw the scars."

Carson wiped tears from her face and nodded. She wasn't able to speak.

A moment later the dolphin emerged close to Carson's paddleboard. Atticus watched in silent awe as the dolphin leaned to its side parallel to the board, her beautiful almond-shaped eyes studying the woman on the board.

"Delphine!" Carson exclaimed, looking back into the dolphin's eyes. "It's me."

Suddenly the dolphin made a high-pitched whistle and dove. A second later she emerged, leaping high into the air and splashing noisily back into the sea.

Carson laughed loudly and raised both arms into the air. "Woohoo!" she shouted, and turned to Atticus, her eyes shining. "She recognized me!"

Atticus's fist pumped the air, as though he'd leaped with

the dolphin. Something about this creature forged a feeling of kinship. He didn't remember the last time he'd felt such joy.

Delphine swam rapidly back to Carson's paddleboard, then made two tight circles around it, eyeing her. Atticus tried not to interfere, staying low on his board. He felt privileged to witness this extraordinary bond between wild dolphin and human.

Delphine emerged beside Carson's board, her dark eyes eager. Expectant.

Carson lowered on the board to bring her face close to Delphine's. She was careful to keep her hands on the board. For several minutes she sat quietly as she rocked, then slowly she stretched out on the board onto her belly. She gazed eye to eye with Delphine. It seemed to Atticus that the dolphin was studying her, as well.

"Poor baby," she murmured. "I'm so sorry."

Delphine merely looked serenely back at her seemingly without judgment.

Other than the faded scars, Delphine appeared healthy. And fat, he thought with a smile.

"So, you're having a baby," Carson said to Delphine. "I guess we were both pregnant last summer. Only *you* kept your baby. Good for you."

Atticus pursed his lips and shifted his weight on his board. He hadn't known that Carson and Blake had lost a baby.

Delphine started making staccato nasal noises and hitting the water with her rostrum.

Carson turned her head to him. "She doesn't understand why I don't pet her." Carson's expression showed she clearly ached for the contact. "She's my best friend. She helped me through some of my worst moments." Carson reached out her hand. Then stopped midair. "No. I mustn't touch her. She's wild."

But Delphine had other plans. She rose in the water to deliberately bump her rostrum against Carson's hand.

Carson laughed despite herself. "I didn't do it. She did!"

Atticus didn't know much about dolphin interactions, but it seemed to him Carson was splitting hairs. He watched uneasily as the dolphin swam slowly past Carson's unmoving hand projected out over the water, swam so close the dolphin's skin glided across the hand. Atticus had to admit he was jealous. He would love to feel the dolphin's rubbery skin against his palm, but again, this was a wild dolphin, and even he knew it wasn't good.

Carson withdrew her hand. For a minute she stared at its emptiness. Then she tucked her arms under her head. At first the dolphin seemed piqued. She splashed the water with her rostrum and made several nasal *eh eh eh* calls. Then the dolphin made a shallow dive to push a wave of water with her tail directly at the board. Carson leaned back against the deluge and laughed, coughing with surprise.

"Delphine is pitching a hissy fit!" she called to Atticus.

"She sure is. But you know what's best for her."

Carson stared at him, hard. Then she nodded in agreement. Slowly, she rose to her feet. A slump-shouldered surrender was in her movements. It was, he knew, a moment of reckoning for her.

She looked at Delphine. "Go on and join your friend." Carson stretched out her arm and pointed to the harbor. "Go on now. Go feed your baby."

Delphine flipped water into the air with her rostrum.

Carson pointed again and said more firmly, "Go."

Delphine backed away in the water, then dove, disappearing in the depths. Carson and Atticus scanned the still water. A few minutes later they spotted Delphine much farther off, swimming with speed toward the second dolphin.

"We should get back," Carson called to him. "Make good our escape. I don't want Delphine to follow me back to the dock."

"Sounds good to me."

Once again Atticus put his back to the work, stroking hard to gain speed against the current. He was out of shape, he realized with chagrin. Sweat formed at his brow but he didn't slow down. They both knew that Delphine could effortlessly cross this distance in no time at all.

By the time they reached Sea Breeze and climbed onto the lower dock, he was sweating inside his wet suit. He wasn't too proud to admit he was glad to see that Carson was winded, too. He helped her pull the eleven-foot boards from the water and carried both of them to the upper dock. They set them in a safe spot, then grabbed towels. Carson's long braid fell over her shoulder as she bent to unzip the wet-suit jacket. She dried her face, then let the towel drop to a bench.

"So, tell me about what happened to Delphine," Atticus said, drying his head with the towel. "How she got those scars."

Carson turned to look out over the Cove for a moment before she said, "That dolphin saved my life. I was surfing and that girl T-boned a shark that was after me. Delphine saved me from a shark attack. I'd heard of things like that happening, but it suddenly became real for me." Carson's voice revealed her affection for the dolphin. "Later, she recognized me out here in the Cove while I was paddleboarding. She's that kind of smart.

We bonded." Carson raised her hand over her eyes. "Oh, Atticus, I did everything wrong. I named her, fed her at the dock, swam with her. I had fun—but Delphine suffered the consequences. There was a huge accident last summer. Delphine got caught in fishing lines. It was awful."

"That's how she got the scars?"

Carson nodded, her face bleak at the memory. "Yeah. Blake flew her to Florida for rehabilitation. He saved her life. Anyway, that explains the scars you saw. Blake and I nearly broke up over it. He was so angry at me. Disappointed. Rightfully so."

"Is that why you didn't want him to know about you coming out to see her?"

"No. I wanted to see Delphine again for the first time without Blake watching. I needed to know if I was strong enough to do the right thing." She laughed harshly. "I didn't quite make it, did I?"

"Don't be so hard on yourself. I think you did."

"Do you think I broke my word to Blake?"

"That's between you and Blake. What I think doesn't matter."

"Why should I tell him?" She looked away. "What would I gain? I don't want trouble between us. I know what I have to do now and that I'm strong enough to do it."

"So why not tell him that?"

She looked at Atticus. "Haven't you ever kept a small secret to yourself? For the good of someone you loved?"

Atticus blanched and looked out over the water. In keeping his own secret, he felt like a hypocrite. "Many times," he confessed. "To my mother, mostly. When I was in high school I lied to her whenever I went out drinking with friends and I told her I was out studying. Or the times I told her I didn't know what happened to missing bottles of alcohol." He laughed without humor. "Once I replaced her bottle of gin with water. She found out during a party when she served very weak martinis."

Carson laughed. "You did not."

"I did." His smiled faded. "And those were the easy lies. The later ones were harder. More serious. Though at the time I blew them off. Trips to the police station for underage drinking. A few fender benders. My father bailed me out, punished me. We decided to keep the truth from her. For her sake."

"That was wrong."

Atticus looked into Carson's blue eyes and saw the truth in her statement. "Yeah." He looked down, feeling shame burn his cheeks. "It was. I see that now." He paused. "Lies are never a good idea. Trust me." He looked at her. "Trust him."

Carson listened. She held Atticus's gaze a moment, then nodded. "Yeah, I will."

After Atticus left, Carson headed back down the dock to collect the boards. As she walked back, from the corner of her eye she saw a movement at Girard Bellows's house. She stopped short to peer at the house next door. Someone was coming out from the house. No, two people.

She could hear voices now, not loud enough to understand the words. But she recognized one of the voices as Mamaw's. Carson raced off the dock, set the boards on the ground, and hid behind the wide fans of a sago palm. Stealthily, Carson peered out from her hiding spot and saw Mamaw and Girard walk out on the patio carrying plates and mugs. Mamaw was wearing her blue bathrobe.

Carson let the palm fan go. It snapped back with a noisy rustle. She turned and walked back up the slope to the deck stairs, one foot in front of the other, her mind in a quandary. It was one thing to see a friend—a contemporary—sleeping at her boyfriend's house. No big deal. But one's grandmother?

At the door of the kitchen, Carson turned to look out once more toward Girard's house. The man they used to call Old Man Bellows until Mamaw made them stop. From here on the porch she couldn't see anything behind the carefully landscaped border of shrubs that was planted just to block the view.

"I guess someone else is keeping a little secret," she muttered to herself. Then she released a short laugh. She couldn't wait to tell her sisters.

Chapter Fourteen

*I realize you may perceive contractual agreements to be
unromantic, but they work as intended. For individuals
with wealth, a prenuptial agreement is necessary.*

*H*arper carried a breakfast tray to Granny James's room.
She looked in the hall mirror and caught a glimpse of a young
woman in tan linen ankle pants and a matching cotton sweater
over which was a pink, ruffled apron. Her hair was pulled back
in a ponytail. Outwardly, she appeared to be the same twenty-
nine-year-old woman she saw every morning. But Harper knew
she wasn't. A miracle was happening inside her. A new life.
Harper realized that she was looking at a soon-to-be mother.

Grinning, she tapped the door with her foot.

"Come in!"

Harper angled herself so her hand could twist the door
handle without spilling the tea. Inside, the drapes were closed,
leaving the room half-dark. Only the bedside lamp was on, cast-

ing a warm circle of light over the French-styled bed on which Granny James sat, supported by many pillows. She wore a floral bed jacket trimmed with lace and tied up with long, slim pink ribbons. Harper recognized the old-fashioned jacket as what her grandmother wore on what she called her "mending days." Those days she spent entirely in bed to read, sleep, watch television, and generally rest up. In her lap lay a small electronic pad.

Granny James looked up to peer at Harper over her reading glasses. "Goodness, darling. All this fuss over me. How silly! Put that tray down, put your feet up. We could use a good chin-wag."

Harper, brimming with anticipation for a long overdue catch-up with her grandmother, obligingly placed the tray on Granny's mattress. After Harper poured tea, they kissed, touching cheeks. Granny looked more rested this morning. Less pale and drawn. She must've been awake for some time. Her face was washed and creamed and she smelled of scent. Even her hair was in place.

Harper pulled a velvet-covered lady's chair from the corner and scooted it closer to the bed. The lovely room had recently been redecorated by Mamaw especially for Dora. Done in the French style, it had wallpaper with broad pink and white stripes, ornate French furniture, and a creamy Aubusson rug that Mamaw had pulled out of storage. The room was delightfully feminine.

"There's Darjeeling tea steeped in water brought to a roiling boil for five minutes. Crumpets, butter and jam, honey—from my own bees, I might add—and a slice of melon. Nothing fancy, but to your liking I hope."

"A feast. You're an angel." Granny James picked up the cup

and sipped. "If I were a cat, I'd purr" was her verdict. "It takes a Brit to know how to make a proper cuppa tea."

"I'm a lowcountry girl now," Harper quipped as she reached for the cup she'd brought for herself on the tray, for she enjoyed a sip of the dark brew.

Granny James sipped again, then set her cup on the tray. "You, my dear, have English history in your blood that is traced back farther than the reign of Charlemagne. Your family is in *Debrett's*. Speaking of which, look on the bureau. I've a gift for you."

Harper rose and went directly to the charming painted bureau. Lying beside Mamaw's jewelry case was a wrapped parcel. She lifted it. "This one?"

"Yes. Bring it here."

Harper did so and settled in the chair once again. Carefully she undid the pretty floral wrapping paper. Inside was a copy of *Debrett's Wedding Guide*. Granny James had given her the *Debrett's Handbook*, a weighty tome of advice with a beautiful red-and-gold embossed front, as a gift when she graduated from high school.

Harper gasped in excitement. "Oh, it's perfect. Thank you, Granny. I've been reading Mamaw's Emily Post guide to etiquette—but I know how much this will come in handy," she hastened to add, not wanting to offend her other grandmother. Harper knew how competitive the two old biddies could be.

As Harper suspected, Granny James's eyes narrowed and she sniffed haughtily. "That's all very nice. But *Debrett's* is the only wedding guide for British brides. Why, it's the British etiquette bible! Guiding brides since the eighteenth century. You'll find you won't be able to make a decision without it."

"But we're having a beach wedding. That's a far cry from an at-home wedding at Greenfields Park. I should think we must relax the rules and protocol a bit."

"We might be personalizing the wedding by having it at the beach," Granny James said archly, "but we will still maintain a proper degree of formality. We're not having a luau, silly girl. No matter where the wedding is held we must apply the rules properly."

A thought crossed Harper's mind. "What does it say in your book about a pregnant bride?"

Granny James's face softened as she looked at Harper's belly. "Oh, Harper, I cannot tell you how much this baby means to me. To your family! To think, the James name will continue with this child."

"The James McClellan name."

"Will you hyphenate your name?"

Harper shook her head. "No. But he or she will have James as their middle name."

"Yes, I suppose that is the way of things. I do hope you'll have more than one. At least one boy. There seems to be a run of girls in the Muir family."

"And boys in the McClellans."

At that, Granny James brightened. "I always hoped Georgiana would remarry and have another child."

"Mummy? Remarry?" Harper was shocked. "She couldn't bear being married the first time. And that only lasted a few months."

"Yes, but we got you out of it, didn't we?"

Harper couldn't help but smile at that. "I'd like to have a

few. Maybe three. Who knows?" Harper sipped her tea, wondering.

"You should. You've never looked more beautiful. Pregnancy agrees with you. Your skin is positively glowing. Though I must say, I could have been knocked over by a feather when you told us the news."

"I was dying to tell you," Harper said, warming to the topic. "I wanted to get past the first trimester, and with you arriving at the same time, I thought the announcement at the party would be special."

"Well, it was. As was the announcement of your minister." At this, Granny James's tone hardened somewhat. "Atticus Green."

"But you didn't have anyone else in mind for the ceremony?"

"No, I didn't. But it might be a problem that he is . . ." Granny James paused.

"What?" Harper asked testily. "Black?"

Granny James snorted. "Don't be ridiculous. I couldn't care less what color he is. I was going to say he is a Southern Baptist. You're in the Anglican Church."

Harper laughed, relieved. "Oh, that. Don't worry." She tapped her baby bump. "We'll make sure it's legal."

"You know"—Imogene picked up a crumpet and lavishly applied butter—"that does bring up a sticky issue. We have to contact our lawyers as soon as possible. You really must have a prenuptial agreement."

Harper shook her head. "I don't want one."

"Come now, Harper, do be practical," Granny James said impatiently. "There are countless reasons why you must get one. Most prominently, you are much wealthier than Taylor. You have your trust, of course, and that is locked tight. But when I die, you will inherit a significant portion of my estate as well. You and your issue. I shall do what I must to protect you from the grasping hands of family members, including, unfortunately, your own mother. But you must take steps to protect your inheritance in this country. In this state. We mustn't be emotional. This is business."

"That's not how I see it. This is family."

"Precisely. You are about to be a mother. You must look after your child in your womb."

"Taylor's child, too. He'd never do anything to hurt our child."

"I don't believe he would, either. And having your financial matters in order will make you both feel much more comfortable and secure as you move forward in your marriage."

"But isn't a prenup mean-spirited? And to spring it on him now, after the invitations have already gone out, it seems . . . premeditated."

"No, I certainly do not think it is either of those things. You are a very wealthy woman, Harper. You must think like one. I realize you may perceive contractual agreements to be unromantic, but they work as intended. We must look not just to our own futures, but the futures of our children. You must consider *them*. When you inherit, the new trust will be set up to include certain provisions to stop any assets from going to your husband or his new wife should, God forbid, you divorce. Or even your child's ex in the event of divorce. The prenup simply prevents your inheritance from me from becoming marital property. Believe me, it keeps things simple. In fact, I'd be very surprised if Taylor wasn't expecting this. He's a sensible man. After all, the house is already in your name."

Harper's face clouded. "Yes. He's never mentioned it, but I sometimes wonder if that doesn't bother him. Grate at his pride a bit."

"It shouldn't. He knows he couldn't afford this house on his own. Where else would you live?"

"We could live in a smaller house. Off island."

"Yes, but that's not what you wanted, was it? You wanted Sea Breeze."

Harper couldn't argue this point. She did want Sea Breeze. Desperately. Not just for herself, but for Mamaw and her sisters.

Granny's voice grew icy. "You can't think there was any way under heaven I was going to lend you millions of dollars to buy this house with his name on the deed? You were not even married then. And even if you were, I would not have done it. I made the arrangements for Sea Breeze because of my love for you. No other reason. The stipulations I set up regarding the house protected you, as well as my investment. I'm quite careful with my money, as well you should be."

Harper felt instantly repentant. "I'm so very grateful for what you did, Granny. You know that. But, I still don't like the idea of a prenup." Harper's chest was constricting and she felt the walls of the room closing in on her. "I trust Taylor. I don't want to think of my marriage in terms of *my* money versus *his* money. It smacks of control. Even superiority. Or worse. It makes me feel like my mother."

"Because she had a prenup signed? Hers is a perfect example of why you need one!"

"Because it was all a business arrangement in her mind. A means to an end."

"Come dear, let's not argue. Bring the topic up with Taylor and see what he says. I feel quite certain you're worried about nothing. And you can make me out to be the nasty person who is insisting."

"Well, you are!"

Granny James lifted her shoulders and bit into her crumpet. She dabbed at her mouth daintily with the corners of the linen napkin Harper had brought. "You'll see I'm right. It's better to get this tied up quickly. Especially with a baby on the way."

"It wasn't planned. It just . . . happened."

"Yes, dear. I know how these things happen."

"Are you happy about it?" Harper asked, suddenly concerned. "You can be honest now that we're alone."

"Ecstatic." Granny patted Harper's hand. "At my age, we don't want to waste too much time waiting for grandchildren."

"Great-grandchildren."

Granny James made a face. "Please, let's keep that fact between us, shall we?" She smoothed the napkin with her fingertips. "Are you going to tell your mother?"

Harper's smile shifted to a frown. "I suppose I must. I'm just not sure how to do it. We don't communicate at all. I'm not sure she'd answer if I called her on the phone."

"You did send her an invitation to the wedding?"

"Of course. She should have received it. Though, I don't know if she'll come."

"She'll come."

Harper twisted her lips. "I'm not sure that I want her to come."

Granny James looked off at the window, shuttered and draped. A new sadness was in her eyes, a heavy cloud over her demeanor that everyone had commented on to Harper since Granny James's arrival. Even Devlin had taken Harper aside and inquired about Granny James's health. "The fire has gone out of the dragon," he'd said. It was meant to be funny but genuine concern was behind it. She'd lost weight and her hands seemed barely strong enough to carry the heft of the large diamond-and-sapphire ring that had been her engagement ring.

Harper had seen photographs of her grandmother when she was Harper's age. She'd been a great beauty with aristocratic bone structure and a tiny, voluptuous body. She was a great lady of a lifestyle that belonged to her generation. She was an excellent horsewoman, a renowned socialite, a champion of causes, and a passionate gardener. She had almost single-handedly renovated the Greenfields Park estate to the show-case it is today. To see her now, tired and crestfallen, Harper felt suddenly afraid for her.

Granny James swung her head back. She was smiling. "Let's give her a ring right now, shall we?"

"Who? *Mummy?*"

"Of course your mother. It's early yet. She should still be at home." Granny James reached for her cell phone and said with a twinkle in her eye as she dialed the number, "She'll answer for me."

Harper suddenly felt sick. She put her cup of tea on the tray, noting that her hands were shaking. Her mother had this effect on her. Somewhere hidden deep inside, and despite all her efforts to be independent, regardless of her successful relation-ship and getting married, becoming a mother, being the mistress of her own house, she still wanted her mother's approval. She clutched her hands together in her lap, watching Granny James sit with the cell phone to her ear, listening to it ring.

Suddenly her face grew animated. "Georgiana, dear. It's me. Good morning!"

Granny James listened a moment. "I'm at Sea Breeze." She paused, then rolled her eyes. "Yes, of course in South Carolina. At Harper's house. We have wedding plans. Very exciting. You got your invitation? . . . Very good. . . . I'm as well as can be expected. . . . Yes, he's settled in the Memory Center. Let's talk about that later. Harper's here, dear. She has some special news to tell you. . . . What? No, it won't take long."

Harper cringed. Obviously her mother didn't want to talk with her.

"Must you always be in such a hurry? You can tell your driver to wait." Granny's voice brooked no disobedience. She looked up to Harper and waved her closer. "Here she is." Granny held the cell phone toward Harper, her eyes bright with encouragement. She mouthed, *Tell her.*

Harper suddenly wanted to throw up. She felt cornered. Trapped. She reached out across the mattress, took the small phone into her hand, and brought it to her ear. Leaning back in her chair, she took a breath as she forced a cheery voice.

"Good morning, Mummy."

"Harper." Georgiana's voice was coolly polite.

So, Harper thought. *She remains unrelenting.*

"You have some news?" Georgiana prompted. Harper imagined her mother glancing at her watch, foot tapping.

"Yes!" *Too much enthusiasm*, Harper told herself. She tried to still her quaking nerves. "I have happy news, Mother. You're going to be a grandmother."

There was silence on the other end of the line.

"Mother?"

"I heard you. I'm just not quite sure what it is I'm supposed to say."

"How about congratulations?"

"Well, I don't know. You aren't married yet. Are congratulations in order?"

"We're very happy about it."

"Then I'm happy for you, Harper. Truly. Congratulations."

Harper couldn't believe her ears. She heard real emotion in the words. Harper's heart soared. What girl didn't want to talk to her mother when she was having a baby? It was only natural.

"Thank you, Mummy," Harper choked out, surprised to feel herself welling up with long-unshed tears. "That means a great deal. I'm so happy."

There was a beat of silence on the other end, then Georgiana made a sound as if she was clearing her own throat, but when she spoke again, her tone was brisk. "You're going to be a mother. Well, well, well. That changes things, doesn't it?"

"Everything."

"Surely you won't stay in South Carolina now?"

Harper wasn't sure she understood correctly. "Yes, of course I'm staying here. Why wouldn't I?"

"You have your child's future to think of now. Not only your own. Do you think living in the backwoods of the South is thinking of your child? What kind of a life are you offering him or her? Consider the opportunities in England. The social connections. Darling, won't you consider moving to Greenfields Park? You would make everyone so happy if you took over the estate. You could raise your child in the very best of surroundings with the very best people."

"I think I am raising my children in the very best surroundings with the very best people. We're really very happy."

"*You're* happy. Aren't you concerned about Granny James? She dotes on you. Has all her life. She's done everything for you. And Daddy, dear man. He's been through so much."

"Of course I'm concerned about both of them. But I don't know that where I live is their decision any more than it's yours." Harper could feel her temper rising, any softened feelings from their brief moment before having disappeared. "Let it go, Mother. This is my home and this is where I'm staying."

"Aren't you being selfish?"

"*Me* selfish? Greenfields Park is where *you* grew up. Yet you turned your back on it and chose to live in New York City. I grew up in New York and chose to live on Sullivan's Island. You can't expect me to feel a binding loyalty to Greenfields Park when you yourself did not. You can even say I'm following your example."

"You really mean to say you have no loyalty to Greenfields Park? That you would see it sold? A place where you've been happy?"

"I was happy there. The times I was allowed to visit. Anything was better than the dorms of whatever boarding school I happened to be enrolled in at that minute. I was happy at Sea Breeze, too. But I don't think you care if I was happy at Sea Breeze because it doesn't suit your plan for me. I was merely a placeholder, wasn't I? To take over your responsibilities at Greenfields Park while you live the big New York City dream you've always wanted. That's why you had me, wasn't it? And do you think that anything in this world could compel me to put my own child in that same position?" Harper paused to quell her rising emotions. "I think not."

Harper glanced at Granny James. She had paled visibly. Her eyes appeared sunken.

After a long pause Georgiana's voice went flat, void of emotion. "I didn't know you felt that way. Pity. Once again, Daughter dear, we do not see eye to eye. Nonetheless I wish you the very best. Again, my congratulations."

"Will I see you at the wedding?" The little girl in Harper, the one who always pictured her mother walking her down the aisle, needed to know. What did she have to lose?

There was a momentary pause, then her mother said in her crisp British accent, "I think not."

When the line went dead, Harper thrust the phone back toward her grandmother. True to her career, her mother really was good with words. She was well aware that by repeating the very words Harper had spoken, cool and without emotion, the dagger would be all the more sharp.

"I don't want to ever talk to her again," Harper said, barely able to speak the words, her lips were trembling so. She had thought she'd grown accustomed to her mother's vitriolic conversations. But today, damn her, Harper had once again slipped into the fantasy—for the briefest, sweetest moment—that her mother was truly happy for her. That she cared. *Fool*, she told herself. *When will you ever learn?*

"What did she say?" asked Granny James in a low voice.

Harper swiftly wiped away a tear from her cheek. "Must we discuss it?"

"Yes, dear, I think we must. Tell me what she said."

Granny was no stranger to Georgiana's ability to cut a person off at the knees. Granny had been there for Harper for all of her life to listen, to console, to reassure her that she was loved.

"Well, first she congratulated me on the baby."

"That's something."

Harper laughed derisively. "Then she proceeded to tell me to sell this backwoods house and move to Greenfields Park. She was quite clear it was my responsibility. Even my destiny. I suppose to fulfill her own sense of duty."

"Oh, this is such a mess. I never expected Georgiana or you to take the reins at Greenfields Park. I'd hoped, of course. But, Harper," Granny James said with annoyance, "we've been through all this long ago and made our peace. You live here at Sea Breeze and I think you've made the right decision because you love it here." Granny smiled a watery smile. "And so do I. Most of all, you're happy."

"Why can't my mother understand that?"

"Oh, Harper, I wish I knew. There's something missing in that woman."

"I know. A heart."

Granny James looked at her hands with pinched lips.

"But what about Greenfields Park?" Tears flooded Harper's eyes. "Did I let you and Papa Jeffrey down? I'd feel horrid if I did."

Granny James reached out to take Harper's hand and pull her close against her chest. "Dear girl, no! Not at all."

Harper leaned back and wiped her eyes, sniffing. "But what will happen to it?"

"I don't know where to begin." Granny James moved the breakfast tray away and pushed back to sit higher against her pillows. Once settled, she placed her hands on her thighs. "It's time I tell you, dear. I've sold Greenfields Park."

"*Sold* it?" Harper was shocked. Greenfields Park was a large estate, a historic manor house filled with antiques, portraits.

"But you knew it was meant to be sold."

"Y-yes," Harper stammered. "But so quickly?"

"Not so very quickly, actually. You see, I've known for some time I might have to sell it. What with your grandfather's Alzheimer's. Georgiana made it very clear she was staying in New York. So I waited for you to decide whether you'd come back to take over the estate. I hoped you would, of course. No guilt," she said, pointing at Harper when she saw the desolate expression on Harper's face. "You're entitled to make your own decisions." Granny James's fingers creased the edge of her sheets. "But once you decided to stay at Sea Breeze, I was free to act on, frankly, several offers that had been floating around for some time. Greenfields Park is quite the plum, you know. There are very few estates like it available." Harper heard the pride in her grandmother's voice.

"I'm not surprised it sold, Granny, only how fast. I'm kind of in shock, to be honest. I didn't get the chance to go back for a last look-see. A farewell. I had some very happy days there. I would have liked to show Taylor the property."

"Oh, there's plenty of time for all that. It's going to take me a while to settle everything and parcel out all of the treasures inside. There are so many decisions to be made, not only by me, but by you and Georgiana." Granny delivered a firm look. "I want to keep the important family pieces, of course. You'll have to come soon to choose what other pieces you want. Then I'll pass some on to nieces and nephews. The nonfamily pieces I'm selling with the house. A sheikh from Saudi Arabia bought the place and wants everything possible included. Can you imagine?"

Harper could very well imagine. The collection of furniture was not only rare but had taken her grandmother a lifetime to amass. "Don't be taken over a barrel. Some of your pieces are priceless."

Granny James delivered a withering look. "Really, Harper. Do you think I don't know my business?"

Harper smiled, her eyes filled with amusement. Imogene James was never one to be swindled. Harper suddenly felt pity for the sheikh.

"What about Papa Jeffrey?"

Granny James scoffed. "He doesn't remember me, much less the house."

Harper faltered at the raw emotion in her words. "Is . . . is he settling into the new home?"

Granny James grew pensive, the sad look in her eyes returning. "Yes, dear, as well as can be expected. He is not the same person he once was. The home has become his new world. The people who care for him. He doesn't need me anymore."

Harper was alert to the catch in Granny James's voice. "You've done all you could. For such a long time. No one could have been more attentive. More loving."

"I did try my best."

Harper steered the conversation back to the estate, wanting to distract Granny James. "What will you do now that the house is sold? Where will you go?"

It was Granny's turn to falter. "Well, I was rather hoping I could spend some of my time here."

"At Sea Breeze?"

"Yes, at Sea Breeze. You're my family. And now with a baby coming, I'd like to be closer. Oh, don't look alarmed," Granny said with a nervous laugh. "I'd only be here for a few months at a time. I will still spend summers in the Hamptons with Georgiana. And I can stay at her condominium in New York, as well. We get along well enough. She works all day and spends evenings out, after all. And, she is my daughter. Plus I want to travel. So I wouldn't be underfoot."

Granny James paused and let her gaze float about the room. "But I'd like for this to be my base. I've become quite fond of the lowcountry. Sea Breeze in particular. There's an aura about this place that's quite seductive. And of course, *you're* here."

Harper listened, processing Granny James's response but not quite ready to offer up an answer. She needed to mull it over and consult with Taylor first. Sea Breeze was a big old bear of a house—there had to be a space for Granny James that would satisfy them all.

Granny James grew aware of Harper's hesitation, and suddenly her tone became more urgent. "You understand now why I was so disappointed to find Marietta in my cottage. I'd thought it would be the perfect arrangement. Me in the cottage, giving you and Taylor your space, out of the way and all that."

"Mamaw had the same idea."

"Right," Granny James said with annoyance. "And she beat me to the punch, as they say."

Harper sighed and leaned back on her arms.

Granny James adjusted the ribbons of her bed jacket. "We don't need to decide anything now. Don't give it another thought. We've a wedding to plan, after all. Lists to make."

"Granny James . . ."

"Don't we have an appointment at the bridal shop this afternoon? I must get up and dressed."

"Granny—"

"No!" She put her hand up. Tears flashed in her eyes. "No more talk."

The tears in her grandmother's eyes frightened Harper more than anything she'd said. Granny James was the bulwark never faltering in the family. The rock upon which every ship rested upon for safe harbor. To see her crumbling now shook Harper to her very foundation.

"Off you go, dearest. But do have that conversation with Taylor about the prenup. Now you understand why time is of the essence. I'll take care of the legalities, don't you worry. You have enough to think about now."

Harper left to go to her own room. She was grateful that Taylor was at work and she was alone. There she closed the door, curled up on the bed, and had a good cry.

Chapter Fifteen

Isn't that what a wedding is all about?
The gathering of family. The sharing of stories.
The linking of arms. For better or for worse.

Carson was sitting at the kitchen table, her laptop open, an empty bowl of cereal beside it and a half-finished cup of coffee at her fingertips. She was doing her usual morning routine of reading the *Charleston Post and Courier* and checking e-mails. The sky was gray and heavy with thin, dark clouds so she'd decided not to go to the ocean and had instead lingered over a second cup of coffee. She jumped when her cell phone rang.

She checked the time: 6:46 a.m. Who would be calling her so early? she wondered as she answered.

"Hello, this is the Isle of Palms police station. Is this Carson Muir?"

Carson stiffened. "Yes."

"We had a report of a dead dolphin on Isle of Palms. Or at

least they think it's dead. Between Third and Fourth Avenues. Can you take that?"

She climbed to her feet, her blood racing. "Yes, of course. Right away. Thanks."

Carson put the phone in her pocket and took a second to collect her thoughts. She had only just completed the one-day workshop. This was her first call. Without delay she hurried to her room, tugged a T-shirt on, and slipped into cutoff jeans, buttoning them as she scoured the floor for her sandals. Slipping into them, she grabbed the backpack that she'd prepared and headed for the door. Carson had spent a lifetime racing to the ocean to catch the dawn. Mamaw used to tell her she dressed faster than a nun late for mass.

Outside, she caught her first whiff of the new day. The air was moist and cool, with a hint of the warmth that would come later. A good omen, she thought as she hurried to her car. Another positive sign was that no car was blocking her in this morning. The Blue Bomber was a baby-blue convertible with sexy tail fins. She was a beauty, old but in good condition, and the best gift Mamaw had ever given her. Sliding into the white leather seat, Carson fired the powerful engine and was on her way.

Carson breathed in the ocean's breeze when she stepped out onto the beach. The sea was gray like the sky, and just a few people were on the beach, most no doubt kept away by the weather as Carson had been. One woman walked her small dog on a leash. Carson's eye was drawn to where two other women stood shoulder to shoulder near the shoreline, looking down at something on the beach. One bent and reached out to touch something. Cursing under her breath, Carson took off on a trot. Part of her job was to keep the public from touching the carcass. As she drew close to the women, her gaze shifted to the sand. There lay a small, pristine dolphin. Her heart lurched at seeing it.

The women turned to look at her with skepticism. They clearly felt in charge. They were middle-aged with soft bodies and reddish dyed hair tucked in hats that matched the pastel colors of their nylon jackets. Even behind their sunglasses Carson could tell they were checking her out.

"It's a dead dolphin," the woman in the pink nylon jacket told her with authority.

"So it seems." Carson slipped off her backpack and dropped it on the sand, then knelt beside the tiny dolphin, hoping she was wrong. In truth, it didn't look dead. It was a neonate, likely just born, still with its folded dorsal fin and faint neonate stripes. It was perfect, not a bite nor a mark on it. Just a sweet baby with that sweet smile dolphins had that melted the heart. Immediately she thought of Delphine and fear shot through her that this might be her calf.

Carson opened her bag and pulled out her stranding-report form, a pen, and plastic gloves.

The women watched her carefully. "Are you with the dolphin team or something?" the woman in the aqua-blue gym jacket asked with suspicion.

"Yes," Carson replied, trying to be friendly. "I just have a few things to check off my list. Do you mind stepping back a bit? . . . Thanks."

"We're the ones who phoned it in," the lady in pink informed her with an air of self-importance. "We were taking a walk and found it and called the police."

"I tried to push it back into the ocean," the lady in blue said in a woeful tone. "I didn't know if it was dead and wanted to save it. But the waves just pushed it right back on the beach. Look at my pants." She lifted her left leg. The nylon pants were indeed wet to the calf.

Carson put her gloved hand on the dolphin. Without question it was dead. Poor baby, she thought as she took measurements, then filled out the forms. Male neonate. Thirty-nine inches in length.

She looked over her shoulder and spoke to the women behind her. "Thanks for calling it in. You did the right thing. But in the future if you see a stranded dolphin, please don't touch it. Stranded animals are often sick, and diseases can be transmitted to humans. Not to mention, they could bite. Best to call it in, like you did, and wait for help."

"You're touching it," the lady in blue argued.

"Yes, but I'm trained to do this and I'm wearing gloves."

The woman in pink harrumphed softly. "It could've died while we waited for you." They watched a few minutes longer, then apparently bored, the women meandered on.

"Thank you again," Carson called after them, but they didn't respond. She finished the form, then put her supplies back into her backpack. Now all that was left to do was wait.

Thankfully, she didn't have to wait long. She'd sent out the NOAA pager, as directed, but she'd also called Blake directly. It helped to know the guy in charge, she thought as she watched his pickup driving toward her along the shoreline. Carson waved her arms overhead.

Blake climbed from the truck and strode straight toward her.

Even though it was only April, he was already tanned, wearing shorts and a navy NOAA T-shirt. He had that laid-back, old-fashioned masculinity that always set her blood thumping. His dark eyes lit up when he wrapped his arm around her and pulled her in for a kiss. "How's my girl?"

"Sad." Her lips turned down in a frown.

His gaze shifted to the beach where the dolphin lay. "A neonate." He dropped his arm and walked directly to the dolphin. "Yeah, it's always sad to see one of these."

Carson followed Blake. "Look at him. He's so cute. He looks like he should just swim off with his mama."

Blake pulled gloves from his back pocket and slipping them on, bent at the knees to survey the animal while Carson watched. Without speaking he went to his truck and pulled out a case, then returned to the animal. He spread out a thick piece of blue plastic and lay the small dolphin on this. Blake was as precise as a surgeon as he took blood and skin samples and placed them in tubes. Then he wrapped the tarp around the dolphin.

"Would you grab the case?" he asked as he carried the wrapped dolphin to the truck. He placed the carcass and case inside, then closed the tailgate.

"Where are you taking it?"

"To the NOAA offices. Wayne McFee will do the necropsy. Researchers are able to gather a wealth of information from strandings that will help support the live ones out there."

Thinking again of Delphine, she asked, "Why do you think it died?"

"For neonates, if it isn't a shark attack, the culprit is usually water quality. The toxins in the water build up in the mother. When she gives birth, she purges the toxins from her body through the calf. Thus the stillbirth."

"Could that happen to Delphine's calf? Could it be hers?"

Blake lifted a shoulder. "I don't know. It's a fresh birth. I'll only know when I see Delphine next."

Carson looked out at the sea. These were tough times for all the animals in the oceans. But Delphine was her friend. She cared about this dolphin. "I hope not."

"I don't think it is," Blake added reassuringly. "I can't be sure, my guess is she has a ways to go yet." Blake took his gloves off and tucked them into his pocket. "Hop in, I'll drop you off."

"I'm parked on Third, but I'll ride with you." Carson hopped into the cab of the truck. The truth was she wasn't ready to be alone just yet, needing Blake's comforting presence a bit longer after witnessing that heartbreaking scene of the dead calf.

The truck rocked on the uneven surface as she looked out at the sea. Though the day was gray, there were no waves to speak of. Still, one young man in a wet suit was out there. Probably someone on vacation determined to practice. Carson had surfed since she was sixteen, usually right here on Isle of Palms. She glanced at the man beside her. He clearly hadn't shaved yet. The dark stubble rimmed his jaw. Was it only a year ago that Blake had taught her how to kiteboard? She smiled, remembering. That might've been when she knew she could fall in love with him.

"This would make carting all my boards and kites onto the beach easy," she said, tapping the truck with affection.

"Yeah, right?" He laughed lightly. "But don't get any ideas.

I can only do this on official business." He reached out to push back a lock of hair that had escaped from her dark braid. "You done good today, Carson. I'm proud of you."

She basked in his compliment. "You didn't see me duke it out with the two ladies who phoned it in. They were none too pleased I told them not to touch the dolphin."

His smile came slow, teasing, aware of her frankness. "Just be nice. We're ambassadors out there."

"I'm always nice," she replied, ignoring his snort. She felt the time was right to bring up another dolphin story. "Blake, there's something I've been meaning to tell you. Last week when I was paddleboarding, I saw Delphine." She glanced over at him. He was busy maneuvering the truck off the beach along the narrow beach path for trucks.

Once they got to Ocean Boulevard, he turned onto the pavement and headed back to Third Avenue. Blake shifted to look at her. "Yeah? So how is she?"

"She looked good. Fat." Carson chuckled. "She was swimming with another female out at the mouth of the harbor."

"She's fit right back into the clan." Satisfaction was in his voice.

"So it seems." This was what they'd wanted for Delphine. The reason she was released back into home waters. Carson licked her lips. "She recognized me."

There was a brief pause. "Yeah? What she do?"

"Oh, the usual. She whistled and splashed. She pitched a hissy fit when I wouldn't engage. It near broke my heart to ignore her. I know it was best for her, but how can I explain that to her? So I lay down on the board and we just looked at each other for a while. Eye to eye. It was pretty powerful. I knew we were connecting and she must've, too, because she calmed down and just looked right back at me."

"Cool. I wish I could've seen that."

"Atticus did."

"Atticus?"

"Yeah, I invited him to come out with me. Remember him talking about how he had that experience with a dolphin? I was hoping we'd see Delphine. Thought it would mean something special for him."

"Did it?"

"Yes. I think so. But to be honest I also wanted someone else with me the first time I saw Delphine again. I thought it would make it easier not to reach out to her if I wasn't alone."

They arrived at Third Avenue. The Blue Bomber was parked in the sand off the street. Already two other cars and a golf cart had filled parking spaces.

Blake parked the truck beside the Bomber. "So what happened?"

Carson puffed out a plume of air. Now she was getting to the hard part. "I messed up." She saw a quick flare-up in his eyes and his face grew somber. "I started putting my hand out to touch her. It was instinctive. Selfish, I know. But I stopped, Blake. Halfway, my hand just stopped. I was about to pull it back when Delphine rose up and bumped my hand with her rostrum. It made me laugh. Then she circled around and swam past me, right close to the board so she would brush against my hand. I swear, Blake, I didn't move it forward. Not so much as an inch. But I felt her skin under my palm. I told myself I didn't do it, that *she* did. But I was kidding myself. I let my hand hang there off the board. I was encouraging her, allowing it to happen."

Blake waited for her to finish.

"Then I tucked my hand back in, climbed to my feet, and when she started making noises at me, I gave her the signal to go. And"—Carson ended with a sigh—"she did. We watched her make a beeline for her friend farther in the harbor. The last we saw of her she was swimming off with her friend."

Carson turned her head to study his profile as he looked out the windshield, so strong and seemingly so rigid.

"So," he said after a few moments of silence. "You're telling me she came to your paddleboard and tried to engage you. And then you touched her."

"Yes. That was my first challenge, the one I was most afraid of," she said in a rush, trying to explain herself. "Now I know that I can do it. As hard as it was to see her again, it was harder to watch her swim away."

Blake stretched out his arm. "Come here."

Carson sighed and slid into the crook of his arm. He tightened his arm around her and kissed her head. "I know that was hard for you to not engage with Delphine. But you did it." He squeezed her shoulders. "And you told me. That means a lot to me. I love your honesty. And that you trust me with your feelings."

"I always want to be honest with you. Even if I'm worried you'll be mad."

"I might get mad sometimes. You might get mad at me. Babe, we're going to have a lot of issues to face in the years ahead. When we have children, you know we're going to see things differently from time to time. But as long as we can talk about them, air our feelings out, and not be afraid if the other person will get mad, we'll get through them."

She smiled up at Blake and, looking into his eyes, sighed with deep relief and even hope. Whatever roller coaster their marriage might be, wherever they decided to live, whatever she decided to do as a career, she sensed that she and Blake were going to be just fine.

Midmorning that same day, Marietta sat on the back porch under the uncompromising shade of the black-and-white-striped awning. She was enjoying a rare third cup of coffee. Over the rim of her cup she glanced across the water to see Girard's dock. His Boston Whaler was hanging above the water in a lift. His small johnboat was tied up to the lower dock, bobbing on the water like a pelican. Her lips stretched to a smile beside the rim of her cup as she recalled the first two cups of coffee she'd enjoyed this morning with Girard.

A splash caught her attention, and Marietta diverted her gaze to the pool. Imogene had been swimming laps for the past quarter hour. Back and forth, her arms pumping like a piston. Too much emotion was in those strokes for it to be just idle exercise. Something was bothering the woman. Marietta had noticed a change in Imogene since she'd arrived, despite how she'd tried to cover it up.

Marietta sipped the coffee, disappointed in its tepidity. She worked on the newspaper's crossword puzzle a bit, then looked again at Imogene in the pool. Her strokes were slower now, weary. Could she be so upset that Marietta had moved into Lucille's cottage? Marietta hadn't missed that glare Imogene had directed her way upon finding out her beloved cottage was already occupied. If that was, in fact, the reason behind Imogene's change in attitude, well, that was absurd! Marietta bristled. First of all, the cottage wasn't hers to be upset about. This had been Marietta's home, after all. For more than fifty years. And her husband's family's beach house for a hundred more. If anyone asked her, Imogene was just a prima donna, making a tempest in a teapot. So what if her money had bought the house? It was Harper's name on the deed of sale. The decision had been Harper's to make. And make it she did. Marietta adjusted her seat on the chair, letting out a little humph of righteous indignation. If Imogene James thought Marietta was going to kowtow to this little show of pique, she was sadly mistaken.

Marietta continued to watch Imogene swim until at last the woman ran out of steam. With weary steps, Imogene climbed from the pool and reached for her towel. The temperature was only in the seventies on this beautiful first day of spring, but Harper had heated the pool to a toasty eighty-two degrees. All for Imogene—and it was costing Harper a fortune, Marietta thought with distaste.

She picked up a magazine and pretended to be reading as Imogene walked up the stairs to the upper deck. She strolled to the table. Marietta looked up with a welcoming smile. Imogene's white hair with hints of auburn was slicked back from her face, and the large towel engulfed the woman like a blanket. In the stark morning light it shocked Marietta to see how tired and old Imogene appeared. She'd lost weight since her last visit. How could Marietta have missed that? And her usual spark of life, her bravado, seemed to have fled, leaving something of an empty shell behind. In a rush, all Marietta's previous pique fled in the wake of compassion.

"Imogene, do sit down. I'll get you a cup of hot tea to warm you."

"No, thank you, I've brought water. But I will join you for a moment."

Imogene collected her water and returned to the table, moving her chair to sit in the sunshine. She closed her eyes and lifted her face to the sun.

After a moment, Marietta wondered if she'd fallen asleep. "Imogene?"

Imogene brought her head up. "Yes?"

"Are you all right?"

Imogene released a short, tired laugh. "No."

Marietta's brows furrowed in concern. "Do you want to talk about it?"

Imogene released a long sigh and slowly shook her head. "I've made a muddle of things."

"Why not tell me what's bothering you? It helps to talk about it. Or so Lucille used to tell me."

Imogene sighed. "I suggested Harper call her mother with the good news about the baby."

Mamaw wanted to jerk Imogene's tail. But she pursed her lips and looked at her hands, giving Imogene the chance to finish.

Imogene tightened the towel around her neck. "It didn't go well."

"How could you expect it would?" Mamaw asked with annoyance. Then in a softer tone: "What happened?"

"It was bloody awful. Georgiana suggested that Harper move to Greenfields Park."

"*Suggested?* I bet it was stronger than that. That woman is as subtle as a Mack truck."

"Well, I only heard Harper's end, so I don't know exactly what was said. But from what I could glean, Georgiana thought Harper more or less owed it to the family . . . to me . . . to take over Greenfields Park."

"But she's already bought Sea Breeze." Mamaw felt a little panic stir.

"Georgiana, I'm sure, sees that as a rectifiable mistake. She pressed on the poor girl to think of the child's welfare. They waffled and it went downhill from there, I'm afraid. She must've said something that really set Harper off, because she rallied and told her mother she wasn't doing her duty, or something like that. She pretty much told her mother to sod off."

Marietta nodded approvingly. "Good girl."

"Then, when Harper asked if Georgiana was coming to the wedding, Georgiana replied that she was not."

Marietta made a fluttering motion with her hand as though waving away a pesky fly. "Frankly, I would be surprised if she'd accepted."

"All the same, Harper is hurt. She seems to have an infinite ability of being hurt by her mother."

"And doesn't Georgiana know it." Mamaw was fit to be tied about that woman. She only wished she could have had five minutes on the phone with her.

"She can be difficult," Imogene conceded, shifting the towel on her shoulders. Looking up, her face was grave. "But she is my daughter. And Harper's mother. Regardless of what you and I think, I would like to try to help the two of them get past this argument. For Harper's sake. She may not say it aloud, but of course she wants her mother at her wedding."

Marietta was instantly contrite. "Of course, you're right. Surely we can put our heads together and figure something out."

Imogene sipped water from her bottle.

Mamaw watched her, going over in her mind what Imogene had said about Greenfields Park. "Does Harper have a responsibility to Greenfields Park?" Mamaw asked at last, unable to conceal her worry. "I thought that issue was put to bed when Harper bought Sea Breeze last fall."

"Oh, blimey, no one has any responsibilities!" Granny James put her forehead in her palm. After a second she let her hand drop and faced Marietta. "I've done it all. Though I haven't yet told Georgiana. You see, I've sold Greenfields Park."

Marietta was stunned by the news. "Sold it?"

Imogene brought Marietta up-to-date on the sale of the estate, concluding with how she was, for the moment, homeless.

"But wherever will you live?"

Imogene smiled cagily. "I thought I'd move here for a while. Just until I find something suitable. I wouldn't be here all the time, of course. I would visit Georgiana."

"Good heavens, Imogene. Who do you think you're fooling? No one can spend time with that woman. I'm sorry, but that's the truth."

"Sadly, there is truth in what you say." Imogene looked off.

"But Georgiana is so busy, always running out to some luncheon or dinner, she's never around anyway. We'd be like two ships passing in the night. It wouldn't be for long. I'll find my own place, perhaps on Sullivan's Island. I want to travel, too. I'm free! For the first time in a very long while." Imogene smiled and looked again at Marietta, lifting one shoulder. "As I said, Sea Breeze would just be a place to hang my hat. My base." Imogene's face sobered. "The last thing I want to be at this point in my life is a burden."

Marietta understood this emotion so well. It had been her greatest worry with the sale of Sea Breeze.

"I confess, I want to be near my only granddaughter. And my new grandchild." Imogene smiled at the thought of the upcoming baby. "Is that so wrong?"

"Of course not. We all feel the same way."

Imogene nodded, accepting that.

Marietta leaned back in the large black wicker chair and considered all Imogene had told her. "Now it's all becoming as clear as day," Marietta said with a huff of incredulity. "That's why you're so upset about my living in the cottage. That sweet li'l space was to be your . . . your 'base,' as you put it."

"Of course it was! That was the plan all along." Imogene reached out her finger to point accusingly at Marietta. "And you knew it! But did that stop you? No! Not bloody likely."

Marietta laughed.

Imogene sat up in her chair, insulted. "What's so funny?"

"You're right. I did know that."

Imogene was appalled. "I knew it."

"It wasn't why I moved into the cottage. But"—Marietta shrugged as a sly smile eased across her cheeks—"knowing I'd be skewering you a bit in the bargain made the move all the sweeter."

Imogene stared at Marietta as one unable to believe what she'd just heard. Then her lips twitched and she burst out laughing. "I'd have done the same thing!"

"Don't I know it!"

"Gawd, what a pair we make. Maybe we should move in together."

"We'd kill each other."

"But what sport we'd have!" Imogene reached for her bottle of water and took a long swallow. She put the bottle on the table and made a face. "You wouldn't happen to have any of your special tea, would you? The family recipe?"

Marietta chuckled and shook her head. "Not now. But how about a game of cards tomorrow afternoon? I'll make it special."

"You're on. Make a pitcher. Make two. I need a purge."

The air of a truce floated between them as they settled back into their chairs. They lapsed into a thoughtful silence. Marietta studied the woman across the table from her. Once again she'd leaned back into the cushions and looked off at the Cove. Imogene just didn't have the same vitality she'd had the last time she was here. Imogene shivered under the heavy towel. Her hair, drying in the sun, blew in soft wisps, exposing a pinkening scalp. They were old soldiers, Marietta realized. Comrades-in-arms. They'd fought many battles in their years. Seen their triumphs, too. But the woman across from her appeared near broken.

"Come sit in the shade. You're getting a sunburn," Marietta said.

"I'm too chilly."

"Then wear a hat." Marietta reached beside her, grabbed her floppy beach hat, and handed it to Imogene.

Imogene took it and flopped it on her head with an exaggerated push. "Happy now?"

"Yes."

"You're a bossy bitch."

"So I've been told."

Imogene adjusted the hat on her head and settled into a brooding silence.

When it appeared she had nothing more to say, Marietta prompted her, "Why do you feel the need to come to Sea Breeze? You have so many options. Money isn't a problem. You could move anywhere. Imogene . . . my friend . . . what's got you so shaken?"

Imogene's eyes watered and she brought her hand to her lips. The coral polish was chipped. "I feel lost," Imogene said softly. "For the first time in my life."

"Lost? How so?"

"You know very well how I feel," Imogene said reproachfully. "When your husband died . . . I'm sorry, what was his name?"

"Edward."

"Yes, when Edward died. Didn't you feel lost?"

"Yes, I did." Marietta recalled the deep depression she'd slipped into after his death, so close after the loss of her son. She'd felt she was drowning in her sorrow. Lucille had saved her with her trademark compassion, care, and unwavering diligence. She wouldn't let Mamaw go under.

"You had a good marriage, didn't you? Happy?"

"As happy as can be expected. Naturally we had our ups and downs."

"But of course you did," Imogene said impatiently. "No couple can be married for some fifty years and not have ups and downs. Hell, even thirty years. A long marriage can be a battlefield. We had bloody blowups, I can tell you. There were times I hated Jeffrey. Wished he would just die. I'd be free without the scandal of a divorce." She laughed shortly. "I can't count the times I'd planned to leave him. And he me. He cheated on me, you know. Several times. He felt somehow entitled to a bit of dalliance, don't you know. His own father did, and his father did the same thing to his wife before him. We wives are meant to look the other way. Excuse their flirting about as simply a man's way. The self-important pricks," Imogene muttered under her breath. "I suppose that's what happens when a man's wealthy and successful and powerful in his business. And has a title to boot."

"'Power tends to corrupt and absolute power corrupts absolutely.'"

"Oh, I couldn't agree more." Imogene nodded vehemently. "Jeffrey was decent enough looking, to be sure. But it's that other stuff that was the aphrodisiac to young women. We muddled through, however. Age has a marvelous way of mellowing one, doesn't it? In the end, we found great comfort in each other's company. The reward of perseverance." Imogene picked lint from the towel. "I admired him. Jeffrey was a brilliant man." She stilled her hand and looked vacantly at the pool. "Then came the Alzheimer's. It's a dreadful disease. I hate it. It stole Jeffrey from me. Not all at once. Bit by bit. It's terrible to watch a luminous mind implode like a black star and not be able to do a single thing to stop it." Her voice broke and she reached for her water bottle.

Marietta felt her own eyes moisten at Imogene's unexpected display of emotion. "I'm so sorry."

"I am, too." Imogene sipped water, then licked her lips. As she screwed the top back on the bottle, her voice grew thin. "That wasn't the worst of it, though."

Marietta leaned forward to hear her voice, which had grown as soft as a breeze.

"I did my best to care for him at Greenfields Park. I hired a full-time nurse. A nutritionist. Therapists. No expense was spared. I thought if I couldn't cure the disease, I might be able to slow it down a little. At the very least make Jeffrey comfortable and feel safe. They get quite frightened at times, you know. When they don't remember things or get lost. These things I was prepared for. There are loads of books published on the subject. I must have read them all.

"What I wasn't prepared for were the small daily hurts." Imogene paused in recollection. "Jeffrey was a publisher, you know. Years back. He was a very fast reader. Had an extensive library. Reading was his world. I'd watch him as he sat and read. He'd set the book down, then pick it up again a bit later and begin reading from the beginning. Over and over. He didn't remember what he'd just read. It was painful to watch. Eventually he stopped reading altogether. He couldn't make sense of the words. A part of him died that day." Her lips trembled. "And a part of me died the day he didn't know who I was."

"Oh, Imogene," Marietta said with feeling.

She waved away the sympathy. "In the last two years, he

deteriorated rapidly. You recall I couldn't bring him here last summer. Nor the Hamptons before that. He loved going there. Loved the sea." She smiled wistfully. "He would have liked it here, too. He'd have called the scenery primitive." She laughed at Marietta's expression. "Jeffrey was a terrible snob, you know. If it wasn't British, it wasn't up to snuff." There was a small pause. "He was also fastidious about his personal habits. A spot on his cuff would drive him to distraction. So imagine the horror I felt for him when he dropped his pants in the middle of the front hall and relieved himself. He proceeded to remove the rest of his clothing and refused to put them on again. There was quite a struggle. He'd decided he liked being stark naked." Imogene laughed, but there was sorrow in it. "I knew then that I'd reached the end of what I was able to provide. He needed more. He had to go to a Memory Center."

Imogene adjusted her position in the chair, trying to find a comfortable spot. When settled, she folded her hands on the table and looked at them. "That place is his home now. The people who care for him are the ones who matter. They're his family now. There's no place for me there. I'm no longer important to him. He doesn't even know me." She brought her fingers to her cheek as though seeing the scene again. "Driving away that morning, leaving him there . . . it was the hardest thing I've ever done." She looked up and her eyes were watery. "I've lost my purpose. My rudder. I feel adrift."

Marietta rose to come to her side. She lay her hand on Imogene's shoulder, felt the sharp bone beneath the towel. "Of course you were right to come here. To Sea Breeze. Not only to Harper. But to Taylor. And to me. In time, you will find your strength again, but until then you need the comfort of family and friends. We're here for you, my dear friend. You belong here. With us. At Sea Breeze."

Imogene was listening, her eyes wide and vulnerable.

Marietta smiled with encouragement. "After all, isn't that what a wedding is all about? The gathering of family. The sharing of stories. The linking of arms. For better or for worse."

Imogene choked back a teary laugh. "Till death do us part."

"Let's not go that far! It's a bit too close to home. Come dear, let's get dressed. The girls are expecting us to be at our best. We mustn't disappoint. The wedding must go on!"

Chapter Sixteen

A young bride looks sweet in a cloud of white tulle. But a bride in her thirties or older would do well to choose a creamy or off-white color. As would, perhaps, a woman who is already sharing a home with her intended.

Dora, Carson, and Harper parked the car in the lot and walked along the crooked sidewalk on East Bay through the bustling crowd. Spring was in full flower and Charleston was a destination city for vacations. Tourists fled the snowy North and were hell-bent on wearing shorts, T-shirts, and flip-flops, even in the city.

The Muir girls, however, wore dresses and heels. Harper even wore a hat. They were all in a festive mood, helped along by the champagne—and sparkling cider for Carson and Harper—that they'd consumed at SalonSalon hair salon, where they'd tried out hairstyles for the wedding. Feeling primped and pretty, they strolled down King Street, going from the hair salon to Studio R to pick up their printed thank-you notes, then straight on to Croghan's jewelry store, one of the oldest jewelers in the city, to pick up the grooms' rings.

Shopping in Charleston always meant a fun day. Boutiques, antiques stores, jewelers, great restaurants, cobbled streets oozing charm and history. Shopping for a wedding dress, however, makes the day stellar. And that's just what the girls intended to do later that afternoon.

But first, they had reservations for lunch at Magnolias. Fresh flowers decorated the tables draped in thick white linen. As usual, the restaurant was filled with locals and visitors alike. The girls were seated swiftly, and a short time later Carson bit into her fried-green-tomato BLT. She closed her eyes and emitted a soft groan of pleasure.

"I'd forgotten how delicious this was," she muttered while chewing. "Does anyone make a better fried green tomato?"

"Not exactly the diet of someone shopping for a wedding dress," Harper said testily.

Carson picked up a chip and devoured it. "I don't care about a dress half as much as I care how damn good this is." She looked at Harper. "How're your chicken livers?"

Harper looked at her plate, barely touched, and offered a quick but unenthusiastic smile. "Very good. I'm just not that hungry."

"Oh, baby, do you have morning sickness?" asked Dora, eyes round with concern. Harper resisted the urge to roll her eyes. Dora had been clucking around her like a mother hen since she'd announced her pregnancy. Besides, she wasn't feeling sick. More sad and confused by her argument with her mother earlier that morning. That and the prenup. The thought of asking Taylor for one hung over her like a thundercloud about to burst.

"Yes," she lied. "I should have ordered something bland." At that thought, suddenly the smell of the liver made her stomach turn for real.

"You just hold on a minute, sugar." Dora raised her hand and signaled the waitress. "I'm sorry, but could you remove her plate, please, and bring us some toast with avocado and sea salt?"

"Oh, yes, of course." The waitress picked up the offending plate with alacrity and nodded demurely, whisking it away and hurrying back to the kitchen.

Harper smiled weakly. "Thank you."

"You should've ordered a crème brûlée while you were at it," Carson said. "If you didn't finish it, I'd help you out."

"How can you eat like that and keep your figure?" Dora asked.

Carson shrugged. "High metabolism, I guess. And lots of exercise. It's always the exercise. Sorry. No secrets there. By the way, are you still running?"

Dora looked slightly embarrassed. "I was until recently. I'm just starting work with Devlin's company and I've got a lot to learn. I'm running around like a chicken without a head. On top of that, I've got Nate's schedule to juggle. You'd think I'd be losing weight, nervous energy and all, but I'm not. I'm gaining. But," she added with more pride, "Nate's joining clubs at school and he has new friends! Oh, he's doing so well. It warms the cockles of my heart to set up playdates."

"He's doing so well at the new school," Harper said, feeling genuinely happy for the ten-year-old boy who'd been so lonely before Dora had moved to Sullivan's Island.

Dora nodded her assent. "The private school is costing me an arm and a leg, but it's worth every penny."

"How's Cal taking it?" asked Carson. "Still complaining about the tuition?"

Dora rolled her eyes. "Of course. That man can't utter a sentence without attaching a whine to it. But it's in writing. You gotta love a good lawyer."

The waitress returned with the toast for Harper and a basket of warm rolls for the table. The scent of biscuits lured Harper, suddenly ravenous, to reach for one immediately. She looked up to see Dora staring at the rolls.

"Oh, go ahead," Harper told her. "Today's special."

Dora thought a moment, then shook her head with resolution. "Nope. I have to try on a bridesmaid gown. And I'm standing up there next to you two beanpoles."

Carson chuckled and took another large bite of her sandwich. "You look beautiful, Sister mine. And happy. That's what matters. How's it going with ol' Dev, anyway?" Carson and Devlin had been friends for years. She had prodded a reluctant, withdrawn Dora to go out to meet him the previous summer.

"Our professional relationship is fine. There were a few noses out of joint at the office when I first arrived. Some of them thought I was getting preferential treatment. Sleeping-with-the-boss kind of thing. Devlin put a stop to that right quick. By the way, Mamaw offered to introduce me to her friends, and we all know how important that is. So, I'm feeling hopeful there. And Devlin and I work well together. We're like peas and carrots that way. Our personal lives, however . . ." Dora shook her head and twiddled her fork in her fingers. "All this marriage talk is making him testy."

"Meaning he wants to get married?" Carson said, swirling her iced tea.

"Right." Dora skewered an olive. "He doesn't understand why we don't join the fray."

"Frankly, Sis, I don't either." Carson looked at Harper for agreement. She was busy chewing a roll and only nodded.

Dora abandoned her fork and instead reached for her white wine. "I just don't want to get married right now. Should I feel guilty about that?"

"Hey, I have no problem with that," Carson said, heading off an argument. "It's Devlin who's having the problem."

"I can handle Devlin. Just lay off, okay?" Dora sipped her wine, frowning. "Sorry. I'm a little sensitive about that subject."

"I understand," Carson said.

"The thing that's got me seriously worried is he's made some noise about selling the cottage."

"*Your* cottage?"

"Technically it's not my cottage. I rent it from Devlin, at a ridiculously low amount."

"Ooh, that horrible man," Carson teased. "Cruel and unusual, making you pay only token rent."

Dora grinned and acknowledged the tease with a nod of her head. "We both understood from the beginning that I was doing him a favor by renting the house. I was taking care of the place until the market improved and a good offer came up."

"And he was doing you a favor," Harper pointed out.

"For sure."

"And you believed him that it was a real estate agreement?" Carson asked skeptically.

"Hell, no. I know I'm a kept woman, but it's a good excuse, isn't it?"

Carson burst out laughing.

"He loves me and I love him. I know we'll get married someday, and this cottage bit is just business. That's the deal. We flip houses to make money. I get part of the profit. But, shit," Dora said under her breath, "I love that little cottage. So does Nate."

"Can you afford to rent it for more money?" Harper asked.

"No." Dora shook her head. "No way. I'm scared I won't be able to afford rent for a crappy place off island as is. I won't be able to stay on Sullivan's, for sure. And no!" Dora said sharply, pointing at Carson, who was about to interrupt. "I'm not moving in with Devlin. He's already asked and I told him no. I can't live with him before I'm married. I couldn't bear the gossip."

Dora's eyes widened as she realized what she'd just said. She swung her head around to face Harper. Her sister was sitting straight backed with an unreadable expression on her face, but her already-fair skin had visibly paled another shade. "Oh, Harper, I didn't mean anything by that. I don't care if it's just me living with him. It's Nate I have to think about. School and all. Kids can be so nasty."

Harper shook her head. "Don't be silly. I understand. Though frankly, I couldn't care less about gossip."

"Good for you." Carson raised her glass of iced tea.

"Really?" Dora challenged with a cool gaze. "You're not living with Blake."

"Oh, I'd live with Blake, no problem. I just like it better at Sea Breeze." Carson chuckled, then took a healthy swallow.

"And if you tell him that, I'll deny it." After they finished laughing, she added, "Hey, Dora, I'm in the same boat as you are. Blake and I are undecided about where to live. We could stay in Blake's apartment after we get married. We both love Sullivan's and being close to y'all. But he's hankering to move to John's Island, closer to work. He wants to buy a house." Carson shuddered. "And nothing says forever like buying a house together." She grimaced. "It all sounds so permanent."

"Sister mine," Dora told her, leaning in, "that's what marriage is. Permanent." She lifted one shoulder in response to Carson's questioning glance. "Well, it's supposed to be," Dora backtracked, acknowledging her own divorce. "Hey," she suddenly said with excitement. "If Blake lets his place go, let me know. It's one of the few affordable places on the island. I might be interested."

"Sure, but hold your horses, Sister. I like it there, too.

"Deal."

"Okay, subject change. Can I just ask what our opinion of Reverend Green is?" Carson asked, eyes twinkling.

"Besides the fact that he's GQ material?" Dora asked. Carson hooted in response. "I mean, heavens above, how is a man like that a minister? And not married?"

"He can get married," Carson told her.

"Then why hasn't someone snatched him up?" Dora speared another piece of lettuce. "Anyway, I like him. He seems like real folk. Plus he's a friend of Mamaw's. There's something about him that makes him so easy to talk to. Do you feel that?"

"Very much so," Carson acknowledged.

Dora swung her head to check out Harper. "How about you?"

"Oh, sure, I like him, too." Her voice was flat.

"You okay?" Dora asked her, her voice laden with concern. "You're awful quiet over there, Little Mouse."

Harper smiled, hearing the old nickname her sisters used to call her. "Yes." She paused, then shook her head. "No."

"What's going on?" Carson asked.

Harper picked up her knife and idly started tracing lines on the tablecloth. "How do you two come down on the subject of prenups?"

Carson and Dora both sat back and exchanged a quick, commiserating glance. "I don't like them," Carson said firmly, right off the bat. "If you're making the decision to get married, for better or for worse, richer or poorer, tossing in a prenup is kind of like you saying, 'But just in case, I'm throwing in a safety net. For me.'"

"That's easy for you and me to say," Dora said. "Neither of us has any great fortune to protect. We're just looking to make a life together with the person we love. But Harper does. A pre-nuptial agreement is important for people like her who have to protect multimillion-dollar financial interests. And not just money, but her family estate. Things that have been in her fam-ily for generations. And ours! Let me remind you, Harper owns Sea Breeze now. God forbid, what if she dies young? The house would go to Taylor. It would fall out of the family."

"Taylor's a good guy," Harper said defensively. "He would never do anything untoward. Especially with a baby. He'd have a family to think about no matter what."

"All true. But he's also young," Dora reasoned. "And hot. He'd get married again. And he and his pretty new wife would have children. On his death, or divorce, Sea Breeze would be out of the family."

"Damn," said Carson, appearing worried for the first time. "I didn't think of that."

"Most brides don't," said Dora. "Let me tell you, I wish I'd signed one with Cal. We didn't have a pot to pee in, but we both promised the other that, if we ever got divorced, we'd split the money up even-steven, but he would keep his family antiques and I would keep mine. It made sense we'd want those pieces that were part of our histories. Sentimental, you know? But lo and behold, once Cal figured out how much some of my pieces were worth compared to his during our divorce, he got the lawyers to claim all as community property. That's how I lost some of my furniture, my silver, and my art. I only wish I had the money to buy them back. Just saying, you don't know how nasty divorces can get." Dora picked up her wineglass. "Like they say, 'Marriage is grand. Divorce is fifty grand.'" With that she swallowed down the rest of her wine.

Harper appeared troubled. "I hear what you're saying and see the sense in it. But I feel like asking for a prenup is saying to Taylor that I don't trust him."

"I think you can make your prenup about anything you want it to be. My Lord"—Dora giggled—"you'd be surprised what some prenups include. I heard of things such as how often you have sex, too much weight gain, housekeeping chores, who gets the pets."

"That's horrible." Harper's face reflected her feeling. "Why are they even getting married? Seems like they're entering nothing more than a contractual agreement."

"That's what marriage is," Carson reminded her. "A contractual agreement. Legally binding. If you don't want a prenup, you could always opt for cohabitation."

"No." Harper shook her head. "That seems so lacking in commitment. I want to marry Taylor and be his wife. I love him and my child, and I want us to be a family." Tears started filling her eyes.

"Spoken like a bride," Dora said with a hint of warning.

"Aw, honey, don't let this upset you." Carson reached across the table to put her hand over Harper's.

"She's right, honey. And for what it's worth, my backwoods beliefs about prenups is that it's no big deal. It's like prearranging anything, even your funeral. Which, girls, you should both do. 'Cause remember, the reality is that up to fifty percent of marriages end in divorce. And of those that don't, one hundred percent end in death."

"And on that happy note"—Carson put her napkin on the table—"we have to scoot. As you're so fond of telling me, there is so much to do. We picked up the rings, nailed the venues and the bands. But now you have to put 'get a lawyer' on your to-do list." She snorted when she saw the dismay on Harper's face.

"Oh my God, look at the time," Dora said, checking her watch. "We're supposed to meet the grandmothers at the bridal salon at two. It's nearly two now."

Harper pulled out her wallet. "Tell you what, I'll pay the bill to save time."

"You don't have to do that," Carson said, reaching for her wallet.

"Done!" Harper flagged down the waitress and handed her a credit card.

"I'll pay you back," said Dora, rising to her feet. "You know what they say. When women have problems or get depressed, they eat or go shopping. We did both."

Carson piled some cash on the table for a tip. "Men invade a country."

Dora smiled. "Well I, for one, would rather do the former. Less mess and way more fun."

Feeling buoyed by the luncheon, the girls walked to King Street to the bridal salon where Harper was scheduled for a fitting of the wedding dress she'd ordered months earlier. They plowed past the afternoon crowds and one tempting boutique after another, not daring to stop at a window if they were going to arrive in time for their appointment. When they arrived at the small white door of LulaKate on King Street, they pushed through the door, feeling as if they were gaining exclusive entrance. Mamaw and Granny James were already there, sipping flutes of champagne and looking quite relaxed.

From the moment she stepped into the salon, Harper felt like a bride. A floral scent floated around the room, not cloyingly sweet but more fresh and springlike. Rows of gorgeous white gowns were lined up against an exposed redbrick wall, each one promising to make its bride a princess for a day. The boutique salon had achieved that delicate balance between elegant chic and charming lowcountry. Exactly what Harper had hoped she would achieve with her wedding. She felt her spirits rise as her sisters made cooing noises and immediately headed toward the gowns and began sorting through them.

Then Harper looked toward the far wall where the finished gowns were waiting to be united with their owners, tailored exactly to each bride's specifications. Gowns that were slim-fitted, looking almost doll-like on their padded hangers. And very, very unforgiving in the waistlines.

Suddenly that toast and avocado from Magnolias wasn't sitting so well. "Excuse me," she asked the pretty salesclerk urgently, quietly. "Is the bathroom unlocked?"

The pretty saleslady took one look at Harper and, eyes widening slightly, nodded and turned on her heel to quickly lead Harper to the bathroom.

"I'm Lauren. Let me know if there's anything you need," the saleswoman said as she discreetly closed the door.

Harper clung to the rim of the sink and took deep breaths, stilling both her roiling stomach and her racing heart. She was nervous her dress wouldn't fit. And even if by some miracle it did, what if they didn't like it? She'd bought the dress on an impulse when she'd come in alone one afternoon in the first flush of wedding plans. Putting her hand on her baby bump, she thought how much had changed since that afternoon several months ago.

Harper ran a hand towel under the cool water from the marble faucet and patted her cheeks, breathing slowly. Then she stared at herself in the mirror. She was paler than usual and her blue eyes were rimmed with smudges of fatigue.

There was a soft knock on the door. She heard Granny James's voice. "Harper? Are you all right?"

"Yes. Fine. I'll be out in a minute."

There was a long pause, then: "Very well. I'll wait for you with the rest of the girls."

Harper took several more deep breaths, rearranged her hair, and left the bathroom. Lauren was waiting for her and guided her to a large dressing room with white chairs and heavy, white-framed floor-to-ceiling mirrors. She immediately saw her gown hanging on a hook, waiting for her. Her breath caught on a sigh as she hurried to the dress and tentatively reached out to touch the embroidered bodice.

"It's as lovely as I remember," she said softly.

"Of course it is," Lauren said cheerfully. "It's one of my favorites. Feeling better?"

Harper turned to face her and shook her head. "I don't think I'll be feeling better for several more weeks." She smiled. "I'm pregnant."

Understanding flashed across Lauren's face, swiftly followed by concern. "How far along are you?"

"Second trimester. Near four months."

"And the wedding date is when, remind me?"

"The end of May."

Lauren began counting on her fingers. "Well," she said in a long, tentative drawl, "by then you'll have a baby bump." She glanced at the gown. "With some gowns, like an A-line or Empire style, we can make alterations to the dress quite easily. But with the gown you selected, I fear it will be difficult." Lauren grimaced. "The bodice is intricately constructed with embroidery, and the waist is so tight."

Tears stung Harper's eyes. "I know," she said softly. "I've been worried about that."

"Oh, don't cry." Lauren rushed for a tissue. She strove for optimism. "Let's try it on, shall we? You're so small, perhaps we can make it work. We won't know until we see what we have to work with, right? I'll put you in the dress, then I'll call for our alterations head. Alva is a miracle worker."

Lauren was efficient at smoothly slipping Harper into the gorgeous gown, but Harper could already feel the gown pulling at the waist, where months before the folds had fallen across her frame in perfect harmony. Harper sucked in her breath, but it didn't make any difference. Her baby bump was barely visible yet, but it did make the small waistline of the gown feel extremely tight. Nonetheless, Lauren managed to fasten all the buttons. Harper could barely breathe. She turned to face the mirror.

It was a moment she'd never forget. Her heart melted at seeing herself in the luminous gown. The sweetheart, strapless neckline featured a heavily embroidered bodice in old-world guipure. The bodice was corseted to fit tightly, accentuating her small waist before exploding in tulle. Little girls, herself included, dreamed of seeing themselves in a gown such as this. Yet seeing it again, Harper didn't quite remember its being so . . . so the dress of a Disney princess.

"Shall we show your family?"

Harper nodded, lifting the folds of fabric as she followed Lauren into the waiting area, imagining how she would possibly move in this dress on her wedding day. The dress was heavy and constricting, especially at her waist where the stays dug into her skin.

Great shafts of light flowed into the room through the large front windows. With the brick walls, the wood floors, and bouquets of fresh flowers, Harper felt as if she were a deer walking into an open meadow. Carson, Dora, Mamaw, and Granny James were sitting waiting for her in the plush chairs, arms and legs crossed. Harper pasted a wide smile on her face and walked with studied grace onto the small platform set before a wall of mirrors. She pirouetted daintily, then dropped the fabric from her hands and looked at her entourage expectantly. Carson's brow was raised with indecision. Mamaw's head was tilted in thought. Granny James's face was a classic study of the old British stiff upper lip. Only Dora wore a broad smile on her face.

"Well?" Harper asked breathlessly. "What do you think?"

"I love it!" Dora exclaimed with unbridled enthusiasm. "It's so beautiful. You look just like a princess!"

Harper smiled tremulously. That was just the comment she'd been hoping not to hear. She looked to Carson.

Carson said thoughtfully, "It is a beautiful gown." She paused and her brows furrowed. "But . . . a princess gown? Tulle? You always wear very minimalist, chic styles. I don't know, Sis, it just doesn't seem like *you*."

Harper felt this criticism stab at her heart. Her smile fell and she looked to Mamaw, expecting support.

"It's lovely, dear. You are a beautiful bride," Mamaw said sincerely.

Harper heard hesitation. "But . . ."

"Well, I don't know, dear. The dress feels so . . . naïve. Is that the right word? A young bride looks sweet in a cloud of white silk and tulle. But according to Emily Post, a bride in her thirties or older might do well to choose a creamy or off-white color. As would, perhaps, a woman who is already sharing a home with her intended." Mamaw paused, then said delicately, "And is in a family way."

Harper felt the color drain from her cheeks.

"Mamaw!" Dora exclaimed, breathless with shock. "What

era are you living in? Women wear all colors these days. White, cream, pink, blue, even black. And by the way, Harper's only twenty-nine."

"I'm aware of that," Mamaw said, clearly ruffled. She lifted her chin. "I'm only telling you what I was raised to believe. What others might very well think."

"I can't believe you just said that, Mamaw," Carson said hotly, reproach ringing in her voice. "You just shot a volley over all our bows. We're all sleeping with our *intendeds*, as you put it. Does that mean none of us can wear white? And by the way, so are you! Only he's not even your intended."

Mamaw's mouth slipped open in shock. "What?"

Granny James, who had remained remarkably silent so far, swung around to stare at Mamaw with more amusement than surprise.

"I saw you having breakfast with Girard," Carson said. "In your robe. On his porch. And your bed wasn't slept in. I know. I checked."

Dora chuckled and wagged her brows. "My, my, my. Look who's calling the kettle black."

Mamaw's cheeks flamed and she clenched her hands together. "I'm sorry if I've offended you with any impropriety, Carson."

"Oh, for heaven's sake, Mamaw," Carson said, frustrated. "No one's offended by what you're doing with Girard, but by what you just said. Words can be hurtful." She looked pointedly at Harper.

Harper stood quietly on the stage, appearing a lost waif in all the fabric.

Mamaw's face fell with remorse. "I'm so sorry. I didn't mean . . . Don't pay me no mind. I'm just an old fuddy-duddy. Truly, Harper dear, it wasn't meant to hurt you."

An awkward silence followed until Lauren tried to take back control of the appointment. "Choosing a bride gown is always an emotional event. Let's try to remember that Harper is the bride and what matters is what *she* wants. And, yes, brides wear every color today. The only question of white today is simply a matter of how well it looks against the skin of the bride. And I think the dress is beautiful on Harper."

"Granny James?" Harper called out, trying to keep up a positive façade despite the lackluster overall reaction of the group thus far. "I haven't heard your opinion."

All heads turned to the woman sitting at the end of the line of chairs.

Granny James had maintained a stoic silence during the outbursts. Too silent. Her face was solemn. "If you love the dress, then that's all that matters."

Harper felt a surge of gratitude. It was short-lived.

"However"—Carson swung her head and looked over her knee to stare at Granny James with a glare of warning. It went unnoticed—"it is a beach wedding. That dress, while lovely, is clearly more formal. Are you sure it's in theme with the wedding? I'm not sure that it is. But"—she waved her fingers delicately in the air—"it's entirely up to you, of course."

The room fell again into silence. Tears filled Harper's eyes and she lowered her head, defeated. No one liked the dress, save Dora. And bless her heart, Dora would love any dress Harper put on.

"Perhaps if I jack her up," Lauren said, forcing cheer into

her voice. "Put on a veil, add some jewelry. You'll get the full effect."

"No," Harper said. "Thank you. I don't feel up to it. I'd like to take it off now, please."

Lauren cast a sad glance tinged with disapproval at the entourage. "Of course." She lent her hand to Harper and helped her off the platform.

After Harper left, the room went deathly silent.

Eventually Granny James said, "Tell me, Marietta, what edition of Emily Post was it that said a bride had to be a virgin to wear white? The one published in the 1920s?" Granny James shook her head disbelievingly. "*Debrett's* is quite clear on the subject. A bride can wear any color she chooses, and these days she does."

"Oh, don't be a hypocrite," Mamaw shot back. "You know as well as I do that no matter what the book says to the young people today, people of our generation will be thinking about the old rules. We have to face that Harper will be visibly pregnant on her wedding day. I just wanted her to choose a dress that was more . . ."

"Concealing?" asked Carson with pique.

"I was going to say *appropriate*, but, yes, *concealing* works even better."

"What do we care what anyone else thinks?" Carson responded. "All I know is that she's feeling badly right now."

"Perhaps I should go talk to her?" Mamaw asked softly.

"I think it's best to let her be for a few minutes," Granny James said, concern for Harper in her tone. "She'll feel better once she gets that dress off." She sighed. "I have to agree with you on one point. There's no possible way they can adjust that cut to fit her when she's five months along."

"You might've all thought of that before y'all started baying like hunting dogs," Dora said reproachfully. "The end would've been the same. She'd have figured out she needed a new dress all on her own. But, no, you had to tear that dress to shreds first."

No one spoke, the silence hanging heavy over the room.

Lauren came back out a few moments later and asked brightly, "Carson, you're the next bride, is that right?" The woman was trying to be positive, but the buoyancy of the day had clearly popped like a balloon. "Have you tried on dresses before?"

"Yes," Carson said without enthusiasm. "A few."

Dora guffawed behind her palm.

"Ah, good. So you have an idea of what you're looking for?"

Carson shook her head. "Not a clue."

Lauren's face fell. Still, she was not dissuaded. "Let's bring you on back to the fitting room and we'll try on a few styles and see what you like."

Carson shook her head. "Not today, thanks. I'll reschedule." She glanced down the line of chairs, nailing Mamaw and Granny James with a hard gaze. "I'd rather come alone."

Chapter Seventeen

Being married means we're in it together. Married couples ought to protect each other by being fair and generous in all ways, including financially.

The moon was rising over Sullivan's Island, bringing with it an ethereal glow that rivaled that of the shimmering stars. Despite the glory of the night, however, not all was peaceful on the earth below.

At Sea Breeze, Harper stood at her bedroom window staring out at the Cove. She never tired of the way moonlight seemed to dance over the water. The sight usually calmed her, but tonight she felt as though the water were dark and stormy and she were being tossed about as helplessly as a piece of driftwood.

She closed the slats of the plantation shutters and let her glance take in the small anteroom that was attached to the master bedroom, the silver-framed photographs of the family on bookshelves and tables. When Mamaw lived here, this had been her sitting room. Harper fondly recalled the many heart-to-hearts she'd shared with her grandmother in the cushy upholstered chairs here. Mamaw had surprised Harper the summer before by redecorating the sitting room into a bedroom so that Harper would have her own room at Sea Breeze. Mamaw had put in sliding doors to separate the two rooms, effectively cutting off half of her own space, just for her granddaughter. And now, only a year later, the room was undergoing another change.

This was going to be Harper's baby's nursery. She was filled with butterflies whenever she thought of her sweet infant soon to be in this room. It was empty now, painted a soft gray and white. Harper walked across the soft white carpet, imagining where she would put the baby's crib, the changing table. Would she highlight the room with the color pink or blue? She smiled, knowing they'd wait till the baby's birth to find out.

Harper looked beyond the nursery to her bed. Taylor lay there reading a book, bare chested and wearing only flannel pajama bottoms, as was his way. He saved the matching tops for Harper—on her small frame they went almost to her knees. Her heart filled with love for him. That's how she saw them, two parts of the same piece. How was she going to ask him for a prenup? Would he accept it without a care? Or would it be like a knife that cut the fabric that bound them? She sighed heavily and brought her hands to her face.

The bedroom was aglow with soft yellow light from bedside lamps on either side of the bed. She switched off the lamp on her side of the bed, then climbed in. Taylor absently reached out to slip his strong arm around her and tug her close. She nestled against his broad chest, her cheek against his skin.

Harper stared at nothing as she reviewed the events of the day in her mind. She'd hoped the visit to the bridal salon with her grandmothers and sisters would have been the springboard for the joy of the wedding season. She'd pictured them loving her dress, fawning over every detail of it as she had when she'd first put it on.

It's not you, Carson had said.

It doesn't fit the beach theme of the wedding was Granny James's opinion.

And Mamaw's old-fashioned ideas, straight from an ancient *Emily Post's Etiquette* book, simply hurt.

Only Dora had been kind, clearly recalling how sensitive and vulnerable the bride could feel, posing in a dress with her heart on her sleeve. She'd never forget Dora's support. When she'd tried to thank her privately after the appointment, Dora had kissed her cheek and told her it was simply payback for the kindness Harper had shown her the previous summer at a certain dress salon. Sisters, Harper thought. What would she do without them?

And Harper knew that Carson always had her back. Harper trusted her. The hard truth was that, after all the comments, Harper had felt uncomfortable in the gown she'd selected, as if she were wearing someone else's dress. Someone younger, more naïve—the very word that Mamaw had used. Harper knew she was many things—smart, occasionally timid, reserved, and, yes, perhaps she did possess a certain innocence, but she was *not* naïve. Perhaps Carson had been right. The dress was not *her*. Harper could no longer see herself walking down the aisle in it.

Taylor shifted his gaze from his book and kissed the top of her head. "What's the matter, honey? Can't sleep?"

At the sound of his master's voice, Thor stopped his sonorous snoring and abruptly lifted his head, ears alert.

"No," Harper replied in a broken voice.

Taylor lowered his book and turned slightly to face Harper. With his finger, he lifted her chin to study her face. Harper tried to look away, but his hand was firm. He frowned when he saw the tears.

"What's the matter?" he repeated, this time with intent. "More wedding woes? Because if it is, I swear, Harper, we'll elope. I don't want you upset by all this nonsense. It's not good for the baby. I don't care about how we get married. I just want to make you my wife. The sooner the better."

Harper offered a tremulous smile filled with gratitude. "It's not the wedding that has me upset. Well, not entirely." She paused, remembering the afternoon. "We all went to the salon today. Me, the girls, and grandmothers. I showed them my dress." She paused. "They hated it."

Taylor seemed surprised, even angry. "Who the hell cares? You're the one wearing it."

"I know. But now, I hate it, too."

"Don't let them bully you. It's your dress. I'll love it no matter what."

She didn't respond. She appreciated his support, even expected it. But she didn't want to discuss her wedding dress with him. Bless his heart, but he didn't know the first thing about wedding dresses. She patted his chest idly, finding strength. Rather than get distracted by the dress, she wanted to bring up the topic at the forefront of her mind.

She moved from the crook of his arm to sit cross-legged beside him. The pajama top rode high up her thighs. Harper tugged at the sheet, covering her legs. Seeing that she was intending a serious discussion, Taylor marked his place in the book and put it on the bedside table, then turned to give her his complete attention.

She felt the power of his green-eyed gaze and licked her lips, finding the strength to continue. "Today was tough. Aside from what happened with the dress, to start off, this morning I had tea with Granny James, and she came up with the brilliant suggestion that we call my mother to tell her the baby news."

"What?" Taylor sounded both surprised and angry.

"I know. Stupid, but we did. Mummy was cool at first, which was no surprise. But then, when I told her about the baby, she actually said she was happy for me. And congratulations. That's all it took for me to melt into a blubbering pool. I was so *grateful*. Can you imagine? Grateful my mother told me congratulations. Oh, Taylor, when will I ever learn?"

Taylor shook his head in sympathy, eyes trained on her, his facial expression unmoving but his green gaze glowing like embers in a fire.

"Then she used the baby to make me feel like it was my responsibility to take over Greenfields Park for Granny and Papa. That's when I lost it. I told her off." Harper smiled at him. "It felt good."

Taylor's face softened and he leaned in to kiss her. His lips were soft yet strong, comforting. "That's my girl. I knew you had it in you. I don't mind telling you, that was a long time coming."

"Yeah." Though inside Harper's heart, she didn't feel her struggles with her mother were over. Far from it. She looked over at Taylor. His handsome face was relaxed again and he leaned back against his pillows. "Taylor, there's one more thing. My grandmother wants us to sign a prenuptial agreement." Harper didn't mean to blurt it out like this. She'd practiced how she would broach the subject, but the words just tumbled out.

Taylor's eyes widened, but he didn't comment. He moved back into an upright position, resting his elbows on his thighs, and stared unseeingly at some point in the room, silently taking in all that the words implied.

At length he said with a short laugh, "Have to admit, I didn't see that one coming."

"Nor did I."

"Explain, please."

Taylor was always most calm and succinct when he was tense. This was but one of the many things she'd learned about this man during the past year. Things such as how he liked her to fall asleep on his shoulder at night, the slanted gaze he sent her way when she was teasing him, his stoic silence when he was angry, how he didn't like cologne and yet smelled so good just with shaving cream, the way his brows creased when he concentrated or was worried, the idle way he stroked Thor's head when the dog sat beside him, and the way he let his fingertips glide along her arm when she talked to him. He was extraordinarily thoughtful and kind. It was as though with his being so large, his gentleness provided balance.

"It started with Granny telling me that she sold Greenfields Park. I know," Harper said, seeing Taylor's surprise. "That's huge. And with Papa Jeffrey in the home without mental acuity, Granny's in the process of making significant changes to her will." Harper took a breath. "She suggested—more like demanded—that we have a prenuptial agreement in place as soon as possible."

His gaze hardened. "Demanded, huh?" He reached back and grabbed a pillow and squeezed it in his hands. "I wish I could say I was surprised by that. She's never fully believed I'm not after you for your money."

"No, Taylor, that's not it at all. She loves you. She even told me that she had faith that you'd have no problem with this because you're so strong and practical. And you love me. Granny is just looking toward the future. She has to. She has a huge estate to protect. The way she put it is that by doing this, family money stays in the family to be passed down from generation to generation." Harper had been thinking about this all afternoon, and the idea of a prenup was beginning to make sense to her. "Why should all that my grandparents built be at risk when someone new marries into the family?"

"At risk? That's how you see marrying me?" Taylor tossed the pillow across the room.

"No!" Harper suddenly felt sick. She could see Taylor beginning to blow up. This was her worst nightmare coming true. "Of course not. I love you. I trust you."

"But you don't trust me with your money."

"I do!" Harper cried, and put her hands over her face. "I don't care about my money. You know that. I never have. But it's not just the money, can't you see? It's the estate, the family property. That's more important than just money. Granny James is rather insisting. Oh, Taylor, I don't know what I should do."

Taylor rubbed his forehead with agitation, then let his hand drop. He reached out again to bring Harper close to his chest. She slunk into his arms and wrapped hers around him.

"I don't want this to come between us," she said miserably.

"It won't," he said in a low voice. "We won't let it."

Harper sniffed and wiped her eyes, feeling suddenly a world better.

"It's just the way I see it," Taylor continued, "is being married means we're in it together. Married couples ought to protect each other by being fair and generous in all ways, including financially. So it strikes me that starting our marriage with financial negotiations and withholding property isn't a very good way to begin a relationship that should be built on love, trust, and mutual protection."

"I agree with the heart of what you're saying. Really, I do, and I said just as much to my sisters earlier this afternoon. If I weren't the heir to the James estate, we wouldn't even be having this discussion. But the fact is, I am. That puts a different slant on things. But a prenup would be simply protecting property that has been in my family for generations."

"Still, there's no way it won't disturb the balance of power in our marriage. You'll control all of our finances. I'll always feel like it's your money at the end of the day, your decisions. That'll make me feel less than an equal partner."

"Taylor, Sea Breeze is already in my name and you don't have a problem with that."

He looked at her, his brow raised mockingly. "I don't?"

"What?" she exclaimed, shocked. "Do you?"

"Of course I do. But your grandmother bought you this place. What was I going to say? No, I won't live here with you?"

"I'm going to repay Granny once I get my trust fund."

"What difference does it make? I didn't buy the house. Nor could I. Not in several lifetimes. And you using *your* trust-fund money"—Harper didn't miss the emphasis he placed on *your*—"to repay your grandmother won't make Sea Breeze feel any more like mine. Like ours."

"Don't you like living here?"

"What's not to like? Except, it feels like I'm living in *your* house. Because, frankly, it is."

"I didn't know that's how you saw things." The words slowly dropped into her brain like stones into a deep, empty well. She was silent a moment, then asked in a whisper, "Do you want to move? Is that what you want?"

"Frankly, as long as you're asking, I have to say I wouldn't mind it."

Harper moved her head to look up at him. She couldn't believe what she was hearing.

"Harper, look. It hasn't been easy moving into this place, knowing it was paid for by you. It's beyond anything I could afford. Hell, I'm not even paying rent."

"That's not true. You're paying for all the maintenance and household bills. You buy the groceries. It's an expensive house to maintain."

"Well, I can afford those ancillary expenses," he replied flip-

pantly, "especially since I didn't even have to buy you a ring."
He picked up her left hand and let his thumb run over the large
mine-cut diamond on her ring finger. It had been a gift from
Mamaw on her engagement, a ring that Harper had always
loved. "Some would say your grandmothers have made my life
very easy. I'm sure some think it in not the kindest way, either.
But they'd be wrong. I feel like a freeloader."

"Oh," Harper said, crestfallen. She didn't know his feelings
about all this ran so strong. "I'm sorry. I had no idea."

"I didn't want you to feel I wasn't grateful or that I was
being small-minded. It's a great house. I just don't feel like it's
our house."

Harper slid down beside him on the bed and laid her head
again on his shoulder. She didn't want him to see the crushing
disappointment on her face. "Maybe we should consider selling," she said in a choked voice.

"Maybe we should."

Harper swallowed hard, closing her eyes tight. She'd
expected him to counter her offer, to tell her, *No, of course not.
This is our home.* Or something along those lines. The thought
of selling Sea Breeze, leaving this place she loved, filled her
with despair. She moved from his shoulder to her side of the
bed, her back to him.

There was no point in trying to deny her true feelings. "I
love this house," she said in a shaky voice. "This is more than
just a place to live to me. It's my touchstone. I have memories
here. Family. I spent the past year tending the house and garden
with thoughts that it would be our forever home. Where we'd
raise this baby, and hopefully others. Where you and I would
grow old together."

For a long time Taylor did not say anything. Then he reached over to turn off his bedside light and settled on his back on his side of the bed.

"Let's sleep on it," Taylor said into the darkness. "This is a lot to think about. In the meantime, I'll talk to Imogene about this whole prenup business."

"No, I will."

"No," Taylor said in a voice that brooked no further discussion. "I will."

Chapter Eighteen

*What being a good parent is about—what being a spouse is about—
is no longer thinking only of yourself or your self-interests.*

*T*he month of May had arrived as fast as sand through
Carson's fingers. With Dora's stalwart support and unfailing
advice, Carson and Harper had crossed off items on the to-do
list one after the other. Carson was beginning to get into the
flow of being a bride. She still hadn't found her dress, but her
goodie bags were done, her hairstyle set, and Blake's ring was
in the safe. She was sitting at her bedroom desk going through
today's mail. The RSVPs were beginning to roll in and most
were acceptances—even a few she'd thought would be a no.
Apparently Charleston was a destination people wanted to
visit, on top of wanting to celebrate with the young couple.

Her phone rang. She reached out to grab it, eyes still on her
acceptance list. "Hello?"

"Hello, is this Carson Muir?"

"Yes, it is."

"Hi, Carson, this is Jennifer at the aquarium."

"Oh!" Carson felt a flutter of excitement. She sat straighter, her attention focused. "Thank you so much for getting back in touch."

"I'm sorry we kept you waiting. I'm calling you to tell you that after much discussion, we've decided to go in a different direction and we won't be hiring a PR director at this time. You were one of the strongest candidates and we'd like to keep your résumé on file should something else open up. But for now, I'm very sorry that we don't have a position to offer you."

Carson listened in a daze as the flow of words floated in one ear and out the other. The only words she fully caught were *I'm sorry*. After that, nothing else mattered. She didn't get the job.

After several more moments of platitudes, she and Jennifer bid each other a polite good-bye, and Carson dropped her phone on her bed. A moment later, she, too, fell on the bed and covered her face with her palms. She didn't have a job. No job. She'd waited for several weeks for them to get back to her, fully expecting to be hired. Precious time that she didn't have, with no other real prospects on the horizon. What was she going to do now?

Without pausing to think, Carson picked her phone back up and dialed the number she knew by heart.

After she hung up the phone, Carson spent an hour staring despondently at her bedroom ceiling, then rinsed her face with cold water and drove to Blake's apartment on Sullivan's Island. He was working on a report at home so she knew he'd be there.

His apartment building was once a bachelor officer quarters, built around 1900 when the island had a large military presence. The old white wood building had since been converted to apartments. Typical of a wooden building near the ocean with a brick foundation, the exterior needed some work, but with its long porch and the ocean nearby, Blake was lucky to have his apartment, as these were some of the few for rent on the island.

Carson knocked on Blake's door and heard the familiar gruff bark of warning from Hobbs. The door swung open and Blake's face was before her. His hair was unbrushed, curls askew. His dark eyes widened when he saw her, unexpected, at his door.

"Hey, baby," he said as a crooked smile of pleasure eased across his handsome face. "I didn't expect to see you till tonight." Leaning forward, he kissed her. She tasted something deliciously bitter and tangy on his lips and, looking down, saw he carried a beer in his hand. He was careful not to drink when she was around, an effort she deeply appreciated, and he now tried to discreetly tuck the bottle behind his back. Hobbs immediately came to sniff it.

"Don't stop on my account," she said irritably, passing Blake as she walked into the room. "Better yet, why don't you have a drink for both of us."

Blake's smile collapsed to a frown. He held the door a moment, inhaled deeply, then closed the door and followed her into the small living room, pausing only to set the beer bottle on top of a stack of mail on the front table.

Carson went to the brown nubby sofa that seemed ubiquitous in bachelor apartments. She plopped down and idly glanced around, her fingers tapping her thighs.

This, she thought, was the place she was supposed to call

home in a short while. She felt a cloud of dismay float over her. It looked more like a college student's apartment than a career man's home. How could he not see that books and magazines sat everywhere in tilting piles, that his torn leather La-Z-Boy looked more like a holder of laundry? The sisal rug had been chewed in one corner by Hobbs, and she didn't even want to count the food stains. In the corners and under tables were tumbleweeds of Hobbs's hair.

Her gaze roved to the galley kitchen, which was part of the open plan of the apartment. He didn't have dirty dishes lying everywhere, thank heavens. Blake was careful about bugs. But he was clueless about the purpose of cabinets. The counters were cluttered with boxes of cereal, bags of bread and rolls, and electronics plugged into the wall.

The trouble was that she was as bad as, or worse than, Blake at housekeeping. Didn't couples try to find someone who was the opposite so that they complemented each other? How would they ever manage living together? Suddenly Carson felt desperate that she'd be leaving the spacious and beautiful Sea Breeze for this cramped, bland apartment.

The whole wedding—the thought of getting married—suddenly made her feel anxious and just plain scared. She used to be able to tone down her insecurities with a drink—and she craved one now more than she had in months. It was a physical ache. So she clenched her hands and knees and tried to physically hold herself together. It felt as if she were holding back a bomb about to go off.

Hobbs ambled by, tail wagging, and gently nudged her knee with his nose. It was wet, cold, and slobbery. She usually gave the dog a good rubdown when she came in, but today she couldn't. "Go away," she barked at him, pushing his big block head away.

The big yellow Lab stood for a moment, looking wounded, as though wondering what was wrong.

"Hobbs, settle," Blake ordered as he drew near.

Hobbs cast a final baleful look at Carson and obeyed the command, his nails clicking on the hardwood floor as he trotted to the corner where his bed lay. He settled onto the cushion with a grumpy grunt.

Blake didn't sit. He leaned against the kitchen-island counter, resting his elbows on it. His dark brows were gathered and he was watching her warily.

"Carson. Tell me what's going on."

"I didn't get the job at the aquarium."

He sighed in understanding. Pushing himself from the counter, he took long strides and was at her side in an instant. "I'm sorry."

"Me, too."

"It's only one job. You'll find another."

"Yeah, sure."

He paused, taking in her mood. "Okay, your dukes are up. You're looking for a fight. I don't want to fight." He rose to his feet. "Want some coffee?"

No, she wanted to scream. She wanted some tequila. Vodka. "Sure. Thanks."

She stared out the window, through the cheap vinyl blinds, at the trees outside, listening to the noises coming from the kitchen. She knew what she wanted to tell him, but knew if she said the words, Blake might end their engagement. She clenched her hands. She really, really wanted that drink now.

She heard the clicking noises of his automatic coffeemaker and a moment later caught the scent of java in the air. "Smells good."

"Milk and sugar?"

"Thanks." Her voice was still petulant.

Blake carried the mug of steaming coffee to the wood coffee table. "Careful, it's hot. Better let it cool a minute."

Carson stared at the creamy brown liquid, her hands clasped between her knees.

Blake grabbed an armchair and sat in it, his eyes on her. "Carson?"

"What?"

"What did they say?"

"They're going in a different direction. I have a great résumé. They'd like to hang on to it. But no."

"Okay, that's a good rejection."

"Oh, yeah, it's really great," she snapped sarcastically.

"I know it's not what you were hoping would happen. I'm disappointed, too. But it's not the end of the world. Hey, something just popped up this week. Something you might really like. Maybe even better."

"Not now, Blake."

"Why not now?" Urgency entered his voice. "Just listen. It's with Waterkeepers of Charleston. They're a great nonprofit. They—"

"I already have another job."

Blake silenced and tilted his head to look at her with a guarded gaze. "What job is that?"

"You know what job. With Jason Kowalski. I called him to find out what the status was. He told me it was a good thing I'd reached out because he was in the process of getting his team for the film together. It's going to be a major film. Big budget."

It felt as though the temperature in the room had just dropped twenty degrees. Blake's face was set. "So you took it?"

"I told him I'd let him know by the end of the week."

Blake looked vaguely out the window. "I thought you were going to give us until the wedding to find you a job. That's a month away. We'd agreed."

"I know." Carson looked down at the table. Saw the coffee cooling. A scented candle, already half-burned off.

"Then why are you rushing it?"

"I'm not rushing anything. I called to check in. I have to make a decision by the end of the week or this job is gone."

Blake swung his head around. "What the hell do you care if this job is gone?"

Carson didn't look up. "I care. I think I want to take it."

Blake reached out and put his hands on her shoulders. "Carson, look at me and explain why you want to take this job, knowing what that would mean. For us."

Carson leaned back so Blake's hands fell from her shoulders. She still couldn't meet his eyes. "You know how I feel. I . . . I wanted things—to change. I hoped—I'd find something here." She looked up at him. "But it's not happening. You say you have another job possibility. We both know it will end up being the same story: I won't have the right credentials, or I'll not be right for what they're looking for, or it's really just a courtesy because they already have someone on the inside they want to hire. This can go on for months and months." She stopped and said loudly, angrily, "I can't just keep applying, and hoping. And waiting. I'm not good at standing still, Blake. You know that. I have to keep moving." She shook her head in confirmation. "I can't just sit around and do nothing. I can't."

Blake looked off again, his jaw working furiously. When he turned back to her, his face was rigid. "Are you breaking our engagement?"

She looked at him in shock. "No." She shook her head. "I'm asking you to still go through with the wedding if I take this job."

Blake leaned back against the cushions, his shoulders drooped in defeat. "I'm sorry, Carson. I can't do that. I know I don't have the right to make this decision for you. I only know I can't go through another six months like the last."

So, Carson thought to herself. It sounded as if they were giving each other their bottom lines. She wondered what Atticus would advise now. "What do we do?" She looked down at the diamond on her hand.

"Are you asking out of politeness, or do you really want my answer?"

"I want your honest answer," she said bluntly. "Of course."

He looked at her, and though his face was calm, his eyes were dark with intent. "Okay then. I know what I think you should do. Contact Charleston Waterkeepers, the Coastal Conservation League, NOAA, and every other nonprofit and profit organization that deals with environmental subjects you can sink your teeth into and send a blitz of résumés out there. Frankly, you sat on your ass for the past month and assumed you'd get the aquarium job. Well, you didn't. Now you say you've only got a few days to decide. So you'd better get cracking, girl. That's what I think you should do. Fight for us, baby." Blake took a breath. "Or break it off now. Don't make me hope if there's nothing to hope for."

Carson sucked in her breath. She heard what he was asking, knew it was fair. Blake was always fair. Now she had to be fair, as well. She looked down at the ring on her finger, the small diamond bordered on each side with a sapphire. The ring that had been his mother's. The ring that had helped keep her sober when she was out of town because when she looked at it, she saw Blake's face.

"All right, I will. I do want to marry you. I don't want to break off our engagement."

Blake released a sigh. "Do you still want that drink?"

"Yes," she replied honestly. "But then I always want a drink. I don't want it as badly as I did when I walked in."

"Do you need to call Bill?"

Bill was her sponsor. She shook her head. "I'm okay. I thought I needed to, but not now. Though, I might give Atticus a call."

"Sounds good. I'm glad you feel you can talk to him." Blake reached down and took her fingers and held them in his. Gently he stroked the inside of her palms with his thumb. "You can always talk to me, too, you know."

"I know." Then she laughed shortly. "Except I need to talk about you."

"Okay." He laughed, too, though there was no humor in it. He brought her fingers to his lips. "Are we still on for dinner?"

"I don't want to go out. I want to get cracking, as you put it. Want to come over and we can work on them together?"

"Yeah," he said, brightening. "I'll bring sushi."

"Sounds great."

They'd reached an impasse. There wasn't anything left to say.

Carson rose to leave. In the corner, Hobbs saw the movement and immediately climbed to his feet and trotted toward her. Carson, hoping to make up for her rude behavior earlier, gave him a generous pat and back scratch, sending tiny golden hairs flying in the air.

"See you in a little bit," Blake said, and kissed her gently on the lips. She felt his warm breath, waited, hoping he would kiss her again.

But he didn't.

Carson felt the chill when his arms slid from her shoulders. She smiled quickly as she said good-bye, then turned and walked head bent to her car, aware that he was watching her. She'd found a parking spot not far from the house, yet by the time she'd reached the car and turned to wave once more, Blake was already gone.

Atticus was sitting at the dining-room table of his condominium writing a sermon for Sunday. He'd been asked to fill in for the pastor of Morris Baptist Church while he went to a conference. Atticus gladly agreed. He needed to get back in the pulpit. Preaching gave his life purpose and meaning. The Reverend Manigault at Ebenezer Baptist Church in Atlanta had been wise to urge him to take a sabbatical in the lowcountry for as long as he needed. Atticus was doing more than forging new relationships. He was forming a new identity.

His sermon was on honesty. Something he'd spent a lot of time praying about in the past weeks. During that time he'd slowly gotten to know the Muir family, though he knew he'd only scratched the surface. A lot was bubbling underneath that he wanted to tap into. He'd spent several hours chatting with both couples—Carson and Blake, Harper and Taylor—but for the most part everyone was being on their best behavior in the small groups, keeping things vague. No one was digging into serious issues. Usually Atticus would have taken the gloves off by this point and started probing deeper, getting the couples to open up more. He felt that he hadn't seen anything real, raw, and truly honest since that morning out on the water with Carson and Delphine.

Yet in all fairness, he'd never before been in a situation like this. First, they weren't parishioners. Second, they weren't even Southern Baptists. And third, how could he ask for honesty from them when he was living a lie, or omission—whatever he chose to call it.

He didn't know if he could continue the charade much longer. The dishonesty of the arrangement with Mamaw tainted everything he did or said with his sisters. And even if he wanted to tell them the truth, the question was, how could he? How could he drop the news that he was their brother after having spent the past weeks denying them that knowledge?

His cell phone rang. He reached for it.

"Hi, Atticus?"

"Harper?"

A light, nervous laugh. "Yes, it's me."

His heart warmed for this particular sister, close to his age, tenderhearted. Of his three sisters, she seemed the most fragile. He readily understood Taylor's inclination to be her knight in shining armor.

"What's going on?"

"I really need to talk to you. In person. Do you have time?"

"Is it urgent?"

"Yes," she said in a soft voice.

He heard the anxiety in her voice as though she'd shouted the word. "I'm working now. Can I swing by in two hours?"

"Thanks." Her relief was audible. "I'll make tea. See you then."

He hung up the phone and started back at his sermon. Then the front doorbell rang. Who could that be? he wondered, pushing back his chair and rising. He crossed the tiled floor and swung open the door.

Carson stood at the door carrying two Starbucks coffees. "Surprise."

"Come in," he said, glad to see her, but curious what she'd come for. Other than Dora, no one in the family had come by his condo yet.

"Nice place," she said, looking around. Like him, she was drawn immediately to the view. "I always love the view of the Cove until I see the view of the ocean. I go back and forth. But this is pretty up here. How long do you have it for?"

"Till June."

"Then what?"

"I go back to Atlanta. At least until I get my permanent location. In the meantime, I'm working at a few local parishes, helping where I can."

"While you do your research."

"What?" he asked, uncomprehending.

"While you do your research. That's what you said you were in Charleston to do."

"Oh, yeah," he said quickly, remembering what he'd told them the day he'd arrived. "Of course."

"What are you working on now?" She walked toward the table filled with papers, several of them balled up in the trash.

"My sermon for Sunday."

She studied him a moment. "Do you ever get nervous up there? With all those people listening to you, hoping to be inspired. I'd think it would be daunting."

Atticus shook his head. "Maybe before I speak I get a little nervous. Not stage fright exactly. More that I hope that my message is received. That I find the right words. Once I begin to preach and feel the spirit of the Lord, I just let her rip."

She nodded, lips pinched, and looked out the window to the ocean.

"So, what's up, Carson? Want to talk about anything in particular?"

"You must be so bored of hearing my problems by now."

He laughed. "What? No way. They're mesmerizing."

"Very funny. Seriously, we Muirs are really keeping you on your toes."

"It's par for the course with weddings," Atticus said, hoping to reassure her. "Brides and grooms always end up having more questions than they thought. You wouldn't be normal if you didn't. So sit down and let's drink that coffee. It smells great. Then you can tell me what's on your mind."

Carson sat at the table and pried open the lid of her coffee. Atticus sat across from her and took a sip of the hot brew. He felt the caffeine flowing through his veins, waking him up a bit after his struggles with his sermon.

"So, I had some news."

"Good news?"

"Bad. I didn't get the job at the aquarium. But I did get the job in California. So now I have to decide if I'm going to stay here and find a job and marry Blake. Or"—she stretched out the word—"I take the film job and break off my engagement."

"You've been bouncing back and forth on this issue since I met you."

"Yeah, well, I've been bouncing around pretty much my whole life."

"Why do you think that is?"

She looked at him as if he were stupid to ask. "My father."

"Parker?" Atticus was keenly interested in learning about their father. "How is he responsible?"

Carson snorted derisively. "I'm sorry, I just have a hard time hearing the name *Parker Muir* with the word *responsible*. He was anything but."

Atticus didn't respond. He picked up his cup and took a long sip, allowing Carson time to continue.

She looked at her cup for a minute. "Parker—my father—struggled with his alcoholism all his adult life. Unfortunately, it fell to me to care for him rather than the other way around. I was only eight when we moved to California. It was a pretty ghastly childhood. I spent a lot of nights going out to bars looking for him so I could bring him home. I cleaned the house, bought the groceries. Money was always tight. I used to take some out of his wallet while he was sleeping just to have money to buy us food. He made some money on his writing. God knows he tried hard. And there was always that monthly check from Papa Edward. But he couldn't manage to pay his bills. So"—she brought the cup to her lips—"we moved from place to place a lot." She drank her coffee.

Atticus was stunned. He hadn't thought it could've been so

bad for her. "Your grandmother let you live like that without interfering?"

"She didn't know. I only told her the truth about it all after Parker died."

Atticus didn't want to criticize, but he thought her grand-parents were neglectful not to have kept better tabs on their grandchild. And that Carson was tragically loyal to a father who didn't deserve it.

Carson sat silently staring out the large porch window. He often found himself staring out at the sea. It was calming, like pressing a delete button in your brain.

"When did he die?"

Carson turned back to Atticus. "When I turned eighteen, I moved out on my birthday. Happy birthday to me," she said flippantly. Then her face grew serious again. "Parker died a few years after. Alone and drunk." She looked into Atticus's eyes, almost as a challenge. "I had to go to the morgue to identify his body."

"I'm sorry you had to do that."

She placed her hands around her cup as though seeking warmth. "I don't think I've entirely forgiven myself. Or him."

"What do you have to forgive yourself for?"

Carson looked up from the coffee. "For leaving him, know-ing what he was."

"Now you're taking on too much responsibility. *You* were the child."

Carson shrugged. "Maybe. But from that time on I had a hard time making a commitment of any kind, not to a boy-friend or a pet. I didn't even take a long-term rental apartment." She drank the dregs of her coffee and set her empty cup on the table. "One diagnosis would be attachment disorder."

She was being curt, something he recognized as a front for her vulnerability. "Did a doctor make that diagnosis?" She shook her head. "Then neither should you."

"Whatever you call it, the scars are there. I'm still skittish about losing my independence. Sticking to one place, one guy. It's causing problems between me and Blake. Why else am I so afraid to commit? To settle down? It's got to be because of my shitty childhood. Because of *him*."

"You're still angry at your father."

"Hell yeah, I'm angry at him. He screwed up my life!"

"Carson, carrying around all that anger will only keep you tied to that tragic past. It's like some heavy chain wrapped around your mind and your heart. The only way to release yourself from the anger and fear is to forgive him."

"Forgive him for what? His whole life?"

"That's a good question. Of all the things you're angry with Parker about, what is the easiest to forgive?"

Carson scratched her head while she looked off. At first she seemed irritated by the question and wouldn't answer. Then she looked at Atticus. "I suppose . . . it would have to be his alcoholism."

"And the hardest thing to forgive him for?"

Tears unexpectedly flooded her eyes and her lips began to tremble. "For not taking care of me."

Atticus was moved by the child's cry he heard in the woman's answer.

Carson wiped her eyes with quick strokes, trying to bring

herself under control. "Isn't that the responsibility of a parent?" she asked angrily. "To take care of his child?"

"Of course it is. Hey, I'm not a parent. I'm not even a spouse. But I know this much."

Carson stilled to listen.

"What being a good parent is about—what being a spouse is about—is no longer thinking only of yourself or your self-interests. By that criterion Parker wasn't a good parent. Or, apparently, a good spouse." Atticus reached out to put his hand over hers. "But forgive his alcoholism. Start there."

Atticus rolled into the Sea Breeze driveway a few hours later. He saw Carson's Blue Bomber parked next to Harper's Jeep—a car he found curiously incongruent with his image of its petite, proper owner. When his foot hit the pavement, he heard the thunder of paws against gravel as Thor came trotting from around the house to check out the new arrival.

"Hey, big boy," Atticus called out, holding out his arms.

Thor bumped into him, sending Atticus tottering back with the weight of the huge dog. The Great Dane mix whined with pleasure at seeing him as Atticus scratched his ear.

"You know who I am, don't you, old boy?" Atticus wished he could be as honest with everyone else at Sea Breeze. "Time to find out what's bothering your lady, okay? Come on, boy, lead the way." Atticus pointed to the front door.

When they reached the porch, Thor sat on his haunches beside the door and watched as Atticus knocked several times. There was no answer. Finding the door open, he hesitated. If Harper knew he was her brother, would he be able to stroll right in, like Carson and Dora? Would she still have reservations?

He glanced at Thor, wondering how he'd react to a home invasion. "You okay with this, old boy?"

Thor lay down on the porch and put his head on his paws.

All right then, Atticus thought, and pushed open the door a crack. "Hello?" he called out, sticking his head in. "Harper?"

Thor was instantly back on his feet, curious.

Atticus heard the sound of footfalls running toward him. In a flash, Harper appeared in tan pants and a flowing green print top. It was the first time he'd seen her wearing maternity clothes, and he thought she looked wonderful.

"You're here! Come in!" She walked up to him. She kissed his cheek in welcome, then turned to Thor. "Not you. You stay outside." She nudged Thor back out the door and ushered Atticus inside.

The usual fresh flowers were in a vase on the hall table. The house was filled with light and the scent of polish. Harper turned to Atticus. "Thank you for coming right over. You made good time. I hope it was no inconvenience."

Atticus thought of the unfinished sermon on his table. "No problem."

"Let's go in the library." She led the way down the hall. "We can talk there."

The library was a handsome room, masculine with peckycypress paneling and walls of bookshelves filled with books, some new and some quite rare. Yet it had a strong feminine touch, clearly an effort of Harper's since Atticus knew she'd claimed this as her office where she wrote. Her signature style was everywhere. An English chintz lined the windows and covered the chairs, a worn, muted Oriental rug had rose and creamy hues, and standing proud in front of the large windows was an exquisitely beautiful writing desk with cabriole legs. Harper had lit a fire in preparation for his visit. It snapped and crackled and created a cozy atmosphere. A pot of tea and mugs sat on the glass cocktail table along with a plate of cinnamon scones.

"I thought we'd be more comfortable in here, rather than the living room."

And more private, Atticus thought to himself. Away from curious ears. "So many books." He ran his fingertips along the spines. "I've always loved books. Felt I could get lost in them."

The feminine chintz-covered chairs sat side by side near the fire. Atticus took one at Harper's invitation. He squeezed in, but just. This was definitely a woman's office.

"I'd like to begin with a silent prayer for guidance."

Harper looked a bit surprised, but after a moment willingly nodded and bowed her head.

Atticus similarly bent his head and let his eyes flutter closed, silently asking God for the knowledge to help this young woman in whatever way he was able. Upon finishing, Atticus felt the cloak of calm that he always did when his prayer was heard. Looking up, he saw Harper sitting at the edge of her chair, having lifted her head, eyes wide open. "You seem a little uncomfortable with prayer. Do you believe in God?"

"Yes, I believe in God," she replied hastily. "I was raised in the Anglican Church. Granny James goes to church . . . on occasion." Harper's lips twitched. "I expect my grandmother feels she can commune with God directly."

Atticus chuckled. "And you?"

Harper shook her head. "I never had that kind of relationship with God. I've always thought He wasn't much concerned with what's going on with us peons on earth."

"Are you at all curious about religion?"

"I wasn't before, but now that I'm pregnant I'm feeling more interested in finding out more. I've been doing some research. I'd like to raise my child with some spiritual foundation for his or her future. And, well, I definitely want to baptize the baby. I have this fear that if I don't, well—" She paused and her cheeks colored fetchingly. "Promise you won't laugh?"

"Promise."

"I'm afraid if I don't and the baby dies, it'll go to limbo."

"*Limbo?*" Atticus snorted in disbelief. He couldn't help it. "You mean the place where babies who die without baptism go?"

"Yes, I suppose."

"That's an old Catholic teaching, and even they abandoned it."

"Still, mothers think of these things. I read about it on the Web."

"The Web," he repeated knowingly. "Do you know what medical schoolitis is?"

Harper shook her head.

"It's the phenomenon of medical students thinking they've acquired the many diseases and illnesses they're studying. Happens on the Internet, too. Everyone self-diagnoses based on articles they've read. Sounds like that's what you're doing. Maybe you should lay off the Internet a little."

Harper nodded and looked at her hands. "You must think me a complete idiot."

Atticus reached out to take her slim fingers in his large, strong grip. "Quite the opposite. Listen, I don't know much about pregnancy, but from what I do know, being curious about all stages of your baby's growth and development—physical, mental, and spiritual—is natural."

Harper smiled. "Thanks. I needed some support today."

Atticus released her hand and bent to pick up his tea. "You know Charleston is called the Holy City? There are churches here from most every denomination. Why not check a few out? You never know. You might find one you like."

"I will. I've always been curious. Taylor's open-minded, too. My mother didn't guide me in matters of religion. Let's just say that was one more area of neglect. Speaking of Georgiana, the other day I called her to tell her my good news. I didn't expect much, maybe a simple congratulations." Harper paused. "She actually asked if congratulations were in order. As though I might not be happy about the pregnancy and might consider getting rid of it."

That took him aback. "And what did you tell her?"

"In so many words, to stick it where the sun don't shine."

He smiled into his cup. "Can't say she didn't deserve it."

"I'm back on my mother's blacklist. She doesn't approve of my engagement or my wedding. And as for my pregnancy, well"—Harper snorted in an unladylike fashion—"let's just say she sees it in limbo. You know"—Harper looked out the window—"it's hard, even at my age, to realize my mother has no concern or sympathy for anything that makes *me* happy."

"I'm sorry." From what Atticus was hearing of Georgiana so far, he was far from impressed. This was the same woman who had treated their father miserably and fired his mother. She seemed irredeemable. "I do understand, though. I had a distant relationship with my father. He wasn't what you'd call an affectionate guy. First, he worked all the time. But even when he was home, he didn't hug or share his thoughts. He cared, don't get me wrong. Just . . ."

"You didn't feel loved?"

"Not as a kid. He was a formidable personality with a big voice and staunch principles. He could be intimidating at home as well as in the courtroom. He was generous with charities, a deacon in the church, and took on a lot of pro bono cases," Atticus added, wanting to round out his father's character. "I admired him. When I got older, we communicated on a grown-up level. We had a few good moments. But that's also the time I started getting in trouble." Atticus sighed. "I was a constant source of disappointment to him."

"That's how I felt with my mother. No matter how hard I tried, nothing I ever did seemed good enough."

Atticus felt a connection with this sister. She understood his loneliness and displacement. That something was missing from their lives.

"But now you have a chance to start fresh. You can't change your mother. Maybe not even your relationship with her. But you've already changed your own life. You've created this warm and inviting home. You won't make the same mistakes with your child."

Harper shook her head, eyes filled with new hope. "No, I won't," she said with conviction.

He smiled, glad that he could offer her some consolation.

He suddenly felt hope of his own that he could make a change in his life, as well. With Mamaw and his sisters.

Harper returned the smile, then bent to pour the tea. "How do you take your tea?"

"Cream and sugar, thanks."

He watched her graceful movements as she poured, added milk, a teaspoon of sugar, then handed Atticus his cup. It was good tea, a blend of some kind, strong with a heady scent.

"But, you see"—Harper picked up her cup—"the phone call brought up a tough conversation I had with Granny James. This is what I really wanted to talk to you about." She paused. "Granny wants me to get a prenuptial agreement."

"A prenup." Knowing Harper's finances, Atticus wasn't entirely surprised. "How do you feel about that?"

"At first I was against it. It's hardly romantic and I'm worried drawing one up will cripple my marriage before it even gets started. But I can see Granny's point, too. The James estate is vast, and it is her responsibility to ensure that the estate is kept in the family. It's a unique situation."

He set his cup on the table. It sounded to him as if she was trying to persuade herself out loud. "What does Taylor think about all this?"

She held her cup in front of herself like a shield. "He didn't like the idea. He said it makes him feel like a lesser partner in the marriage." She took a sip of her tea, then cast a glance at Atticus.

"Well, he is the one with the lesser money. You hold the purse strings."

She set the teacup back on the table. Her huge diamond caught the light, brilliant as a giant star.

"For any guy," Atticus said, "but especially for a southern male, that's tough. And, the vow does say 'for richer or poorer.'"

"I do trust him." She made a face. "It's his future wife I don't trust."

"What?" Atticus laughed in disbelief.

"If I died young and he remarried, I don't want *her* to get my money. I want it all to go to our baby. See, that's Granny James's point—keep the family fortune in the family line. It's beginning to make sense to me."

"Hope for the best, but plan for the worst."

"That sounds horrible, but yes."

"Harper, you're the one who has to live with the consequences of your decision. You have to decide for yourself what you want and need and hope Taylor will understand no matter what. Because he loves you."

Atticus remained silent as Harper sipped her tea and contemplated what he'd said. He sipped his tea and looked around the room, taking in the shelves of books.

"I've always wanted a library like this," he said abruptly. "I love books. I've always been a great reader."

"Me, too! My sisters used to tease me for hiding out in my room with my nose in a book. That's how I got the nickname Little Mouse."

"Did you always write?"

"Good heavens, no." Harper laughed. "At least not openly. I suppose I always made up stories, but I was terrified my mother would find out. When I was eight, I finally worked up the courage to give her one of my silly stories to read, and she called me into her office and told me quite plainly that I didn't have talent. Of course I believed her. She was the head of a major publishing house. I was groomed to be an editor, and I liked editing. I still do. I'm good at it. But it wasn't until I moved here last summer that I truly explored writing, freely without fear. You might be surprised that this Little Mouse had a lot to say."

Atticus cracked a wry grin. "So the mouse roars?"

"She damn well does." Harper sipped her tea. Atticus saw her eyes sparkle over the rim of her cup. She lowered her cup to the saucer and returned it to the table.

Atticus leaned forward. His mother had worked for her father. She was pregnant with Atticus at the same time Georgiana was pregnant with Harper. They were both connected to the same damn novel. He wanted to know more about this father he never knew.

"Wasn't your father a writer? Parker Muir."

"He was. Never published, though. That's how he met my mother. She never said so, but I think she was supposed to edit his book. There was only one. A lifetime's work."

"Did you ever read this book?"

She shook her head. "No. It breaks my heart that Carson lived with him all those years, but she never even picked it up. I can't imagine not grabbing it and reading it under the covers at night with a flashlight. Anything . . . just out of curiosity. But Carson's not much of a reader."

"What happened to the book?"

"Parker destroyed it. Such a waste," Harper said with feeling. "The only copy. He must've hit rock bottom."

"That was the only copy?" Atticus asked, astonished.

"Yes. And it's lost." She sighed. "I would have liked to have read it. Good or bad."

"Do you remember your father?"

"Yes, but we didn't have many precious father-daughter moments. Mummy wouldn't allow it. She hated him, you see. Still does, and the man has been dead for years. She never wanted me to so much as mention his name growing up. I couldn't even keep a photograph of him. So you can imagine how she felt when I told her I was writing a book. She went nuclear, told me—again—that I had no talent. Mummy can be so supportive," Harper said with heavy sarcasm. "Her hatred of him is positively pathological."

"That sounds harsh." Atticus was shaken by this description, knowing the facts of Parker's affair.

Harper shrugged. "It's the truth. Like I said, anything to do with Parker Muir was anathema to her. And by association, his mother, Sea Breeze, and the entire South. As I mentioned, we had a big argument on the phone, and the gist of it all is, she said she's not coming to the wedding."

Atticus knew that the mother-daughter relationship loomed large during the wedding process. And that children of neglectful parents were, unbelievably, often all the more attached to them.

"How do you feel about her not coming?"

Harper's mask of bravado slipped off to reveal a face of sorrow. "Sad," she said in a soft voice. "There's a part of me that still wishes she could be happy for me. Of course I want my mother at my wedding. I don't have my father, either. Or a grandfather." Harper sniffed so hard for a moment that he feared she might burst into tears. But she held herself together. She lifted one shoulder in a halfhearted shrug and said in a wobbly voice, "Who is going to walk me down the aisle?"

Atticus looked at her, and his steady eyes met hers. "Who

do you want to walk you down the aisle? It doesn't have to be a man," he prodded gently.

Harper had such an expressive face. He knew the moment the answer came to her. There was relief and lessening of grief followed by a look of wonder.

"Granny James," she said clearly, her mouth breaking into a wide grin. "And Mamaw. Can I have two women walk me down the aisle?"

"You can have whatever you want."

"Then of course. I want my grandmothers."

Chapter Nineteen

*It is inconsiderate as well as impolite not to send a reply
to a wedding invitation which includes R.S.V.P.*

—Etiquette, Emily Post

*T*he MacKenzies are a yes?" Granny James exclaimed, flabbergasted. "That old laird hasn't left his castle in twenty years, but he's coming all the way from Scotland for the wedding?" She shook her head. "If this keeps up, we will have to rent another tent."

"At least they responded," Harper said. "I can't believe how many people haven't yet. It's so rude!" The two women were sitting together at the desk in Harper's office, accompanied by a crackling fire and a tea service, sorting the invitation responses.

"What's happening in a world where people don't RSVP to something as important as a wedding? The planning involved, the cost . . ." Granny James sniffed haughtily. "Raised by wolves."

"What do I do with all the ones we haven't heard from yet?"

Granny James lowered the cards in her hand and looked up, her glasses slipping down her nose. "I suppose we can try and follow up with a phone call. But I tell you, my dear, if anyone waltzes into the wedding without having responded, they'll be escorted out! I don't care if they did fly in from Europe."

"Watch your blood pressure, Granny," Harper said with humor in her voice. Then, setting down her pen, she said with feeling, "I don't know how to thank you for all you've done. I had no idea how difficult things must have been for you this past year. And you still finding time to plan my wedding. I've been so selfish, thinking only of myself."

"Not at all, child. You weren't meant to know." Granny James smiled. "You're the bride. Besides, the wedding has been the one bright spot in a long annus horribilis."

"Granny James," Harper began hesitantly, remembering the scene in Granny's room the other day that had ended with the older woman near tears. "I know you're not happy Mamaw is in the cottage. That you'd expected to be in there." She added ruefully, "You've made that abundantly clear. But I hope you know that you are welcome here—for as long as you want. This is your home."

"Thank you, dear. I appreciate you saying that. And Marietta and I seem to be managing just fine," she said lightly, sifting again through the response cards.

Harper paused. "Do you remember you asked me to talk to Taylor about a prenuptial agreement?"

Granny James looked up, fingers stilled. "Yes, of course."

"Well, he doesn't want to sign one."

"He doesn't *want* to?"

"No. We had quite a heart-to-heart." Harper gathered her strength. "And if he doesn't want to sign, I won't make him."

Granny folded her hands on the table. "I see."

"He also told me he feels uncomfortable living at Sea Breeze because it's my house. Not ours."

"Well, dear, the house *is* yours."

"Actually, it isn't. Not until I turn thirty when I pay back the loan. It's yours."

Granny looked at her sharply. "What are you trying to say?"

"I love Taylor, more than any house or any amount of money. If he's not happy, I'm not happy. So, what I'm suggesting is that you make Sea Breeze your home. Taylor and I will move."

"*What?*" Granny James's voice was sharp. She whipped off her eyeglasses. "Don't be silly. That's not what I want at all."

"But it makes sense. You need a place to live. You already paid for the house. Taylor has some money saved, and a nice income from his job, and I've made money off the book. Although not much," Harper added with a laugh. "We can rent a place."

"You'll do no such thing. I realize you're pregnant, but really, Harper, must you be so dramatic? We're British. We don't let our emotions rule. Let's table this discussion for another time. Neither of us is going anywhere for the moment. Do I make myself clear?"

Harper sat back, unaccustomed to Granny's sharp tone.

Granny's face appeared contrite. "Forgive me. It's that I'm quite flustered. Please, be a good girl and don't mention this again. Sea Breeze is your home. If anyone should go, it will be me. Now"—she slipped her glasses back on—"tell me again how many yes responses came today?"

Harper hesitated, then lowered her gaze and resolutely began counting the list of names on the paper. Granny James took a breath, relieved that Harper didn't notice her hands were shaking.

Later that afternoon Imogene was on her hands and knees in Harper's garden, Harper's wide-brimmed hat on her head and a sharp spade in her hand. She'd been attacking weeds with a vengeance. Her conversation with Harper had her so vexed she needed to get outdoors and put her hands in the soil. If the word *soil* could be applied to whatever she was digging in now, she thought wryly. As far as she could tell, it was all sand and mud.

Imagine, Harper telling her that she could live at Sea Breeze. She'd think her insolent if she hadn't said it so sincerely. Imogene paused, leaned on her hands, and caught her breath. In truth, she did feel homeless. She missed her extensive gardens at Greenfields Park. Now *that* was soil, she thought wistfully. Her gardens had been her private sanctuary, which she'd tended carefully for more than forty years. If she closed her eyes, she could see the rows of perennials, touched by dew when she took her morning walk. This time of year the air would be crisp and fragrant.

Imogene opened her eyes and wiped the sweat from her brow. But she wasn't at Greenfields Park, she reminded herself, shaking from her doldrums. She would never live there again. That part of her life, her life with Jeffrey, was finished. This was her new life, here in the lowcountry. She rested her spade and looked out over the Cove. The sun was shining in a sky a piercing blue. For as far as she could see, water and sea grass swirled together with as much color and energy as a painting by van Gogh. The view was so different from the rolling fields of England. Yet she would never tire of it. Of this she was certain. The mystery and magic of the lowcountry, unlike anywhere else, she found unusually comforting. She sighed and, with a half smile, thought she could use a little mystery and magic in her life now, after so many years facing harsh realities.

She heard a birdcall and looked up, her eyes darting about trying to spot the source behind the unique sound. She loved the variety of birds along the coast, especially now as birds migrated, choosing their summer range. She'd seen plenty of the winter residents—cardinals, sparrows, mockingbirds, and blue jays—but she was eager to spy a bluebird or yellow-throated warbler, a South Carolina wren, and most especially a ruby-throated hummingbird.

Instead of a bird, however, she spied Taylor. He was coming her way carrying a tall glass. Dear boy, she thought, feeling her thirst acutely. She tugged at her gardening gloves and looked up, smiling, as he approached.

"You are an angel of mercy," she told him, reaching up to accept the glass.

"Granny James, do you have a minute? I'd like a word."

Imogene drank the glass of tea to the dregs. She had an inkling what Taylor might want to discuss and suddenly wished this tea had some of Mamaw's secret additive in it.

"Help me up, then," she said briskly, offering Taylor her hand. "I'll get a crick in my neck if I have to look all the way up at you."

She offered her hand, and with an easy pull Taylor had her

standing on her feet. They walked together to the porch, where she sat in a large black wicker chair under the welcome shade of the awning. Granny sank into the cushion with a weary sigh and fanned her face with her gloves. Taylor, she noticed, did not sit. He stood wide legged with his hands behind his back, his face completely unreadable. If she didn't know better, she'd think he was about to salute her.

"So, Taylor, what is so important that you pull me from the garden like some old weed?"

"I spoke with Harper the other night about the prenup," Taylor said in an even voice, not mincing words. "I don't like it. Just saying."

Granny James tsked with impatience and opened her mouth to speak, but Taylor put up his hand to silence her. "Let me finish."

Granny James snapped her mouth shut, but her eyes narrowed.

"The James estate means nothing to me. But I gave it a lot of thought, talked it over with Blake, and he helped me understand why it means a great deal to you. Back in the day, Blake's family once held a large plantation here in the lowcountry. The Legares tried to hold on to it for generations, keeping the land in the family. It was considered a sacred trust. But in time . . . the war, it was sold off, bit by bit. Now it's no longer in family hands." Taylor looked out at the Cove. When he turned back, he met Granny James's eyes levelly. "So I can understand you wanting to keep your property in the bloodline. Still, the balance of power shifts to Harper within this arrangement. She already owns the house."

"You knew that going into this."

"I did. I guess I figured we'd work it out between us. Despite what you might still think, I'm not interested in Harper's money."

"I never thought you were." She paused and looked at him, searching for an honest answer. "Will Harper marry you if you don't sign?"

"Yeah." His face softened. "She's got her heart in the right place. Which is why I want to meet her halfway."

Granny James liked what she heard and cocked her head. "I'm listening."

"I called a friend of mine, a lawyer, and he said we could isolate specific things, like the James trust and the house—and leave out the rest. That way after we're married, any money Harper makes and any money I make we pool together and make decisions just like any other normal married couple. And I get to keep my balls in the process. If your lawyers can whip up a prenuptial agreement that spells that out, I'll sign it."

Granny James resisted a smile at the boy's cheeky choice of wording and pursed her lips. She brought to mind Harper's earlier suggestion that she and Taylor move from Sea Breeze. "To be clear, you'll agree to live in this house with Harper? Even though it's in her name?"

"Yes."

Granny James refrained from revealing her relief. She chewed the tip of her glasses. "What made you change your mind?"

He shrugged one shoulder. "It's simple. I love Harper. She loves Sea Breeze. I want her to be happy."

Granny James slipped her sunglasses back on her head and rose with agonizing slowness to her feet. She keenly felt the past hour she'd spent on her knees. "Very well, young man. I'll call my lawyers and it shall be done as you've requested."

"Thank you, ma'am." Taylor turned to leave.

"Taylor!" Granny James called after him.

He spun on his heel to face her.

"You are a remarkable young man. And Harper is a very fortunate young woman."

His stern face at last eased into a begrudging smile. "Thank you, ma'am."

She watched him turn again and walk with long strides back into the house before she broke into a wide grin of her own.

Atticus slept in boxers with the doors of his bedroom wide-open, leading to the porch. Beyond the doors the great blackness of the ocean sky blanketed him, the gentle breeze better than any fan and the gentle roar of the ocean a soothing white noise. He had to hand it to Dora for finding this place. He'd never slept so well before in his life.

But in the morning he paid the price of open curtains. The sun rose smack outside his window and, like any star performer, demanded he rise to his feet and appreciate her glory.

Atticus rose with the sun and gave humble thanks. Then he headed for the shower. A short while later he took a last slurp of his coffee, laced up his running shoes, grabbed his sunglasses and ball cap, then headed outdoors.

Stepping into the morning air, he felt the moisture of the ocean on his face. He stretched and slipped his cap on, back forward, and headed toward the shoreline. This early in the morning the sand was smooth and undisturbed by footfalls.

Shells and wrack littered the high-tide line, which formed a wavy dark line across the glistening, pristine beach. His spirits lifted as he caught his stride and he felt the truth in the old adage *the world was his oyster.*

He'd run nearly two miles and was approaching the southern tip of the island where Breach Inlet separated Isle of Palms from Sullivan's Island. Up ahead he spotted two male runners heading his way. They were tall and fit, and behind them trotted two big dogs, one yellow, the other black as night. They made quite a sight, as testified by the two women in jogging attire who had stopped running and turned back to stare at them after they passed.

"Hey, bros!" he shouted, lifting his arms to greet Blake and Taylor as they approached.

"Atticus, my man," Taylor called as he jogged to his side. They were both dressed in running shorts and T-shirts spotted with sweat. Taylor's T-shirt was worn, torn, and had USMC in bold letters across his chest. "So," he said with approval in his gaze, "the Rev runs."

"Every day." Atticus took deep, gulping breaths. These guys must've run all the way from Sea Breeze on Sullivan's Island and were barely winded.

"You should join us," Blake offered. Then he cracked a wicked grin. "If you can keep up."

"Oh, I can keep up." Atticus laughed, trying not to openly pant. He glanced over Taylor's shoulder. "Don't look now, but your fans are coming," he said in a low voice, nodding.

Taylor looked over his shoulder to see the two twenty-somethings walking their way. The blonde, her luxuriant hair pulled back into a long ponytail that swished jauntily left to right when she walked, seemed to be forcing the darker woman to accompany her. The blonde had her gaze set on Taylor. The other woman's hair was black and her ebony skin glistened with a fine sweat from her run. Atticus remembered his mama telling him that ladies didn't sweat, they glowed.

"Nice dogs," the blonde said, lifting her arms to point out the two dogs frolicking in the surf, oblivious of their admirers. "Are they yours?"

"No, they just followed us," Taylor replied.

"Really?" she answered, eyes wide. "Don't they scare you? They're so big."

Atticus met Blake's eyes, and it was all they could do not to laugh.

"No, I'm just messing with you," Taylor said. "They're our dogs."

"They're beautiful," the black-haired woman said, eyes on the dogs. "It's nice to see animals so fit."

"Indeed it is," the blonde echoed, and her double entendre didn't escape anyone.

"The golden one is obviously a Lab, but the other? Is it a Great Dane mix? Maybe some Lab there, too?" the other woman pondered.

She knew her dogs, Atticus thought.

"Yeah, that he is," Taylor said. "That's Thor. He's my dog." At the sound of his name, Thor stopped and turned toward his master. "The other dog, Hobbs, is Blake's."

"I'm Ashley," the blonde said, smiling with invitation, "and this is Vivian. Are you boys from around here? Your accent says you are."

"Yes, ma'am," said Taylor, who was answering for the team. "We're here to celebrate our weddings."

"Oh." Ashley's disappointment was clear in her voice and on her face. "*Y'all* are getting married?" Her hand made an encircling gesture to include all three men.

"Everyone but the Rev here," Blake said. He winked at Atticus, knowing he'd just opened the door for him. "He's here to marry us. We keep it friendly."

Atticus glanced at Vivian. She was a stunner, lean and intelligent looking with fine cheekbones that gave her dark eyes a lilt. "Are you here on vacation?" he asked her.

"I live here. I'm the local vet."

"Really?" he said, surprised.

"We best be going," Taylor said, jabbing Atticus in the ribs. "You coming?"

"Uh, yeah, sure."

Taylor nodded to the women in farewell. "Ladies."

Blake turned toward the surf and gave a piercing whistle. In an instant, Hobbs and Thor were at their heels. They took off toward Atticus's condo.

"I got to get myself a dog," Atticus said, picking up the pace.

"That you do," Taylor told him. "For lots of reasons."

"Hey, my cousin's Lab is having pups," Blake offered. "Real pretty chocolates."

"Not yet. I'm only renting the place."

"I wouldn't wait. Not with a vet like that on duty," Blake said.

"I'll just borrow Hobbs for a day. Rent a dog," Atticus called back.

"You don't want a puppy," Taylor said. "Get a rescue. They're so grateful."

"Is that what Thor is?"

"He sure is. But he's more than a rescue. He was trained for the Wounded Warrior program. I got him when I got back from Afghanistan."

"You had PTSD?" Atticus asked.

"Yeah. I was in pretty bad shape." Taylor looked at Atticus, and the pain was visible in Taylor's pale green eyes. "Nuff to say that I wasn't sure I wanted to keep going. That guy back there"—Taylor pointed over his shoulder to Thor—"got me through it. I used to have these bad dreams. Real bad. I was back in the war. Reliving it. Ol' Thor could tell when I was having a nightmare. He'd lick my hand, my face, wake me up. Got so I couldn't sleep without the dog by my side." Taylor glanced over his shoulder to check on his dog. Thor was trotting comfortably behind him in an even stride. "Best damn dog in the world."

Atticus was well aware of the trauma of PTSD. He'd counseled several parishioners suffering from it, not as many servicemen as battered women, accident victims, and others who'd experienced the many traumas of life. "How are you doing now?"

"Good. Thanks."

"You don't have nightmares?"

"Nope, not in a long time. I was worried when Harper and I moved in together. You can imagine. I would've been okay with separate rooms, but she wouldn't have it." Taylor grinned, obviously thinking of his bride. "For such a mite of a thing, she's got a backbone of steel when it comes to me. She's going to make the best mother." Taylor's love for Harper shone in his face.

Atticus wondered if they'd resolved the prenup issue. "What about her mother? Have you met her?"

"Georgiana?" He said the name as if it were a curse word, followed by a guttural grunt. "Shit, no. Don't want to. That woman's a piece of work. I'm glad she's not coming to the wedding. Not sure I'd be able to be civil."

They drew close to Atticus's condo and he started to slow down. "This is my place." Atticus pointed out the building. "Want some water? Coffee? That's about all I have to offer."

"Man, I'm starved," Taylor said. "I need some real food. Let's run back to Sullivan's. We can eat in town, and they have water for the dogs. It's civilized."

"Aren't we due at Sea Breeze at nine?" Blake asked.

"Look at him," Taylor teased. "Tethered to the leash already."

"Hey, you're the marine. You understand taking orders," Blake fired back.

Taylor laughed and held his palms up in surrender.

"I get my orders from higher up," Atticus told them. "And that, gentlemen, is why I'm still single." Grinning, he took off in a sprint in the direction of Sullivan's Island. Looking over his shoulder, he called, "Last man there pays the bill."

Atticus paid the bill. Not because he'd come in last, which he did, but because he was happy to pay. Happy to be part of the brotherhood. He'd been missing his buddies in Atlanta. As much as he enjoyed spending time with his sisters, he needed time with his boys. The banter, talk about sports, jokes, and just the general feeling of male camaraderie.

They ate breakfast sandwiches outdoors on the patio of Café Medley, their long legs stretched out under the small tables.

When their appetites were sated and conversation lagged, Blake rose to go. "I've got to bring Hobbs back home first, and then I've got a phone call coming in. Thanks for breakfast, Rev."

Blake gave a whistle that had Hobbs scrambling to his feet. Atticus watched the handsome dog trot beside his master and thought to himself maybe he did need a dog after all.

Taylor rose from his chair. "Hold on, we'll walk with you."

"Yeah, notice he said *walk*, not run. My dogs are barking," Atticus complained.

"We'll come by for you again tomorrow. Keep in shape, man." Blake checked his watch. "But I've literally got to run or I'll miss my call. You know the way. See you there." He took off at a trot.

Thor was already on his feet, erect, eyes glued to Taylor.

Atticus and Taylor walked at a comfortable pace past quaint shops in the lowcountry-style buildings, past the Sandpiper Gallery windows filled with local art, the park with the tennis courts, and the cherry-red fire station to where the neighborhood quieted to private homes hidden behind oaks, palms, and shrubs.

"You know Harper asked for a prenup," Taylor said, turning his head to search Atticus's face.

"Yeah, she told me."

"It was a lot to swallow. I can't lie. I talked to Granny James about it."

Atticus hadn't heard about this part. If he was a betting man, he'd bet on old Granny.

"She has her lawyers working on a prenup we can both live with."

"Really?" Atticus was extraordinarily pleased. "That's great, man."

"We'll see. But I'll tell you this, Rev. You're on duty to marry us. One way or the other. Damn the prenup."

"You're a good man, Taylor. I have high hopes for your marriage."

"There's still the problem of the house."

"Sea Breeze?"

He nodded. "I love the house. Who wouldn't, right? But the house is solely in Harper's name. Technically she's the owner, it needed to be hers for the estate, blah blah blah. I get that. But between us men, you can see how I might feel like I'm a . . . What's the word for a guy who's kept by a woman?"

"A gigolo?"

"Yeah, that's it."

Atticus stopped in the street. "Aw, come on, bro. No one thinks you're a gigolo. They wouldn't dare."

Taylor stopped a few feet ahead, hands on his hips, and turned to face Atticus. "I don't care about anyone else." Taylor drew a huge breath. "It's how I feel."

Atticus walked toward Taylor and patted his back. They both started walking again. "Can't argue with how you feel. So okay, then." Atticus summed up what he knew. "You like the house but you feel like it's Harper's, is that it?"

"That's it."

"You know that's not how Harper sees it. She sees the house as both of yours, together."

"One thing you've got to understand about Harper." The gravel crunched loudly underfoot. "She's eager to please. Her mother would say jump and Harper would say how high. I don't want Harper to feel like she has to make me happy at the expense of her own happiness. I'd leave Sea Breeze tomorrow. But it means too much to her." Taylor walked a few steps. "So I'm going to stay. Harper says it's our home, and I'm going to have to believe her, even if inside I'm not fully on board."

"What would it take for you to make the house *feel* like yours?"

"Like, what could I do to it?"

"Yeah. If it's your house, you can make it yours, right? You redid the kitchen already. That's a start."

Atticus could tell by Taylor's expression that he had never before considered the situation in this light. He kept his gaze straight ahead while the muscles in his jaw worked. A few cars passed. A man walked by talking loudly on his cell phone.

Taylor's green eyes were alive with an idea when he turned to look at Atticus. "Thanks, Rev." He slapped his big palm on Atticus's back with such enthusiasm he almost knocked him over. "I know just the thing."

Atticus and Taylor showed up at Sea Breeze a couple of hours later, practically running into Blake on his way inside, looking just as disheveled as the other two despite his stop at home. Not until they reached the kitchen did Atticus realize they'd unwittingly walked into a party. The kitchen table was filled with alcohol bottles, and dozens of tiny sip cups and plastic glasses were filled with amber-colored drinks. Girard was looking over Mamaw's shoulder, telling her something as she poured champagne into two flutes. Carson and Harper were bent over a notepad on the counter, glasses in hands, and Dora and Devlin were debating about the contents of their glasses. Toward the back of the room, a strange woman was shaking a mixer as if she were dancing the cha-cha.

Atticus thought how the three men had not stopped talking all morning—as they ran, as they devoured a hearty breakfast, and later as he and Taylor had walked back to Sea Breeze. This sight, however, silenced them all.

Mamaw looked up and, seeing them, set down the champagne bottle and called out in her cheery southern drawl, "Well, it's about time you boys joined the party!"

Everyone else turned his or her head, grinning.

"There you are!" Harper hurried over to Taylor to take his arm and drag him into the room, her gaze taking in their running clothes. "You look like you're coming from the gym. Honey, I told you nine o'clock. We couldn't wait any longer. Erinne only has so much time, you know."

"The cavalry's arrived," Carson called out, waving Blake and Atticus into the room from where they hovered by the door. "We need some more men's opinions." She gave their running clothes a once-over. "And you guys look like you could use a watering hole."

Taylor wasn't smiling. "Can I just ask what in Sam Hill y'all are doing?" Taylor looked at the glass in Harper's hand. "Are you drinking alcohol?"

"No, silly, of course not." Harper giggled. "It's ginger beer.

Carson and I are working on a nonalcoholic drink." When Taylor still looked confused, she said with a huff of frustration, "We're creating our signature drinks for the weddings. Don't you remember? We talked about it."

Taylor shot a glance to Blake. He lifted his shoulders in a classic *Huh?*

"Men," Dora called out with mock frustration. "Hopeless."

"Nah," Devlin called out, coming over to greet the men. He handed them each a glass. "Be gentle with them, ladies. They just realized that there's no one less important during wedding plans than the groom."

"Blake, meet Erinne," Carson said as Erinne walked up with her shaker. "She's from Firefly Distillery and brought all these goodies for us to taste."

"I don't need an introduction to Firefly." Blake took a sip from his glass. "Sweet tea vodka is a staple in my house. Okay." He set down the glass and rubbed his hands together, eyes feasting on the choices. "I'm at your service, ladies. Though I have to say, I don't usually drink at nine thirty in the morning. What've we got here?" He picked up a smaller bottle in the shape of a large mason jar. "Moonshine?"

"Really?" Taylor came closer. "Nothin' says wedding in the South like a little moonshine."

"It's a specialty of ours." Erinne joined them at the table. "We have more flavors than just this one, but I brought some peach moonshine specifically for the wedding cocktail." She offered them two flutes. "This is the drink the group liked for the wedding. Sparkling wine and peach moonshine. Now *that's* lowcountry."

Blake and Taylor each took a swallow of the wine.

"Good." Blake looked at the glass. "Mama's going to love that."

"Real good," Taylor agreed. "For the ladies. But we need something with more bite for the guys."

"See?" Harper said. "That's why we needed you. Get busy, boys."

Dora leaned over to Mamaw and said in a stage whisper, "She didn't say *chop-chop*."

Erinne poured two more cups of liquid from her shaker. "Try this, guys. It's not so sweet. This is a mix of Cannonborough ginger beer and Firefly sweet tea vodka."

Taylor tried a swallow. "Now we're talking." He smacked his lips. He stepped closer, getting into the mood. "Can I get in here and mix a bit?"

"Look who just became a mixologist," Blake teased.

Erinne laughed. "That's what you're here for. Both of you. Dive in."

As they did so, Carson stepped closer to Atticus and handed him a glass of iced ginger beer. "You're gonna love this. You won't miss the alcohol, it's so good."

He met her gaze and they shared a look of mutual support. "Thanks." He took a sip and it was extraordinarily delicious. Not too sweet. He looked at her again, noticed she looked better. She had some color from her time out on the water. But more, she'd lost the sullenness that had cloaked her features the last time they'd talked.

"How are you doing?" he asked. They both understood this was a follow-up question to the long discussion they'd had after her last argument with Blake.

"Good." She couldn't hide the sparkle in her eyes. She

looked around and saw that everyone was clustered around the table, talking, laughing, tasting. "Actually, do you have a minute?" When he nodded, she led them out the kitchen door to the porch, where they could talk privately.

The air felt warmer outside than it did inside. Atticus took a deep breath as he looked out over the majesty of the Cove. Spring had really set in now. He'd never realized that one could notice the change of seasons along the coastline as one could in the North. It was just more subtle, but when you knew where to look, the signs were obvious. The cordgrass was a deep green at the bottom, and as it grew, all the wetlands would be like the great prairies, waving green in the sun. The lowcountry was setting roots in his heart.

"That's a new look for you, Rev," Carson said, taking in his running shorts and sweaty T-shirt, his ball cap on backward. "I like it."

"Yeah?" He chuckled. "We all met up on the beach. Had breakfast together. Have to say, they're great guys. I really like them."

Carson beamed. "Yeah, they are. They like you, too."

"How can you tell?"

"I can always tell. If Taylor doesn't like someone, he puts on his marine face to scare them away. Blake is more subtle. He just ignores you. Politely, of course. His mama raised him right. But you, they treat like one of the family."

Atticus swallowed down the rush of emotion that comment elicited. "Yeah, we're going to start some pickup games of volleyball or something. So, what's up?" he asked, gently leading her back to the topic.

"I got a second interview with Charleston Waterkeepers. It's this really great nonprofit that focuses on local water quality. The pay is nothing, of course." She laughed. "But I don't care about that. It's a job I can really sink my teeth into. I can make a difference, and that's what I need." She grinned with pride.

"Are you going to take it?" he asked, knowing full well what that meant.

"If they offer, yes."

"Good decision."

"I know." She gave a short laugh. She took a sip of her drink, then after a minute said more seriously, "Thanks, Rev."

"For what?"

"For helping me say yes. To the job, to Blake, to my future."

Atticus thought he'd never been paid a better compliment. He reached out to slip his arm around her shoulders, feeling more than a minister to her or even just a friend. He felt like her brother.

"There you are," Harper called from the doorway leading out of the kitchen. "The guys settled on a drink. They're calling it the Firefly Cannonball. Has a ring to it, doesn't it?"

"I like it." Atticus grinned. "But I'll stick to the straight ginger beer."

"Atticus, glad I caught you." Harper looked over her shoulder and let the screen door silently close behind her. She hurried over to where Carson and Atticus stood. "Listen," she said in a low voice. "I need to ask you a huge favor."

"Yeah?" Atticus's voice rose slightly in anticipation.

"I told you about how bad the last session at the bridal salon was, right?"

He nodded.

Harper met Carson's gaze and she nodded in agreement,

egging Harper on. "So we were thinking, Carson and I, on going to the salon again, only this time without the entourage."

"Okay," Atticus said slowly, not liking where this was going.

"We want you to come, too."

"Whoa, ladies." Atticus back-stepped with one palm up. "You've got the wrong guy for this. I don't know the first thing about wedding gowns."

"You have good taste," Carson pressed. Then snickered. "Present outfit excluded."

"You think we didn't notice your fine wool suits? And your shoes," Harper added wryly.

Atticus was feeling cornered. "But why me? Ask Dora."

Carson glanced at the door, then lowered her voice. "Dora likes *all* the dresses, bless her heart. You don't have to know anything. You'll be like the tiebreaker in a sports game. Thumbs-up or thumbs-down."

Atticus almost had to laugh at the idea of him in a bridal salon with his half sisters, who didn't know they were his half sisters, giving dress advice. His buddies would never let him live this down if they found out. "Ladies, I don't know."

"We need you there more for moral support than your fashion opinion. Right, Carson?" Harper looked pleadingly at her sister.

"Right." Carson put her hands together like in a prayer. "Pretty please?"

Atticus closed his eyes. They got him.

Chapter Twenty

I'm only ever truly happy when you're here with me. And I want you here with me every day. Every night. Isn't that love? Isn't that the basis of a good marriage?

*T*he following afternoon Imogene carried a bottle of the Firefly sweet tea vodka in one hand and held the railing with the other as she painstakingly made her way down the front stairs. She was a fool to have overdone things as she had in the garden. She'd needed to work out her frustration. But now her old, tired body was certainly giving her what for about it, and she needed something to take the edge off. Only one person could help her.

She walked across the gravel driveway and up the three short stairs to the cottage front door. She looked with distaste at the rusted pineapple knocker, which she tapped briskly. She would have to change that, she thought to herself as she let her gaze wander the porch. She spied the two rocking chairs and the small wood table. Those would do for what she had in mind, she told herself, then whipped her head around as the front door opened.

"Marietta!" she exclaimed with a broad smile.

"Goodness, Imogene, I didn't expect you. What brings you here this afternoon?"

"Do you have iced tea? I seem to recall that's a staple in your house."

"As a matter of fact, I just made a batch."

Imogene lifted the bottle of vodka. "Good!"

Marietta laughed, eyes sparkling. "Oh, yummy. '"Will you walk into my parlour?" said the spider to the fly.'" Marietta stepped aside to allow Imogene space. Her eyes swept through the room, picking up details she'd forgotten. It was the same sweet place she remembered. Nothing had changed, she thought with contentment.

Marietta followed her into the living room, moving quickly to fluff up a pillow and pick up her used tea glass and lunch plate and carry them to the kitchen sink.

"You have cards, I presume?" Imogene asked.

"Of course." Marietta opened the vodka, poured a liberal amount into the pitcher of tea, then gave the concoction a good stir. After putting ice into two tall glasses, she filled them with the spiked drink, then dropped a sprig of mint into each. She handed a glass to Imogene.

"To the weddings." Marietta lifted her glass.

"To Sea Breeze."

As they each sipped, Imogene noticed Marietta studying her circumspectly over the rim of her glass.

"Can we sit down?" Imogene asked.

"Of course."

"How about on the porch? There are two pretty rockers there."

"Follow me."

"Don't forget the playing cards!"

Marietta led the way to the two rockers, picking up a deck of cards from the desk en route. Imogene groaned softly, again, as she lowered to the seat.

"Are you all right?"

"I'm a twit. I was working in the garden and may have been a bit overeager." Once settled, Imogene took a long sip of her drink. "That's better. For medicinal purposes, of course."

Marietta took a long draw from her drink. "Of course. And there's plenty more where that came from." She set down her glass and skewered Imogene with her gaze. "Okay, old girl. What's this all about? This isn't my first rodeo with you."

Imogene sat back and rocked her chair with her foot. "Oh, I just experienced my own personal O. Henry play."

"Would you care to elaborate?"

"You recall 'The Gift of the Magi,' where the young couple each give up what's most precious to them so they can buy a gift for their loved one?" Imogene paused, bringing the story to mind. "I believe it was her hair and his watch."

"Yes, of course I remember it. O. Henry was an American short story writer," Marietta added with smug pride.

"Whatever, the characters in this particular homespun play are our own Harper and Taylor. And the item being given up was Sea Breeze."

Marietta became suddenly alert. "What about Sea Breeze?"

"Harper said she and Taylor were going to move." Imogene was not too proud to admit it brought her quite some pleasure to see Marietta's face pale.

"Move?"

"It was all a big misunderstanding. We sorted it out," Imogene hurriedly added. She didn't want Marietta to pass out on the floor. "You see, I suggested Harper get a prenuptial agreement."

"You didn't!"

"I did," Imogene confirmed archly. "Surely it can't be a total surprise to you, a woman of your property. Harper discussed it with Taylor, and, in his words, he didn't like it."

"I should think not."

"Will you stop interrupting, you daft cow? Anyway, this morning, Harper tells me that she is not signing a prenup and that I should make Sea Breeze my home since I'd paid for it. And because Taylor feels that the house is not his, she declared that she and Taylor were moving."

"Oh, dear Lord . . ." Mamaw put her chin in her palm.

Imogene skewered her with her gaze. "Anyway, yesterday morning, while I was digging in the garden, working up a lather, I might add, Taylor comes out and informs me that he *will* sign the prenup—although a more limited version than I would like—*and* that he will continue living in Sea Breeze." Imogene was gratified to see Marietta's eyes well at this conclusion to the story. "It seems," Imogene said, her tone softening, "that those two are very much in love and would do anything to make the other happy."

"Oh, Imogene, that's just as sweet as sugar," Mamaw crooned.

"I confess, it made me teary eyed to witness." Imogene

reached out for her glass. "God, I do love happy endings." She took a hearty drink.

Marietta's expression shifted to bewilderment. "But why would Harper think you would want to live in Sea Breeze?"

Imogene lowered the glass. "I might have mentioned something about the cottage. . . ."

"Oh, Lord, you're not still nattering on about that?"

"I know, I know." Imogene gave a sorry shake of her head. "I was acting like a spoiled child. But you knew very well my intention was to stay in the cottage. You were supposed to go to some"—she wagged her hand—"some retirement home."

"Really, Imogene, you must let the cottage issue drop."

"Easy for you to say," Imogene muttered. Then she pointed her finger at Marietta. "You know, if they do still somehow decide to move, I could end up your landlord," Imogene said smugly.

Mamaw merely shrugged and smiled beatifically. "Squatter's rights. They hold firm stateside."

Imogene reached for her sunglasses and slipped them on. "Careful, dear, your pirate's blood is beginning to show."

"It's our heritage, you know. They called him the Gentleman Pirate. That's because the story claims he never killed anyone." Marietta smirked and wagged her brows with meaning. "But how likely was that?"

"I thought as much." Imogene rocked forward in her chair, then reached out to tap the deck of cards with her nail. "Care to play for it?"

Marietta appeared taken aback. "Play for what?"

"The cottage, of course." While Mamaw's eyes widened with shock, Imogene picked up her glass and relished the moment, taking a sip. She leisurely set her glass on the table, then leaned toward Marietta. "You like to brag about your pirate's blood and how good you are at gin rummy. Well, matey, put your cottage where your mouth is."

"You can't be serious."

"I'm always serious when I talk about cards. Here are the terms. If I win, I move into the cottage and you go to the main house. If you win, I'll buy another house on the island."

"Wouldn't it be simpler if you just did that anyway?"

"No," Imogene said succinctly. "Now don't delay. Yea or nay?"

Marietta's back stiffened and she reached for the cards. "Yea."

Two hours later, Marietta lay down her discard and called out, "Gin!"

Imogene stared at the two of hearts on the pile for a moment, then tossed down her playing cards on the wood table. She leaned back and with her foot shoved the chair into a rocking motion. "That's two out of three. You won," she said glumly. "Fair and square." She stopped rocking and looked at Marietta sharply. "Or did you? I'm a bit blitzed, to be honest," she slurred. She pointed at Marietta. "How much did you have to drink?"

"Enough," Marietta replied, trying hard to enunciate.

From the main house the relentless hammering that had been going on for the past hour picked up again.

Imogene put her hands to her temples in agony. "What in the name of all things good in this world is that unholy racket?" She turned in her chair to look back at the house.

Marietta waved her hand. "Oh, that's just Taylor. He said he's starting some project up in the attic. Bedrooms, he said." Then her eyes widened and she burst out with a laugh. "Oh! Maybe for you!" She giggled again, then hiccuped. "Oops." She covered her mouth with her hand. "Pardon me."

Imogene smirked. "You Yanks. Every time you say that, we English have to laugh. We say *pardon me* when we burp or break wind."

Marietta laughed heartily at that bit of knowledge, and Imogene joined in.

"Are you really looking for a place to live on the island?" asked Marietta.

"I'd already talked to my man Devlin after I saw that my cottage had been taken," Imogene said archly, ignoring Mamaw's eye roll. "In fact, he said he has a pretty little cottage on the creek he's putting on the market. Great views. He owns it and can work out a special price."

Mamaw stopped rocking and pushed herself forward. "Not Dora's cottage? You can't be saying you'd buy the house she's renting right out from under her?" Marietta's tone was accusatory.

"Dora's cottage?" Imogene tried to sit up but slumped back against the chair. "Devlin never mentioned anything about it being Dora's cottage. Why would he be selling his girlfriend's house?"

"Well, it has to be. They're having a squabble about it. Oh, Imogene, you take the cake. You know Dora's as poor as a church mouse. She can't buy that place but she loves it. And you, richer than Croesus. Isn't it just like you to spark another fire?"

"If you hit me with one more colloquialism"—Imogene's eyes flamed—"I'm . . . I'm going to slap you from here to Sunday!"

Marietta caught her breath, then tilted her head, recognizing what Imogene had said as yet another southern expression. Imogene's eyes were bright with amusement. Once again, they burst out laughing. Marietta hadn't laughed so hard since the last time they'd had a good drink together the previous summer.

"I could really get to like you, you old hag," Imogene said.

"Ditto, you crone."

They rocked a bit, wiping their eyes, then sat listening to the blessed peace now that Taylor had stopped hammering.

"Marietta, of course I wouldn't interfere between Devlin and Dora. Do you think I'm that dodgy? But you're right." Imogene sounded down in the mouth. "I do seem to be a source of squabbles, as you call them, among the young lovers. Truly, dear friend, I don't mean to be a bother to you or anyone. And I'm a good loser." She looked fondly at the cottage. "I'll stay for the wedding, then say my farewells."

"Where will you go?"

"I don't know," Imogene replied honestly. "Georgiana's I suppose."

Marietta suppressed a shudder. She couldn't imagine a worse fate for anyone.

The hammering commenced again, more vigorous than ever.

Imogene tilted her head to listen. She turned to Marietta and smiled like a Cheshire cat. "You don't suppose he's building a mother-in-law suite?"

Across the driveway in the main house, Carson was sitting at her desk wearing thick earphones as she worked, not for music but to mute the sound of Taylor's incessant hammering. On the computer was the long list she and Blake had compiled of nonprofits and companies with possible jobs for her. Over the past four days Carson had gone out on two in-person interviews and talked on the phone to another two groups that had responded favorably to their query blitz. This morning she'd had a second interview with Charleston Waterkeepers. They'd e-mailed her that they would call before the end of the working day. Blake had been right when he'd told her she'd find the company in sync with all she'd hoped to work on with water quality. The people were smart, informed, aggressive, hardworking, and friendly. This small group believed they could make a difference.

Carson saw rather than heard her phone light up with an incoming call, and she quickly took off the earphones and pressed accept, feeling a churning in her stomach. "Carson Muir."

"Hi, Carson, it's Cyrus from Charleston Waterkeepers."

"Yes, hello, Cyrus. I was expecting your call."

"I have to say, you've really impressed all of us."

"Thank you. The feeling is mutual."

"We followed up on your résumé and the recommendations were glowing. There was one from Jason Kowalski. Between you and me, I was wired to get his e-mail. I'm a big fan of his movies. Thought you'd like to know what he wrote. After he sang your praises, he said . . ." Cyrus paused, then read, "'I don't want you to offer Carson a job because I'm hoping to hire her myself. But that said, you should fight for her. She's worth it.'"

Carson clutched her phone tighter, stunned by the generous praise.

"You've got the credentials. But more than that we all thought you were a great fit. Your enthusiasm, your personal story. We're a small group. Like a family. And we all agreed you'd be a great addition. I hope you'll join us."

Carson sat still as a stone, dazed. "You're offering me the job?"

Cyrus laughed. "Yes, Carson. We're offering you the job."

Carson couldn't talk to anyone quite yet. Not even Blake. She had to hold this news close, to slowly digest it before she could share it. She slipped out of her dress and into yoga pants and a fleece jacket. The soft fabric felt like a security blanket around her. She tucked her hands into her pockets and walked out the back door to the dock. Dusk was just setting in, lending a lavender cast to sky that was reflected in the water. It was a mystical time, those fleetingly brief moments before day ended and night began.

She sat looking at the racing water below the dock, struggling to find the words she'd need to tell Blake of her decision. To thank him. He'd never lost hope. He'd worked tirelessly by her side, leaving no stone unturned. His faith in her—in the two of them working together—had convinced her they needed to be together. More than she needed any job. She would stay in the lowcountry and marry her lowcountry boy. Her mind was at last in sync with her heart.

From below the dock came the unmistakable sound of air pushing out from a blowhole. Startled, Carson gripped the dock railing and bent over to see Delphine swimming below. There was no question it was her. Even in the lavender light, the sorry scars were visible.

Carson hurried to the lower floating dock. Delphine spotted her and immediately brought her large gray head out from the dark water, revealing her limpid dark eyes. Her mouth was open, revealing rows of pointed teeth. Carson stood at the edge of the dock, close to Delphine, staring down at her. But she didn't speak. Did not call out her name.

Delphine tilted on her side and swam leisurely alongside the dock, exposing her belly. Carson chuckled to herself, amazed at how bloated Delphine had become. Blake had confirmed that the neonate Carson had been called to on the shore last week was, in fact, not Delphine's baby, and Carson was thrilled to see that Delphine looked happy and pregnant as ever. She was likely to give birth soon, which was a risky business in the wild. There were sharks, for one thing, and other threats. Carson wished she could be there for the birth, to witness and to support her friend.

But Carson knew there was one way she could help Delphine. As with her decision with Blake, her heart was in sync with her mind. With a final look at Delphine's beguiling face, Carson turned and, without a word, walked away.

Delphine made a series of clicking noises and whistles. She splashed the water with her rostrum to show her displeasure.

Carson couldn't understand the language of the whistles. No human could. She only knew that dolphins were smart and excelled at communication. Underwater they released myriad vocalizations with meaning, such as a signature whistle for a newborn calf that was akin to a name. Throughout the waterway, the dolphins maintained family and community bonds through sound.

Yet, in her own humble way, Carson could understand the *emotion* of Delphine's sounds. Her *eh eh eh* noises when she was happy; the clicks and guttural growls when she was not. And the whistles—high-pitched queries, short bursts of surprise, and now the plaintive calls of beckoning. Oh, yes, Carson heard and understood the heartbreak. Tears ran down her cheeks.

This was the moment of truth for Carson. There was no going back on the decisions she'd made today. She'd given her word that she would help Delphine remain wild. She'd also given her word to Blake that she would be his wife and settle here in the lowcountry. And, too, she'd promised herself that she would stay sober, true to herself. A lot of promises, she realized. These promises would be the foundation upon which she'd build her new life.

With her heart filled with lavender light, she walked toward Sea Breeze. Her footfalls reverberated on the dock with the force of her steps. She loved Delphine enough to keep walking away. Only when she reached the door of the house did Carson dare to turn and look back. Delphine was cloaked in the silvery shadows, but Carson could still hear the dolphin's mournful whistles and clicks.

Inside the house, sounds of dinner preparations and con-

versation sang out from the kitchen. Carson remained standing at the door, listening, chilled to the bone, until, at last, the
whistles stopped. A deep quiet descended in the purple sky.

Only then did Carson walk to the center of the porch and
peer out over the water of the Cove. In the dim light she could
barely make out the sight of a dolphin's silvery dorsal fin far out
in the purpling water. A single dolphin, swimming farther away
down the creek toward home.

"Good-bye, Delphine."

In another house on Sullivan's Island, Mamaw stood at the window staring out at the moonlit Cove. Her long white gown
appeared gauzy in the filtered light. One hand lay against the
window glass, cool to the touch. Tonight, however, instead of
being drawn to the water, her attention was on the opposite
shore where the deep shadows appeared looming and unfath-
omable, like the thoughts running through her head.

"Marietta, you seem troubled." Girard came up behind her
to rest his hands on her shoulders. "Care to talk about it?"

She felt his hand, so strong and so comforting, and leaned
back against him. He rested his chin on top of her head.

"It's Imogene. We played cards today and you'll never guess
what the prize was."

"I give up."

"The cottage."

"The cottage? *Your* cottage?"

"Yep." She laughed lightly at the reality of how high the
stakes had truly been.

"Save me from the suspense. Who won?"

She turned in his arms, slipping hers around Girard's neck. "You had to ask? Me, of course."

Girard chuckled and his gaze was admiring. "I never should have doubted you."

Marietta dropped her hands to his chest, patting over his heart. She thought about Imogene's face when she'd called out, *Gin!* The obvious defeat, and something more . . . a complete and utter sense of loss.

"I'm so fortunate to have you in my life. I'd be terribly lonely without you," Marietta told him. "Poor Imogene. Despite her British stiff upper lip, she is suffering. It's been very hard for her to put Jeffrey into the Memory Center. After fifty years of marriage, it feels to her like a divorce. Or even a death. Only she can't mourn him, which leaves her with no closure whatsoever. It's no wonder she wants to be near Harper now. She's her only family."

"Doesn't she have a daughter in New York?"

"Georgiana?" Mamaw sniffed. "She's a cold one. Imogene would find little comfort there. No, it's Harper she needs. And now with the baby coming, it's a lifeline." Mamaw turned to look again out the window toward Sea Breeze. "Imogene is desperate to be in the cottage. It's become a fixation in her mind. She can afford to move anywhere in the world, but all she can see is that small, insignificant cottage."

"Not so insignificant in her mind."

"No, you're right about that. And there I am, roosting in it like a fat hen when it was Imogene who was the goose that laid the golden egg in the first place. Without her, we'd all be living somewhere else. Seems rather heartless of me not to let her move into the cottage. I could take the guest room in the main house. I should. After all, I spend most nights here anyway."

"I have another idea."

Mamaw looked up quickly.

"Why not move in here with me?"

"Move in? With you!" Mamaw held up one hand to her chest, genuinely aghast at Girard's suggestion.

"Why not? We both know you don't want to stay in the guest room at Sea Breeze. You said yourself you'd feel like a third wheel, always in the way. And I'm rattling around in this big old house by myself. Moving in together makes sense."

"I suppose, when you put it in that light, it does." But she was still caught off-balance.

Sensing her hesitation, Girard pressed on. "You do like it here, don't you? It's a rather nice house," he said modestly of his impressive home, larger than Sea Breeze. "I know Sea Breeze will always have a special place in your heart. That this house won't be the same. But you won't be far. You can look out the window and there it is. You'll still be close to Harper, Dora, and Carson."

She reached up to place her palm against his cheek. "You are the dearest man."

"But I don't want you to do this if it makes you at all uncomfortable, Marietta. I wouldn't want you to be embarrassed in front of your friends."

Mamaw laughed and shook her head. "Hardly. They'd be terribly jealous."

His lips twitched with amusement. Then his face grew still. "I have another idea. A proposal, if you will. I'm only ever truly happy when you're here with me. And I want you here with me every day. Every night. Isn't that love? Isn't that the basis of a good marriage?" Girard took her hands. "Marietta, would you do me the honor of becoming my wife?"

"Marriage?" Mamaw was utterly floored.

"Of course. Unless you'd rather live in sin," he added wryly.

Marietta laughed. Her heart felt infused with the moonlight, as though it could soar right from her body directly into the heavens. She smiled at this old friend who had reappeared as a gift to her in the later years of her life.

"Oh, Girard, my friend, lover, neighbor. I love you. With all my heart. But marriage? I don't want some fool snickering about a triple wedding. At our age. As if . . ."

"Why not?" Girard said with a twinkle in his eye. "Apparently, you can wear white."

She slapped his chest, blushing. "Oh, don't remind me of what I said. I'm so ashamed."

"Wear red, if you have a mind to. Just marry me, Marietta. I've loved you from the first moment I saw you all those years ago. You know that."

Marietta nodded as a wry smile eased across her face. "I suspected. And I daresay Edward did, too. He loathed you. Kept a gun by the door in case he saw you sneaking around."

"You're kidding," Girard said unsurely.

"Of course I'm kidding." She paused. "Or am I?" Marietta laughed again, then looked up and cupped his face in her hand. "Dearest Girard, I don't want to get married again," she said gently. "It's all so complicated at our age. Your children will be up in arms, claiming I'm after your money."

"What money? I've given them just about everything

already. The only thing they still have their greedy eyes on is the property in the Adirondacks."

"What? You still have that gorgeous, virginal property up North?"

"Yes."

"Girard, that land is priceless! Invaluable to the wildlife in that overdeveloped area. You know what you have to do. Tell me you do."

"If you're suggesting I put it into conservation, lock, stock, and barrel, like I did with my property in South Carolina, my children will disinherit me. They've been after me for years to sell it to developers. They'll make a fortune. Though I have to wonder how much money do they need."

"The little vultures." She saw his brows furrow and was instantly contrite. "Did I say that out loud? Sorry."

"Don't change the subject. I believe I just asked you to marry me."

"Must we get married? I'm inclined to go with your other suggestion. To live in sin."

Girard barked out a laugh. "You'd do that?"

"Of course I would! I'm a modern woman, haven't you heard? No more Emily Post for me."

"I'm fine with that. If that's what you really want."

"It is."

"You drive a hard bargain. You press me to offer a second proposal."

"What proposal is that?"

"Oh, just something that might appeal to your pirate's blood." He tugged her closer against him and smiled leeringly. "A bounty."

Marietta was intrigued. "I'm listening."

"What would you say to a swap? My land in the Adirondacks for your consent to marriage."

"What?" Marietta was stunned and confused. "What do you mean?"

"I will put the virginal land, as you so appropriately called it, into conservation if you say you will marry me. Call it my bride's price."

Marietta couldn't believe what she was hearing. "You'd do that? The land has to be worth countless millions."

"You're worth that and more to me. And"—he grinned wryly—"I'm no fool. It's a good tax break." He drew his face closer, so close she could feel his breath upon her ear. "Besides, don't you know when I put all that land in South Carolina into conservation, I did it for you?"

Marietta gasped and looked into his eyes, as pale a blue as the wispy clouds crossing the light of the moon.

He smiled. "All for you."

"Girard, you take my breath away. And all my objections. Yes, I will marry you. But," she said with a gentle kiss on his lips, "not a word about this to anyone until after the girls' weddings. Do you promise?"

His eyes kindled and he said with import, "I do."

Chapter Twenty-One

For a bride, her wedding dress was the transition article of clothing that took her from girlhood to womanhood.

*H*arper struck a silly pose in the long gilded mirror, hands on her hips as she turned this way and that. She dissolved into giggles as she moved the delicate scrap of lace from where it was covering her eyes. She had returned to the LulaKate bridal salon with Carson and Atticus. The girls had been disappointed that the cheerful Lauren was off for the day, but they had a more than suitable replacement helping them decide on their gowns: none other than Kate McDonald, the designer of the beautiful dresses.

"Women still wear these?" Harper, disentangling the face veil from its perch on her head and handing it back, asked Kate.

"Some people think the face veil is old-fashioned. Back in the day, a very young bride might be shy to face the congregation and the young man she barely knew unveiled. Today, if a bride wants to wear a veil over her face, it's more because she prefers the look of it, or wants to maintain tradition. In any case, the veil is taken off by the maid of honor when she gives the bride's bouquet back to the bride at the conclusion of the ceremony." Kate smiled guiltily. "Personally, I've always loved the face veil. I think it's dramatic."

Kate had appeared surprised and none too pleased when she'd seen Atticus walk in the salon with the women. Her eyes flashed and she tucked her long dark hair from her face. "It's like bringing a fox in the henhouse," she'd declared. But the brides had insisted, and there was no arguing with that.

Atticus tried to shrink into the background on this warm and breezy afternoon in the lowcountry. Taylor had called for a pickup game of volleyball, then razzed him when he found out Atticus would be stuck on King Street in Charleston surrounded by white tulle.

Kate suggested, "Girls, we're getting ahead of ourselves. Let's select the gowns before the veils."

"Of course." Harper became serious and turned to Kate. "You know our situation. We've run out of time. We all agree we'll never get the dress I'd selected to look right with my baby bump." Harper slid her palm around her belly, already considerably larger than on their last visit. "And Carson is at ground zero. What are our options at this late date?"

"Not many, I'm afraid," Kate replied. "You're limited to our samples, and of those you'll have to select something that needs minimal alterations. We're slammed going into peak wedding season. This is Charleston, you know. The number one destination-wedding spot in the country." Kate sighed with compassion as she checked her appointment book. "I'm going to try and squeeze your alterations in. Though, thank heavens, we've already allowed time for your other dress in the calendar, Harper, so that's something."

"Just grab me a white dress that fits," Carson said. "Or rather, an off-white dress." She winked at Harper.

"Don't pay her any mind," Harper said. "Though, with her figure, she really could wear any dress and she'd look gorgeous. Can you show us what we have to choose from?"

Kate guided them to the sample racks. "I've seen a lot of wedding dresses on a lot of brides, and one thing I've learned is that the right dress can transform a bride from beautiful to extraordinary. It has a lot to do with the bride feeling good about herself in the dress." She turned to Harper. "You don't want to settle on any dress just because you have to. Tell me a little about your sense of style."

Carson piped up, "She's all high style. Never showy or ostentatious but always in good taste."

Atticus spoke up. "Something elegant and understated. Only the best-quality materials."

Harper turned to look at Atticus, wonder etched on her face.

Carson crossed her arms. "I didn't know you brought Mr. Frigging Dior to our fitting."

Atticus lifted his brows and shrugged.

Carson flashed him a wide grin of approval. "Okay then." She cocked her head in challenge. "What do you see for *me*, fashion king?"

Atticus heard the challenge and didn't back down. He put his hand on his chin and studied Carson. She was wearing a cream-colored dress featuring a mix of lace and cotton with a full sweep skirt and dramatic hi-lo hem. On her feet were calf-high cowboy boots. He thought of the sheath of white silk she'd worn at the engagement party that revealed her long, incredibly fit body. Only a woman confident of her looks could wear such a bold choice.

"A vintage look," he told her with authority. "Not frilly but avant-garde. You know what you like and don't care if anyone else likes it." He looked into her eyes and saw the sudden vulnerability. Atticus had a flash of intuitive insight. "The dress has to hold memories," he said more softly. "One that reminds you of someone very dear to you." He took a breath as he felt the connection. "Family."

Carson blinked slowly, almost like one coming out from a trance. "Yes," she said softly. "That's it exactly."

There followed a moment's silence.

Then Kate put her hands on her slim hips and said to Atticus, "Hey, are you looking for a second job?"

Atticus laughed with the others and shook his head, feeling a bit sheepish for having spoken at such length. "Sorry." He ducked his head and backed up. "I'll shut up now."

Kate said, "Let me go back and see what I can find in stock." She held up her hands as she headed to the stockroom. "Lord God in heaven, let there be something there. Y'all help yourself to some champagne. I'll be back in a few minutes."

The three of them strolled to the table where champagne and bottled water were on ice. They all automatically reached for the water, laughing as they realized their common choice.

"So, how do you do that?" Carson asked, unscrewing the top of her water bottle. "I felt like you reached into my brain, sorted through the mess, and pulled out what you were looking for."

Atticus only smiled and drank from his water bottle, then wagged his brows. "It's Spidey sense."

Carson released a short laugh, but it wasn't dismissive.

"Ladies!" Kate was waving the two women back into the fitting room. She had several gowns in her arms.

While the brides were in the fitting room, Atticus took a moment to stroll through the racks in the main room. With so many different dresses, so many different styles, no wonder a young woman's head spun at the prospect of choosing only one.

He flashed back to the time his father had taken him to Tyrone's tailor. It was a favorite memory, one of the few good moments Atticus had had with his father. Atticus had turned eighteen and Tyrone had explained to him that this was a rite of passage. Inside the small men's shop in Buckhead, Atlanta, the air was thick with the scents of cedar and wool. Heavy wooden racks along the walls were filled with men's suits in different fabrics, sizes, colors. Atticus had been what his father called a flashy dresser. Brand names were de rigueur for everything—clothes, shoes, watches, sunglasses, even the logo on Atticus's ball cap. On this day, however, his father wanted to show him the quiet power of a bespoke suit.

Tyrone was welcomed into the shop with a handshake. When Atticus was introduced to Mr. Sydney Ball, he could tell that the old man with the wizened face, white hair, and eagle eyes was already mentally taking his measure. Mr. Ball led them through the shop and opened the door to a back room. They entered a walnut-paneled dressing room—old-school with crystal decanters filled with amber liquid and a single tall mirror hanging from an elaborate brass frame. Atticus undressed, then stood on the small platform as instructed, feeling nervous and exposed in his boxers. Mr. Ball came up to him and, without a word, held his hand up to Atticus's mouth.

Atticus startled and looked into the old man's eyes. There was no question there. He saw respect in those rheumy eyes. Respect for his craft.

Atticus promptly spit out his gum.

His father then offered him a crystal glass filled with a small amount of bourbon.

It was a coming of age, he'd realized years later. He learned that day to respect the beauty of skill and talent. A month later, Atticus received the most beautiful suit he had ever owned or would, likely, ever own again.

"This suit," his father explained, "is your transition article of clothing. It will take you from boyhood to manhood." When Atticus had put it on, his father had looked at him with pride. "This is your ceremonial honor. You are a man now. Equipped to go into battle."

Remembering that day now as he stood peering at the racks upon racks of delicately spun silk and tulle, Atticus understood the importance and value of a wedding gown. For a bride, her wedding dress was the transition article of clothing that took her from girlhood to womanhood. It had to be right. It had to reveal to all that she was a woman of value, worthy of respect. It had to give her the confidence to lift her chin high as she walked down the aisle to commit herself to her life's companion.

He kept up his tour around the salon, idly looking at the veils, jewelry in glass cabinets, blingy belts, and other accoutrements while he waited. In the back of the salon, the door to an office was open. He peered in, more out of idle curiosity than anything else, and stopped short.

Hanging on a hook in the office was the gown he'd been wanting for Harper. Boldly he stepped into the office to look closer. The stunning, simply cut gown had pearls delicately beaded over Thai silk. A sheer bolero jacket of the same fabric buttoned at the neck and had an edged Peter Pan collar. The dress was very French. Very haute couture. Very Harper.

He picked it up, carried the dress to the fitting room in the back of the salon, and knocked gently.

Kate opened the door. Her eyes widened when she saw the dress in his hand. "That's one of my new designs."

"Can you show this to Harper?"

"I suppose." Kate's face was troubled. "It's a sample, so it's small and I don't know if it can be altered. All that beadwork. But"—her eyes brightened—"it is a fit to flare. And Harper is small, even with her baby bump. It might work. What's the point of being the owner if I can't do as I think is best for my bride?"

Harper came to the door to see what all the discussion was about. When she saw the dress in Atticus's hand, her face lit up. "Oh, I love it! I absolutely love it. That's my dress!"

Several hours later, Atticus opened the door to Sea Breeze for Carson and Harper, then followed them single file indoors. The house was redolent with curry. His mouth watered as he followed the girls into the kitchen.

"Oh, Granny James!" Harper exclaimed. Immediately she

launched into a vivid description of the dream dress that Atticus had found her, gesticulating wildly and pulling out her phone to flip through the dozens of pictures she'd taken.

"She's one happy bride," Carson remarked dully.

Atticus looked at her face. She was putting on a brave smile, but he wasn't fooled. He'd known Carson wouldn't find her dress at the salon today. What she was looking for couldn't be found in any bridal salon.

"I'm going to go to my room for a while," Carson told him. "I'm pretty tired. Stay for dinner, won't you? It's curry. Granny James is mad for it. She's British, you know. Curry is mother's milk to them. See you, then." Carson turned and walked away down the hall.

When he was alone, Atticus turned and left the house to walk across the gravel drive to the cottage. Pansies filled pots by the door, cheerful and colorful. Two rockers sat side by side on the porch. Between them a book lay half-open on a small wooden table. Someone was home, he thought. He knocked gently on the door.

A moment later he heard footfalls and the door swung open.

"Atticus!" Marietta exclaimed, delight brightening her blue eyes. Her hair was pinned in a twist, as usual, and she was dressed for dinner with a blue linen tunic over tan pants. "Do come in. What a surprise."

"Am I interrupting?"

"No, not at all. Girard likes to come over for a cocktail before dinner, so he might be by soon. You are joining us for dinner, aren't you? Imogene has made curry."

"I smelled it in the house and I can't wait."

"Can I offer you a drink?" Then, remembering, she added

easily, "I have iced tea. I make it myself. With simple syrup, of course."

"I'd love some." He eyed the platter of cheeses laid out and his stomach growled. While Marietta went to fetch his drink, Atticus moved toward the cheese and helped himself to a thick slice of Camembert on a cracker. Chewing, he looked around the cottage. So this was the prize these two grandmothers were fighting for. It was nice enough, spare but cozy with its white-painted walls and white furniture. But hardly worth World War III. Over the fireplace he recognized the large, colorful painting dominating the wall as a Jonathan Green. Atticus was impressed.

"Here we are." Marietta walked toward him with a glass of iced tea. "Please, make yourself comfortable."

He slid into a thick upholstered chair near the fireplace. Marietta poured herself a cocktail from the crystal pitcher. She came to join him in the chair opposite his.

"It's a lovely space."

"It is, isn't it? Lowcountry on the outside, Santorini on the inside." They shared a brief laugh. "The girls helped me decorate it after Lucille passed. It was very different when she lived here, chock-full of knickknacks. I probably would have left things the way they were, but those girls . . ." She shook her head. "Put them together and they're a force of nature."

"I'm beginning to understand that."

"Are you?" she asked cautiously. She didn't press the point. "I feel freer out here in my little cottage, detached from all the belongings I cared for all those years. Possessions can be a burden, you know. They distract from what's important in life. Here I live like a monk. With certain privileges . . ." She hoisted her drink in the air. She laughed. "But I can walk across the drive to the big house and see everything in place, only now Harper has to tend to them. Big houses, like young children, belong to the young. It all takes so much energy." She took a sip from her drink. "But I do go on. You've come here for a reason. I'm all ears."

"Actually, I did want to talk to you about something. Do you know I went to LulaKate with Carson and Harper today?"

"No, I didn't." She clapped her hands together and laughed. "My goodness, dear, I'm afraid I just can't picture you amidst all that lace and silk. Although, better you than me, I'm afraid. I made a rather poor showing in front of my granddaughters."

"They told me about that. We all make mistakes, Marietta. I wouldn't worry yourself over it. And the good news is, Harper's found a new dress."

"She isn't keeping the other one? But didn't she buy it already?"

"She's going to sell it. Besides, I don't think that's an issue for her. She's inside telling Imogene all about it. I'm sure you'll get all the details over dinner."

"That's very good news. And Carson?"

Atticus paused. "Carson didn't find anything there."

Disappointment flooded Marietta's features. "I swanny, she's tried on every dress in the city!"

Atticus placed his palms together. "It wasn't that Carson couldn't find a dress. She couldn't find a dress that was meaningful to her." He glanced up to see if Marietta understood. Her blue eyes were bright. "Beneath Carson's confident exterior lurks the heart of a frightened woman. I saw it in the way her hand trembled when she fingered the gowns in the salon.

Heard it in the cavalier way she said she'd wear any old dress, as though it didn't matter. Felt it when I'd looked into her eyes at the salon and realized she was holding on by her nails. Marietta, what is she so afraid of?"

"Commitment. Loss of independence," Mamaw answered simply with a wave of her hand. She sighed, slumped deep into the chair's cushions, and looked at her hands. "I realize now I turned a blind eye when she was young and living in Los Angeles with her father. Edward and I sent monthly checks, but it was all, shall we say, *convenient* for Edward and me to live in ignorance on the opposite coast." A sparkle of hard-won wisdom flashed in her eyes. "I suspect . . . no, I know that's why I'm trying to make amends now." She stopped for a moment, lost in her thoughts. Then she brightened and said with more cheer, "Last summer, though, Carson made great strides. She faced her alcoholism and joined AA, she went back to work, and she became engaged to Blake."

"Big commitments."

"Exactly. The wedding plans are going smoothly enough." Marietta smiled. "The Legare Waring House is a well-oiled machine at events. Yet, I don't see any of the excitement or joy one expects in a bride when planning a wedding."

"Fear has a way of numbing a person."

Marietta brought her hand to her cheek. "Yes, of course. I see that now." She looked to Atticus. "What can we do to help her?"

Atticus told Marietta how, in a flash of insight at the salon, he'd understood that Carson, more than Harper, needed to wear something that had meaning to her. A dress filled with memories. One that would remind her of someone dear to her.

He moved forward on his seat and rubbed his palms

together. Their eyes met. "I was wondering . . . hoping, really . . . Marietta, do you still have your wedding gown?"

Atticus knocked on Carson's bedroom door.

"Come in."

Carson was lying on her side on her four-poster bed flipping through a magazine. Her shoes were off and her dress was high on her long thighs. A slim circle of light poured out from her bedside lamp. The large, airy room had broad windows dressed with plantation shutters. Seeing Atticus, she sat up quickly and pulled her skirt down over her knees.

"Sorry. I thought it was one of my sisters."

"I didn't mean to bother you, Carson, but I have a message. Your grandmother Marietta would like to see you. In the cottage."

"Now?"

"Yes." He smiled. "As she put it, *lickety-split.*"

Mamaw had telephoned Girard and headed him off, telling him she'd meet him at the house for dinner. She wanted some privacy with Carson.

She was atwitter. So much so she didn't feel the shame she knew she ought to for being such a horrible grandmother not to have seen Carson's dilemma from the beginning. She, who thought she knew her granddaughters so well. It took Atticus, a young man who had known them for such a short time, to identify the problem. Such a perspicacious man her grandson was, she thought with pride. And such a fool he had for a grandmother.

She approached the large box resting on her dining table with trepidation. The box hadn't been opened since 1951. The box was made of acid-free cardboard and was completely enclosed in a natural muslin bag. Marietta fooled with the stiff metal clasp that bound it, cursing under her breath when she nearly broke a nail. It was careful work, and once the clasp was undone, it took some effort to drag the bag off the large box.

Catching her breath, she surveyed the box. To her dismay, it had yellowed over the years. Worried that her dress had met the same fate, she gripped both sides of the top and lifted it off the box. She sniffed cautiously, half expecting to smell the telltale scent of mildew or mold. To her relief, she did not. Inside, thick layers of acid-free tissue had not yellowed and still felt miraculously stiff. Encouraged, Marietta gingerly unfolded the first layer of tissue, feeling like a child opening a Christmas present that she hoped was what she wanted. She said a quick prayer that the dress was in good shape, for Carson's sake. Then she lifted the gown from the box, just enough to peek. Her lips eased into a grin of relief.

A soft knock came at the door. She gently returned the bodice to the box, gathered the tissue paper over the gown once more, and hurried to answer the door. Carson stood at the entry, looking a bit tired and perhaps even a little annoyed with having been summoned.

"You wanted to see me?"

"I do. Come in."

After closing the door, Mamaw clasped her own hands,

barely able to contain her excitement. This had to be handled correctly. She didn't want to pounce on the poor girl, thrust the dress at her, and risk Carson's saying no.

"Would you care for some iced tea? I've made a fresh batch."

"No, thank you. I think dinner is about to be served." Carson glanced back at the door, as though ready to leave.

"Oh, they can wait. It's curry. The longer it sets, the better."

Carson looked around the room idly, clearly not in the mood for a chat. She glanced at the table where Atticus's glass of iced tea sat beside a glass of rum and tonic.

"You had company?"

"Yes, Atticus stopped by for the briefest chat."

"What about?"

"We talked wedding dresses." Mamaw clasped her hands again so they wouldn't shake. "He told me that you didn't find anything you liked."

Carson shook her head. "No. Harper did, though. It's perfect for her." In one fluid movement Carson slid down on the sofa and curled like a cat, her legs tucked under and her head resting on her hands along the back of the sofa. "Oh, Mamaw," she said despondently, "I give up. I'll never find a dress in time. Maybe I'm not meant to be a bride."

"Nonsense. Finding a dress has nothing to do with whether you're meant to be a bride."

"Doesn't it?" Carson replied obstinately, eyes averted.

"No. You're ready to be a bride, Carson. You've worked very hard for this moment. Sacrificed, struggled, dug deep, and persevered. I know, because I watched you do it."

Carson didn't respond, but with some reluctance, she looked Mamaw in the eyes, seeking affirmation.

Mamaw pressed on in an upbeat tone. She didn't want to derail the purpose of tonight's visit. "Atticus was telling me that you thought you might like a vintage gown. One with memories and connected to the family."

"Where will I find such a gown?"

Mamaw's eyes brightened with her news. "How about right here?"

Carson looked confused.

"Come, lazy girl, sit up." Mamaw reached out to lend Carson her hand.

"Mamaw?" Carson raised her head to peer over the sofa at the large box that rested on the dining-room table. "What is that?"

"That, my dear, is my wedding dress."

Carson's mouth slipped open in a soft gasp. She pulled herself to her feet. "You still have it?"

"Of course I do. It was customary for brides in my day to save their dresses for posterity." Mamaw walked to the box on the table and gazed inside, gingerly touching the tissue. She spoke wistfully. "One always hoped her daughter would want to wear the gown. I, of course, never had a daughter. But, Carson . . ." Mamaw paused, and a tremulous smile eased across her face as she looked at Carson. "You're the closest thing I've ever had to a daughter. You're my granddaughter, true. But more a daughter than anything else."

Carson's lower lip wobbled. "I've always felt that, too."

"My dear girl . . ." Mamaw opened her arms.

Carson followed the same path to her grandmother's arms that she had as a child. Tears stung Mamaw's eyes as she caught the scent of the perfume they both shared.

"This is not a time for tears!" Mamaw laughed lightly. "Take a look! The same rules apply. If you like it, then it's yours. If you don't, don't feel beholden to wear it."

"I just hope it's not white," Carson said with a wry grin.

It took a moment for Mamaw to catch the joke, and when she did, she giggled and waved her hand dismissively. "Oh, you. As a matter of fact, it's not. It's ivory. Now go ahead, darling," she said, anxious to see the dress. "Open it."

Carson approached the box with care. Reaching out, she spread open the folded tissue with fingertips. Mamaw held her breath, eyes wide, one moment looking at the dress, the next checking on Carson's reaction. Suddenly she felt afraid Carson wouldn't like the gown. She'd think it was old-fashioned, nothing a modern girl such as Carson would like.

Slowly, reverently, Carson lifted the dress from the box. Huge mounds of tissue paper that had carefully been tucked between the folds of the dress fell away like birds, taking flight to scatter on the floor. Yards of creamy satin flowed from the box. Carson took a step back and held the dress in front of her, arms straight out, while she studied it.

As did Mamaw. As she saw her gown again, heady memories of that glorious day in 1951 came rushing back at her. Her wedding was one of the most talked about of the season. Her and Edward's union had marked the blending together of two historic Charleston families. At that time, most of her friends wanted to look like Elizabeth Taylor or Grace Kelly: the fashion was tight bodices with sweetheart necklines and full, layered skirts. Her dress was quite the opposite, a sleeveless gown of duchesse satin, V-neck and V-back. Carson held the gown to her body. The ivory color complemented her tanned skin and dark hair. The dramatic cut would show off her tiny waist and the graceful curve of her back, as would the covered buttons that trailed to the court train.

Mamaw sighed, feeling again like the young bride. The dress was as beautiful to her now, and as precious, as it was when she'd worn it on her wedding day.

"Do you like it?" she dared to ask. "The veil is all French lace. That was the rage then, postwar."

Carson fingered the soft fabric and said softly, "Vintage satin . . . lace . . . It's everything I wanted."

Encouraged, Mamaw brought Carson to the bathroom so she could look into the picture mirror. "It should fit you. We're the same height. And once upon a time I had a small waist, like yours."

Mamaw flicked on the bathroom lights and, for a moment, blinked in the brightness. Carson held the gown in place against her body. She stood staring, unblinkingly. Mamaw held her breath.

To Mamaw's surprise, tears began flowing down Carson's cheeks. As she looked at the gown, her expression was as if she couldn't quite believe what she was seeing in the mirror—her very own fairy tale.

"Harper told me I was supposed to feel like this," she said with a choked laugh. "But I didn't believe her. Look at me! I'm crying. *Me!*" She laughed again. "And so are you!"

Mamaw brought her hand to her trembling lips and nodded.

"Oh, Mamaw!" Carson then said the words she'd come to believe would never cross her lips: "I've found my dress!"

"There's one thing more." Mamaw reached out to pick up a small navy velvet bag from the bathroom counter. "I want you to have this."

Carson took the velvet bag, which was surprisingly heavy. As she tipped the bag, a large piece of jewelry fell into her palm. The large circular brooch had diamonds in a starburst pattern around a large sapphire. Carson could only stare, speechless, it was so stunning.

"My mother gave it to me to wear on my wedding day. It's been in the family for ages. Bought at Croghan's back in the day the store was still in Mr. Croghan's home. That piece is a part of your history."

"Oh, Mamaw, it's too much."

"Now, Carson, that brooch is meant to be worn with that dress, and it will give me the greatest pleasure seeing you wear it as I did. Right here." Mamaw touched Carson's left shoulder. "You can't wear your black pearls on your wedding day. It wouldn't be seemly. You don't want to wear pearls anyway. That dress was designed to show off my swan's neck. Or rather, like it was, once upon a time." Mamaw smiled tenderly. "Wear it, dear. It's your something blue."

Chapter Twenty-Two

*This is our adventure, right? Our weddings. We've
never been afraid before. Let's not start now.
Like you said, the future begins today.*

May arrived with a heat wave. The lowcountry shot from
spring to summer. By the end of the month the trees had
exploded with color, flowers overflowed their boxes, residents
caught short were racing to plant their gardens, and local children were crossing off days on calendars till the school doors
opened and they were set free. Talk on the streets was of how
warm the waters were already, always a predictor of hurricanes. Some thought the sea-turtles season would begin early.
Folks were selecting programs for the upcoming Spoleto Fes-
tival.

At Sea Breeze, however, the only thing on the ladies' minds
were the impending weddings.

Outside Sea Breeze, large tents were being erected for the

rehearsal dinner the following night. Mamaw was standing on the deck at a safe distance overseeing the workmen. She didn't have any directions to give them, per se, but felt they needed watching nonetheless. The house would not be open to guests, but a crew was inside buffing the floors and washing the windows until they sparkled in the sunshine. The porch had been transformed. The wicker table and chairs had been removed, to God only knew where, and replaced with a handsome bar and several long tables that a woman was now covering with a pile of silvery linens. Men were delivering potted plants, and three women in green butcher aprons emblazoned with WILDFLOWERS INC. were hanging lush ivy, greenery, and flowers from a poled framework over the porch. All this under the direction of a bubbly, talkative, happy-go-lucky woman with the eye of an eagle.

Dora, her blue eyes bright with excitement, came to join Mamaw on the deck. Dora was dressed to work in white pedal pushers and a blue T-shirt that had SEA BREEZE BRIDES in script across her breast. The girls had ordered T-shirts for all of them, but Mamaw couldn't bring herself to wear hers.

"Mamaw!" Dora exclaimed. "There you are. Isn't this exciting? It's all beginning. It's wedding time!" Her enthusiasm could not be contained.

"I might get excited once I see the tent securely up. There's mud back there." Mamaw shook her head. "I hope it will hold."

"Don't worry, Mamaw, these guys know what they're doing. What can I do to help?"

"Thank heavens you're here. Would you supervise what's going on in the living room? I can't be in two places at once. Carson is inside talking to the Legares. Cru Catering hasn't received the shrimp from the Captain yet. I know they've been culling the best shrimp from the crop and I'm grateful, but they have to get a move on. You can't make a Lowcountry Boil without shrimp!" Mamaw brought her handkerchief up to dab at her brow and upper lip. "Is it just me or is it hotter'n Hades out here?"

"It's hot. Don't get flustered, now, Mamaw. Harper's given everyone a time line with strict instructions to follow it. We all know where to be when."

Mamaw fanned herself with her clipboard. "Let's hope so. Harper doesn't want any surprises."

Harper was in her office finishing wrapping up the cookbooks she had created from Lucille's recipes. She was proud of the project. When she'd blithely come up with the idea, she had no idea of the number of hours of concentrated labor all the testing of recipes would take. Just deciphering the yellowed and stained cards and scraps of paper she'd found with Lucille's chicken scratch all over them was a labor of love. Harper had made what she called "loving changes" to the recipes, partly because she didn't want to cook with bacon fat or lard and partly because she couldn't read the writing. But she was finally done. She stood back and admired the wrapped books with pride. She was giving them to her sisters, as well as all the ladies in the family, tonight as wedding gifts.

"Harper!"

Taylor's voice boomed through the house. He was in the attic working on his project. She smiled, thinking of him up there doing what he needed to do to make this house feel like his own. Although, she thought with a sigh, why he had to start the project right before their wedding was beyond her.

She hurried to the hall in time to see his head pop out from the attic. "What is it, honey?"

"You'd better come up and take a look at this."

Something in his tone told her not to waste any time arguing. She hurried to the pull-down stairs and climbed monkey-style up into the attic.

Taylor took her hand and helped her climb up at the top. The air in the attic was thick with dust motes shaken up from all Taylor's hammering and moving things around. It was nearly empty now. Mamaw had cleared the attic of all her belongings when she'd moved out the previous fall. They'd had quite a party sorting through the boxes of memorabilia. Only a few unwanted pieces of furniture had remained. These Taylor had shoved out of the way of his labors until he could get help moving them out. Some of them were immense, which was the reason they'd remained in the attic.

Taylor led her to the far left end of the attic. "Careful where you walk," he called out.

"Oh, look at that!" she exclaimed, mesmerized by the small fort that had been constructed in the corner. It was shabbily built of miscellaneous pieces of wood nailed together. Its door opening was so small that an adult would have to crawl through to get inside. Most arresting, however, were the letters—large, malformed, and crudely written—and drawings in paint. There was a sun, a moon, stars. A rough sketch of a skull and crossbones, and a long grassy mound that looked like a mole's tunnel.

"I found it behind the bookcase when I moved it," Taylor

told her. "That thing was heavy as hell. Hadn't budged in years. Was this your playhouse?"

"No." She shook her head in wonder. "At least not mine. I don't know about Carson and Dora. But I doubt it." She pointed. "It says NO GIRLS ALLOWED." She clutched Taylor's arm. "Oh my God, Taylor. It must've been my father's."

She bent at the waist to peer in. Its window was grimy with dirt, but some light peered through, giving her a glimpse of the space. Someone had constructed a wood floor and painted more drawings on the inside. There were words, too, that stood alone—COURAGE, MAGIC, BELIEVE, HEART, PERSEVERE. These were written in a neater, more mature script. Other than a ratty-looking red blanket piled in a corner, it was empty.

"Have you gone in?" she asked Taylor over her shoulder.

"Not yet. Not sure I can squeeze through the opening."

This was one of the times Harper was glad she was small. She got down on all fours, relieved she was wearing jeans today.

"Be careful," Taylor warned.

"I'll be fine." She slowly crept into the fort, eyes on the lookout for mice or spiders. Once inside, she sat Indian-style and looked around. The space was tight and cozy, a right proper fort, she thought to herself, and smiled. Just the kind of place she would have loved to hide out in as a child.

"See anything?" Taylor was on his hands and knees, peering in.

"You can fit through. But it might be tight." Poised to leap back, she reached out and gingerly lifted the red blanket, half expecting a mouse to scamper out. She released a long sigh when one didn't, but she was surprised nonetheless. Under the blanket was an ashtray filled with butts.

"That's weird," she said.

"Not really. Parker probably came up here to sneak a smoke."

Nasty habit, she thought as she leaned over to grab the ashtray. The floor under the ashtray teetered beneath the weight of her hand. Catching her balance, she set the ashtray aside, then lowered her head and inspected the floor.

"The wood floor in here has been cut. I wonder . . ." She wiggled the wood a bit, getting one side to rise up a few inches. Grabbing the edge, she lifted the board off. "I knew it. It's a secret compartment!" She was filled with admiration for her father's cleverness. It's exactly what she would have done if she'd had a fort like this.

"What's in it?"

"Just a minute." She wiped her brow, feeling the heat of the attic. Behind her, Taylor had climbed through the door to his waist and was watching over her shoulder with keen interest. She handed him the pieces as she pulled them out.

There were three watches sans bands. A black velvet bag. A few empty gun shells. A World War II medal, a few pennies so green with age she couldn't make them out. On the bottom of the compartment were three slim books. She pulled them out and set them on her lap.

"Are they yours?"

Harper was wildly wondering the same thing. Could her father have gotten hold of books she'd written as a girl, perhaps from Mamaw, and had them printed? "Wouldn't that be lovely?" she said with a child's delight. To think he might have read them, cherished them enough to bind them up. Her hands were dusty. She wiped them on her apron before inspecting the first book on her lap. She carefully opened the navy cover.

"It's not mine. It's a self-published book. Oh, Taylor, this might be one of *his* books. My God, it might be the only copies we have of something Parker wrote." Her heart beat faster.

She reverently turned the page and read the title. *Tideland Treasures*. She looked up at Taylor and grinned with anticipation. She began to read aloud.

> On a small barrier island there lived children who sat
> only on towels when they went to the beach, swam only
> in chlorinated swimming pools, who never picked up
> a fishing rod, and who never, ever ventured from the
> paved path.
> And then there was Atticus and his sisters, Dora, Car-
> son, and Harper.

Harper's voice faded until the last word, her own name, came out a mere whisper. She felt the heat of the room like a furnace, and her head grew dizzy as all the comments, gestures, glances, and clues that had been floating in her head the past few weeks fell neatly into one inevitable conclusion.

Those eyes. Those incredible Muir-blue eyes.

She looked at Taylor. His green gaze was hooded, masking his emotions so he could better gauge hers.

Harper closed the book and licked her parched lips. "We'd best get Mamaw."

Atticus sat at the granite counter of his condo, hands folded, head bent, praying for guidance.

Mamaw had called to tell him the cat was out of the bag. His sisters had discovered he was their brother. Something about a fort found in the attic and a book Parker had written. *Tideland Treasures* was the story of a boy named Atticus who had three sisters: Dora, Carson, and Harper. How ironic, Atticus thought bitterly, because none of the three were mentioned at all in the terrible book he had read. He looked at the marked-up, tattered manuscript lying on the counter.

He dropped his forehead to his palm. He felt overwhelmed with shame, panic. All that he'd built with his sisters—trust, confidence, even affection—would be soured by this. They'd only know that he'd lied to them.

Why hadn't he just told them the truth? He'd asked himself this same question over and over for weeks now. What madness convinced him to agree to that lie in the first place? And how did he and Mamaw think they wouldn't be discovered and not hurt the very ones they had hoped to protect? Now nothing was left for him to do but man up and face them. To let them vent their anger.

He looked outside the window at the ocean sparkling in the distance. He'd come to love living here, being near his new-found family. God help him, he was going to miss having them in his life. Leaving them—leaving the lowcountry—would be the hardest thing he'd ever had to do. Mamaw and his sisters had filled the hole inside him. And now he'd ruined it. They'd never trust him again. Atticus squeezed his eyes tight, feeling the hole in his heart opening again, fathomless.

After a moment, he reached out to pick up Parker's manuscript from the table. This, he now knew, was the only copy of their—and his—father's book. It was the treasure for which the girls had been searching for so long. Not because it was an outstanding novel and would bring great wealth; sadly it wasn't. But because the book was Parker's life's work. That made it priceless. At the very least, he could give them their father's book as a parting gift. He slowly set down the manuscript, resting his hand upon the tattered pages. At least with that, having met him wouldn't be a total loss for them.

The Muir women congregated in Harper's office, seated on chairs clustered around the coffee table. Everyone hastily called to this gathering and pulled from a wedding task on an already busy day now sat stunned and wide-eyed at the news that their father's old fort had been found in the attic, with the children's books authored by him nestled within. Outside the room, the calls of workmen echoed and the hammering was distracting. Inside the office, it was as silent as the grave. Tension crackled in the air as Harper read the line from their father's book:

"'And then there was Atticus and his sisters, Dora, Carson, and Harper.'"

The silence continued. Mamaw looked at each girl's face. Dora sat far back on the settee, her blond hair pulled back in a sloppy ponytail and her eyes wide as saucers. Carson sat beside her and dropped her face in her hands. Harper closed the books and sat stiffly, ankles together and lips tight, like a marionette.

"He's our brother," Dora said in a flat voice. "Our *brother*!" she exploded. "Daddy's illegitimate son, born just months after Harper. Both women must've been pregnant at the same time. For God's sake, didn't Parker ever keep his pickle in the jar?"

"Dora!" Mamaw exclaimed, shocked. It was one thing to think it, another to shout it out so crudely.

"I can't believe Atticus lied to us," Harper said, her voice high with emotion. "After all his talk about honesty."

"I know," Carson agreed. She shook her head disbelievingly. "I should've trusted my instincts. There was something about him that seemed like we'd met before, a deeper connection than just a minister or a friend. And then, those blue eyes. And you, Mamaw"—Carson pointed her finger at her grandmother accusingly—"you covered for him. That's what threw me off the scent."

The three girls turned their heads to look reproachfully at Mamaw.

"I did *not* cover for him," Mamaw said sternly. "There was no covering up at all. He came to see me that first day, and we decided, Atticus and I, not to tell you the truth about all this until after the weddings. In fact, it was my idea in the first place not to tell you. Atticus didn't like the idea of lying. And by the way," Mamaw said with emphasis, "we didn't lie. I told you that Atticus was a minister and that I asked him to marry you. All that is true."

"You just omitted the little part about him being our brother," Carson spat out.

"Only temporarily. We were going to tell you after the wedding. I thought it would be too stressful for you to deal with."

"And this isn't?" Harper's voice was an octave higher than normal.

"You weren't supposed to find out."

"Well, we did," Carson fired out. "And I feel like I've been betrayed. That my trust was betrayed. I told him very personal feelings. I believed him."

A knock sounded at the door.

"Taylor is furious," Harper added. "I had to stop him from going over and having it out with Atticus."

"It's not Taylor's issue to deal with." Mamaw's voice was harsh with outrage. "I will not have it."

The knock sounded again. "Mrs. Muir?" a voice rang out from behind the door. "It's Beth from Wildflowers. I have a quick question for you."

Mamaw closed her eyes tight a moment, then composed, called back, "I'll be there in a minute." She felt the tension rising in the room. Everyone had a million tasks to attend to, which only exacerbated the already-short tempers. This had to be the worst time for the news to come out.

"You stirred the pot," Dora said to Mamaw. "Bringing Atticus in here under false pretenses. Of course we're upset. What did you think would happen when we found out?"

"I didn't think that far ahead," Mamaw admitted honestly. "I was so thrilled to meet my grandson. And I was so pleased with the way you were all getting along. You did get along. You can't deny it."

"But it was all based on a lie."

"I don't want him to marry us. Who knows if he's even a real minister?"

"He was taking advantage of us."

"How do we know he really is our brother?"

The girls' voices all rose over each other until Mamaw couldn't bear the backbiting any longer. She clapped her hands. "Stop it! Be quiet," she said in a controlled fury. She looked at each of her granddaughters without hurry. "Atticus Green *is* your brother. The only brother you have. And he is my grandson. And as such he is as dear to me as every one of you."

The three women stared back at their grandmother, summarily silenced.

Another knock sounded on the door. "Excuse me, Mrs. Muir. It's Dan with the tent. Would you come take a look?"

"One moment!" she called back in a frustrated shout. She could feel her heart accelerating. Everyone seemed to want a piece of her today. And it felt as if her granddaughters were ganging up on her. It was all too much. She looked down at her hands and saw them shaking. Clasping them together, she lifted her chin and faced her granddaughters.

"I pray that none of you have to endure the agony of burying a child." Her gaze lingered on Harper. "You never fully get over it. And Parker was my only child." She looked across the room at the rows of books on the shelves, recalling how Parker had loved to read in this very room.

Mamaw's face softened with memories. "You never forget any of the things they'd done or said, no matter how trivial. The sound of his laugh, the feel of my arms around him, his arms around me. That morning when I opened the door and saw Atticus standing there, I thought I'd seen a ghost. I called out Parker's name."

"Oh, Mamaw," Carson said with sympathy.

Mamaw placed her hands on her lips to still the trembling. "I saw my son in his son. I still think back on that moment with a degree of disbelief and awe."

"But why did you feel you couldn't tell us the truth about Atticus?" Dora asked.

"Atticus didn't want me to tell you. We made a promise."

"But why? I don't understand." Dora looked both confused and hurt.

"He had only just discovered the truth of his birth a week before. Imagine how *he* felt learning that the father he'd known his entire life wasn't his biological parent? His father had died some years ago, his mother had just passed several months prior, and he'd thought he was alone, without family, only to suddenly learn in a letter from his mother's lawyer that he had a grandmother and three half sisters he'd never known existed. He didn't know how we'd react to the news of his not only being your illegitimate brother, but one who was black. You have to put yourself in his shoes."

"It wouldn't have mattered that he was black," Harper said dismissively.

"It might have mattered to some people," Dora argued. "He's a black man from the South. Of course he wondered."

"Dora's right," Mamaw said. "I'm not sure he believed me when I told him it wouldn't matter until he met you, Harper. Then you, Carson. After that, he agreed to go along with my plan. It seemed harmless at the time. I don't think either of us realized how quickly he would come to feel like one of the family. By then it was too late."

"It doesn't matter. You should have told us," Harper said, frowning. "Atticus preached honesty, and now it all feels like a sham. All of it. And it's all the worse now because we feel that you lied to us, too. I don't know if I can forgive him."

The door knocked again. "Mrs. Muir?"

"Coming!" Mamaw called out sharply, at the end of her patience. "I have to go before they knock the door down," she said irritably. She put her fingers to her temples, took a breath, then slowly rose to her feet and rounded the sofa. She paused, hands on its back. She turned to her granddaughters sitting before her, her face grave.

"Your father, God rest his soul, is dead. We were blessed to find these treasures. And more than blessed to discover he had a son." She took a breath. "I have a grandson! And you have a brother. Be careful, girls. You're all self-righteous now. But think. How has Atticus helped you these past few months? Whenever you called, he came running—and you called him often. You couldn't have asked more from him if you did know he was your brother. In matters of the heart, he couldn't have been more true."

Across the room the three women's faces were introspective more than angry.

"Where is Atticus now?" Dora wanted to know.

Mamaw was pleased to hear Dora's tone was conciliatory. "On his way here. I called him. He should be here soon. I think"—Mamaw walked toward the door—"that you should all talk amongst yourselves before he arrives. I'll make tea."

Atticus slipped in the front door without anyone's noticing him. Men and women were buzzing everywhere like worker bees, traipsing across paper walkways that protected the newly buffed floors. He ducked his head and walked quickly down the hall to Harper's office, where Mamaw had told him the girls had congregated when she called him to come.

He knocked three times, firmly, on the office door.

The door opened and he was face-to-face with Harper. She looked trim and tidy, but her face was chalky with fatigue. He was sorry to see that. She should look happy the day before her wedding festivities began. Elated.

"Come in," she said in a flat voice, void of her usual charm.

Across the room, Dora and Carson sat side by side on the settee. Neither of them smiled when they saw him. Nor was Mamaw in the room. He could have used her support. His heart sank as he walked in, but his shoulders were straight with determination. He knew what he had to say.

Harper shut the door and followed him across the room. When they reached the group, she said graciously, "Won't you sit down? There's tea. Would you like a glass?"

Always the proper hostess, he thought. "No, thanks. I prefer to stand."

Harper's brow rose but she accepted his decision and went to sit in the chair beside Carson. Atticus faced his three half sisters. They made a united front, and he'd never felt more the outsider. He took a deep breath.

"I'm sorry I didn't tell you who I was. There were many times over the past months I wanted to, believe me, I really did. But the lie had grown so big I couldn't tell you without you feeling"—he paused, then continued with regret—"without you feeling exactly the way you do now. This isn't what I wanted to happen. Your grandmother and I both had the best intentions when this ruse started. And, ladies"—he paused, then said with heart—"*Sisters*, I hope you know I care about you. Deeply. I would never do anything to intentionally hurt you. I realize now that the road to hell is paved with good intentions."

They all were looking at him, hands folded in their laps, sitting on the edge of their seats, listening. But not one of them spoke. If this was his jury, he'd just been found guilty. They were cutting him off without uttering a word. And he couldn't blame them. He felt embarrassed, ashamed, alone.

"I'll go. I'll make arrangements with a local minister to officiate the weddings, so I won't be leaving you stuck at the eleventh hour. There's just one more thing." He lifted the plastic grocery bag in his hands and pulled out the manuscript. "I received this from my mother's lawyers. Along with birthday cards your . . . our . . . father sent me every year. He put dollars in the cards, to match my age." Atticus laughed shortly. "I never got more than eight dollars. Of course, I never received them as a child. Not until the lawyers sent me the letter from my mother after her death. When she told me about Parker Muir being my father."

He took a breath and began telling them the full truth. "My mother was an assistant editor in New York. Her name was Zora Green. She worked for your mother, Harper."

Harper gasped and clutched her sister's arm.

"Georgiana ordered my mother to edit your father's manuscript. That's how they met. How they fell in love. Neither of them planned for her to get pregnant, but she did. With me. My mother returned to Atlanta where my real father raised me as his own. And as you know, Georgiana divorced Parker."

"That's why she hated him," Harper said with new insight. "He cheated on her."

Atticus shook his head. "Apparently she wasn't too fond of him before that. According to my mother's letter, their marriage was on the rocks already."

Harper put her hand to her forehead. "That, sadly, sounds more like Georgiana. She no doubt hated him all the more for embarrassing her."

"We'll never know. I don't care, to tell you the truth. But you should know your father did the honorable thing. He asked my mother to marry him. But she refused. All she asked of him was that he never contact me. Other than the birthday cards, which my mother saved for me, he never did. She also saved this."

Atticus carried the manuscript to the coffee table. The pitiful-looking pile of papers, curled at the edges, was heavily marked in blue, cut and pasted old-school with scissors and tape, all bound by two thick elastic bands.

"What's that?" Dora asked.

"Your father's manuscript. My mother edited it. This was her copy."

Harper let loose a squelched sob and rushed for the manuscript, holding it in front of her with disbelieving eyes. "This is his book?"

Atticus nodded. "Yes. I wanted to give it to you earlier, but I couldn't without y'all knowing everything. So . . ." He let his explanation wither. They knew the rest.

Harper's eyes were filled with tears. "Why didn't you just tell me? I would have kept your secret. Didn't you trust me?"

"Or me?" Carson asked, the anger in her tone betrayed by her trembling lips. "We shared so much. I bared my soul to you. And you held back. That's what really burns me."

Atticus was glad to hear the anger and the hurt. These were honest emotions he could deal with, much better than the cold silence.

"I couldn't tell one without telling you all. I was stuck between a rock and a hard place with no salvation between. I'm sorry."

"What bothers me is how you talked about being honest. And you weren't being honest," Harper said.

"I'm being honest now. I am Parker Muir's son." It felt empowering to say the words. Freeing. "This is the first time I've said that out loud. I am your half brother. Regardless of what you think of me, this is an immutable fact. I think each of you is a fine, remarkable, good woman. I'm proud to be your brother. You've brought a lot of happiness to my life. And meaning. You've made me feel part of your family. You know, I thought when I came here that I had a mission to help you. I see now I had it all wrong. You saved me. I'm only sorry that I may have destroyed my chance to continue being a part of your family. I'm sorry."

"Stop apologizing." Harper rushed forward to put her arms around him. "It's all in the past. The future starts right now."

Atticus felt a shuddering relief and hugged his sister without restraint. Dora came hustling around the cocktail table to wrap her arms around him in a sweep of emotion. Atticus looked over Harper's shoulder at Carson. She remained seated on the sofa, slump shouldered. Their gazes met. Atticus saw in her eyes the fierce war raging within her. Carson, so strong, so tough. She, perhaps, had been hurt the most by his deception. They'd shared a deeper bond, bound by the inherited gene of alcoholism. If he should have told anyone, it should have been her.

I'm sorry, he mouthed to her directly, and held out an open arm.

Carson rose and, her face crumpling, came to his open arm. For that brief moment of connection, wrapped in his sisters' arms, Atticus felt whole again. When they separated, no shyness or awkwardness was between them, only a newfound happiness.

"So you're my brother." Carson wiped her eyes.

"Your half brother," he corrected.

"Don't let Mamaw hear you say that," Dora warned. "She hates that phrase. She says blood is blood and there's no watering that down."

"So I guess we still have a minister for the weddings?" Harper asked him hopefully.

"If you'll have me."

"It's either that or walk us down the aisle," Carson told him. "You are the only surviving male Muir."

"I'm still Atticus Green. That hasn't changed."

"No, of course not," Carson amended. "But you're also a Muir."

"I am."

"We have to tell Mamaw," Harper said. "She'll be so pleased. She didn't tolerate us berating you in front of her."

"Which of course we did freely and viciously," Carson said.

"Nothing more than I deserved." Atticus looked at the brides. "So the weddings are still on as scheduled?"

Harper looked at him suspiciously. "Of course. Why do you ask?"

"Well"—Atticus held his hands behind his back—"now that everything's out in the open and being that I'm your brother and all, I figure I can voice my opinion openly, too."

"Okay," Harper replied warily.

"Since full and complete honesty is being called into question today, let's all come clean. Like Harper said, the future begins today."

They looked back at him, curious and mildly amused.

Atticus grinned and pointed his finger at Harper and Carson. "You two aren't being honest about your weddings. In particular, about where your weddings are being held."

Dora perked up, catching on. "Amen, Brother! I've been after them about this forever. You've been like two hens picking at seed. All you do is talk about each other's wedding, not your own. Girls, be honest like Atticus said. Neither of you want the wedding you're having. You both know you want to get married at each other's venue."

"What are you saying?" Harper's eyes were wide with disbelief. "You aren't suggesting we cancel our weddings?"

"No, not cancel." Atticus held his arms akimbo and looked at her from under gathered brows.

In their prolonged silence, Carson and Harper looked at each other, neither taking a breath.

"Switch?" Carson asked in a whisper.

"Why not?" Dora asked.

"No!" Harper said, getting her back up. "That's ridiculous. Everything is set. It can't be changed now."

"Of course it can," Dora argued. "Stop being so rigid. You can do anything you want. You're the bride! It's about time you realized that. And with your efficient brain working on it, you'll have new lists for us to start checking off in no time. This is your wedding, Harper. And yours, Carson. You've both been trying so hard to please everyone else you neglected yourselves. Now's the time to be honest, right, Rev?"

Atticus chuckled at hearing Dora call him by that nickname.

"Right." He put on his serious face. He liked seeing this bossy side of Dora, playing the elder card. It suited her.

"Tell me the truth. Carson, do you want to get married on the beach?"

Carson blinked, took a breath. "Yes."

Dora's face flooded with satisfaction, even as Harper's shifted to shock.

"Now you, Harper," Dora said. "Do you want to get married at the plantation?"

"It doesn't matter. Granny James—"

"I'm not asking Granny James," Dora interrupted. "I'm asking you. For once, Harper, tell us what *you* want." When Harper hesitated, wringing her hands, Dora nearly shouted, "Where's your spine, girl? Damn the torpedoes."

"Yes!" Harper shouted back at her. "All right? Yes, I wish I was getting married at the plantation. So what? All this talk of a switch is nothing more than crazy."

"Why is it crazy?" Carson grinned happily. "Come on, Harpo. This is our adventure, right? Our weddings. We've never been afraid before. Let's not start now. Like you said, the future begins today. Okay, Brave New World." Carson straightened her shoulders. "I want to get married on the beach."

Harper dropped the manuscript, she was so shaken. She stood, hands at her side, wide-eyed, frozen in indecision. She looked at Atticus for guidance, her large blue eyes limpid in fear.

Atticus shrugged and shook his head, indicating this was her decision to make. He'd led her to this point, but could go no further.

"It's time to put the mouse to rest," Dora said to her gently. "You're not that little girl anymore."

"If I do this, I'll feel like a rat."

Carson and Dora laughed.

"You're going to be a mother," Dora said. "You're a lioness."

Carson put out her hands to capture Harper's. She gave the smaller hands a squeeze. "What do you say, Sis? You and me again on another adventure on Sullivan's Island. Will you switch with me? Do you dare?"

Harper's eyes flashed and she smiled a crooked grin. "You bet I do."

Chapter Twenty-Three

*In nothing does the present time more greatly differ
from the close of the last century, than in the unreserved
frankness of young women and men towards each other.*

—Etiquette, 1951 edition, Emily Post

*D*ora fluttered about her sisters like a mother hen, giving
orders, creating new to-do lists. It seemed to Atticus that she'd
found a new calling as a wedding planner. And speaking of
wedding planners, they'd called the wedding planner, Ashley
Rhodes, and, after assuring her that, no, they had not lost their
minds, filled her in on their plan to swap wedding venues.

"I'm a professional and managed countless weddings, but
I have to tell you, this is one for the books." Ashley released a
muffled laugh over the wire, one tinged with resignation. "But,
okay, if it's what you want to do. My duty is to make my brides
happy."

Mamaw and Granny James were not so amenable.

"But you can't!" Granny James exclaimed. "I planned every detail. My guests are arriving from Europe!"

"Exactly," Mamaw told her in no uncertain tone. "*You* planned everything. *Your* guests are arriving. What about Harper? It's *her* wedding, after all."

"And *you* didn't plan Carson's wedding?" Granny James fired back.

"I absolutely did. Every detail." Mamaw turned to Carson. "Though why in merciful heaven didn't you tell me what you wanted sooner?"

Carson shrugged sheepishly. "The same reason Harper didn't. You were having such a good time, and I felt I owed it to you to plan the wedding. And I was living under the delusion that it didn't matter where I got married. But I was wrong. It does."

"Blake can't be happy about this," Mamaw said with import. "His family has been married at the Legare Waring plantation for generations."

"Oh, he's happy about it." Carson grinned. "He loves the beach as much as I do. It's where we fell in love."

Mamaw harrumphed. "Well, his mother won't be happy, that's for true and certain."

"But *you*, Mamaw?" Carson asked with trepidation. "Are you okay with it?"

Mamaw stepped forward and captured Carson's face in her hands and kissed her soundly. "I just want you to be happy." Mamaw dropped her hands and repeated the gesture with Harper. "And you." She turned to look at Granny James. "Imogene and I will move mountains to make it happen. Won't we?"

Imogene didn't smile but she lifted her hands in surrender. "I'll agree on one condition. Taylor must agree."

"He will," Harper said readily.

"And, in the future, when we look back on this weekend as the *wedding debacle*, you will both admit you were wrong."

Mamaw laughed lightly. "Oh, that is easy to agree to because I'm never wrong."

Granny James threw her hands up in the air. "Oh, sod it. I agree."

"Oh, Granny, thank you!" Harper exclaimed, homing in to her grandmother's arms to kiss her cheek.

Granny James accepted her kiss and put up a good front of refusing to be mollified. "Though I can't imagine what I'm going to tell the guests."

"We've thought of that already." Harper hurried to her desk to grab her omnipresent clipboard. "Everyone is gathering here tomorrow night for the rehearsal dinner. We simply hand out new printed programs informing each of them of the change in venues. It will all be clear as day."

"Printed? On that copier with the cheap paper?" Granny James asked, horrified. "But we already have the most beautiful programs. With gilt edging." It was more a whine of regret than a serious complaint.

"They won't care if the printout doesn't have gilt," Harper said gently. "And after we make the announcement, they'll just be happy to know where to show up."

"You make it sound so simple."

"Because it is. It's done, Granny. You simply have to accept it, and the rest comes easily. If it hadn't been for Atticus making us realize how we truly felt, this farce would have continued, and neither Carson nor I would have looked back on our wedding day with the complete and utter joy that it was everything we both wanted. And now we will." Harper looked at Atticus. "We owe a lot to him."

"So you're the instigator of this conspiracy?" Granny James skewered Atticus with a look where he was lounging on a chair, happy as a clam.

Atticus grinned. "Guilty as charged."

Granny James narrowed her eyes. "Of course. You're a Muir, too, I understand."

Carson went over to put her hand on his shoulder. "He's our brother."

Granny James sniffed and said archly, "It figures." But her eyes held mirth.

Mamaw clapped her hands. "Ladies! We have plenty of time to rehash all this later. Right now we've more work to do than I can shake a stick at. Let's get back to business, shall we?"

In the flurry of activity, Mamaw drew Atticus aside. "I'm so happy it's all out in the open. At last. I was such a ninny to suggest it in the first place. Now I can shout out to the world that you're my grandson. I'm so very proud of you."

He smiled warmly. "The truth will set you free." He noted with some concern that she appeared tired and drawn. Her eyes didn't shine with their usual brightness. "Are you feeling all right? Are you truly okay about all this?"

"Me, oh, I'm just tired." Mamaw sighed. "But one is only as happy as her least happy child." She looked toward the door. "Dora's left. She just got a text from Devlin. He's not coming to the dinner tomorrow night. I don't think he's coming to the weddings, either."

"The hell he isn't." Atticus bent to kiss her cheek. "Hold down the fort, I'll be right back." He squeezed her hands.

Atticus hurried from the room, unnoticed by all save Mamaw. This late in the afternoon most of the worker bees had left to return tomorrow morning. The house was quiet as he rushed through the rooms.

"Powwow over?" Taylor asked as Atticus came upon him in the kitchen. He was standing at the counter, making himself a sandwich.

"Yes, for now. Hey, you okay with the wedding switch?"

"What wedding switch?"

"Ah," Atticus said, quickly backpedaling. "You might want to check in with your fiancée. There's news afoot."

"What now?" Taylor asked warily.

"How do you feel about a plantation wedding instead of a beach wedding?"

Taylor snorted. "You had me going there for a minute. As long as I don't switch brides." His laugh quieted and he said sincerely, "I fell in love with Harper the moment I saw her. Hit me like a thunderbolt. There's no one else for me. Harper just has to tell me where to show up and at what time and I'm there. I'm marrying *her*, and whether it's at a beach or under some tree, what the hell do I care? And for the record, I'm betting Blake feels the same about Carson."

"Good man." Atticus tapped the doorframe. "You seen Dora?"

"Yeah. She just grabbed her purse and headed out."

Cursing under his breath, Atticus picked up his pace as he ran out the front door, in time to see Dora's car slowly backing out. He darted down the stairs and rounded her car to stand in front and slap his palm down on the hood.

Dora braked with a jerk. "What the heck are you doing?" she called out, shocked. "You could've gotten yourself killed!"

Atticus hurried to her door and opened it. "Come on out, Dora. You're not going anywhere until we sort things through."

She sat looking out the windshield. "You and I have nothing to sort out."

"But you and Devlin do."

She shot him a guarded glance. "What do you know about me and Devlin?"

"I know that you're about to make the biggest mistake of your life." Her eyes flashed but he pressed on. "Dora, let's talk. Just for a minute."

Dora slid her hands from the steering wheel and nodded. "Okay," she said reluctantly.

Atticus noticed her SEA BREEZE BRIDES shirt, stained now with dirt from the plants. "Nice T-shirt."

She tugged at the hem of the blue shirt. "You're the only one that thinks so. I'm the only one wearing it."

"Everyone got caught short today. Your sisters will wear the shirts tomorrow."

"You mean *our* sisters, don't you?"

He smiled. "Our sisters," he corrected himself, feeling the impact of the moment. "By the way, it was nice seeing you be the older sister up there. You have a lot of strength."

She seemed surprised by the compliment. "Thanks. Lucille once called me the rock. I forget that sometimes."

"I wish I could have known her."

"You would have loved her. We all did."

There followed an awkward silence. Dora lifted her hands

to the steering wheel. Her fingers tapped it; she was clearly nervous.

Atticus got right to the point. "So tell me why Devlin isn't coming to the weddings."

Dora didn't question how he'd heard the news. "He says he can't."

"Can't why?"

"He says he can't pretend anymore. He can't pretend he's part of the family when I won't let him be."

"Because you won't marry him."

She nodded. "Right."

"Dora, *why* won't you marry him? I'm new here and even I can tell you two should be married."

"I'm not ready. I have to feel settled first. Find a new place to live. Sell the house in Summerville—"

"That sounds like a to-do list, not reasons not to get married," Atticus interrupted. "You demanded honesty from your sisters a little while ago. And honesty from me. So I'm going to demand that same honesty from you now. Do you love him?"

"Yes."

"Do you want to marry him?"

"Yes—someday."

"There is no someday, Dora. There's now, or I'm guessing never."

Her lips tightened and she looked down at her hands.

"You want to know what I hear? I hear you give a lot of reasons why you can't get married. I hear you being cautious and practical . . . and selfish."

"Selfish?"

"Yes, selfish. While you're compiling that long list of things you want to get done before you get married, have you ever stopped to ask yourself what Devlin might want? What he might be feeling?"

Dora didn't answer, but she had a haunted expression.

"Devlin's a good man. Ask yourself—honestly—if any of your reasons are worth losing him. And if your answer is what I think it will be, stop procrastinating and go after him."

"Go after him?"

"You love him. You want to marry him—then just do it!"

Dora burst into a wide grin, one of relief, he thought. And joy. Definitely joy. She fired up the engine, gunning it once with a laugh.

"Marry that man!" Atticus shouted. "Carpe diem!"

Dora beeped the horn twice and was on her way.

The parking lot was nearly empty in front of the white wood house with black shutters. A huge oak tree with thick boughs almost obscured the building from Palm Boulevard, but the large black-and-white sign that spelled out CASSELL REAL ESTATE and was shaped to look like a medieval castle was clearly visible from the street. Dora parked her car and went directly to the door, jiggling the keys in her pocket.

The door was unlocked. Inside, the six desks of her fellow agents were cluttered with paper and a few Styrofoam cups. The room smelled of burnt coffee. Her own desk in the last row was relatively neat, not because she was tidy but because as yet she had few clients. She walked to the back of the room to where one office was enclosed. The name DEVLIN CASSELL was on the door. She lifted her hand to form a fist, gathering her courage to knock. *You can't chicken out now,* she told herself. She heard Atticus's voice ring out in her head: *Carpe diem.*

She gave a cursory thump, but the door wasn't completely shut and the force of her knock pushed it open enough for her to see Devlin sitting at his enormous desk, arms stretched out and hands around a cut-glass tumbler.

He looked up at the noise and, seeing her, leaned far back in his chair. The springs squeaked with the effort. He eyed her without surprise, indeed without any discernible emotion.

"What are you doing here?"

She stepped into the room and closed the door behind her. "Hello to you, too."

Devlin scowled and took a sip of his drink. She heard the ice clink in the silence.

"Can I pour you one?"

"Yes, please."

His brows rose, seemingly surprised by her response. Over the past year she'd nagged him to cut back on his drinking, and he had. For her sake. Devlin obligingly rose to walk to the walnut cupboard and retrieve another cut-glass tumbler. He filled it with ice from the automatic ice maker, then returned to his desk and poured her a splash of bourbon. Devlin tilted his head and looked at her with question, bottle tilted over the glass.

"Just a scotch more." Dora lifted her fingers to indicate a small amount.

Devlin poured in another splash.

"Maybe just a scotch more."

Devlin almost smiled and poured her a liberal amount. He

handed her the glass, his eyes studying her speculatively as he leaned back against his desk. "What's the occasion?"

Dora looked at her glass, feeling her stomach tie up in knots. All her life she'd been told to act the lady. To let the man lead, to take charge. Her mother had instructed her countless times that no man wanted a pushy woman. But today she'd watched her sisters stand up for themselves and voice what they'd wanted. They weren't pushy in the least, they would simply no longer be pushed around. She saw Carson and Harper as strong and honest women. Didn't Atticus tell her she was strong? Didn't she have the same right to speak her mind? she asked herself. She took a bolstering mouthful of bourbon, coughing slightly at the burn as it slid down her throat. Atticus's words flashed again in her mind, as they had over and over during her drive here.

There is no someday, Dora. There's now, or I'm guessing never.

Dora wasn't looking for never. She wanted forever.

Taking a breath, she looked up into Devlin's eyes. He was waiting, watching her closely.

"I'd like to ask you . . . Devlin, will you marry me?"

He froze for a moment, staring at her as one who wasn't sure he'd heard quite correctly.

"You're asking me to marry you?"

"Yes. Or rather, I am. I believe you're the one who's supposed to say yes in this scenario."

Devlin's eyes were sparkling with amusement blended with love. "Hell, yes!"

Dora smiled, embarrassed and happy and unsure what to do next. She looked at her glass. "Good. Real good." She sighed in relief. "I wasn't sure you were going to say yes."

In silence, Devlin took her tumbler, then set both on the desk. Then he took her hands in his. "Woman, why in the world would you think I'd answer anything but yes?"

"You gave me a scare when you said you weren't coming to the weddings. Set me to thinking. Really thinking. For a year I've been telling you what I needed in order to say yes to your proposal. And you kept waiting, helping me, helping Nate. I kept putting you off and you bore it as few men would. Never losing faith." She paused, gathering strength for honesty. "I felt I needed to prove to myself that I could take care of myself and my son. Then I would feel worthy of being your wife."

"Worthy?" Devlin said with disbelief. "Don't you know I worked hard all these years, raised myself up from nothing, just to make myself worthy of you?"

Dora squeezed his hands and smiled tenderly. "What a pair we make. Devlin, it must've been hard with the two weddings coming, reminding you of how I've been making you wait. That was selfish of me. I'm sorry. I see now how I should have put your needs and wants first. That's what love is. Selfless and unconditional. And it's about trust. I was burned. We both were. But because of you I know I can trust a man again. I trust you."

She stepped closer, placing her left hand on his chest. "Devlin Cassell, I love you. I always have and always will. So, if you still have that ring, I'd be proud to wear it."

Chapter Twenty-Four

*Two lowcountry weddings—one at the beach, one at a plantation.
Each venue is as unique as the bride, yet each is equally
bound by the traditions and values of the lowcountry.*

*I*t was a perfect night for a party. The temperature was balmy,
with that moist, tropical breeze that smelled of night jasmine
and a hint of the sea. It gently caressed her skin, heated after
an evening of dancing and drinks.

Mamaw sat on the rocker of her front porch. Edward had
always told her to leave the party at its height. And so she
did, making her unhurried way down the front stairs across
the gravel to her own sweet cottage. She was still fully dressed
in her fancy silk underclothes, black silk nylons, the dreaded
girdle that seemed tighter every time she put it on, and the stiff
and constricting black taffeta gown with elaborate beading that
caught the moonlight and shimmered with her every movement. The dress was an old warhorse brought out of mothballs

for the party. That was the advantage of couture gowns, she thought. Vintage never went out of style. And at her age, she thought it unseemly to struggle to keep up with the latest fashions when classic always struck a dignified note.

She was tired and a bit woozy from the several Lowcountry Wedding signature cocktails she'd enjoyed. They had a bit of a kick in them, as Lucille liked to say. But who was counting? What a party it was! She had to laugh when she recalled the shocked looks on the guests' faces when Carson and Harper announced the switch of venues. The staff discreetly and swiftly handed out the newly printed programs directing Harper's guests to the Legare Waring plantation and Carson's guests to Wild Dunes Resort. She thought poor Linda Legare looked ready to pitch a hissy fit. Mamaw chuckled again. But it all went off as planned, and after the music picked up again, the party resumed without a hitch.

Carson and Harper had never looked lovelier. Their faces shone with excitement and anticipation, befitting fiancées on the eve of their weddings. Yet, Mamaw thought with a wry grin, Dora may have stolen the limelight tonight. When she walked in flashing her stunning diamond engagement ring, the party's excitement shot to new heights. At last, Dora had come fully into herself. She was a woman in love, every bit as radiant as the brides. Though the one who might've looked even happier was Devlin. He accepted the congratulations like a rooster crowing at the sun.

And speaking of love . . . Atticus had never left the side of a certain attractive woman he'd escorted to the dinner. Word spread fast on this little island, and Mamaw had already learned that she was the local vet. From what Mamaw could tell, Atticus looked like a hound dog that had caught the scent. She chuckled to herself. If Lucille were here, they'd already be matchmaking.

Oh, the parties this house had seen, she thought, looking out from her cottage porch to Sea Breeze, alight tonight with the festive fairy lights and live music of the rehearsal dinner. Her dear home had been polished and primped as it hadn't been in years. Tonight Sea Breeze appeared as breathtakingly shimmering and filled with golden light as any bride.

Her Sea Breeze.

Contemplating that she would be leaving it after all was bittersweet. Though she would be only a stone's throw away, she felt the apron strings tug at her heart. In this house she'd reigned as hostess to parties, baptisms, graduations, weddings, even funerals. She'd watched her granddaughters grow from carefree children into women she was proud of. Under the roof of Sea Breeze she'd welcomed Blake and Taylor and Devlin to the family. She had met her grandson, Atticus. The future appeared bright on the horizon.

She'd said her farewells here, too. Her mind conjured up a vision of dear Edward, wiry and tanned, laughing as he carried a towheaded Parker on his shoulders to the beach. *Parker.* Thinking of Parker, she always saw her son as a young man in his twenties—in his prime. So full of life and dreams. So confident of his position, his good looks, his talent. She could think of him now without pain. Rather, she felt a comfort keeping his memory alive. He would have been sixty now had he lived, likely white in his hair, wrinkles here and there, the proud father walking his daughters down the aisle. She sniffed and reached for the handkerchief she kept in her sleeve. But that was not to be, she told herself, stopping herself from slipping into the maudlin. This was a night for joy. Carson and Harper had bestowed on her the honor of walking them down the aisle. A particular pride was associated with that, she thought with a sniff.

Finally, she remembered the brown, wise, yet maddeningly unlined face of Lucille, her large eyes flashing with humor or a scold. Tonight the past was as alive in Mamaw's heart as the present. So many changes, she thought, kicking off the rocking motion with her foot.

"What did you 'spect?" came a voice in her mind's ear.

It was often like this when she sat alone on the porch of the cottage, especially on a soft night such as this when the ringing of laughter wafted down from the big house. Marietta was not superstitious. But she was Charleston born and bred and had seen and heard too much in those old houses not to know that spirits came and went at their pleasure. Still, she told herself she only imagined her dear Lucille sitting here with her, as she had so often throughout their lives together. So many years of coming up with one harebrained scheme after another, playing hands of gin rummy, and just passing the time as old friends did. When Marietta heard a voice in her head, it did not cause her apprehension nor did she feel haunted. She simply accepted the voice as a comfort in her old age. Welcomed it.

"I suppose I expected things to go on the way they were . . . forever," she replied.

She heard a rustling in the leaves that sounded like laughter. "Them girls were going to get married, start lives of their own someday," Lucille said. "You knew that. Well, that day's here, so no use bellyaching about it."

"I'm not bellyaching," Mamaw said indignantly. "Can't an old woman get teary eyed with nostalgia?"

"Sure she can. Only not too much. You'll spoil your makeup. Your fella is going to come lookin' for you pretty soon."

So like Lucille, always looking out for her. "You like him, don't you?"

"Always did. Girard's a fine man. Got what I call character. And he's a looker, too."

Mamaw smiled and curled her toes at the memory of how handsome Girard looked in his dinner jacket tonight.

"The weddings begin tomorrow," she said, not quite believing the day had finally arrived. "Two lowcountry weddings—one at the beach, one at a plantation. Each venue is as unique as the bride, yet each is equally bound by the traditions and values of the lowcountry. Oh, Lucille, I wish you could stand by my side at the ceremonies."

"I'll be there," came Lucille's voice on the wind. "I'll be right beside you, same as always."

Marietta felt the breeze glide across her face and sighed. "I know you will. We did it, Lucille. We've seen our Summer Girls married and settled. Happy. Oh, I know there will be bumps in the road ahead. There always are. But I have high hopes for them."

"I do, too. And from where I'm sittin' I got a good view."

Mamaw smiled, reassured by that. "What do I do now, old friend?"

A bird cackled in the old oak, shrill and high.

"Lucille?"

"You keep on living, old girl," came the voice, fading now as the sound of footfalls rose louder. "Tomorrow you pick up your skirt and dance!"

Mamaw, distracted by the sound of laughter, looked up to see her three granddaughters walking her way, arms linked, their long dresses flowing in the breeze, their faces shimmering in the night like the stars overhead. They were laughing and calling her name.

"Mamaw!"

"I'm here!" she called back.

They hurried up the stairs and surrounded her, wrapping arms around her, enveloping her in their scents, kissing her cheeks, scolding her for running off. She closed her eyes and heard their voices as a symphony of her life—highs and lows, dissonance and consonance, solos and duets, staccato and grave.

"We've come to fetch you back to the party," Carson said, tugging at her arm.

"It's not a party without you," Dora added.

"Up now, Mamaw!" Harper exclaimed, helping her from the chair. "You are and always will be the hostess of Sea Breeze. Everyone is waiting on you."

Standing on her porch, Mamaw looked out and saw a young man walking toward her, cloaked in shadow. Her breath caught. Tall and slender, he walked with his hands in his pockets, his gait elegant and achingly familiar. *Parker,* her heart called out. Standing in the arms of his daughters, she felt his presence keenly.

Yet as the young man drew nearer into the light, she recognized his darker skin, his broader forehead, his fuller lips. This man was no one's ghost. He was his own man, she realized, seeing his eyes light up at the sight of her and his sisters. Her grandson.

"Atticus." She reached out her hand.

"Mamaw." Atticus kissed her hand. "Come. The night is still young. The party has just begun!"

Snapshots

Legare Waring House

Harper felt as though she was in a dream as she rode in the white horse-drawn carriage down the long alley of ancient oaks. Moss dripped from the boughs like bridal lace. It was twilight and a hush fell over the lush, historic gardens of the Legare Waring House as though the earth held its breath for her wedding. She heard the *clop clop clop* of the hooves, was enveloped in the heady scent of jasmine, and everywhere she looked she saw signs of the lowcountry she had come to love and call home.

The sound of the hooves alerted the guests gathered under the drape of oaks. Everyone stood and turned toward her. Harper felt her heart flutter in her chest like a caged bird eager to take flight. Granny James and Mamaw came to her side, each dressed in beige lace. Linking arms, she felt their wisdom, strength, and love support her. The string quartet started to play, and with her grandmothers, she began her walk toward a small white tented pavilion decked with seasonal flowers. Hanging from ropes, mason jar lanterns lit her way. She smiled when she saw Carson and Dora standing side by side in long dresses of coral.

Then she saw Taylor, standing straight and tall in his Marine dress blues, her knight in shining armor. Their eyes met and with a gasp the trembling bird in her chest broke free to soar. As she walked, smiling, toward her husband, she heard the whispers of the past rise up to wish this lowcountry bride a loving present and a bright future.

Wild Dunes Grand Pavilion

Who is that woman? Carson wondered as she stared at her reflection. Her long dark hair was curled, braided, and looped around her head with pearl pins. Large teardrop pearls fell from her ears. With her hair done up and dressed in the vintage gown, Carson thought she could be looking at the portrait of her ancestor Claire, the founder of the Muirs of Charleston.

She smiled at the thought and felt the confidence she always did when she saw the Muir blue eyes that represented generations of southern women who called the lowcountry home. In these final moments as a single woman, Carson searched for talismans to help her transition to wife. Soon she would unite with Blake in the eyes of her family and her community.

The door to her room opened and Mamaw, Dora, and Harper rushed in, a blur of aqua blue dresses, singing out a chorus of *oohs* and *ahhs* at seeing her in her bridal attire. Harper and Mamaw attached the French lace veil to the back of her head. Dora handed her a bouquet of white roses and blue hydrangeas. Grasping it, Carson felt a shiver of anticipation laced with anxiety. It was time.

Mamaw took her hand and led her out of the townhouse, one of a row of quaint and colorful townhouses along the board-walk at Wild Dunes. Her heart pounded in her chest and she felt the balmy air of the early evening envelope her as she made her way to the Grand Pavilion. She had always been afraid of commitment and here she was at the precipice of making the ultimate commitment—to love, honor, and cherish one man all the days of her life. She felt her footsteps falter. Mamaw clutched her hand tight.

Then she heard the call of the ocean. She followed her instincts and, picking up her hem, rushed down the remaining yards to the pavilion. The vista opened up to reveal the radiance of the sun sparkling on the blue ocean. She went directly to the gazebo railing to clutch it and stare out beyond the cluster of palms and shrubs. The long stretch of sandy beach and the ruffling white surf welcomed her. She sighed and felt her panic abate.

People clustered near four white pillars decorated with palm fronds and flowers. Her gaze zoomed to one dark-haired man, tall and slender, in a navy blazer and tan pants. Though he stood with his back to her, her heart saw the piercing dark eyes that were searching, waiting, she knew, only for her. Carson breathed deep the salty air and smiled with the calm of knowing. The water, the beach—this man—was where she belonged. She'd been right to get married here.

In a rush Carson felt her courage and joy rise up to crest in her heart and flow through her blood. She ran to the center of the pavilion, stretched out her arms and, letting her head fall back, twirled in a dance of joy while Mamaw, Harper, and Dora laughed and clapped.

"I'm getting married!"

Dora and Devlin held hands and snuck away from the reception. The band was playing "My Girl" and couples swayed slowly under the great gazebo overlooking the ocean. The moon was high and the stars were bright, lighting their path beneath the palms to the waiting car that Devlin had phoned to pick them up. They climbed into the backseat, giggling like kids.

"You sure you want to do this?" Devlin asked in the backseat. "That was one helluva wedding. You sure you don't want one like this? Or like Harper's? Just say the word and you'll have it."

"I've had the big wedding and I don't want another," Dora told him. "I only want you. Besides," she said, snuggling closer, "I think this is ever so much more romantic."

His eyes sparked as he bent to kiss her lips, the first of many to come.

"Where to, sir?" asked the driver.

"The airport," Devlin told him. Then, smiling his crooked grin, he looked into Dora's eyes and called out, "Las Vegas, here we come!"

Epilogue

It was a rainy June morning in the lowcountry. The soft rays of dawn were obscured by thick clouds the shades of blue and gray. They hung low with a mist that hovered over land and sea like a down blanket. From the harbor the sonorous foghorn of a towering cargo ship bellowed as the behemoth lumbered out to the open seas. The pungent, amniotic scent of the wetlands hung heavy in the air.

These were the magic hours for the lowcountry wildlife. Before the humans descended to the meandering creeks and racing rivers with their roaring boats and prying eyes. The tide was low and the mudflats presented a bountiful feast for the birds. Higher in the sky the great ospreys soared over the water searching with their binocular vision for a fish to bring home to the fledglings waiting in the nests.

In the Cove, all was serene. Not a paddleboard in sight. A dolphin swam at a leisurely pace against the current, arching gracefully, its silvery gray skin camouflaged by the steely color of the water. The dolphin journeyed to a particular dock she knew well. She could hear the rhythmic bumping of the lower dock against the wood pilings as it rose and fell with the waves. The dolphin's dark almond eyes searched the dock, circled again, and seeing no one, released a loud and plaintive whistle. A high-pitched, beckoning contact call for one particular human. A tall female with long dark hair and eyes the color of the skies on a cloudless day.

But no one answered the whistle. The house was quiet. Void of sound. The dolphin did not sense any human presence in the great house beyond. Still, she whistled once more, then waited.

A small calf, fragile and tender, nudged its mother. The dolphin knew she could stay no longer. The woman would not come again. Nor would the dolphin. Without another whistle or click, the dolphin turned and with one effortless sweep of her tail headed back up the creek, farther away from the dock and the tall woman, the memory of whom was already beginning to fade. As the dolphin swam, she scanned the water, alert, all her senses, her whole being, focused on the safety of her calf. At her side the newborn calf was attuned to its mother, already learning the dolphin ways. Together they swam deeper into the mysterious waters of the Cove in a fluid lowcountry ballet. A graceful celebration of the beauty of all things wild.

Acknowledgments

This being the fourth book in the Lowcountry series (*The Summer Girls*, *The Summer Wind*, *The Summer's End*) I have journeyed not only with the characters for these several years, but also with so many people who have helped me create the books.

First and foremost, I'm blessed with an extraordinary editor and publishing team. For their love, support, and brilliance, thank you to my stellar team at Gallery Books: Lauren McKenna, Louise Burke, Jennifer Bergstrom, Jennifer Long, Liz Psaltis, Jean Anne Rose, Elana Cohen, Kristin Dwyer, Diana Velasquez, Jennifer Robinson, Steven Henry Boldt. And to my equally grand team at Trident Media Group: Kimberly Whalen, Robert Gottlieb, Tara Carberry, Lauren Paverman, Sylvie Rosokoff. As well as to Joe Veltre at Gersh.

For arranging my tour schedules and speaking engagements and for writing such great articles, thank you Angela May, Kathie Bennett, and Susan Zurenda. Thank you to Lisa Minnick, Ruth Cryns, Charlotte Tarr, Linda Plunkett, Jeanette Turner, for more support than I can list.

Again, sincere thanks and appreciation to Dr. Pat Fair at

NOAA and to the wonderful team at the Dolphin Research Center, Grassy Key, Florida, for my education and training with dolphins.

A heartfelt thanks goes to Amy Sottile, a longtime supporter and friend who, with the support of Wild Dunes, has graciously thrown me book launch parties at the resort that took my breath away.

The Lowcountry Wedding Giveaway involved so many wonderful companies and people who stepped up to proudly display a glimpse of the charm and unparalleled beauty of a lowcountry wedding. I remain humbled by your enthusiastic response. Thank you: Wild Dunes Resort and The Legare Waring House at Charlestown Landing. Firefly Distillery for creating the signature cocktails *A Lowcountry Wedding* and the *Firefly Cannonball*. Cannonborough, Kate McDonald Bridal; LulaKate; Brackish Bow Ties; Charleston Tuxedo; Wildflowers Inc.; Studio R; Stox & Co.; SalonSalon of Charleston; Cru Catering; Christy Loftin; Charleston Virtuosi and Kiral Productions; Squeeze Cocktail & Beverage Catering; Sweet Lulu's Bakery on Wheels; Charming Inns (John Rutledge House); Carolina's Executive Limo Line; Riverland Studios; EventWorks; Ashley Rhodes Event Designs; Croghan's Jewel Box.

And as always, my love and thanks to the man I married—Markus. I couldn't have finished this book without your love and support and meals! Come and grow old with me, for the best is yet to be!

A
Lowcountry
Wedding

Mary Alice Monroe

This reading group guide for A Lowcountry Wedding *includes an introduction, discussion questions, ideas for enhancing your book club, and recipes. The suggested questions are intended to help your reading group find new and interesting angles and topics for your discussion. We hope that these questions will enrich your conversation and increase your enjoyment of the book.*

Introduction

This is the fourth book in *New York Times* bestselling author Mary Alice Monroe's Lowcountry Summer series about three half sisters and their grandmother living on Sullivan's Island.

After finding love and new beginnings, Marietta Muir and her granddaughters, Dora, Carson, and Harper, are facing their lowcountry weddings. While new careers and dual wedding plans bring insecurities to the surface, it's the unexpected arrival of Reverend Atticus Green who introduces an unknown family secret into their midst.

As personal crises and two weddings converge, it will take the Muir sisters' strong bond to persevere and appreciate how compassion, honesty, and commitment are fundamental for marriage.

Topics & Questions for Discussion

1. When Mamaw was first married, her mother, Barbara, told her, "[A]t the root of all etiquette and manners is kindness" (p. xiii). Do you agree? Etiquette and manners have evolved since the 1920's Emily Post. What do you think women of Dora, Carson, and Harper's generation would say about their great-grandmother's view of the world? How about Granny James?

2. Early in *A Lowcountry Wedding*, we learn that Marietta believes that the purpose of marriage is to be "an institution set up by society to protect the concept of the family" (p. xvii). Do you think her opinion is informed by her generation or by her personality? How do you think her beliefs regarding marriage evolved by the end of the novel? Discuss what you believe the purpose of marriage is.

3. Were you surprised by Dora's initial response to Devlin's proposal? Whose side of their argument do you find yourself agreeing with more?

4. Atticus Green arrives at Sea Breeze unannounced. What was your initial reaction when he was introduced to the Muir sisters? How did his role as marriage counselor support the brides and the family?

5. Take a look at how everyone is dressed at the rehearsal dinner, beginning on page 182. What do you think their choices say about their personalities and roles within the upcoming weddings? How about within the Muir family at large?

6. "[S]he could not have imagined a happier ending to this evening's play" (p. 195). Why does Mamaw call Harper's rehearsal dinner a play? If this is a play, who is the main character(s) and who, if anyone, should we consider the antagonist? Discuss if you think the proceedings of a wedding can be likened to a play—characters with roles to play, lines to say, costumes and rehearsals.

7. Much of Atticus's personality and habits, including his alcoholism, can be traced back to his genealogy. Yet he also places much store in the strong family values he learned from his parents. What do you think Mary Alice Monroe is trying to tell us here in the nature vs nurture debate? Contrast Atticus and Carson's way of dealing with their alcoholism with Parker's. Why do you think they were arguably more successful in living with this disease?

8. Early in the book Mary Alice Monroe writes that "Weddings bring out the best and the worst in people" (p. 114). Share

with your book club stories of best and worst behavior at a wedding you've attended (or your own!).

9. While Harper is initially against signing a prenuptial agreement, Granny James raises some valid points for protecting the family assets for Harper's future children. Whose viewpoint—Harper, Granny James, or Taylor—do you find yourself agreeing with most? Would you sign a prenup?

10. Taylor and Harper live in Sea Breeze together, but to Taylor, since Harper owns the house and her name is on the deed, "It feels like I'm living in *your* house" (p. 275), rather than a house they both have equal control over. Do you think Harper would feel the same way if the roles were reversed and Taylor owned all of Sea Breeze on paper? Or if she lived in Taylor's ancestral family home that he owned and connected with fond memories? How does gender, society, even region, influence the roles a man and a woman assume in marriage today?

11. What do you make of Harper's renewed interest in religion and how she relates to God? How does this compare with the role of religion in Atticus's life? How common is it for young mothers to reconsider the role of religion, and baptism, in their new family?

12. Were you at all surprised by the direction Mamaw and Girard's relationship went? In what ways does their relationship mimic, and in what ways does it differ from, Dora and Devlin's relationship?

13. Consider Parker's written legacy: "It was the treasure for which the girls had been searching for so long. Not because it was an outstanding novel and would bring great wealth; sadly it wasn't. But because the book was Parker's life's work. That made it priceless" (pp. 370–71). Why is it important for the Muir sisters to understand their father? Why does a person's life's work take on the mantle of "priceless"? Do you think Parker deserved the elevated status his daughters give his novel? Finally, why do you believe Parker wrote, and hid, his children's book, *Tideland Treasures*?

14. The novel describes two classic lowcountry wedding venues—the plantation wedding and the beach wedding. Which would you prefer?

15. Delphine's role in the novel, while understated, rounds out the series's theme of appreciating and protecting wildlife. Why do you think Mary Alice Monroe wrote the epilogue in the dolphin's point of view? Discuss the ways you can support dolphins in the wild.

Enhance Your Book Club

1. Fun drinks feature prominently in the rehearsal dinner and at Harper and Carson's wedding. As part of your club's meeting, bring ingredients for the cocktail created by Firefly: "A Lowcountry Wedding" or the "Firefly Cannonball" (recipes follow).

2. *A Lowcountry Wedding* is the fourth book in the Lowcountry Summer series. If you haven't already, check out the first three books about the Muir sisters, *The Summer Girls*, *The Summer Wind*, and *The Summer's End*. Or reread the books as a group and refresh your memory on how Mamaw, Dora, Carson, and Harper all began their journey to finding Sea Breeze and one another again.

3. Create the delicious lowcountry dishes mentioned in the book: "Lowcountry Gumbo," "Lowcountry Pickled Shrimp," and "Pecan Tassies" (recipes follow). Don't forget the cornbread!

4. Have book club members bring photographs of their weddings to share. Perhaps have a prize for the worst bridesmaid dresses!

RECIPES

All recipes from *Rise and Shine!: A Southern Son's Treasury of Food, Family, and Friends* by Johnathon Scott Barrett and courtesy of Mercer University Press.

A Lowcountry Wedding Cocktail

3 ounces sparkling wine
or prosecco

1 ounce Firefly Peach Moonshine
1 orange wedge

Firefly Cannonball

3 ounces Firefly Sweet
Tea Vodka

2 to 3 ounces Cannonborough
Ginger Beer
¼ slice of lemon, squeezed

Add ingredients to shaker to blend. Pour over ice, and enjoy!

Lowcountry Gumbo

1 pound shrimp, peeled and deveined, shells reserved*

2 quarts low-sodium chicken stock

½ pound smoked sausage, such as andouille, sliced into ½-inch rounds

4 teaspoons creole spice,** divided

½ pound boneless, skinless chicken thighs

2 tablespoons olive oil

1 scant cup chopped onion

½ cup each chopped celery, green bell pepper, and red bell pepper

¼ teaspoon each salt and freshly ground black pepper

1 tablespoon minced garlic, packed

1 (14.5-ounce) can diced tomatoes, no salt added

1 teaspoon Worcestershire sauce

½ teaspoon Texas Pete or other hot sauce

4 bay leaves

1 tablespoon minced fresh basil

2 teaspoons each minced fresh thyme and oregano

1½ cups sliced fresh okra, cut into ¼-inch rounds

2 teaspoons filé powder

6 servings of cooked rice

½ cup chopped fresh parsley

Place shrimp shells and stock in a pot; bring to a boil, reduce heat, stir, and allow to simmer for 15 minutes. Set aside.

---

* Instead of shrimp, you may also add or substitute 1 pound of lump backfin crab. Because the crab is so delicate, I recommend stirring it in at the very end of the recipe until just heated through.

** Harper makes this recipe a little lighter by cutting out the sausage or using chicken andouille sausage. Panfry ingredients in a little olive oil instead of bacon grease to cut back on the fat.

While waiting for the stock to simmer, brown the sausage in a Dutch oven. Remove the sausage and set aside. Drain all but 1 tablespoon of the accumulated fat.

Rub 2 teaspoons of the creole spice onto the chicken thighs. Add olive oil to the pan and bring to medium-high heat.

Add chicken, browning nicely on each side, turning occasionally until done, about 10 minutes. Set aside with the sausage.

Keeping the Dutch oven on medium-high heat, add the onion, celery, and bell peppers, along with the salt and pepper. Cook, stirring constantly, for 2 minutes.

Add the garlic, stir, and cook another 4 to 5 minutes, until the vegetables are soft and the onion becomes translucent.

Strain the stock into the pan, pushing down on the shells in your sieve to get the juices.

Cube the chicken into bite-size pieces.

Add the tomatoes, Worcestershire sauce, hot sauce, bay leaves, basil, thyme, and oregano and the remaining 2 teaspoons of creole spice. Bring to a boil, and reduce heat, stirring.

Add okra, sausage, and chicken and continue cooking for 20 minutes, stirring occasionally.

With the gumbo on a steady simmer, add your shrimp, stirring occasionally; cook for 3 to 4 minutes, until just done.

Sprinkle filé powder over the stew, stirring, and allow to cook 2 to 3 minutes more; the gumbo will thicken slightly.

To serve, pour into a bowl, top with ½ cup rice and sprinkle with parsley. Serve with a hot biscuit to sop up the gravy.

Serves 6

Lowcountry Pickled Shrimp

This dish is a fixture on Savannah buffet tables and sideboards; usually served in large cut-glass bowls, it makes a beautiful presentation. There are a number of variations on the dish—some with capers, maybe green bell pepper, some spice it up with red pepper flakes. Tom likes to throw in cherry tomatoes and fresh bay leaves to give it a bold splash of color, particularly at a Christmas party. But the basics are always the same: lightly poached shrimp, oil, vinegar, onions, and celery. I enjoy the taste of fresh dill with shrimp and include it in this recipe.

3 quarts water

¼ cup Old Bay Seasoning

3 pounds large shrimp, peeled and deveined, tails removed

3 stalks celery, sliced into 2-inch julienne strips

1 medium Vidalia or red onion, very thinly sliced into rings

1 (4-ounce) jar sliced pimiento, drained

6 to 8 fresh bay leaves

3 tablespoons capers

¼ cup minced fresh dill weed, packed

1½ cups good quality vegetable oil

¾ cup apple cider vinegar

½ teaspoon Dijon mustard

1 teaspoon salt

¼ teaspoon freshly ground black pepper

3 to 4 large sprigs fresh parsley, for garnish

Bring the water and the Old Bay Seasoning to a boil in a large pot. Add shrimp, stir, cover, remove from heat, and set aside for 5 minutes. The shrimp are done when the tail section curves up and almost touches the head area. Drain thoroughly in a colander; do not rinse.

Place the shrimp into a large airtight container, along with the celery, onion, pimiento, bay leaves, capers, and dill. Toss to mix.

In a bowl, whisk together the oil and remaining ingredients except the parsley. Pour over the shrimp mixture and toss to coat. Cover the container and refrigerate 8 hours or overnight. Stir once or twice during the chilling process.

Before serving, drain the shrimp in a colander. Place in a decorative crystal or cut-glass bowl and garnish with sprigs of parsley.

Pecan Tassies

CRUST

1 cup plus 1 tablespoon
  unsalted butter, at room
  temperature, divided

2 cups all-purpose flour
¾ cup confectioners' sugar
Pinch of salt

FILLING

4 large eggs
2 cups granulated sugar
⅓ cup freshly squeezed
  lemon juice
2 teaspoons finely grated
  lemon zest

1 teaspoon baking powder
¼ teaspoon salt
¼ cup all-purpose flour
3 tablespoons superfine
  or confectioners' sugar, for
  decoration

Pecans?

INSTRUCTIONS

CRUST

Preheat oven to 350°F.

Grease a 9 x 13-inch baking dish with 1 tablespoon of butter.

Mix the 1 cup of butter, the flour, sugar, and salt in a bowl; stir well until thoroughly combined.

Place dough in the baking dish and pat down the mixture into the bottom of the dish with your hands until evenly distributed.

Bake for 15 to 20 minutes, or until the crust is golden. Remove from oven and allow to cool.

FILLING

Beat the eggs and sugar until smooth.

Add the juice, zest, baking powder, salt, and flour; stir until well incorporated. Pour the filling over the crust.

Bake for 25 to 30 minutes, or until the filling is set.

Allow to cool to room temperature. Sprinkle with sugar and cut into bars. Can be stored for several days in an airtight container.

Serves 16 to 20